GAIA'S GAME

A HORROR NOVEL

KEN STARK

OTHER TITLES BY KEN STARK

"Similar to the Alfred Hitchcock thriller The Birds, Keeter's Bluff is under siege and no one is safe in Gaia's Game by Ken Stark, prompting us to take notice of our ecological practices. Expertly written, it contains a compelling and suspenseful plot, solid and personable characters, and a definitive and climactic story arc that builds to a dramatic and chilling conclusion. It is a phenomenal horror story that promises to thrill... Outstanding!"

- Reviewed by Susan Sewell for Readers' Favorite

CHAPTER

I

W hat the hell..."

Jake Peluso pulled his Pontiac to a stop in the alley behind his rooming house even as they emerged from the darkness. There were three, from what he could make out in the dim light thrown down from above. He climbed from the car with a grunt, flicked the stub of his cigarette to the ground, and barked a curse while satisfying an itch just north of his ass crack.

"Get lost, would'ja?" he growled. "Go on, now! Fuck off! Go home!" But for all of his snarling and scowling and both oversized hands already curling into fists, the three of them just stood there, staring dumbly up at him with their dark, expressionless eyes.

Well, okay then. If that's the way they wanted it, maybe he'd just teach them a lesson they'd never forget.

He strode straight at them, intending to either barge his way through or begin the day's schooling, but he never got the chance for either. He only became aware of the fourth one hiding in the shadows when a sharp sting in the small of his back brought him nearly to his knees, howling in pain.

"Son of a *bitch!*" he roared, spinning around to pour out his anger on anything within reach. "Are you fucking *kidding* m—"

A sudden pain near his temple silenced his tongue and clouded his vision with a crimson haze. As he doubled over, something sharp pierced the skin behind his right ear, and a warm gush of blood began to soak down the back of his shirt.

He tried to fight back, but it was like battling an octopus. Every time he turned on one, the others closed in from somewhere else. He swung at one, and something sharp hit him in the ribs. He threw a back-handed punch at another, and felt a slash near his crotch. He spun around in an absolute rage, but then something heavy bounced off the back of his skull, and his entire world started to spin.

Battered, dazed, and bleeding from a dozen places, Jake 'the Snake' Peluso finally shook himself free and bolted back toward his car, but it was no use. They were right on his heels. In the time it would take him to fish the keys out of his pocket, they would be on him. So, he did the only thing he could do. He pivoted midstride, abandoned his car where it sat, and ran for his very life.

He ran like no man had ever run before. He ran until his side ached, and until his breath came in tight little gasps. He ran until his legs were numb, and until he could taste bile at the back of his throat. He ran with the determination of a man knowing his own life was about to end, but even with street after street blurring past, those horrible things gained more ground by the second. In desperation, he tore across the road and barged through a used car lot, hoping against hope that dodging rows of vehicles might gain him an extra second or two, but they stayed right with him. He barreled through the back gate and sprinted down Laurel Avenue as fast as his feet could carry him, but with the huffing and puffing from behind growing louder by the second, he knew that his time was running out.

Then he saw his chance. An expansive yard overgrown with weeds as high as wheat sprawled out at the bottom of the hill. If he could make it that far, he might just make it through this night after all. With a final burst of energy, he sprinted the last thirty feet and allowed himself to be swallowed up by the suburban jungle. He bulldozed his way through, swatting weeds away from his face and all the while throwing frightened glances back over his shoulder. Then a door miraculously appeared before him, and without a single concern as to where it might lead or what might be on the other side, he threw himself bodily into that door and crashed straight through it.

But it was already too late. The things descended on his bloodied, crumpled form, and the last the world ever heard from Jake Peluso was a wet, gurgling sob, lost in the darkness.

That, and the squealing.

CHAPTER

II

J esus, Mary and Joseph..."

Carl Rankin stood in the doorway of the Elk's Hall, sur-
veying the carnage. Everywhere he looked, he saw red.
The floor. The walls. Even the ceiling hadn't been spared
from random spatters of gore. And in the middle of it all was
Sheriff Cooper, down on one knee, examining a pair of tiny,
broken bodies.

Cooper sensed his young deputy approaching and
looked up.

"Carl, you look like a cow that's just come across a new
fence. Shut your damn mouth and get in here. Just watch
where you step."

Rankin tiptoed over the threshold and picked his way
through the carnage, then he hovered over Cooper and
hushed the single word, "Jee-*zuzz!*"

Cooper made no reply. He simply knelt there, staring
down at the pair of broken bodies.

At last, he stood up, shook his head, and uttered a long, slow sigh.

"She's going to kill me for this, Carl. I swear to Christ, that woman is going to hand me my everlovin' ass."

He bent down and scooped up the tiniest bit of crimson gore from the floor, and then he did a most curious thing. He brought that tiny bit of detritus up to his nose and had a sniff. Then, he stuck out his tongue and gave it a lick.

"Mmm... Cherry," he said with an approving nod. But as the horror returned in full, he threw back his head and howled, "*Damn* it, Carl! The reception's in six hours, and I have single-handedly destroyed the biggest and most expensive wedding cake this town has ever seen. How the hell did I fuck this up so badly? I mean, look at it, Carl. *Look* at it!"

The deputy gazed down at the tiny broken bodies that had once graced the top of a grand five-tiered wedding cake, and he tsk-tsked aloud.

"Don't reckon Fancy'll be too happy about it, and that's a fact. Reckon the Judge'll have somethin' to say about it, too."

Cooper swallowed hard.

"Carl, I am officially screwed. How do I replace a wedding cake in six hours?"

"Dunno about wedding cakes, Sheriff, but did you ever try one of them ice cream logs from Dairy Queen? Tell you what, I'm always the man of the hour when I show up at one of my niece's birthday parties with an ice cream log from the DQ."

Cooper hung his head and sighed.

"Carl, you're a goddam genius. An ice cream log to celebrate a union of souls and wish them a lifetime of wedded bliss. I wonder why no one's ever come up with that before."

All sarcasm lost on him, Rankin simply shrugged.

"Dunno, Sheriff. Twenty bucks for a whole lot'a happy don't seem like a bad deal to me."

"Carl, Fancy ordered this wedding cake six months ago. It set her old man back over a thousand dollars. Marigold had to bring in extra people just to get the frosting done right because of drooping, or wilting, or whatever the hell. Five layers, Carl. Five! Each one with pink rosettes all around, and cherub's perched along the edges." He collected the pair of tiny bodies from the floor and cradled them gently in his hand. "These were hand-carved by a master craftsman back in Boston, Carl. *Hand*-carved mind you, then Fed-Exed all the way here. This little pecker-ass bride and groom cost an extra hundred bucks each. *Each*, Carl! The usual plastic deal-ies might be good enough for everyone else, but Fancy heard about some guy who could carve the happy couple out of marzipan, and she wanted them. And like Judge Whittacker always says, what Fancy wants..."

"...Fancy gets," Rankin finished the quote. "But Jee-*zuzz*! Two hundred bucks for two little dolls? Man a'livin', what's this world comin' to?"

Cooper ran his hand through hair turning white with age and thinning far too much for his liking, and regarded the broken figures in his outstretched palm.

"I have no idea, Carl. Maybe he charges by the pound."

In fact, the bride and groom did look a little like a tiny Fancy Whittacker and a nearly as tiny Gordon Harshwaldt. The bride was double-wide, with extra marzipan around the middle and a chunk or two spilling out on either side. The groom was even closer to the genuine article. Tall, skinny as a rail, and how the guy managed to carve those Buddy Holly glasses and massive Jimmy Durante schnozzola, Cooper hadn't a clue.

He unfurled a handkerchief from his back pocket and wrapped it gently around the broken marzipan bodies like a funeral shroud.

"She trusted me, Carl. Fancy trusted me with the single most important part of her special day. All I had to do was pick up that damn wedding cake and deliver it here. And as hard as I tried, I still fucked it up."

"I'm sure you tried real hard, Sheriff..." Rankin started, but that was as far as he got.

"The damn monstrosity was too big for my cruiser, so I borrowed Doc Jenkins' wagon. Marigold and three of her girls helped me get it out to the van on a dolly, and we loaded it in just as carefully as you please. And on the way back, I drove as slowly as I've ever done, Carl. I swear to you, I drove that van with Fancy's cake in the back slower than I've ever driven a motor vehicle before. I drove so slowly that people were honking at me to get out of the way. Seriously! I drove so slowly and so carefully that ordinary citizens were honking at the coroner's wagon to get the hell out of the way, and flipping the town's Sheriff the bird as they tore past. Can you believe it?"

Rankin tucked his thumbs behind his belt buckle and clucked a disheartened, "Tsk, tsk, tsk..."

"I got it all the way here in one piece, Carl. Not one rosette dislodged, not one cherub disturbed, and Fancy and her beanpole of a beau completely intact. Then I had to get that massive son of a bitch out of the van and into the Elk's hall, and it took the help of an entire herd of Elks to get it done. But we did it, Carl! We actually delivered Fancy's ugly-ass monstrosity in one piece!"

Rankin stepped casually aside as a dollop of icing peeled away from the ceiling and splatted to the floor, inches away.

"Uh, but if you got it here safe and sound, Sheriff..."

"It was my kryptonite, Carl. My *goddam* kryptonite. We were just hoisting that rosette-covered, cherub-lovin', pink slab of hernia-generating self-indulgence onto the table when I saw it. "

"You don't mean..."

"Carl. I don't know what I did in a past life to warrant the universe giving me a punch in the ball sack every chance she gets, but I swear she does. I don't know, maybe I kicked a puppy in a previous life or something. But just as we were getting that pink behemoth onto the table..." He paused a beat, took a breath, and skewered Rankin to the spot with tight, hooded eyes. "It was big, Carl. And I mean big! A good foot across if it was an inch. My hand to God, Carl. Now, I can handle those little green bastards in the garden. Mostly. And I can deal with an occasional daddy long-legs because I tell myself they're nothing more than crane flies with their wings torn off. But *dammit* Carl, that motherfucker was as big as my hand! No, *bigger!* It was like Thing from the Addams Family, you know? But black. Jet black. And with extra fingers. And hair. And a whole shitload of beady red eyes. I only saw it once we were lifting that damn cake onto the table, but then it started to skitter towards me with its legs all going everywhere at once, and... and... *Fuck*, Carl!"

Rankin laid a gentle hand on Cooper's shoulder.

"I understand, Sheriff. I've never been particularly afraid of spiders myself, but phobias are a real thing, and I want you to know that I support you. You know, as a person. As a fellow human being. I do not see you as any less of a man just because you are afraid of itty bitty insects. No sir, I respect all my fellow citizens of this planet Earth as individuals, and just because you happen to be deathly afraid of something that mostly scares little girls does not diminish you one iota in my eyes. We are all equal here on this beautiful blue planet drifting through the black void of space, and if you happen to be afraid of something that anyone else might squash with the heel of a boot and scrape off on a patch of grass, then that is just part of the magic and majesty that is you."

Cooper narrowed his eyes at the man.

"Carl, you been watching Oprah again?"

"Nuh uh. Mindy-Lou posted somethin' like it on my Facebook page. Pretty, ain't it?"

"Oh yeah, Carl," Cooper replied, deadpan. "Goddam beautiful."

Rankin grinned triumphantly, and Cooper began to pick his way through the pink minefield to the door. He stopped at the threshold and swung back, darting his eyes from one corner of the room to the other, just in case his kryptonite might still be hanging around.

"Carl, any word yet on Jedediah?"

"Actually, that's what I come to tell you, Sheriff." Rankin whipped a notebook from his breast pocket and flipped to the correct page. "Captain Callahan from the State Troopers called in a while ago. Two of his men made the trek up to Lake Habersham and found Jed's campsite. Said it looked like a bear'd gone through it, and no sign of old Jed."

"Any blood?"

"Not a drop, but what with the rain last night, that's not surprising. The boys found his truck down at the turnoff where Agnes said it'd be. The doors were locked, and no sign suggesting Jed tried to make his way back down there. Captain

Callahan called in Search and Rescue from up in Jolene. Said he'd let you know when they figure out what's what."

"Well, the man practically grew up in those hills. If anyone knows how to take care of himself out there, it's Jedediah Smithers."

"Reckon so," Rankin agreed. "According to the missus, he's made the same trip every June for the past forty years. First day of hunting season, he's up there tryin' to bag himself a buck or two."

"And he never comes back empty handed, either. Alright, keep me informed. And hey, Carl, we need this place to be spotless for Fancy's reception. Grab a few Elks and see to it, alright? I have to go find something approximating a wedding cake, or Fancy and the Judge will tear me apart like a pack of hyenas."

With that, he swung back around, launched himself through the door, and was back in his cruiser before Rankin could utter a word in protest.

Barely had he laid the broken, shrouded bodies of Fancy and Gordon on the passenger seat when his phone jingled. And barely had he pulled the thing from his pocket when the car's radio crackled.

"Base to KB-one, over."

It was Grace, back at the station. He checked the caller ID on his phone. Shit. Grace Tolliver at both ends. If she was that determined to get through to him, it meant more than a kid caught at the Tasty Mart with a hot Twix in his pocket.

He chose the lesser of two evils and unhooked the microphone.

"Go ahead, Grace."

"Sheriff, where the *fuck* have you been?" Grace asked in her usual refined fashion, punctuating the question with a smoker's cough and subsequent phlegmy spit into the waste can. At least, he *hoped* it had been into a waste can.

"I'm dealing with Fancy's wedding cake, Grace," Cooper reminded her as politely as possible. "We had some last minute hitches, so I don't have time to waste. Just tell me what and where."

"Well, I wouldn't know about the wedding now, would I?" Grace snarked back. "I mean, it's not like *I'll* be going, is it? Even though I received a personal invitation in the mail and had my best taffeta dress altered and all, not only will I not be attending the nuptials, but I will not be attending the reception, too! Uhhh... *either!*"

"Lucky bitch..." Cooper hushed under his breath, then he thumbed the button and said aloud, "I'm sorry, Grace. It couldn't be helped. Someone has to man the phones. Please just tell me what and where."

He counted the seconds in his head.

Eight.

Nine.

Ten.

Ten seconds before the radio crackled again. Yup. she was pissed, all right. Hell, with Fancy and the Judge on one side and Grace Tolliver on the other, he'd be lucky to make it to midnight with his testicles still intact.

Grace's voice came through cold enough to frost the cruiser's windows.

"10-91 Victor. The Carlin place, out on 50."

Damn. Another one. Just what he didn't need. 10-91 translated to an animal complaint. Tack on the 'Victor' and it became a *viscous* animal complaint. Normally, it could mean anything from Mabel Kutner's cat digging in old man Wilson's garden again, to Rick Grimes leading a herd of walkers straight down Main Street. Considering the day he'd had so far, and that this was the eighth 10-91 Victor since he'd come on duty, he assumed it would be closer to the latter than the former.

Before he could ask for clarification, the radio crackled again.

"And before you ask... *Sheriff*, I was not given sufficient details to advise you further. The boys are all on other calls, so how's about you get your skinny ass out there and ask Ada yourself what the problem is? I mean, unless you're too busy, what with the royal nuptials and all."

Cooper keyed the mike, but he let the button go before uttering a word. He gathered his thoughts until he was certain of his response, even rehearsing it in his head a few times, then he keyed the mike again. And again, he released it before saying a single word. At last, he keyed the mike one last time, spat out a simple, "Copy," and let the microphone fall to the floor.

As he pulled out of the back lot of Keeter's Bluff's one and only Elk's Hall, he could almost hear Grace Tolliver back at the station, laughing her big old head off, and ending it all with a wet, phlegmy cough and a spit into a waste can.

CHAPTER

III

He took in every bit of the Carlin place as he drew near. Driveway clear. Garage door closed. Lawn carefully manicured, as always. Shrubbery running alongside the driveway and skirting the house. Junipers. Chrysanthemums. One big oversized rhododendron bush in full bloom at the top of the drive. Garbage cans alongside the house, nestled in their own picket fence corral. Both untouched. Lids intact. Massive oak tree dominating the property as it always had, but thank God now minus the tire swing. Eight years since little Sean died from the cancer he'd been born with. About time Jim and Ada took down that *damn* swing and got on with what was left of their lives.

He pulled into the driveway and barely had time to crack his door open before Ada Carlin came rushing out of the house. He met the woman halfway, just managing to catch her before she collapsed to her knees.

"Tom!" the woman panted. "Thank heavens you're here.

Is it gone? Is it gone?"

Cooper bundled her in his arms and helped her regain her feet.

"Now now, everything's alright, Ada," he assured her. "You're okay. Just tell me what got you so worked up."

The woman said nothing, but Cooper could feel her entire body suddenly stiffen. And just as suddenly, he had to redouble his hold on her just to keep her from retreating back toward the house.

"Ada, what..." he started to say, but then he looked into her eyes and the pure, unadulterated fear he saw there silenced his tongue. He followed her goggle-eyed stare back over his shoulder, and now he could see it too. There. Nearly lost among the riot of blossoms pouring from Ada's prized rhododendron bush. A light pink triangle, fringed with black.

He had only seen such a thing once before, but once had been enough. As the rest of the thing came slowly into focus between, around and amongst the blossoms, his blood turned ice cold.

Dull pink triangle. White flash below. Tawny brown above. And there, just where he knew they'd be, a pair of golden orbs, pierced through with the blackest black on Earth.

His first instinct was to run, but to run was to die. He looked to the house and saw the front door still hanging open, but it was thirty feet away. Too damn far. If he was alone, maybe. But not with Ada. No way. Ada Carlin tipped the scales at close to two hundred pounds. If she tried, she'd fail, and he would then have the onerous distinction of watching one of Keeter's Bluff's citizens ripped to shreds on her own front lawn.

There was only one option. The cruiser was closer than the house. Ten feet. Twelve at most. The doors were unlocked and the windows were up. If he did this right, they might just make it. Two seconds to get to the car. Another two to fumble for the handle and squeeze Ada inside. One more to pile in after her. Yes. If they moved fast enough, it might just work.

Either way, it was their only chance.

Ada was still straining to break free from his grip, so he reeled her in close and wrapped his big arms around her, pinning her to his chest. Then, despite her desperate struggles, he began slowly and cautiously inching her farther away from the safety of her home and toward the cruiser.

The bush shivered, and a single rhododendron blossom dropped to the ground. Cooper clapped a hand over Ada's mouth just in time to stifle a scream and forced her to take one more half-step to the side. Now, the front of the cruiser was almost in a direct line with the rhododendrons. If he could just ease the two of them far enough onto the lawn, he could put two thousand pounds of metal between them and that dull pink triangle. It might not be enough, but at least it was something.

He kept a hand clapped tightly over Ada's mouth and used every ounce of strength he possessed to move the woman another foot. Then another, and another. Then their time ran out.

The branches parted just enough to let the pink triangle glisten wet in the sunlight, and the bush gave one last almighty shiver right down to its very roots as a dark, tawny blur exploded directly toward them.

Cooper threw the woman at the car, shouting, "Ada, get inside!" even as he drew his pistol, but barely had the weapon cleared its holster when a flash of gold streaked up to the far side of the car and bounded over its roof in a single powerful leap.

Cooper had only ever seen a mountain lion up close that one time. He'd been camping in the mountains when the smell of bacon cooking over a campfire drew it in. The half-starved cat had come to within a dozen yards of his campsite, and he'd thrown it a few strips of raw bacon. It had grabbed the bacon and ran off, leaving Cooper with his heart pounding out a rhumba beat and filled with a singular sense of privilege at having experienced such a rare encounter. But in the single heartbeat it took for this other animal to hurdle his big fat Oldsmobile, he knew only dread. This cat was twice the size of that scrawny, half-starved little female, and far from being cautious and aloof, it made straight for him with blood in its eyes.

With no time or space to draw a proper bead on the thing, he fired blindly, hoping that the sounds alone would be enough to scare the cat away. But aside from tearing up twin divots in Ada Carlin's lawn, the explosions had no effect whatsoever. The cougar cleared the cruiser's roof with room to spare and barely touched down before it was airborne again, this time on a trajectory that would bring it down on top of Cooper before he'd have time to say a single Hail Mary.

Certain that his life was about to end, and with the only lingering question being how gruesome and painful that end was likely to be, Cooper's only thoughts were of Ada. But somewhere through the flurry of sensations and flood of endorphins, he became dimly aware of the sound of a car door slamming shut, so he had to assume that he'd done his job right. He had saved a life. He had served and protected, just like he'd sworn to do all those years ago. Well, bully for him. Maybe he'd even get a plaque on the wall back at the station, because he sure as hell wasn't going to be around to accept it in person. With his squad car as the backstop in this particular shooting range and a member of the public hunkered down within said backstop, he simply couldn't risk taking another shot. All he could do now was die.

He caught the briefest glimpse of a mouth filled with long, white fangs, and knew it would be the last thing he would ever see. But then there came a sudden roar from off to the side, and he was thrown violently backwards as a flash of blue filled his vision. He hit the ground hard, slamming the back of his head on the hard-packed soil violently enough to nearly shake his teeth loose, and there he waited for the big cat to drop on him like a stone.

He took a deep breath, thinking it would be his last. Then he took another. And much to his surprise, another. And before he knew it, he was raising himself awkwardly to his elbows, completely flummoxed as to why he was not yet dead.

It took several seconds for his brain to catch up to his eyes and make out exactly what he was seeing. Oddly enough, it looked like words. Odder still, those words were accompanied by what looked for all the world to be a giant rodent. Then a man stepped into his field of view and gave the whole thing away. He was tall and lanky, with long blond hair, two weeks worth of scruff around a cheesy handlebar moustache, and clad in an ancient Frank Zappa t-shirt and Adidas shorts he might have been hanging onto since high school.

Austin Granger. It had to be. No one else in town had such a keen eye for the very worst in fashion and manscaping.

Cooper raised a hand to shield his eyes from the glare of a sun grown suddenly intense and had another look. Sure enough, behind Granger sat his old Toyota Landcruiser. Rust pooling around the wheel wells. Ugly blue canopy. A snarling cartoon rat painted on the door inside a red circle with a slash through its snout. And beneath it, four words in bold type. Keeter's Bluff Animal Control.

A hand reached down, he took it gladly, and as he was pulled awkwardly to his feet, a look of abject horror came over Granger's face.

"Coop? Jesus *Christ*, Coop! What the *fuck?*"

With his mind beginning to clear and his vision coming into real focus, Cooper was finally able to make sense of what had seemed to make no sense at all.

Granger's Landcruiser butted up against Ada Carlin's front porch. Huge tire marks gouged into her perfectly manicured lawn. His own person, undead and undisembowled. And more importantly, a sickening pool of blood widening around the front wheels of the Ratmobile.

"Austin?" he said, shaking the last of the cobwebs away. "Where did *you* come from?"

"I got a call from Haddy Winfield about a pack of dogs running loose in Hamilton Park," Granger explained, his long moustache quivered with every syllable. "She said there were a bunch of kids around, and she was afraid one of them might get hurt. I was just heading there when I saw you. And I saw the cat. And I didn't even think. I just acted on impulse. Jesus Christ, Coop, what the fuck did I *do?*"

Cooper dropped to a knee and peered under the Toyota. Sure enough, there it was, wedged between bumper and porch. His heart literally ached at seeing the big cat dead, but not nearly enough for him to wish that their roles had been reversed.

"I'll tell you what you did, Austin," he said, climbing back to his feet. "You just saved my damn life, that's what you did."

He clapped the man on the shoulder, and said nothing as he casually wiped a palmful of sweat onto the leg of his pants.

"Is it dead? Oh dear Jesus, did I kill that magnificent animal?"

"Trust me, Austin, that magnificent animal becomes decidedly less magnificent when you know it's going to be the last thing you ever see."

"But you know me, Coop. I don't kill God's creatures. I've never killed a living being in my entire life. I trap them, then I drive them out to the country and turn them loose. I would never kill an animal. Never! Oh dear Jesus, what the fuck did I *do?*"

He could understand what the man must be feeling. Other than arachnids, Cooper would never hurt an animal either, but on this day, he was perfectly willing to make an exception.

"You saved my life, Austin," he said again, and though he was about to clap the man once more on the shoulder, he reconsidered on the fly and instead faked working out a kink in his elbow.

They both crept up to the front of the Toyota to have a closer look. Granger's charge across thirty feet of Ada's lawn might have been the desperate act of a man with no other options, but somehow in that mad jumble of mathematics, the big cat's trajectory and the Toyota's front bumper had come together with absolute precision. The cat was dead, sure enough, but it had happened in the blink of an eye. The animal hadn't suffered for a fraction of a second. It's delicate skull had come apart upon meeting hardened Detroit steel, and the rest of it was all just gruesome Biology 101.

"It was hiding behind the rhododendron bush," Cooper explained, trying hard not to let his voice hitch. "I barely had time to throw Ada at the car when it attacked. The damn thing came straight at me."

The only response from Granger was a cocked eyebrow and a single harumphed, "Huh."

"What, you don't believe me?"

Granger ran a trembling hand through his pockets, but having sworn off cigarettes nearly a year ago, he came up frustratingly empty.

"I don't have to believe you, Coop. I saw it for myself. But you weigh what, one-eighty?" He threw a cautionary glance over his shoulder at Ada still huddled in the squad car and lowered his voice to a hush. "And Ada's no Tinker-bell herself."

"I guess it must have been one hungry cat," Cooper concluded, relieved to put a period at the end of it all, but Granger wouldn't have it.

"No, no, no, you don't get it. You see, there's a reason no one ever sees these animals in the wild. Mountain lions are lone hunters. Ambush predators. You'd only know one of them was stalking you when you felt its claws grab hold and its fangs sink into the back of your neck. But in town? In broad daylight? With dogs barking on every street? No way. Not a chance. Even if it was injured and unable to hunt its usual prey, a *felis concolor* would stay as far away from humans as it could get. Even if it somehow got confused and found itself lost in town with an empty belly, it would go after a stray cat or a chicken coop *long* before it would ever attack a grown man, much less both you *and* Ada. This is impossible, Coop. Ain't no way on God's green Earth a cat would attack two humans together, and it sure as *shit* wouldn't attack them from the front."

"Rabid, maybe?" Cooper suggested.

Granger stroked his moustache as he considered the notion.

"Well, I don't see any obvious signs, but that's the only thing that would make any kind of sense. I'll have to get him back to the shop to know for sure."

"Any recent reports in the area?"

"Reports? Hell, there's no end of reports. Me and Jermaine have been run ragged all day. All of a sudden, it's like every critter in the county's got a hate on. First thing this morning, Enid Farrier down on Hampton called in to report that a gang of squirrels had chased Stefan all the way across the yard and into the house. Can you believe it? Those were her exact words, too. A *gang* of squirrels. Jermaine and I almost came to blows over which one of us was going to go. Ultimately, we both went just so we could see for ourselves what manner of street thug, skinhead, leather-jacketed squirrel gang could chase big Stefan Farrier across his yard like a frightened schoolgirl."

Cooper allowed a half-grin. "And?"

Granger stuck out his bottom lip. "Sadly, the *gang* was gone by the time we got there. Jermaine said they must've gone off to rumble with the Jets, whatever that means."

Despite the growing sense of unease roiling through his belly, Cooper couldn't help but picture a gang of adolescent hoodlum squirrels dancing through a carpark, singing *Breeze it, Buzz it, Easy does it,* and he had to stifle a chuckle.

"Actually, I meant reports of rabies, Austin. Anything in

the county? The state? Any reports of rabies at all?"

"None that I've heard, Coop. I'll call Keith up in Jolene to make sure, but rabies doesn't exactly slip under the radar. There would've been a bulletin. Sheriff's Office would've gotten it, too."

"Well, it wouldn't be the first time someone screwed the pooch," Cooper reasoned. "How long before you know?"

Granger did the math out loud.

"Let's see... Ten minutes back to the shop, maybe thirty more to retrieve tissue samples from the brain stem and cerebellum. Normally I'd Fed-Ex the samples up to Jolene, but there's a veterinary diagnostic clinic in Piedmont that'll be able to do the DFA. Figure an hour's drive to Piedmont, another two for the test..." Granger checked his watch and Cooper followed suit. "Chances are, I can give you an answer by five o'clock."

"Alright, call me when you know either way. Actually, you should probably text me. If I can find a cake, I'll be at a wedding. If not, I'll be on Doc Jenkins' slab." Cooper held out a hand, Granger took it, and the two old friends shook. "Thank you, Austin. I owe you big time."

"Hey, all in a day's work, right?" Granger tried to joke the horror away, but then a sudden revelation had him spinning around. "Oh shit! Ada!"

On cue, the car door cracked opened, and Ada Carlin's puffy white face emerged out into the open.

"Tom?"

"It's alright, Ada. You can come out now."

Slowly, nervously, Ada creaked the door open inch by inch. At last, she threw it wide, leapt out like an oversized acrobat, and rushed into Cooper's arms, nearly knocking him back to the ground.

"Oh, Tom! Thank you, thank you!" she gushed into his chest. "I thought it had gone, but it must have been hiding. Oh Tom, I thought for sure..."

"Oh, now now, Ada," Cooper tut-tutted, patting her back and adding her sweat to Granger's on his pants leg. "It's okay. The cat's dead. He's not going to hurt you. And for the record, *I* didn't do anything. It was all Austin Granger."

The woman released Cooper and threw her big beefy arms around Granger, nearly swallowing him whole.

"Well then, thank you, Mister Granger! Thank you, thank you, thank you!"

"Uh, I didn't do..." Granger started to say, but then he clamped his mouth shut and simply held Ada's big, plump body against his spindly form, drinking in the warmth.

CHAPTER

IV

"H ayley, what the hell are you doing?"
Cooper stuck his head through the open window
of Hayley Abbott's rusty old '62 Falcon, resting his
folded arms on the door.

The woman behind the wheel was even older than the
car. Eighty-plus, and counting. Cooper had known her his
whole life. The Abbott's had lived in Keeter's Bluff since forever. Most of the family had either died off or moved out of
the 'Bluff through the years, but there was one granddaugh-
ter still living in town. Samantha Abbott. Sam ran a dress
shop downtown, and gave manicures out of her house on
the side. She was a sweet lady. Absolutely nothing like her
grandmother, currently sitting there in that ratty old Ford
with a scowl on her face, flooring the gas pedal despite the
car's rear wheels hanging high in the air.

"Hayley, I don't think that's going to do it," Cooper informed her with a sigh.

"Mind your own damn business, flatfoot!" the woman howled back, hoisting a middle finger and snarling through ill-fitting dentures. "I've been behind the wheel since before your daddy was born, so don't you be telling me how to drive my own damn car! Goddam Five-O. The only thing you cops are good at is spending my hard-earned tax dollars to harass honest, law abiding citizens!"

Time was, Hayley Abbott taught second grade at King Ed Elementary. She eventually rose to the rank of vice-principal, and when old Ben Horn kicked the bucket, she'd taken over. Twenty years she spent in that job, then another twenty at the public library. If even some of the rumors were true, half the people in town owed that woman not only for their education and their love of books, but for every cuss word they'd ever known and a predisposed affinity for menthol cigarettes.

He stepped back from the car and had another look. Clearly, the old gal had been coming north on Main and had tried to make a left turn into the Esso. But she hadn't seen the new concrete median, courtesy of a small town council with big city ideas. Now the car was riding high atop that median, balanced on its centerlink. It wasn't going anywhere. At least, not without a tow truck and a whole lot of scarred concrete.

He stuck his head back through the window and tried again.

"Hayley," he said as gently as he could while still being heard over the racing motor. "Hayley, would you stop, please? You're hung up. You aren't going anywhere. How about you turn the engine off, and you and me pop across the street for a cup of coffee while we wait for Harlon to come and pull you off the hump. Fair enough?"

In answer, the old gal stomped her foot to the floor, sending the straight-6 motor into hyperdrive. Then, with the engine racing and blue-grey smoke billowing from the car's ancient exhaust pipe, she calmly retrieved a cigarette pack from her sweater pocket, tongued out a Kool, and lit it with a Bic. As she blew a double stream of smoke through nostrils crowned by a delicate pair of pince-nez, she raised her middle finger again and aimed it directly Cooper's way.

"How about you shove that coffee up your ass, pig!" she growled with a threatening clack of her dentures. "That's where all you flatfoots keep your brains, so maybe the caffeine will do you some good!"

Cooper sighed and withdrew from the car for good.

Locals were coming out from shops and restaurants all along Main Street to watch the strange goings-on, but he paid them no mind as he walked back to his squad car, reached through the window for the mike and thumbed it to life.

"KB-one to dispatch."

Only dead air came back, and he let it. Grace was a good woman and a valued member of the team, but she could be as moody as hell at the best of times, and considering the cause of this latest snit, he wasn't about to push it. He counted off the seconds in his head, and when he had almost reached sixty, at last a gruff, whiskey-hardened voice answered back.

"What?" it said. Bluntly.

Cooper was ready. That extra minute had given him time to rehearse what he was going to say, so he keyed the mike again, barked out the words, "11-85 at the corner of Dunwich and Main, best possible speed," then he tossed the mike back inside and stepped away from the vehicle before he could hear whatever glorious thing Grace came up with in response.

He watched the old Falcon spin its wheels and belch out smoke until Hayley Abbott's extended finger became lost in the haze, and with the crowd continuing to build, he dodged a trio of kids charging down the middle of the sidewalk and made his way up the street to Jeeter's Cafe, two long, wonderful blocks away from the scene.

Jeeter's Cafe had a dubious past. It started out life as the Main Street Saloon, but the eighteenth amendment saw to that. So it had become a speakeasy, flouting Hoover's heavy-handed tactics and making a buttload of cash for all the wrong people in the process. After the death of prohibition, the dive had taken some time to find its place in the world. Bar. Juke joint. Malt shop. Diner. It was that last incarnation that had finally stuck. The food stunk, the coffee stunk, and the place itself stunk, but Jeeter Hodges was smart enough to hire the best-looking girls in town to wait tables, and his own wife, squirrelly little Anita Hodges, sewed uniforms personally tailored to each one that straddled the line between skimpy and downright obscene. So yeah, the place did all right.

An old-fashioned bell over the door tinged, and on cue, every eye turned to see which one of the townsfolk was hungry enough and stupid enough to brave Jeeter's menu. Cooper nodded to Ben Stanton, gave a chin-jut of recognition to Ferrel Gimpley's boy Mike, then he strode up the counter, perched himself on a stool, and leaned across to the gorgeous young thing on the far side with a pencil stuck behind her ear and every ounce of her ample assets on full display.

"Hey, Janice," he said, trying not to leer.

"Hey, Sheriff," the girl smiled, showing off the delightful little gap between her front teeth. "What can I getcha? Coffee? Pie? I'm supposed to recommend the meatloaf, but I gave it a sniff this morning, and pee-*yew!*"

"Janice!" Jeeter appeared around the corner, wiping his hands on a stained and tattered dishrag. "Now, I know we've had this talk before. Nothing in your job description says that you have to tell our customers what to eat and what not to eat. I've got thirty pounds of meatloaf about to go bad, and if I don't move it, I might not be able to make payroll." He looked past the waitress to Cooper and offered him a genuine, "Hey Tom, how's it going? Care for a slice of the best meatloaf in town? It comes with mashed potatoes and enough gravy to float a boat."

"Just coffee, thanks," he told Jeeter, and by extension, gorgeous, gap-toothed Janice.

The girl snapped her gum, sneered derisively at Jeeter, and poured a cup from the pot.

"Good choice," she said with a wink.

She slid the coffee across the counter, and Cooper had to avert his eyes from the single button straining to hold her blouse closed against all of the combined forces of physics.

"You sure, Tom?" Jeeter tried one last time. "You look like you could use a home-cooked meal. I promise, you won't find a better meatloaf in all of Keeter's Bluff."

"No doubt," he answered back, charitably, then he threw the waitress a quick, "Thanks, Janice," while trying to look anywhere at all but at that tiny white button.

The girl leaned farther across the counter, stretching the confines of her blouse to the absolute limit.

"My pleasure, Sheriff," she cooed, snapping her gum and blowing a gentle spearmint-scented breeze his way. "If you need anything else, you just holler and I'll come running."

Those big beautiful eyes and soft, pouty lips said the rest. He wouldn't have to holler. All he'd have to do was crook his finger. Hell, the girl had looks enough to grab the cover of a magazine, but here in small town nowhere, she was just another pretty-as-hell farmer's daughter with ample wares and nowhere to peddle them but on the local yokels.

"Thank you, Janice," he said again, as indifferently as he could and as sweetly as a man as old as her father would dare.

She beamed him one last gap-toothed grin, then she padded out from behind the counter with coffee pot in hand to the general delight of the other patrons, every one of whom was male.

Jeeter's big, sour mug loomed over the counter.

"Tough day at the office, Sheriff?"

"It's shaping up that way. Say Jeeter, do you know anything about cougars?"

"Sure do!" the man smirked. "I lost my nut to a cougar. Hazel May Alcomb. Nearly fifty years old and built like a brick shithouse. She did this thing with her tongue that..."

"No, Jeeter," Cooper cut him off with a sickened grimace. "I mean *actual* cougars. Mountain Lions. Pumas. Catamounts. You know, big *fucking* cats."

"Oh," Jeeter's light finally came on. "You mean like Snagglepuss!"

Cooper tried to keep his eyes from rolling, but he only partially succeeded.

"Sure," he said through a sigh. "Like Snagglepuss."

"Dunno. Not much. Why?"

"You ever seen one?"

"Like, for real?" Jeeter shrugged. "Dunno. Maybe in a zoo somewhere."

"Never in the wild? Maybe out on the edge of town, or up in the hills along one of the hiking trails?"

In answer, Jeeter lifted his prodigious belly in his hands and unceremoniously flopped it down on the counter.

"Well, let's see. Last time I was out mountain biking, I saw what might have been a mountain lion, but I was racing down those trails so fast, I couldn't be sure. After all, I don't go for the sightseeing, I go for the workout."

This time, Cooper didn't even attempt to restrain the eye-roll.

"Forget I asked."

"Done," Jeeter nodded, allowing his belly to ooze off the counter and flop back to its normal position three inches below his belt buckle. "Now, how about that meatloaf? I'll even give you the police discount."

"You don't *have* a police discount," Cooper reminded him.

"Well, I do now. For today only, all members of the Keeter's Bluff Sheriff's Department shall receive twenty percent off the regular price of meatloaf."

"Just enough to cover the cost of Pepto," Cooper mused, not quite under his breath. Then, just on the off-chance, he asked, "Hey, Jeeter, I don't suppose you happen to have a cake back there?"

"Cake? No. I got a peach pie that ain't too bad. Got enough lard in the crust to let you crap through a garden hose."

"Sounds inviting," Cooper lied, "but I need a cake."

"You try Marigold's? If I needed a cake, that's where I'd go."

Cooper's shoulders slumped.

"Yeah, I was hoping it wouldn't come to that, but I suppose it will. Damn! Marigold's going to be just as pissed as Fancy."

"Hey, how about Dairy Queen?" Jeeter suggested with a sudden stroke of inspiration. "Those ice cream logs of theirs are pretty damn tasty."

Cooper ran through the entire gamut of possible responses, none of them flattering, then he discounted them all and downed the last of his coffee in a gulp.

"Thanks for the coffee, Jeeter," he said, hauling himself off the stool and making his way back to the door.

He noticed Janice watching him out of the corner of her eye as she topped up a slavering Mike Gimpley's cup. As he got close, she took one long step backward, effectively cutting him off at the pass.

"Oh, I'm so sorry, Sheriff!" she gushed, fake stumbling into his arms. "I am *so* clumsy!"

His head swirling with the scent of spearmint and now just a hint of baby powder, he helped her steady herself, then he quickly put that one straining button in his rearview mirror without another word.

"You gonna pay for the coffee, Tom?" Jeeter called after him, but Cooper didn't even turn around.

"Put it on my tab," he called back over his shoulder as the bell tinged again.

"Tom, you don't *have* a..." he heard, but then Jeeter's voice was cut off as the door swung shut.

Cooper began slowly retracing his steps back to his cruiser, and got there just in time to see Harlon Abrams' tow truck hooking up to the back of Hayley's marooned Falcon. He stuck around long enough to see the man try to remove the old gal from the vehicle, and to watch her fend him off with purse swinging and middle finger held high, then he side-stepped another knot of kids chasing each other down the sidewalk and used the gathering crowds to sneak back to his squad car. With the Falcon's motor racing, and a cloud of exhaust threatening to swallow the entire street whole, he keyed the cruiser to life and made a quick right, leaving poor Harlon Abrams to deal with Hayley all on his own.

Another quick right, and he was on 2nd Street just as his phone jingled. He checked the screen. It was Judge Whittaker, father of the bride and the man who would soon be tearing him a new hole. He dropped the phone back in his pocket and let the call go to voicemail. A voicemail he would never check.

The dash clock read one forty-seven. The wedding was set for three o'clock, to be followed by a reception at six. Why the long interval, he had no idea, but he had a sneaking suspicion that it had something to do with how long it would take to unharness Fancy from her wedding gown and manhandle her into something that might allow her to breathe. And, of course, to eat.

Four hours. That's how long he had. Four hours. Four hours until he effectively ruined Fancy's big day, and the rest of his life.

The phone chimed to let him know he had a new voicemail as he wheeled left onto Griffin. From there, it was a straight shot up to Marigold's. He had no choice now. He had to face the music. Marigold might come after him with a rolling pin for destroying her prized creation, but so be it. In fact, now that he thought about it, maybe a rolling pin upside the head was exactly what he needed right now. If he was laid up in a hospital bed for a day or two, at least he'd have an out. Not even the Judge would be mean enough to take out his anger on a man nursing a concussion. Or, at least, he didn't *think* he was mean enough. In any event, if Marigold could somehow work a miracle and provide him with a replacement cake, it would be a damn-sight better to have *her* mad at him than Fancy Whittaker and her snarling pit bull of a father.

Lost in his own world, Cooper was paying little attention to the larger world blurring past his windows until a shrill scream came out of nowhere and brought his foot down hard on the brake. The cruiser skidded to a stop in front of the First Evangelical Church, and there Cooper sat as a most bizarre spectacle appeared from behind the church itself.

It was Pastor Raymond in his usual off-hours uniform of clean white shirt, big ol' shorts, knee-high black socks, and matching dress shoes. But this was Pastor Raymond as he'd never seen him before. Normally, the good Pastor was as staid and somber as a mortician, befitting both his age and his position. This other man was flailing his arms wildly about, and prancing in odd little circles across the Church's lawn. But even as Cooper marveled at the odd display and wondered what manner of sacramental wine could have possibly gotten the good Pastor to suddenly take up dancing like a hippie at Woodstock, the man boogaloo'ed close enough that he could finally make out what looked to be a wispy cloud swirling all around him.

In one swift move, Cooper jumped from the car, popped the trunk open, snatched up a small fire extinguisher from within, and ran to the dancing Pastor. And with every step he took, a particularly ominous buzzing sound became louder and louder.

It wasn't sacramental wine that had brought out Pastor Raymond's epic dance moves after all. It was bees. Thousands upon thousands of bees were swarming around the man from head to toe, and though the Pastor was swatting away like a wild man, he might as well have been trying to punch his way out of a cloud.

Cooper triggered the fire extinguisher as he ran, and met the Pastor with a full blast of CO_2 directly in the face. And for one brief moment, it seemed to do the trick. The swarm parted, and Pastor Raymond was able to suck in a desperately needed lungful of air. But the respite was temporary at best. Angered by the blast, the swarm quickly shrugged off the cold and returned in force, only now they had two targets for their aggression instead of just one. Cooper felt a sting on the back of his neck and another piercing the lightweight material of his shirt sleeve, and when a third bee flew straight through the billowing gas to sting him just under his left ear, he finally realized that this was a war he could never win. He dropped the useless fire extinguisher to the ground, threw an arm around Pastor Raymond, and half-dragged, half-carried the poor man ten agonizingly long yards back to his cruiser.

He threw the man into the passenger seat and slammed the door closed, and with the greater part of the swarm suddenly denied access to the Pastor, they turned their full fury on Cooper. They swarmed all over him as he ran around to the far side of the car, and by the time he climbed in and slammed the door shut, he had counted no fewer than twenty stings on his neck and shoulders, and two more on his face, frighteningly close to his eyes. But they weren't out of the woods yet. Hundreds of bees had followed them into the cruiser, and he felt two more stings under his shirt collar even as he stabbed for the climate control to crank the air conditioner up full.

He swatted at his shirt collar and swept several more bees from his face, then he turned his attention to Pastor Raymond slumped beside him. He brushed several from the man's face and swatted a dozen more into paste on his back and shoulders and chest, and at last, with the interior of the car turning ice cold, the onslaught began to peter out. Then it ceased altogether.

"Pastor?" Cooper panted, looking for a place to grab the man in order to shake him conscious, but finding not a single square inch of flesh left unstung.

A finger to the neck confirmed the man's pulse, but it was weak and thready. Cooper's Kevlar vest and thick polyester pants had saved him from the worst of it, but a clean white shirt and big ol' shorts offered little protection. Pastor Raymond was one big open wound, all the way from the tops of his knee-high socks to his rapidly receding hairline.

Outside the car, the air was as thick as smoke. The swarm was still there, swirling and eddying all around the vehicle and covering every window like a shroud. Then, just that, they were gone. All at once, the sun shone bright in a clear blue sky, and Cooper was left with Austin Granger's words echoing in his ear.

What the fuck was that?

CHAPTER

V

The doors to Isaac H. Templeton High School wouldn't open for another eight weeks, but the school year was already underway for Emma Wong. The move from sunny California to the middle of nowhere had already been stressful enough. The last thing she needed now was to be caught flat-footed on the first day of a new job at a new school. She had applied for the posting on a whim, just like how she lived the rest of her life. A firm believer in fate, she had long ago decided to trust the universe to take her where she needed to be, and one month ago, the universe decided that Keeter's Bluff was just that spot. So here she was, for better or for worse.

She sipped her tea, turned the page in her binder, and selected another book from the pile.

History hadn't been her first choice. In fact, becoming a teacher at all wasn't her first choice. She had gone to UCLA on a track scholarship with visions of Olympic gold dancing in her head, but one blown-out knee and a chance meeting at a Pasadena Starbucks later, and her plans were altered forever.

Denise. Denise Fairbanks. Beautiful blonde Denise. Their time together had been wonderful. Magical, even. Besides awakening in her a passion she hadn't known existed, beautiful blonde Denise had awakened something else, too. With all of their talk of a life together, the subject had often turned to the possibility of children. Adoption. Sperm donor. The three-parent technique. All were discussed, and all were considered. Then, one year later, Denise was gone, leaving Emma with zero regrets for one single second of that magical year, but also with one last parting gift. Their talk of children had fueled such a desire in her that when it came time to choose which of life's paths she would hobble down on her busted knee and broken heart, she remembered that beautiful blonde goddess with the heart of gold and a love of children, and her hand had automatically selected the Teaching Credential program. And while she pondered the myriad options available to an aspiring teacher of children, the universe answered once again. Her first choice had been the obvious, but UCLA didn't offer a teaching degree in physical education, so she'd stabbed blindly at the raft of papers littering her dorm room desk, and her fate was sealed. History. She would teach those children history. She would teach them the history that was, and along the way, she would show them the unwritten histories of their own futures. And in that way, she would teach an entire generation of children what she would probably never be able to teach her own.

Now, eight years later, here she was in a new town with a new group of kids. But this year was going to be decidedly more difficult. Instead of expanding the minds of children, she was going to be facing high school seniors who knew almost as much about history as she did. These kids were barely a decade younger than her. They had been through almost as much life as *she* had, so what the hell could she possibly teach them? How was she even going to get them to look up from their smart phones long enough for her to have any impact at all?

But once again, the universe had her back. She had dropped into the Keeter's Bluff library on her first day in town to peruse the shelves for inspiration, and inspiration was exactly what she'd found. Fumbling through shelf after shelf of the Spanish Inquisition and the Renaissance and the lives of Madame Curie and Augustus Caesar and Alexander the Great, she had come across one of the librarians returning books to their proper places, and her eyes had naturally gone to the off-balance cart hobbling along behind her. And on that cart had been her inspiration. It was a stack of returned books, destined for the farthest reaches of the library. Back into those dark corners where reality ended and pseudo-reality began.

Ghosts. UFOs. JFK. The Gaia Theory. Flat Earth. They were all there. All the way from Aristotle's theory of the soul, through the prophecies of Edgar Cayce, and right up to the 9/11 'truthers' movement. It was solid gold. Every bit of it. No, she could never use those books to teach her students actual history, but she could sure use them to get her students' attention. And after they debated between themselves the question of what might be true and what was obvious nonsense, they would absorb the real history she gave them like sponges. And better yet, instead of simply getting them to memorize dates and places and names enough to regurgitate them back for a midterm, that back-end play might just instill in them a genuine curiosity for the world and for the history of these naked apes known as humans. Hell, if she could get even a few of them to start thinking for themselves, what more could a teacher hope for?

She wrote the words 'Gaia' across the top of the page and underlined it twice, then she retrieved the appropriate text and began reading. But barely had she begun when a loud *flump!* rattled the window behind her. Startled, she spun around in her chair, but there was nothing there. Hardly surprising, since she was on the top floor of a three-story apartment building, but still, she'd heard *something*, hadn't she? But then again, maybe she hadn't. New town, new apartment, maybe all she'd heard was a water pipe clanging in the walls, or one of her neighbors slamming a door.

She turned back to the binder and put pen back to paper, but before she'd written a single word, another *thwump!* shuddered down her spine, making her spin around once again. But once again, there was nothing to see. But wait, wasn't there? There, just at the edge of the window, wasn't there just the tiniest bit of *something* on the window?

Yes, she was sure of it. The rest of the glass was hardly spotless, but this was more than just the grey haze of an unwashed window. There was something else clinging there, right at the very edge. A tiny spot of red. Barely there, but there. And what was that holding fast to that tiny spot of red? A bit of dander? A little tuft of fur? Hair? Feathers? Neither?

She put her face right up to the glass and focused on that one tiny spot of red. But just as her eyes began to bring the odd little bit of whatever-it-was into focus, an abrupt pounding on the apartment door startled her enough that she inadvertently smacked her forehead hard against the window jamb. She then watched in pain as that tiny red spot with its little bit of whatever-it-was broke away from the window and spiraled down into the abyss.

"Coming!" she growled, clamping a hand to her forehead and feeling a lump already beginning to grow under her hand.

She took a blurry peek through the eye hole, then she undid the chain, threw back the deadbolt, and swung the door wide open. And there, clad in her pajama bottoms and a UCLA halter top that barely covered the essentials, she met her new principal for the first time, with one hand clamped to her forehead and a tear breaking free to carve a path down her cheek.

"Er... Miss Wong?" the man asked. He flicked his eyes from the woman to the number on the door and back again. "Er... it *is* Miss Wong, yes?"

"Auntie Em?" she said at first, jokingly, but seeing no hint of humor in the man's countenance, she did a quick about-face. "I'm sorry, Mr. Danvers. Yes, I'm Emma Wong. Please come in."

She stepped aside and swept her arm inward in a grand gesture, but the pudgy little man remained just beyond the threshold.

"Auntie Em? What exactly did you mean by that?" he asked in a scowl.

"I apologize, Mr. Danvers," she explained, clumsily. "It was a vain attempt at humor."

"Vain, indeed," the man scoffed. "So, is this what we can expect from you in the future? Is Isaac H. Templeton High School to be your own personal Yuk Yuk's?"

"Not if you're in the audience," she said, barely under

her breath, then aloud, she assured him, "I'm sorry, Mr. Danvers. I hit my head, and when I hurt, I joke. It's a coping mechanism, I guess."

Danvers considered the matter fully, then he harumphed out loud.

"Well, let us hope that you have no further need to, er... cope."

"Agreed," Emma replied, wiping away the tear but keeping her hand over a bump that she could actually feel growing beneath her fingers. "After all, joking could lead to a good mood among the students. And what then? Dancing?"

"I beg your pardon?"

She relented with a sigh.

"Nothing. I'm sorry. What can I do for you, Mr. Danvers?"

"I am here at the behest of my wife, Amanda," he told her plainly. "As principal of Isaac H. Templeton High School, she suggested that it might fall upon me to make you feel at home in your new environs."

She aimed a finger his way. "Wait, I thought *you* were the principal."

"What?" he asked, perplexed.

"What?" she replied, playing along.

"Er, uh, at any rate," Danvers went on undeterred, "I am here to invite you to our home for dinner. We dine at seven. Do please try to be on time. And if vanity should strike you mid-course, encouraging you to deliver a stand-up routine, I trust you will do your best to curtail it."

With that, he spun on his dainty little heels and pranced off, and Emma Wong was left alone in her doorway, huffing, "Oh, I'm sure an evening with you and the missus will only make me weep," to no one in particular. Then, as the pudgy little man disappeared around the corner and down the stairs, she called after him, "Wait! Mr. Danvers, I don't know where you live!"

But it was too late. Danvers was long gone.

She closed and locked the door, and with the lump now growing wet beneath her fingers, she made a quick stop in the kitchen to see if the last tenant might possibly have been kind enough to leave behind a full ice tray in the freezer. Of course he hadn't, but that nameless ex-tenant had been almost as kind. There, in the back corner of the freezer, huddled an ancient package of frozen peas. Expiry date... holy *fuck!* She gingerly unhuddled the peas so as not to disturb whatever life form might be growing within, then she grabbed a tea towel from the counter and carried both items with her to the bathroom.

There, she wetted the cloth in cold water and pressed it against a lump over her left eye the size of a robin's egg, topped by an ugly red gash. Again and again she applied the remoistened cloth, hissing through her teeth each and every time. At last, the flow of blood slowed and finally stopped, but the robin's egg and ugly red gash remained.

"Awesome," she told her reflection in the mirror. "Fucking awesome. New job, new school, new town, same fucking klutz."

She wrapped the bag of peas in the wet tea towel and pressed it to her forehead as she popped open the medicine cabinet, hoping against hope that the ex-tenant who had left the old-as-fuck peas might have left an equally old-as-fuck Band-Aid. But it was not be. And she had only grabbed the bare necessities on her way through town. Milk. Bread. A couple rolls of toilet paper. Oh, and that bottle of vodka, of course. Only the necessities. Things like Band-Aids were *way* down the list. Still, couldn't the last tenant of this rundown, fleabag, so-called 'furnished' apartment have left behind one single Band-Aid?

She slammed the medicine cabinet closed and tried the one and only drawer next to the sink, and her persistence was finally rewarded. There, crumpled up beneath a frayed old toothbrush rimmed with black, was a single My Little Ponies Band-Aid, still in its paper cover. She picked up the toothbrush between finger and thumb and dropped it into the wastebasket with a disgusted, "Ugh!" then she tore open the Band-Aid and laid it ever so carefully across the top of the robin's egg.

"Awesome," she said at seeing the phalanx of Ponies galloping gaily across her forehead. "Yippee ki yay, mother-fucker..."

CHAPTER

VI

H e's in shock, but he'll make it."

This was Kira Melanson, chief resident of Keeter's Bluff General. She made one last note in a chart, tucked the pen in her breast pocket, and told Cooper honestly, "Another ten minutes and he might not have. I stopped counting at two hundred stings. He couldn't have survived many more. Not at his age."

Cooper let out a breath he'd been holding since he got there, and shook the woman's hand, holding it for not one second longer than seemed appropriate.

"Thanks, Doc. Buck checked out the church and found the good Pastor's lawn mower next to an exposed nest. He must've run over it without even knowing it was there."

"The man's lucky to be alive."

"Well, he does have God on his side," Cooper quipped.

"More like a fire extinguisher and a sheriff with balls of steel," Melanson scoffed.

"And a doctor who knows her shit," Cooper scoffed back. "Between you, me, and the fencepost, Doc, I'll take *you* over any old, bearded man in the sky any day."

"Don't let the voters hear you say that, Tom," the doctor smirked. "The next election's only a few months away. Outright sacrilege might not sit well with the locals."

He smiled wryly. "In that case, maybe I'll come work for you. You know, I'm pretty good at reading thermometers."

"Rectal?" she mused, and that put an end to it. "Seriously, Tom, you saved Pastor Raymond's life. You should be proud. Good for you."

He shook his head.

"No, Doc, that was all you. All I did was pull him out of the line of fire. You and your team saved that man's bacon, and I'll be sure the whole town knows it. It might even earn you a free hot dog at the annual Baptist and Methodist Summer Jamboree."

"Huzzah," she said, emotionlessly. Then her eyes softened and she had to ask, "Are you doing okay, Tom? We haven't talked much since... well, since..."

"I'm good, Kira," he told her as honestly as he could. "Really, I'm good."

She took his hand once more and held it gently.

"I'm glad, Tom. You know I never wanted..."

"I know," he said, cutting her off again, but making no move to pull his hand away.

"It looks like our little friends didn't leave you entirely unscathed," she said, delicately touching the skin around the welts near his eyes. "Can I give you something for these stings?"

"Naw, I'm good," Cooper lied, pulling up his collar so that the only woman he had ever loved wouldn't see the worst of it. "I'm sure you're busy anyway."

"Oh, you can say that again," she breathed. "It's been a bitch of a day. We had to call in extra staff just to keep the ER moving."

"Yeah? Some kind of flu bug going around or something?"

"More like a full moon fever. I swear, there are days that feel like whoever's running the program just flipped the crazy switch."

Before Cooper could respond, his phone chimed. He retrieved it from his pocket and checked the number. It was Austin Granger, resident critter wrangler. But little more than an hour had passed since he'd helped load Snagglepuss into the back of the Ratmobile. Far too soon to have any test results back yet.

Reluctantly, he released Kira's hand, swiped his thumb across the green crosshairs, and brought the phone to his ear.

"Austin? Whatcha got?"

"Coop?" the voice on the other end said, but it was weak. Barely even there.

"Austin?" he tried again, and then again, louder, "Austin?"

"Coop, you'd better come down here. The old McIffrin place, down on Laurel."

"Austin? What's going on? The McIffrin place? I don't..."

"Get down here, Sheriff," the voice repeated, just as weakly. Then the phone went dead, and Cooper could do little more than throw Doctor Kira Melanson a quick, "Later, Doc," before running back down the hallway to his waiting car.

The phone rang again while he was pulling out of the hospital parking lot. It was the Judge. Again. He dropped the phone back into his pocket. Again. Then the radio crackled.

"KB-Four to KB-One, over."

It wasn't Grace this time, thankfully. It was Deputy Rankin. He keyed the mike as he wheeled south onto Breckinridge and answered back.

"Go ahead, Carl."

A long pause followed. Rankin was chewing over his words. Not a good sign. He only did that when he had bad news.

"Uh, Sheriff, I hate to tell you this, but the Judge knows. So does Fancy. And I could tell by the way each of them tore a strip off'a me that they ain't exactly happy."

Well, shit. It was bound to happen. He'd just hoped to have more time.

"Copy, Carl. Out," he grumbled, and returned the mike to its hook.

Seven minutes later, he wheeled around one last corner and felt a familiar knot tighten in his belly as he took in the old McIffrin place in all of its hideous glory.

This was the oldest building in the 'Bluff, built way back when the town was just a bend in the road. Perhaps there had actually been a time when those high ceilings and gothic spires were considered stylish, but Cooper couldn't imagine it. To him, the place had always been an eyesore. Too big, too gothic, and after sitting empty and rotting for the better part of eighty years, too rundown to ever be more than the crumbling, ramshackle dump it had always been. And worse, old Hezekiah McIffrin had chosen the worst parcel of land in the entire county on which to build his unstately manor. Locals called this area 'the Dip'. At some point in prehistory, the land here subsided, ending up a good thirty feet below the surrounding area and effectively cutting off any chance at a cross breeze. As a result, the air here was perpetually thick. Heavy. Cloying. Borderline miasmic.

Austin Granger's Landcruiser was parked against the curb in front of the place. Granger himself was sitting on the tailgate, puffing on a cigarette. He made no move to stand as Cooper pulled in behind.

"I thought you quit that shit, Austin," Cooper harumphed, climbing from the cruiser and already struggling to fill his lungs with air as thick as paste.

"I did," Granger replied, exhaling a cloud of smoke that went nowhere at all. He hitched a thumb at a tin canister marked 'poison' and added humorlessly, "Luckily, Jermaine missed one of my hiding spots."

Cooper looked his old friend up and down, taking in every subtle detail. The man was nervous. Visibly trembling. Trying to hide it, but doing a piss-poor job of it. Behind him, six steel cages were shoved up against the bulkhead of the truck, each one containing a rat the approximate size of a schnauzer. There was no sign of the cat.

"I see you got Snagglepuss to the shop."

The man forced a shaky nod. "Jermaine's taking the samples up to Piedmont as we speak. Said she'd call with the results." He tried to check his quivering watch, but quickly gave up. "Shouldn't be long."

"Okay," Cooper replied, adding nothing else. Rather than press the man for the reason for the phone call or for why he was so clearly distraught, he knew Granger would tell him when he was good and ready. And soon enough, he was.

"I have the contract," the man began, clumsily. "I mean *a* contract. You know, from the town council. Someone should've torn this old shithole down years ago, but it's a heritage building, so they can't. I mean, *it* can't. I mean..."

"I know what you mean, Austin," Cooper assured him gently, and left it at that.

Granger took a shallow puff of his cigarette and waved it at the old McIffrin place.

"The town hates this place, *I* hate this place, and anyone with common sense hates this place. This monstrosity should've been dynamited the day Hezekiah McIffrin drove in the last nail. Still should be, if you ask me."

Cooper simply listened, saying nothing.

"But you know who doesn't hate this monstrosity, Coop? I'll tell you who. Or, I mean, *what*. Rats, Coop. Rats *love* abandoned buildings. Unfortunately, rats also love Hantavirus, Salmonella, Tularaemia, and a dozen other delights up to and including a little thing we like to call the Plague. So I was contracted to... to, uh..."

His voice trailed off as he looked back to the house. All at once, his expression grew distant and the unfinished cigarette dropped from his fingers.

"I know, Austin," Cooper said, and left it at that. Again, he waited for the man to explain when he was good and ready. And again, that time came soon enough.

"You know me, Coop. I catch and release. I would no more poison a colony of rats than I would a basketful of puppies. I set the traps, leave them for a day or two, and town rats become country rats. Easy peasy."

Not once did the man take his eyes from the McIffrin place, and now Cooper's gaze followed. But all seemed as it had always been. As far as he could tell, there was no difference between what the place was now and what it had been a month before, or a year before, or back when he was a kid tearing past the place on his bike with all the hairs on the back of his neck standing at full attention. But the look in Granger's eyes said differently.

"You didn't happen to see the ghost of old Hezekiah in there, did you?" Cooper asked, only half-jokingly.

"Not of him, no," Granger replied, tearing his eyes away from the house at last and fixing them directly on Cooper's. "But there *are* ghosts in there, Coop. Well, one, anyway."

The man hauled himself to his feet, tucked his long hair behind his ears, took a deep breath, and without another word, set off across the expanse of chest-high weeds that used to be a lawn. Cooper followed, but not quite so silently.

"Austin, is there any history of mental illness in your family?"

Granger threw a threadbare grin back at Cooper and shrugged.

"I had an uncle who thought he was Saint Jerome. Does that count?"

They reached the front steps, and Granger led the way up. Cooper arrived on the rotting deck just as Granger pushed the door open, but the outrush of fetid air forced him back a step with nose and mouth tucked squarely in the crook of his elbow.

"I know, right?" Granger said, clicking a tiny flashlight to life and shining it into the darkness. "That delicate bouquet is a century's worth of dust, mold, and rat feces, with just a *soupçon* of asbestos and lead paint thrown in for good measure. Intoxicating, isn't it?"

Cooper pressed his face harder into his elbow.

"*Jesus*, Austin! Is it safe?"

"Hell no," Granger snorted. "But if it's any consolation, Coop, you're more likely to be killed by this old shithouse crashing down around your ears than by any of those mold spores currently taking up residence in your lungs."

"It's not," Cooper admitted, but with Granger now stepping through the open door, he had no choice. He drew the flashlight from his duty belt, uncovered his face, and reluctantly followed.

Almost immediately, he regretted his decision. Barely had he set foot across the threshold before a cobweb as thick as rope drifted down across his face, and though he held himself together enough to brush the thing away without the usual whirling dervish dance of a confirmed arachnophobe, one sweep of his flashlight's beam made him question every life decision he had ever made that had gotten him to that exact moment in time and space.

The old McIffrin place might have been teeming with rats, and laden with mold, asbestos, lead paint, and who knows what else, but it was far worse than that. It was also crawling with spiders. Literally. A moving carpet of the horrible things skittered in every direction across the floor and up the walls, and formed great undulating knots of ugliness wherever the two converged. Overhead, the tall, vaulted ceiling was lowered by half by a vast tangle of webs, eight feet thick and stretching from one side of the entranceway to the other, with every inch of that awful false ceiling blanketed by the fattest, blackest spiders he could ever have imagined in his worst nightmare.

Everywhere he turned was another horror show. Naturally, the swarms of spiders fled from the light as soon as it drew near, but that made it even worse. Those little bursts of speed and flurries of legs jittered up his spine like ice, and with so many of the creatures fleeing into the nest above, he began to wonder just how long it would be before the whole thing came apart and rained every last one of those evil bastards down on top of him.

But still, he was the Sheriff, so as hard as it was under such circumstances, he buried his fears and concentrated on the job at hand.

Mostly.

"Let's make this quick, Austin," he said, not bothering to disguise the tremor in his voice as he waved the man desperately on.

"This way," Granger motioned, and set off through a maze of corridors as dark as pitch with Sheriff Cooper in hot pursuit.

And there it was. There, at the back of the house, in what clearly used to be the kitchen. A body. Or rather, what was left of a body. Now, it was no more than a skeleton. Just bones, cartilage, and barely enough connective tissue to keep the thing from disarticulating completely.

With a quick, nervous sweep of his light to make certain they were well and truly alone, Cooper dropped to his knee for a closer look. The bones themselves were pinkish-white. The hardwood floor beneath was stained a ruddy brown. One femur had been gnawed away at the knee, exposing a spongey, red interior. And all around the body as far as his light could reach, tiny four- and five-toed prints were clearly visible in a hundred year's worth of dust.

"This is fresh," he told Granger. "A day at most. Are there enough rats here to do this in that short a time?"

"More than," Granger replied, grimly.

"When was the last time you went through this room?"

"Last night," came the answer.

Cooper peered through the remains of what used to be a human being, then he swept his flashlight over and around the corpse in ever widening circles. But aside from an occasional lone arachnid fleeing like a bandit to the darker reaches of the room as quickly as the light hit it, there was nothing else to find. No wallet. No keys. No phone. Nothing but rags, bones, and those ugly, stained floorboards.

"It's not that unusual," Granger offered, apparently reading Cooper's mind. "Once the meat was gone, they would have divvied up whatever remained of the poor guy's clothing for bedding material. If his wallet was leather, they would've taken that, too. And rats are attracted to shiny things, so it's not hard to imagine them making off with keys and whatnot."

"That's a lot of evidence to lose," Cooper grumbled. "Any chance you could locate the nest so we could get back some of those whatnots?"

"Coop, this whole gothic dump is one *huge* nest. Whatever evidence there might be would have been spread around from attic to basement. You'd have to tear open every wall and rip up every floorboard to have a hope of finding even the slightest trace of who this poor bastard was. It would be easier to burn the place down and sift through the ashes."

Not a bad idea... Cooper considered, but kept it to himself.

As he rose back to his feet, he felt a faint ticking at the back of his neck. Without thinking, he brought up a hand to satisfy the itch, but even if he could have somehow discounted the sensation of coming upon something solid, the thing that subsequently detached itself and plopped to the floor right in front of him couldn't be ignored.

A spider the size of a baseball mitt happened to land directly on top of the fleshless skull, and there it clung, looking up at the human intruders with eight gleaming red eyes.

That was enough for Cooper. He spun on his heels and all but ran back the way he had come, sweeping his flashlight in every direction at once, and feeling the floor becoming more and more slick with every sickening crunch beneath his boots. With one final lunge, he burst back through the open door, and at last he was out in the open air under a bright summer sun. One prolonged cumulative attack of the willies later, Granger was there beside him.

"Like I said, Coop," the man shrugged, locking the door and tucking the key under a loose corner of a rotting step. "This place has at least one ghost now."

As Cooper swept a hundred imaginary cobwebs away from his face, and out of his hair, and from as far around his back as he could reach, he answered Granger back without a word of a lie.

"Damn-near had two, buddy," he said through a grimace. "Damn-near had two."

CHAPTER

VII

He pulled his cruiser into the station's parking lot, and there he sat with a thousand thoughts coursing through his head. Bees. Cougars. Rats. Spiders. A destroyed wedding cake. Each had their own place in a panoply of images, but as always, he boiled all of it down to its most essential ingredient.

The body. The dead body. In spite of all of the crazy shit going on, the DB was top priority. That pile of bones had once belonged to a living, breathing human being, so he had to find out who, how, when, and if the universe allowed such a thing, he also had to figure out why. Had this simply been someone looking for a dry place to spend the night and giving up the ghost halfway through? One of the 'Bluff's less fortunate citizens, maybe? Or maybe a drifter with a bad ticker, *almost* passing through town? Hell, maybe it was just a wayward husband stopping to sleep off a snootful rather than stumble home and face an angry wife, and the dumbass happened to choose just that moment to choke to death on his own vomit. Or perhaps, just perhaps, there might be something much more sinister at work.

It was this last possibility that tied a fresh knot in his belly.

Rankin's report was already in. Once Doc Jenkins took the body away, the deputy had gone over every inch of the place with a fine-toothed comb and come up empty. Whatever evidence there might once have been had been obliterated by thousands upon thousands of scurrying feet. The only signs of human activity Rankin found in the entire place was a single partial footprint, and a broken lock on the rear door. So, with no real evidence, no clothes, no ID, and no fingerprints to run through IAFIS, it was all on Doc Jenkins' shoulders. As coroner and chief pathologist, it was now Jenkins' job to come up with the who, the when and the how. Dental records. DNA. The magic of modern science would give them the answers. All he'd have to do then was put the pieces together.

He climbed from the car and made his way up the steps, knowing exactly what awaited him. And he was right. No sooner had he opened the door than he was met by the stern and decidedly unpleasant face of one Grace Tolliver.

The old gal checked the watch pinned to her blouse and scowled at Cooper over her granny glasses.

"Well, as I live and breathe," she growled. "I thought the royal nuptials were underway. What's the matter, Sheriff? Forget your damn rice?"

He ignored her and passed wordlessly into his office, slamming the door closed behind him with enough force to shake it in its frame. He took a seat in his back-breaking relic of a chair, picked up the desk phone, and called Kira at the hospital. She told him that Pastor Raymond was through the worst of it, so the prognosis was good. Next, he called Doc Jenkins' private line. There was nothing on the victim yet, but X-rays had been sent to every dental office in the county. Two molars had also been sent to the University in Jolene for DNA profiling, but it could be weeks before they knew anything. Jenkins then asked if there was any chance they could get one of those forensic facial reconstruction guys to rebuild the man's face. Cooper reminded him that he'd had to sell his soul just to get a new stapler, and that ended the conversation.

He fired up his computer, but there was nothing to find in the KBSD database for missing person's. In a town of only fifty thousand souls, a missing person almost always amounted to a runaway teen or a drunk husband passed out in an alley somewhere in a puddle of his own urine. Either way, those MP reports invariably amounted to nothing. In the twenty years he'd been on the job, he had only encountered a handful of true missing persons cases, and those few were invariably closed when little Becky-Sue or Jim-Bob got tired of sleeping in doorways and wandered back home.

Hell, this was small town nowhere, not big city America. People didn't go missing here, they didn't get gunned down in schools here, and they sure as *fuck* didn't have the flesh ripped from their bones by a swarm of rats here. Sure, the 'Bluff had its problems, and it had its wrong side of the tracks, but this? *Hell*, no. This couldn't be murder. It simply couldn't be. It had to be some unfortunate bum hunkering down for the night and not quite making it through to morning. After that, it was all a case of nature taking its course. Rats were there, so they fed, and that was it. Nothing more. No grand conspiracy, and no big city crime spree. The man died, and rats had feasted on his corpse. End of story. Case closed.

Well, not quite closed yet, but certainly swinging on its hinges.

A knock on the door made him jump, but thankfully, it wasn't Grace. He knew it wasn't because Grace never knocked. Ever. And besides, the KBSD shoulder crests visible through the windows on both sides of the door gave it away. Only one man under his command could possibly fill so much space.

"Come in, Henry," he called out.

The door swung wide open, but the deputy still had to angle his body to get through the opening.

Henry Greenleaf. Six foot six and built like a Mack truck. Born into the Death Valley Timbisha Shoshone Band, and raised in LA. Enormously proud of both. Criminology major from UCal-Irvine. Varsity quarterback. Smart as hell, as strong as an ox, and as loyal as they came.

"Close call with the cat, huh Sheriff?" the man said, towering over Cooper's desk like a redwood.

"As close as I ever want to come, Henry. Good thing I was wearing my shittin' pants."

Henry laughed a deep, hearty laugh.

"As you know, Sheriff, we've been chasing down 91-Victors all day. Mostly dogs snapping at the mailman and the like, but some of them are downright funky. Ferrell Gimpley swore a black bear tried to get in his kitchen window, but he was three sheets to the wind, so who knows? And Luke Taylor claimed a pack of coyotes tried to make a lunch out of his boy when they were out checking the fences, but luckily, he had his rifle in the truck and a couple of shots scared them off. I tell you, Sheriff, something weird's going on. We've had more animal complaints today than we usually get in a year. And you know for a fact that for every one of those, there are dozens more that someone handled on their own."

"Sounds like full moon fever," Cooper suggested. Wrongly, as it turned out.

"Next full moon's not for another two weeks," Greenleaf corrected him.

"Something in the water, then," Cooper said, waving the matter off.

"Maybe so," the deputy considered, then he harumphed, "I know what my grandfather would say. There's an old Navajo legend about a shaman who summoned evil forces in order to gain the power to transform himself into an animal. Once the deal was done, he could change himself into a bear, or a wolf, or a bird... Anything he wanted. They call him *Yee Naaldlooshii*. The Skinwalker."

"And you believe that, Henry?"

Greenleaf shrugged. "I don't *dis*believe it. But I do believe that shit flows the way it's going to, and there's nothing we can do about it. Some days we get a dribble, other days we get the whole damn outhouse."

"Well, this must be one of the outhouse days," Cooper grumbled.

"Feels like it. You hear from Buck, Sheriff?"

"Not yet. You help him take care of our little friends?"

"I did," he said through a scowl. "Dumb fucker wanted to burn the bees out. Can you believe it? When I got there, he was behind the church, hovering over the nest with a can of gasoline and a pack of matches. He was all set to burn down an acre of trees just to kill a few harmless Hymenoptera."

"Those Hyph... uh, hymen... those *things* nearly killed

Pastor Raymond, Henry," Cooper reminded him, however clumsily.

"They were just doing what they do, Sheriff. The hive was threatened, so they responded. Wouldn't you have done the same thing?"

"I don't know. I'm not a bee," Cooper answered, straight-faced.

"I cordoned it off, twenty feet back. Posted signs, too. Bees don't give a damn about humans unless they're attacked or the hive is threatened, so that should be enough. If we leave *them* alone, they'll leave *us* alone."

"I'm sorry, Henry. Which part of 'nearly killed Pastor Raymond' did you not understand?"

"They're blueberry bees, Sheriff. *Habropoda laboriosa*. They got the name because they evolved alongside native blueberries, and their bodies have become a perfect fit for the flowers."

"I've never cared for blueberries," Cooper mused. "Now, if they were *agave* bees..."

"Sheriff, bee populations are down all over the world. It's called Colony Collapse Disorder. No one knows what's causing it, but we humans do seem intent on murdering every last one of our furry little friends. Pesticides, fungicides, air pollution, neonicotinoids, RF blasting from every cell tower in every city... I tell you, Sheriff, if we succeed in killing off the bees, we will miss them terribly."

The mention of pesticides took Cooper immediately back to the McIffrin place, but he shook off the memory before the willies could creep back up on him.

"Bees or blueberries?" he tried for humor, and failed. Miserably.

"Sheriff, are you aware that thirty-five percent of America's crops are dependent on bees? Yes, blueberry bees primarily stick to their namesake, but like all bees, they pollinate a wide variety of plants. Next time you're sitting down for breakfast, think about what that breakfast would look like without the wheat that made the toast, or the banana you sliced up in your bowl of Cheerios."

"I'm more of a Captain Crunch man."

"Well, you won't be with no more corn and no more oats. And where do you think your morning coffee comes from, Sheriff?"

"A Nespresso pod," Cooper replied without batting an eye. But, ultimately, he relented. "Alright, Henry, I get it. So, okay, the blueberry bees get a stay of execution. For now. But once Pastor Raymond recovers, there might just be hell to pay. That hive is on private property, after all."

"Pastor Raymond's a man of God. I'm sure he'll do the right thing."

"And if not?"

Greenleaf considered for a moment, then he said, simply, "Then I'll have a word with him."

Despite the day he'd had so far, or perhaps because of it, Cooper couldn't help but laugh out loud. The image of big Henry Greenleaf looming over that tiny little man in his big ol' shorts and knee socks was just too damn funny.

"And I'm sure you'll make him see reason," he said at last.

"Might just," Greenleaf replied.

With that, the deputy turned to go, but he stopped just short of the doorway and turned back around.

"By the way, Sheriff, the Judge is looking for you. So's Fancy. Any word on a replacement cake?"

Cooper's heart dropped to his knees. All he could manage

was a meek, "I'm working on it," with a heavy sigh.

Greenleaf squeezed his bulk back through the door, but just as he was swinging the door shut behind himself, he stopped and offered, "You know, Debbie does a pretty mean flan."

Cooper returned a tepid, "Thank you, Henry, I'll think about it," and the door clicked shut once again.

Sadly, it didn't stay shut for long.

"I hear you had a run-in with Shere Khan," Grace blustered, barging through the door like a locomotive on jet fuel. "I guess you picked a bad day to have your good luck tuna in your pocket, huh?"

Damn. Just what he needed. Grace goddam Tolliver in his face with a burr under her saddle. Most days, he could abide her.... *eccentric* sense of humor. Today, not so much.

"You know I almost died, right?" he snarled.

"And that big kitty would've shat you out like yesterday's Cat Chow," she said, returning the snarl three-fold. "Poor thing would probably have had heartburn for a week." She stabbed a chubby finger at the two bee stings perilously close to his eyes and added snarkily, "By the way, you got a little something there."

"What do you want, Grace?" he asked, every bit as rudely as he'd intended.

"Me? Oh, nothing," she replied, hitching her glasses high up on a nose that might once have been dainty. "It just does my heart good to see karma in action."

Again, Cooper sighed.

"I don't give you the day off to go to a wedding, so karma sends a mountain lion and a swarm of bees after me? Sounds a little like overkill."

"Well," she considered with a sideways head bob, "I do

believe the general consesus is that karma is, in fact, rather a bitch."

With that, she tossed a handful of papers down on his desk. Phone messages. Dozens of them. He left them where they lay and used a finger to push the little pink pieces of paper one way or the other to see the names. It was exactly what he'd suspected. The Judge. Fancy. The Judge. The Judge. The Judge. Fancy. Fancy. The Judge. Fancy. Fancy. Fancy. The Judge.

"Anything from Captain Callahan and the staties?" he asked Grace.

"Do you see one?" she huffed in reply.

"Doc Jenkins? Austin Granger?"

She folded her arms across her chest and said nothing beyond the scowl.

"Any chance you know what's good for bee stings?"

"Yes," she said, but offered nothing more.

"Do you happen to have any Aspirin?"

"Yes," she said again, and again, she offered nothing else.

"Uh, do you think it might be possible for me to borrow a couple?"

She glared at him over her folded arms and cocked an eyebrow. But ever the optimist, Cooper felt obliged to take one more shot at it.

"Are you going to stay mad at me forever, Grace?"

Again the glare, and nothing more. Just a face like stone, and the cold glint of murder behind a pair of tortoise-shell, horn-rimmed granny glasses.

Grace *goddam* Tolliver. She did far more around the place than simply answer the phone and dispatch calls. As far as Cooper was concerned, that woman kept the entire department running. In fact, he didn't know what he would ever do without her. Grace Tolliver was quite literally irreplaceable. She was efficiency personified. But God *damn* that woman could channel the Wicked Witch of the East when she was pissed. Still, he couldn't really blame her. At least, not this time. This time, it was all his doing, and with little chance of a house dropping out of the sky to crush her into mush, he let every bit of it go.

Then, he had an epiphany.

"Alright, Grace," he conceded, faking surrender. "You win. Go to Fancy's reception. *I'll* man the phones."

At that, the stone face cracked, but only just.

"I wanted to see her walk down the aisle," the woman grumbled, narrowing her glare to laser sharpness.

"I know you did, and I apologize. Please, let me make it up to you. Go to the reception. Go home, put on that beautiful taffeta dress of yours, fix up your hair, and go. I'll even keep you on the clock for the whole evening."

The arms unfolded, but they didn't go far. The woman balled up both fists and jammed them into her hips, growling, "And what the *fuck* is wrong with my hair?"

"Take money for a cab out of petty cash," Cooper insisted. "In fact, take *all* the petty cash. Enjoy yourself, Grace. Fill up on rum punch. Dance with the best man. Schmooze with the town's elite. Stay as late as you want, and don't worry about coming in early tomorrow. You can sleep in and come to work whenever you feel like it."

Nothing. Just the glare, the glint of murder, and a pair of fists wedged into those wide, spongey hips.

"In fact, don't come in tomorrow at all!" Cooper gave it one last try. "Take the whole day off. Hell, take the rest of the *week* off. Just please, I beg of you, could you please spare a couple of Aspirin?"

At last the stone broke, but not in the way Cooper had hoped. The glare melted away, the fists uncurled, and Grace *goddam* Tolliver threw back her head in a fit of gut-busting laughter that had every one of her chins quivering like Jello.

When she finally managed to suck in enough air to speak, she shook her head at Cooper and kept the Jello moving.

"Nice try, Sheriff, but not a chance in Hell. I believe I will be quite content at my desk, answering phones and filing reports, and imagining you trying to explain to Fancy and the Judge just how you destroyed the most important day of both of their lives."

The laughter returned at gale force as she spun around and stomped out of his office, deliberately leaving the door hanging wide open. Just how he didn't like it.

He brought up the wastebasket from under his desk, and with one great sweep of his arm, delivered every last one of the pink message slips to their final destination. That done, he leaned back in his chair, closed his eyes, and tried not to think about how much the welts on his face and neck itched, or about the growing ache behind his eyes.

Jesus, what a day. Twenty years he'd been on the job, the last fifteen in the Sheriff's chair, and never before had he seen a day quite like this. Cougars. Bees. Rats. Spiders... Damn! Was the whole animal kingdom going to rise up and smite him for not giving Grace the day off?

But, ultimately, he rid himself of all of the background noise and focused again on the one truly important issue. The body. Or rather, the skeleton. But then he added a second thing.

The cat. If Snagglepuss was rabid, it would mean days

and weeks and months of bullshit. The whole town would be on Defcon One. Everyone with a dog or a cat or a hamster would be hounding him for answers, and anyone with a gun would be out murdering anything else that moved. Squirrels, raccoons, skunks and coyotes would all have their heads on the chopping block, and once those were gone, the guns would be turned on the friendlier critters in town. Cats. Dogs. Horses. Cows. By the time everyone calmed the hell down, there likely wouldn't be a four-legged critter left alive in all of Keeter's Bluff.

And somehow, he knew that that would be the 'Bluff's death knell. After all, a town was more than people and houses and businesses and cars. A town was also all of those other things. Dogs. Cats. Birds. Rabbits. Skunks. Yes, even bees. And he had to admit that even the lowly rat and go-dawful spider were in there somewhere. Once every living thing in Keeter's Bluff had been destroyed and consigned to the fire of panic, Keeter's Bluff would be no more. Like blueberry bushes with no bees to carry the pollen, the entire town would simply shrivel up and die on the vine.

He reached for the phone and started dialing, but he stopped just short and dropped the phone back in its cradle. Austin would call when he had answers. As would Doc Jenkins. There was nothing to do but wait.

He checked his watch. Ten minutes past three. He had already missed the wedding, but that couldn't be helped. Even Judge Whittacker would understand, once he pled his case. The reception, though. The reception was something else entirely. Thanks to his ham-handed attempt to get Grace to go in his place, and Grace *goddam* Tolliver's infuriatingly quick wits, he was still on the hook for the reception. His absence would not go unnoticed, and it would most certainly *not* be appreciated. The happy couple would burst through the doors of the Elk's Hall in under three hours, and if he wasn't there with the mother of all wedding cakes, Fancy and her old man would dedicate the rest of their lives to ripping him to pieces and feeding the shreds to the dogs.

After that, it would only get worse.

CHAPTER

VIII

Harvey Denton was always the last to leave. This day being just like every other day, once Judith and Mark and Ivy balanced their floats and brought him their trays, he and Margaret Lowe went through it all one last time to make sure that every penny was accounted for, then they wheeled the cart into the vault to prepare the floats for the next day.

"Ben and I are having a barbecue tomorrow," Margaret idly mentioned while they tallied numbers and checked them against balance sheets. "We'd love to have you and Amy and the kids come. I'm sure Jarod would like to have someone there his own age instead of hanging out with a bunch of old fogeys."

Denton rechecked the paperwork one last time, then he answered, grudgingly, "I'll have to ask Amy. I'm not sure, but I think we have something planned."

"Oh, okay," Margaret feigned her regrets. "But just so you know, Ben is a steak savant. He does this dry rub thing every eight hours for two whole days, and I'm not allowed anywhere near the kitchen until he's got them all tucked safely away again in the back of the fridge. I think he figures that once I know his secret, I won't need to keep him around anymore."

She should have known better. Her attempt at humor was entirely lost on the humorless general manager of the First Financial Bank.

Denton shrugged again and repeated the words," I'll have to ask Amy."

And that was it. Denton checked the paperwork one last time, screwed up his nose at the deplorable handwriting of at least one of his junior employees, and concluded at last that all was in order. But really, it wasn't only the poor penmanship that wrinkled his nose. Thanks to Margaret, he had been subjected to more banal chit-chat in the past five minutes than he cared for in a lifetime. He could talk to clients about retirement savings plans and prime-plus-one and twenty-year offsets until the cows came home, but engaging in small talk in the workplace never failed to rankle him. It was a waste of time, it was a waste of energy, and it allowed his staff to become overly familiar with their manager, which only served to undermine his authority. Imagine Margaret Lee having the nerve to suggest an entire afternoon of that same idle chit-chat around a smoky barbecue. Thankfully, she didn't ask again, but clearly it was time to lay down some ground rules. Come Monday morning, he would put an end to all of this nonsense, or there would be a few new faces behind the wickets. After all, this was a place of business, not a high school cafeteria.

The two of them exited the vault without another word. Denton set the time lock for precisely nine a.m. Monday morning, and swung the big door shut, giving the handle three spins to lock it and one more just to be sure.

"All set, Mr. Denton?"

This was Al Barrow, First Financial's aged security guard, and a constant source of unease for Harvey Denton. First Financial hadn't needed a uniformed guard in it's fifty years of business, but the insurance company insisted. Cue Al Barrow's entrance. The man was older than the bank itself and would be less than useless should anything actually happen, but he greeted customers by name and helped them fill out their forms and directed them where they needed to go, so Denton did his best to think of the old man as more of a Walmart greeter than an actual security guard. After all, there had never been a bank robbery in the entire history of Keeter's Bluff, and he couldn't imagine a time when there ever would be, but if that impossible day ever came, surely any self-respecting gonif would rob the First Mercantile across town before even *thinking* of First Financial. Everything in First Financial's vault put together would barely cover a well-to-do robber's lunch bill.

"Yes, all set," he said, and waited for Al to let Margaret out while he hung back by the alarm panel. Once the doors were secured, he had one last look around, then he punched in the alarm code and watched until it counted down to fifty seconds before flicking off the lights and meeting Al at the door. Without a word, Al flipped the lock, they both left, and Harvey himself locked the door behind them, giving the key an extra half-turn and tugging at the door to make sure.

"G'night, Mr. Denton," Al said, putting a finger to his brow and not waiting for a response before making his way around to the back of the building.

Harvey's Volvo was closer. The parking lot was meant for customers, so all employees were instructed to park in the alley. But leadership did have its privileges, after all. He took six short steps to the Volvo, and as he did every afternoon, he laid his briefcase carefully on the rear seat, closed the door gently, and climbed in behind the wheel. Once in, he thumbed the lock, clicked his seatbelt, and checked his mirrors. Only then did he insert the key into the ignition and bring the Volvo to life. He let it warm up for a full minute while he listened to the news, then he put the car into reverse and crept slowly back until he had room to pull ahead without touching a single painted line.

At the posted speed limit, it was a ten minute drive to his home in the Heights. Denton took twenty. Ever the cautious driver, he would rather brake for a stale green light and watch it turn yellow from the stop line even if it meant suffering the angry blast of a car horn from behind. And though school zone restrictions didn't apply in the summer months, one never knew when children might be about, so it was always better to crawl safely through, unlike those hooligans who barreled past him at a perilous thirty miles an hour while shouting obscenities through their open windows.

Once home, he clicked the garage door open only when he was nose-to-nose with it, then he pulled forward until a tennis ball hanging from the ceiling kissed his windshield with the barest hint of fuzz. He keyed the car off and clicked the garage door closed again, watching it descend in his rearview mirror until the last sliver of daylight disappeared entirely. Then and only then, he unclasped his belt, unlocked the door, climbed out, retrieved his briefcase from the back seat, and closed the door gently. Finally, he fobbed the car doors locked with a comforting *thunk!*, unlocked the door that led from garage to home, and stepped inside, making certain to secure the deadlock behind himself.

"Good evening, Amy," he greeted his wife pleasantly enough as he passed into the kitchen.

"Hello, Harvey," she returned with an appropriate wifely smile. "Did you have a fine day at work?"

"Yes," he replied, loosening his tie just enough to pop open the top button of his shirt. He leaned across the counter and gave his wife the slightest of pecks on her cheek. "It was fine."

Such was the routine they had perfected over the years, very much like every other part of their lives. A short hello, a shorter kiss, then a quick glance at his watch, a needless check with the clock on the mantle, and all was as it should be. Now, Denton would take his briefcase to the den, and there he would sort through the papers he would need first thing Monday morning. Dinner would be on the table at six o'clock precisely. Since this was Saturday, it would be roast beef, mashed potatoes, and carrots. Even now, Amy was preparing the carrots, peeling them to within an inch of their lives and julienning each one into identical sprigs of exacting length. The water was already on the stove, but she wouldn't put them in for another seven minutes. Harvey liked his carrots crunchy, so they would go in at precisely five fifty-four.

Routines worked well for both of them, and as they had both said countless times, a well-run home was a happy home. And there was love there too, of a sort. A quiet, undemonstrative kind of love that extended to both of their children, who just now came exploding through the back door as if blown in by a cyclone.

"Daddy!" Tabitha beamed a smile at her father and held

up her arms.

At six years old, she was already too big for him to lift, so that particular routine had been altered for the sake of his sacroiliac. He set his briefcase down on the floor and bent low enough to allow her to hug him, then he kissed her lightly on the cheek.

"Hello, Tabitha. What sort of mischief have you been getting into today, hmm?"

It was the standard question, and she gave the standard response.

"Just playing, Daddy."

"And what of you, Jeremy?" he asked as the boy snitched the one sliver of raw carrot they allowed him to steal every Saturday at precisely this time. "Were you playing, too?"

Jeremy was nearly ten years old, so he knew what his father wanted to hear.

"Only after I cut the front lawn and watered the back," he answered, as he did every Saturday.

"Very good, son," Denton said, patting the boy once on the shoulder. "You're a fine young man. I wish every adult was as responsible as you, my boy."

"Hey, look at me!" Tabitha hooted, picking up her father's briefcase and proceeding to march to and fro like a tiny businesswoman. "I'm a grown-up!"

Amy laughed at the girl's antics, and though it was hardly the way things were done in the Denton household, Harvey joined in, however stilted and however briefly.

"Why, yes you are," he told her, marveling at how little girls could get excited over the silliest of things.

Jeremy quickly joined in on the merriment by marching alongside his sister, declaring, "I'm a grown-up, too!"

But by then, Denton had had quite enough silliness for one evening.

"Well, if the lady and the gentleman really want to be grown-ups, perhaps I'll allow the two of you to pay the bills from now on," he said, sourly. "Now, please take my brief-case up to the study. I have some papers to go through before dinner."

"Yes, sir!" Lawrence saluted, and the two of them went marching off toward the stairs, giggling as they went.

Harvey watched them go with a wistful air.

"And thus is mankind's eternal curse laid bare. When young, we want nothing more than to be grown up. Once we're grown up, we wish only to be young again."

"Not *too* young," Amy recoiled in horror. "I have no desire whatsoever to relive braces and pimple cream."

Harvey leaned over the counter and graced his wife with an entirely unscheduled and wholly atypical second kiss on the cheek.

"Perhaps just young enough to fall in love all over again, eh?"

"Yes," she smiled sweetly. "Perhaps." Then, as she returned to her carrots, she offered distractedly, "You know, it's funny. I was chatting with Beatrice next door, and she said that her own Patty was playing a game called 'grown-ups'. She said that *all* the children were playing it. Apparently, playing grown-ups is all the rage."

Denton snuck a bit of carrot from under her watchful eye and popped it in his mouth.

"I've never heard of it. What do you suppose they do, shop for groceries and take out the garbage?"

"I've never heard of it either," Amy shrugged. "Apparently, it's brand new. And now they're *all* playing it. *All* of them."

"Well, you know children. One of them starts, and the rest follow."

"Yes, I know, but it's a brand-new game, Harvey. The children only just started playing the game this morning, and now they're *all* playing it."

"Well, word does travel quickly these days," Harvey replied, dismissing it all with a shrug.

"I suppose so," Amy said. "But it's just so strange. I swear, it's like every child woke up this morning playing the very same brand-new game."

CHAPTER

IX

D anvers," Emma Wong repeated into the phone, spelling the name this time in case it helped. "No, I'm afraid I don't remember the first name. I think it started with a J. Or maybe an M. Or a T. Anyway, how many Danvers' can there be in a town this size?" She paused for a moment. "Really? That many, huh? Well if it helps, his wife's name is, uh... Martha, I think. Or maybe Mary. Or Gladys. Something like that. No? Oh! He's the principal of Isaac H. Templeton High School. Does that... Oh, really? Class of '07? Small world, huh?" Another pause, longer this time. "Really? History major?" She pulled the phone away from her mouth, hushing, "And now you're answering phones. Awesome."

The girl gladly provided the number to one Hiram Merriwhether Danvers, and though the two shared a chuckle at the name, it took ten more minutes of cajoling, wheedling and ultimately pleading before the woman at the other end was willing to give up a street address.

Emma concluded the conversation with, "No, don't worry, Bethany. I won't tell a living soul that you bent the rules, I swear. And thank you again for the invitation. I'll think about it. Yes. Thank you."

She ended the call and dropped the phone to the desk with a pained grimace drawing up the corners of her mouth.

She put a fingertip to the bump over her eye as gingerly as a feather. Despite the prompt application of ancient peas, the robin's egg had turned into a golf ball. And her fingers came away wet, which meant that it was bleeding through the Band-Aid again. Plus, the mild headache she'd been nursing for over an hour was quickly turning into a red hot knitting needle shoved through her brain from one temple to the other.

"Fucking awesome," she grunted through clenched teeth.

She made one more futile sweep through the medicine cabinet and the lone, empty drawer, then on the off-chance that the previous tenant might have left something hidden away at the back of one shelf or another in the kitchen, she opened every cupboard door and stood on her tiptoes to reach all the way to the back. But, alas, the cupboards were bare. She even checked the refrigerator for a fourth and fifth time, but aside from the few necessities she'd picked up the day before, the thing was a wasteland. She looked longingly at the bottle of vodka standing front and center, but she didn't dare, what with dinner with her new boss looming so close on the horizon. With no other recourse then, she slipped on her jeans and sneakers, grabbed her wallet and keys, and passed quietly into the hallway.

Aspirin. She needed Aspirin. Or Tylenol. Maybe extra

strength. Maybe even with a hint of codeine. As the pound-ing in her head only increased with every step she took down the stairs, she decided on the stronger stuff. Codeine. Or morphine. Or goddam *heroine* if they offered it. Whatever it took to rein in the My Little Ponies galloping through her skull was fine with her.

Her Mazda was parked out back. Like most of Keeter's Bluff, the lot was surrounded by trees. It was the one thing about this new home of hers that had convinced her that the universe had gotten it right once again. LA was a concrete jungle. Smog. Traffic jams. Plastic people in a plastic world. Here in small town America, a person could breathe. The air was clean, the water was fresh, and the people were real. But even as those thoughts were trampled to dust by a fresh wave of galloping Ponies, she realized that something was decidedly missing from this little corner of Utopia.

She could see birds flying overhead, and she could see them gathered on branches high up in the trees, but not a single one of them was singing. Or chirping. Or cawing. Not a single one. They were all perfectly, absolutely, unnervingly silent. Despite every tree being laden with birds and twice as many more in the sky, the only sound she could hear on this bright summer afternoon was the laughter of distant children, riding along on the breeze.

She unlocked the car door and climbed in, but it was with a general feeling of unease that she slid the key into the ignition. For the life of her, she wouldn't have been able to put a name to what she was feeling, but a sudden crash against her windshield brought the whole thing into crystal clear focus.

The starling slumped over the windshield wiper wasn't dead yet, but it soon would be. The little bit of goo it had left on the glass had seen to that. For whatever reason, the poor creature had chosen just that moment to plummet down from an overhead branch and crash into the windshield right in front of her face, and now she was afforded a front row seat to the poor thing's death throes. And worse, that tiny red spot it had left on the glass looked strangely familiar. It was exactly what she'd seen at the edge of her apartment window, just before giving herself the golf ball. That tiny little spot. Red, with just a hint of something else.

It would have been an easy enough thing to take care of. One sweep of the wipers would have tossed the dying bird to the ground. But as a lover of all things furred, finned and feathered, Emma Wong would never be able to do such a thing. So, she did the only thing she could. She popped open her door, gathered the broken body in her hands, and shed a tear as she brought the thing into her car.

It was a starling. Nothing more. A rat of the sky. No beautiful plumage. No song like a nightingale. This tiny, broken creature would never inspire poetry or love songs. It was just a bird. A dull, black, nothing bird. And yet, as she held that tiny dying body in her hands and watched it take its last breath, she wept. She wept openly, and she wept freely. Not because a beautiful, magnificent creature had just died in her hands, but because a tiny living thing was no more. She would have wept just as much had it been a rare Sumatran tiger or a worm at the end of a hook. This was life brought to a sudden, cataclysmic end, so for the sake of that precious lost life, she wept.

At last, she dried her eyes and laid the poor dead creature on the passenger seat, swathed in Kleenex, and started the car.

Thankfully, there was no repeat performance as she

pulled out of the parking lot. All of the branches on all of the trees surrounding the lot were heavy with starlings and crows and songbirds of every type, but they made not so much as a chirp as the car passed beneath them. They simply hung their heads and watched the woman go.

CHAPTER

X

"Hey, Doyle."

The big man leaned in for a closer look at the welts on Cooper's face.

"Cripes, dude. You going through puberty again?"

"They're not zits, dumbass. They're bee stings," Cooper sneered, setting the matter straight.

Tom Cooper had known Doyle Brannigan since they were kids. Doyle had picked a fight with him on the first day of second grade, and Cooper had laid him out flat. After that, they become instant, inseparable friends.

"Yeah? Well if they ain't zits, my next guess would've been syphilis."

Yup, that was Doyle to a tee. World class smart-ass. And he must have been on the toilet when the Good Lord was handing out mute buttons, because the man not only said what he wanted, but he said it through his own personal built-in megaphone. Seeing as he stood six-foot four and was still made of solid muscle at forty years of age, he got away with it. But beneath all of that bluster and bravado and brashness, Doyle was a good and honest man. He loved Mary-Ellen, he positively doted on Darryl and Maggie, and no man could ever hope to have a more faithful friend than big, loud, pain-in-the-ass Doyle motherfucking Brannigan.

"I missed you at the wedding, dude. So did Fancy and her old man. Gotta say, neither of them was too impressed with you playing hooky. But don't worry, I covered for you. I told them you weren't there 'cause you were passed out drunk."

"Great. Thanks, man. Wait, *you* were invited to Fancy's wedding?"

"And the reception, thank you very much."

"You? Fancy invited... *you?*"

Brannigan waved the matter away.

"Oh, she's forgotten all about that by now. Bygones, and all that. Besides, she went to school with Mary-Ellen, and she couldn't very well not invite her. Me and the kids are her plus-one-through-three."

"Next!" the man behind the counter called, and everyone in line at the pharmacy counter moved up a step.

"You're taking your kids to Fancy's reception? What did those poor innocent waifs ever do to you?"

"Well, for starters they stretched out my wife's vagina."

"Wow, Doyle," Cooper said, deadpan. "You suck as a father."

"Oh, don't get your knickers in a twist, girlfriend. There'll be plenty of other kids there. How can I possibly deny the fruit of my loins a chance to experience the social event of the year? Besides, Mary-Ellen said she'd drive, so I can get as hammered as I want. Did I mention the free bar?"

"I was wrong, Doyle," Cooper harumphed. "You suck as a father *and* as a husband."

"Preaching to the choir, sister." Brannigan held up a fist, and Cooper gave it a bump. "But at least I'm smart enough to know not to go *mano y mano* with a swarm of killer bees."

"Actually, they were hyphen... uh, hymen... uh.... They were blueberry bees."

"And you were just fruity enough for their liking, huh?" Brannigan said with his usual smirk, but it faded quickly. "Seriously, I heard about what happened, Coop. Dude, you saved a man's life. That's pretty fucking cool. What're you gonna do for an encore, defeat General Zod?"

"Sadly, my cape is at the cleaners," Cooper said, trying to joke the whole thing away. But Brannigan would have none of it.

"Uh uh, buddy. Like it or not, you're a hero." He threw his shoulder into Cooper's hard enough to nearly knock him off balance. "Suck it up, princess."

"All I did was get Pastor Raymond to the hospital, Doyle. Kira's the real hero."

"Ah, yes," Brannigan grinned goofily and turned his eyes to the ceiling. "Doctor-hotty Kira Melanson. You sure screwed the pooch when you let that little lady get away. I would *so* do her."

It was bullshit, of course. Doyle Brannigan would see himself six feet underground before he'd ever think about cheating on Mary-Ellen. But Cooper played along.

"Do her what?" he snorted. "Her laundry?"

"I'm just saying that I wouldn't say no to a prostate exam. That little blondie is one *serious* hotty."

"Do me a favor, Doyle," Cooper said, putting a hand on his old friend's shoulder. "Let me be there when you tell her that."

"Sure thing, buddy. Just as long as you make yourself scarce once she reaches for the rubber gloves and lube."

The elderly woman in line ahead of Brannigan sent a puckered look back over her shoulder while uttering a matronly, "Tsk, tsk," but the man had no shame.

"Good afternoon, Mrs. Barrow!" he greeted the woman warmly, but with his volume knob forever pinned at eleven, it sounded more like a shout. "Lovely day, isn't it? How's Al doing? Still kicking, I hope."

Jesus... Yup, classic Doyle Brannigan. Loud, proud, and not giving a shit. Cooper felt embarrassed for all three of them, but he still had to hide a smile at seeing the look of utter disgust on Liza Barrow's pinched-up face.

"Next!"

The elderly Mrs. Barrow practically ran for the safety of the counter, and the two men took another step forward. Brannigan spun around again to continue the conversation, but with one look over Cooper's shoulder, he hushed the words, "Whoa, dude. Speaking of hotties. Check your six," and turned sheepishly back.

This was also classic Doyle Brannigan. He would bluff and he would bluster, but when push came to shove, a pretty face would shut him up like the high school nerd he'd always be.

Cooper took a curious glance over his shoulder, and sure enough, a young woman was coming up from behind. And yes, she was attractive by anyone's standards. Young. Slim. A runner's body wrapped in jeans and a UCLA halter top. He watched her for a few seconds as she scoured the shelves, then she happened to look up and catch his eye, and he spun back around, burying his gaze at some random spot on

Brannigan's big back. But then he caught the faintest whiff of lilacs and vanilla just as he felt a gentle tap on the shoulder, and he had no choice but to turn and face the music.

"Yes?" he said, not trusting himself to say more.

"Hi," the girl said back. "Umm, you're the Sheriff, right?"

Stupidly, Cooper checked his shoulder patches to make sure, then he nodded.

"Yes, Ma'am. Sheriff Tom Cooper. And you are?"

"Emma Wong." she replied. Then she caught sight of his welts and her eyes grew big as she hissed, "Oh, my. Are those bee stings?"

"It might be syphilis," Brannigan chimed in without turning around. "Jury's still out."

Cooper hung his head.

"Yes, they're bee stings," he said, trying desperately not to stare at the My Little Ponies on the girl's forehead and failing tremendously. "Is there something I can do for you, Miss Wong?"

"Nope. I'm new in town, so I just thought I'd say hi." The smile returned, and the girl chirped a happy, "Hi!" But then her eyes hooded over as she put a hand to the raging Ponies.

"Hi," Cooper replied dutifully. Then he had to ask, "Miss Wong, are you okay?"

"It's nothing that a handful of pharmaceuticals won't fix."

"*Legal* pharmaceuticals, I trust," he said, only half-joking.

"Is weed legal here yet?" she asked, joking even less.

"In Mayberry? Ha!" Doyle Brannigan scoffed. Loudly.

"Then legal pharmaceuticals it is," Emma acquiesced. "Bring on the socially approved opiates! At least until we get to know each other better."

Cooper looked her up and down, from the top of her head to the tips of her toes.

"Actually, I think I can say quite a bit about you right now, Miss Wong. From your shirt, you are clearly from California. You favor your right leg ever so slightly, so I'm guessing you went to UCLA on an athletic scholarship, but a blown knee ended your career. So, you changed majors. You look like you have a caring soul, so I can imagine you going for a teaching degree. But not Phys Ed, because UCLA doesn't offer that. Hmm... English, maybe? No, that's not right. History? Yes, that's it. You teach History. And being the adventurous sort, you left everything behind and hauled yourself out to the middle of nowhere, merely on a whim."

Emma was suitably impressed, and she made no bones about showing it.

"Omigod! That is amazing! Yes, I'm a teacher, and yes, I teach history! In fact, every single thing you said was absolutely true! What are you, Sherlock Holmes? How did you *do* that?"

As much as Cooper loved having this beautiful creature regard him with such awe, he ultimately came clean.

"Actually, your new boss is a friend of mine. He told me all about you."

"You mean the inestimable Hiram Merriwhether Danvers?" she mused. "He didn't strike me as the kind of man who would have such a bohemian thing as 'friends'."

"Well, he doesn't have many, that's for sure. But one thing you should know about life in a small town, Miss Wong, is that word spreads like wildfire. No one has any secrets here. You ask anyone in town about anyone else, and you'll get the whole picture."

"Oh please, call me Emma, Sheriff."

"Alright, Emma Sheriff," Cooper said, stupidly. And as Brannigan brayed laughter that sounded not unlike a wounded moose, the young woman simply lifted an eyebrow.

"Wow. That was incredibly lame."

"I knew it even as I said it," Cooper readily agreed. "My apologies, Miss Wo... uh, Emma."

"Better," she said with a nod.

It wasn't, but Cooper let it go.

"Next!"

It was Brannigan's turn at the counter. He handed the man a slip of paper without uttering a word, but the old man in the white coat made a point of reading it aloud for the entire store to hear.

"Viagra, huh? Made out to one Doyle Percival Brannigan of 704 Lansing Street. Fifty milligrams, I see. Having trouble getting the ol' pecker up, eh, Mr. Brannigan? You know Viagra's not covered by your medical plan, right?"

The big man pinned his chin to his chest and nodded, saying nothing.

"So, how did you manage to piss off every bee in Keeter's Bluff, Sheriff?" Emma asked. "You know, just so I don't make the same mistake. What did you do, make like Winnie the Pooh and go after their honey tree?"

"Something like that," Cooper shrugged, desperately holding back from scratching under his collar. "Miss W... uh, Emma, did you know that bee stings not only itch like a son of a bitch, but they also hurt?"

"Believe me, I am well aware," she shuddered at the very thought. "Did you try ice? If you put ice on them right away, it reduces the swelling and pain."

"No one thought to mention that to me," Cooper said through a tightening of his lips as he imagined Grace *goddam* Tolliver back at the station, still laughing her ass off.

A grimace of shared pain swept across Emma's face. She sucked air in through her teeth, then a slender hand came up and touched the skin around the welts close to Cooper's eyes as gently as a breeze.

"Oh, I bet those really hurt. What you need is hydrocortisone cream for the itchiness and swelling, combined with an oral analgesic. Benadryl's good." She looked down to see a bottle of Aspirin clutched in his hand, and she quickly snatched it away. "Aspirin's good, but Naproxen has better anti-inflammatory agents." She returned the bottle to the shelf and selected another in its place. "Here you go. Try this."

Cooper accepted the tiny bottle of Aleve just as the old man behind the counter handed Brannigan his purchase in a nondescript white bag while calling out, "Here's your Viagra, Doyle Brannigan!" Once his old friend scurried sheepishly away without a single backward glance, Cooper stepped up to the counter.

"Hey, Doc," he said, greeting the man in the bifocals the same way he always did. But the monicker had always had more to do with his protruding front teeth than any diploma he might have had hanging on the wall. For all the world, every time Cooper looked upon old Jimmy Stanton, all he could see was Bugs Bunny in a lab coat. "Got anything for bee stings?"

"Looks more like syphilis," the old man snorted, but then a tube of something-or-other magically appeared in his hand, and he passed it over.

"Hydrocortisone cream for the redness and swelling.

You might also want to try an oral analgesic. You'll find Benadryl one aisle over. If you have associated pain, you'll want Naproxen. You'll find Aleve a few steps behind you. Next!"

Cooper stepped aside, but only just, and Emma Wong sidled up beside him.

"Tylenol with codeine, please," she announced, matter-of-factly. "The biggest bottle allowed by law."

Stanton took one look at the Ponies riding high atop a golf ball and produced the bottle forthwith. He rang it in and added the new box of My Little Pony Band-Aids she deposited on the counter with a hushed, "I think they've become my spirit animals," without a second glance.

"That'll be ten-ninety. Debit? Surely."

As Emma Wong scanned her card, Cooper pretended to read the instructions on the back of the tube he'd been handed while sucking in every molecule of vanilla and lilacs from the air. Then, once the transaction was complete and this new girl in town was turning to go, he had a sudden stroke of genius.

"Hey, if you're not doing anything later, how would you like to go to a wedding?"

Clumsy. Stupid. *Fuck!*

He watched the woman's hackles rise up accordingly, and heard her say, ever so politely, "Umm... Thank you, no," but rather than try to explain his peculiar predicament, he simply ate his words.

"Okay," he said with the slightest of nods, then he stepped aside to let her pass. "But just so you know, that didn't come out the way I meant it to. I mean, I wasn't asking you out or anything. Believe it or not, I'm not actually a total creep. You'll find that out once we get to know each other better."

With that, she ran her eyes up and down, from the top of Cooper's head to the tips of his boots, and she said, "Actually, I think I can say quite a bit about you right now, Sheriff. You were born in Keeter's Bluff. You've never been away for more than a weekend, and even then, you didn't go far. Vegas, probably. But not a vacation, because you don't take those. So, bachelor party then. And seeing as it was your one time to let loose, you got drunk as shit, you danced with the bridesmaids, and you had the time of your life. But still, you couldn't wait to get home to your own fridge, your own bathroom, and your own bed. Am I right?"

"It depends on what you mean by drunk as shit," Cooper replied. Again, stupidly.

"Oh, I think breaking out the Disco moves and hitting on the one and only confirmed lesbian at the party qualifies."

Damn...

Bethany. Bethany LeGrange. He remembered that weekend. Or most of it, at least. Well, parts of it, anyway. Individual fragments. Like tiny disparate pieces of a massively huge and massively ugly jigsaw puzzle.

Gambling. Drinking. Bodily removal from two separate casinos. Or maybe three. Glenfiddich, flowing like water. Cuban cigars, smoked openly. Strippers. Loud music. Dancing bodies. And that's where it all went blank. All save Bethany LeGrange in her teensy-weensy skirt and fuck-me pumps, and a scene he wished he could forget.

Bethany worked for Ma Bell, now. And she'd always liked to gossip. The rest of it was obvious.

"You had to be there," he said, simply.

"Oh, trust me, I've been there," Emma grinned coyly. "C'mon." She took him by the hand and led him one aisle over. "Benadryl," she said, unscrewing the top, handing him the bottle, and not taking no for an answer.

He guzzled what he reckoned to be a tablespoon or two, then he felt her hand back in his and allowed himself to be led out of that aisle and into another.

"Calamine lotion," Emma said, grabbing another bottle from the shelf. "Great for itches, and it doesn't stink like Hydrocortisone."

She broke the seal on the bottle and dribbled a little into her hand, then she used two slender fingers to apply a dollop of cream to each of the two welts on his face with a gentleness he wouldn't have thought possible. As the itching miraculously began to subside, he reluctantly pulled back his collar to reveal a dozen more.

"Yowza!" Emma gasped. "You must *really* like honey."

"I don't even like blueberries," Cooper muttered back, but with every touch of those slender fingers, more and more of the festering itchiness subsided. And at last, it was gone, just like that. Only the pain behind his eyes remained, but Emma took care of that, too. She popped open the bottle of Aleve and handed him a tiny tablet, and when she matched it with one of her own and cracked the cap on a warm bottle of Coke, the two of them clinked the pills together as if drinking a toast.

"To pharmaceuticals," Cooper said, gulping his down and passing the Coke to his new best friend.

"To *legal* pharmaceuticals," Emma reminded him. Then she tacked on, not quite under her breath, "At least until we get to know each other better."

CHAPTER

XI

Hermione Alcourt was no shrinking violet. At nearly sixty years of age, she could still best most man at anything from poker to chess, and from arm wrestling to shot-for-shot drinking. Ex-WAC, ex-wrestler, and ex-trucker, Hermione Alcourt was not so much a woman as she was a force of nature.

Deputy Sheriff Santino 'Sonny' Garcia was no slouch, either. He wasn't a big man, but he had the quiet, wiry strength of a bantamweight, and his years in the military had taught him well.

The two couldn't have been more different. They were thirty years apart, they came from entirely different backgrounds, and while Hermione had always been a steadfast atheist, Deputy Sheriff Sonny Garcia never missed a Sunday service. The only trait they shared in the whole world was their abject refusal to take shit from anyone. That, and their love of dogs.

Garcia had two. A German shepherd and a collie, both rescued from the pound. Hermione had four, all the way from a miniature poodle to a Great Dane named Samson. And yet, whenever either of them passed by another dog behind a picket fence or tied up outside of a store or lounging in the back of a pickup, they simply couldn't help but stop, greet that animal as a long lost friend, and give it a few pats on the head for good measure.

And so it was that they both found themselves outside the S&J Food Shop, approaching a parked convertible with the top down and a beautiful black retriever minding the store.

"Hey, Grizz," Garcia cooed, coming up on the passenger's side slowly enough to not spook the dog. "Is Mama inside buying you a big box of Milk-Bones?"

He knew this dog. In fact, he had known him since he was a pup. Matias and Sofia Lopez were members of his church, and good friends besides. He had been to their home countless times, so he'd had the opportunity to watch Grizz grow from an underweight fuzzball comprised of all feet and ears into the beautiful sleek hound he was now. And yet, when the dog met Garcia's eyes, he didn't immediately welcome him in with the usual display of tongue-lolling and tail-wagging joy. In fact, it looked as though Grizz didn't recognize him at all.

"You okay, Grizz? What's the matter, pal?"

Garcia reached in to give his old friend a pat on the head, but he stopped short as the big black dog bared its teeth and uttered a low, rumbling growl.

"Grizz, it's me," he tried again. "Remember me, big fella?" he cooed, but the growling continued.

He snuck a half-step closer, convinced that once the dog

got hold of his scent, he'd be back to his usual slobbering self, but a voice from behind stopped him in his tracks.

"I wouldn't, if I were you."

He recognized the voice. Hermione Alcourt. They crossed paths quite regularly. Jake's Pet Foods. Keeter's Bluff Dog Park. And for one harrowing weekend during a particularly robust tick season two years ago, the two had commiserated over his Stanley and her Samson in the lobby of the Main Street Veterinary Clinic.

But he didn't need Hermione to tell him to stay back. All the signs were there. Direct eye contact. Tail up. Legs apart. Chest out. Ears at full attention. And the growl. That low, throaty growl that promised all manner of mayhem. Friend or not, Garcia had no doubt that if he took one step closer to the convertible, that big, beautiful dog he'd watched grow from a pup would launch itself straight for his throat.

"Not gonna," he told Hermione without once taking his eyes from the dog.

"Good. Now back up slow. One step. Nice and easy now."

He tried, but barely had he moved a muscle before the big dog planted its front paws squarely on the top of the door and glared at him down its slavering muzzle.

"Santino, freeze!"

He did as he was told. He froze perfectly still. He didn't even blink. He stood there unmoving, locked in a staring contest with a hundred-plus pounds of muscle, hair and teeth.

Seconds crawled past on their hands and knees with the dog looming massively large over the side of the convertible. Garcia watched foam build at the corners of the dog's mouth, and he followed each individual drop of saliva as it streaked down Grizz's muzzle and fell to the ground. Then he saw something else out of the corner of his eye. Hermione Alcourt sidling out behind him, taking two infinitely slow steps to the right.

"Don't," Garcia tried, but he knew his words would fall on deaf ears. Hermione Alcourt did what she damn-well pleased, and no man, much less a *law*man, would ever get her to heel.

"*Vete a la mierda*, Santino," she huffed back, and took one more agonizingly slow step to the side.

It was working, but it wouldn't for long. With two targets for its aggression now instead of just one, the big dog was confused, unsure which to attack. But the confusion was a double-edged sword. A confused dog tended to be an angry dog, and with Grizz already frothing at the mouth in anticipation of the kill, it wouldn't be long before he chose his target.

The dog flicked its eyes toward Hermione, and Garcia crept his hand an inch closer to his holster. And again. And then again. Two full minutes later, his hand was on the grips and his thumb on the release. But Hermione was too close. It would take the dog a split second to launch itself at her. A second after that, she'd be on the ground. His best time on the range to draw, acquire a target, and fire was two seconds. With a moving target, double that. So the question was, how much damage could those big teeth and powerful jaws do to Hermione Alcourt in those extra two seconds?

He couldn't allow it. Even if he hadn't sworn an oath the day he pinned on the badge, he could never allow it. He would rather let Grizz tear him apart than see someone else hurt. So, he simply had no choice. Without a word, he unsnapped his holster and took a giant step toward that big slavering dog hanging over the side of that wide-open convertible.

"No!" Hermione cried out, but it was too late. The dog came at Garcia like a missile, and it was all the man could do to stumble back, fumbling for his pistol. But before he had even cleared the holster, a freight train hit him square in the chest and the gun went flying. Between hitting the ground hard and the full weight of Grizz landing on his chest, every molecule of air was knocked from his lungs, and all he could do from then on was watch those ravening, slavering jaws descend.

In the fraction of a second it took him to say goodbye to his mother, and to his sister, and to everyone else he had ever known and loved, there came a sharp, loud *crack!* like a peal of thunder, and a hundred-plus pounds of dog collapsed on top of him. But even as he waited for death, he realized that the dog had stopped growling, and that the jaws had stopped snapping. He dared to open his eyes, certain that it was a trick and that the last thing he would ever see would be a set of long, white teeth burying themselves into his throat, but instead he saw the Grizz he had always known. A quiet animal. A gentle animal. A big, beautiful dog resting its muzzle on his shoulder, just waiting for a kiss on the snout.

Then the dream broke. Hermione stepped into view with a revolver the size of an anti-aircraft gun in her hand and a thin ribbon of smoke curling skyward from its muzzle.

Slowly, almost reluctantly, Garcia rolled the dead body of big, beautiful Grizz off to one side and clambered to his knees. Hermione helped him the rest of the way up, then those two dog lovers looked agonizingly down at that beautiful dead animal.

"Why would he *do* that?" Garcia howled. "I've known Grizz since forever! Why would he *do* that?"

"I have no idea," Hermione hushed, tucking the handgun back in her purse. "Sofia brought him to the dog park many times, and Grizz was one of the sweetest dogs in the world. But I guess we can never know what truly goes on in a dog's mind. I don't know, maybe there's some part of them that will always be wild."

A crowd was quickly forming, so to spare the poor dog the disgrace of having a host of strangers view his corpse as some sort of curiosity, Garcia and Hermione lifted the dog up, carried it to Garcia's cruiser, and slid it gingerly onto the back seat.

Deputy Garcia took one last long, aching look before closing the car door.

"What am I going to tell Matias?"

"Tell him he's a lucky man," Hermione said, handing him back the pistol he'd dropped. "If this had happened five minutes earlier, his own dog would have torn him to pieces."

CHAPTER
XII

Rabies? Are you sure?"

"I don't know what else it could be, Sheriff. A dog doesn't just go bad like that. If not rabies, what?"

The phone was on the hood of the Sheriff's cruiser with the speaker on. Cooper was on one side, Emma Wong on the other. The call had come just as the two were leaving the Pharmadeal, and Cooper couldn't very well ask the new girl in town to take a hike just so he could answer the phone. Now, she joined in on the conversation as if it was the most natural thing in the world.

"I know that some plants can have an adverse affect," she said, leaning into the phone. "Locoweed. Peyote. Salvia. Jimsonweed. Any chance Grizz might've come into contact with something like that?"

Dutifully, Cooper introduced Emma to the others in the group call.

"Carl, Sonny, Henry, Buck, this is Emma Wong."

"Hi!" Emma said, perhaps a tad too chirpily, but Cooper put it down to her socially approved opiates.

The others all greeted her back, each in their own way, but then Grace *goddam* Tolliver broke in on the line, snarking, "Who the *fuck* is Emma Wong?" and Cooper felt his heart drop down into his socks.

"Umm, I'm a teacher," Emma said sweetly, adding an uncertain, "Uh... *ma'am*."

Somehow, Cooper knew it wasn't over yet. Sadly, he was right.

"Oh? And what do you teach, Emma Wong? Botany? Animal husbandry?"

"Umm, history?" Emma replied.

An audible snort came through.

"Are you asking, or telling?"

"Umm, telling?" Emma replied.

A great whoosh of air came through the phone, then Grace snarled, "Alright, that's it for me. I'm going to let you muttonheads try to figure this out on your own. I have filing to do." And with that, she was gone. Thankfully.

He could almost hear the others heave a general sigh of relief. Then Henry chimed in.

"We do have locoweed in these parts, Miss Wong, and of course there's always someone in town growing cannabis. But the swainsonine phytotoxin in locoweed is really only harmful to livestock, and the cannabinoid acids found in the resin of the cannabis plant contain an extra carboxyl molecule that renders it psychoactively inert. Those molecules have to be removed through decarboxylation before the plant can have any deleterious effect. Hence the burning and the cooking. You or I or Grizz could chew a raw cannabis plant down to the roots, and none of us would get so much as a buzz."

"Boxcar *what* now?" Rankin chimed in, but he was promptly ignored.

"Okay," Emma replied, undaunted. "But what if a cow or deer ate locoweed, then it died, and Grizz ate some of the meat?"

It sounded at least plausible to Cooper, but Garcia quickly shot it down.

"Naw, even if it worked that way, Grizz was like a son to Matias and Sofia. He was raised on Ken-L-Ration and Milk-Bones. He wouldn't know what to do with a dead animal if he saw one. Believe me, Sheriff, that dog was one of the sweetest, gentlest animals I've ever had the pleasure to know. Whatever turned him mean worked fast. And I don't mean Usain Bolt fast, I mean Barry Allen fast. Matias said he was the same old Grizz on the drive down to the S&J, and in the blink of an eye, Lassie turned into Cujo."

"Alright then," Cooper concluded, looking furtively around to make sure no one was within earshot. "I guess we're back to the 'R' word, at least until the test results on Snagglepuss come in. Sonny, you'd better get Grizz down to the shop so Austin can test him, too. I don't have to tell you what kind of shitstorm we'll be facing if any of those tests come back positive."

"No sir!"

"Nuh uh."

"God forbid."

"Any word from Callahan and the Staties yet?" Cooper asked as an open question.

"Nothing so far, boss, but I've been monitoring their frequencies," David 'Buck' Rogers responded. "Seems like Search & Rescue lost comms with the team they sent out.

They're trying to re-establish, but they're prepping another team, just to be sure."

"Okay, good," Cooper concluded. "For now, let's just take a breather and put all of today's shit behind us. The priorities now are the body at the old McIffrin place, and the tests on Snagglepuss. Jermaine should be checking in anytime now, so we'll know one way or the other if we're about to have a wholesale panic on our hands. Until then, let's just keep our collective fingers crossed."

"10-4."

"Copy that."

"You got it."

"Sure thing, boss."

"Alright then," Cooper said, ending the conversation. But just as he was about to swipe the call closed, Henry Greenleaf reminded him of what he most desperately wanted to forget.

"You find a cake yet, Sheriff?"

"Working on it," Cooper lied, and ended the call with a swipe.

Once they were alone again, Emma turned to Cooper across the hood of the car and said, "You know, it could be that Grizz just went wild all on his own. I know it's rare, but we've all heard stories of a perfectly happy family dog turning on its owner, right?"

Cooper considered the idea.

"Sure, but that would be a hell of a coincidence, wouldn't it? Grizz losing his shit just when the rest of the animal kingdom seems to be losing theirs?"

"Well, maybe it's something all animals have in common. Something in their genetic makeup. Maybe that violent behavior has been inside them all along, just waiting for the right trigger."

"And we just happen to be the lucky ones that get to see it manifest," Cooper harumphed.

"Yeah, it figures, right? I mean, here I am, putting myself out there, thinking I'm ready for whatever the universe throws at me, only to find myself at the epicenter of all this weirdness. I mean, really, doesn't that just figure?"

"I have it on good authority, Miss Wong, that karma is, in fact, rather a bitch," Cooper replied, distractedly.

"Oh, karma shmarma. I've been in Keeter's Bluff for two days, and in the last eight hours we've had, let's see, a swarm of bees, at least three birds hurling themselves into windows, and a good dog turned suddenly feral. Oh, and let's not forget about our friend, Snagglepuss. Did I leave anything out, Sheriff?"

Cooper's mind swirled with images of rats and spiders and gangs of squirrels, but he kept all of those things to himself.

"I believe you hit the high points."

"What did he mean by 'cake'?"

"Just that. A cake. For a wedding."

"Yeah? Who's getting married?"

"Fancy Whittacker."

"Sounds like a fishing lure," Emma snorted. "A friend of yours, I take it?"

Cooper scoffed.

"Not even close."

"But it falls upon you to bring a wedding cake for this person who's not even close to a friend? Sounds a little odd. Is that a 'small town' thing? "

"No, it's an 'I'm an idiot' thing," Cooper admitted. And then he confessed it all. He told her everything. Every detail of the whole sordid mess, up to and including his own personal Kryptonite. And when he was done, Emma simply stood there gawking and clearly trying not to laugh. Ultimately, she failed, but her laugh was so adorable that Cooper didn't even mind. Well, not much, anyway.

"Like I said," he shrugged. "I'm an idiot."

To his dismay, Emma didn't argue the point. All she said was, "Don't you guys have a bakery in town? They're all the rage, you know. Believe it or not, some towns even have more than one."

"Believe me, Miss Wong, there are three things all small towns have in abundance. Bakeries, butcher shops and bars. So yes, we have a bakery or two in the 'Bluff. But not even Marigold would be able to whip up a wedding cake in the time I have left." He let out a long, slow sigh and shook his head. "Hell, maybe I'll just go with Henry's flan after all."

"A wedding *flan?*" Emma giggled. "Oh my."

"Exactly. So now I have two choices. Either I show up empty-handed and let them rip me a new one, or I don't show up at all and suffer even more because they had to track me down in order to rip me a new one."

"And this is the wedding you invited *me* to? Wow. How incredibly cruel."

In his own defense, Cooper admitted, "To be honest, I thought they might go a little easier on me if there was a new face in the crowd."

The girl's smile remained, but there was genuine concern in her eyes as she asked, "So, what now?"

In an ordinary investigation, this would be an easy question to answer, but until word came from either Doc Jenkins or Austin Granger, there was precious little to be done. Two mysteries needed solving, and all he could do was wait. So, with his frustration level at a peak, the pain in his skull not yet beginning to subside, and the town he had sworn to protect possibly getting ready to tear itself apart, he slapped his hand on the car hood and said, "Now, I'm going to have a drink. Care to join me, Miss Wong?"

He left the cruiser where it was and started off down Market Street fast enough that Emma had to run to keep up.

"Wait a minute, Sheriff. I thought you guys weren't allowed to drink on duty. Isn't that what they say on all the cop shows?"

"If the good people of Keeter's Bluff want my badge, they can come and get it," Cooper scoffed. "At least the Judge won't have it to shove up my ass."

Emma wrinkled her nose. "And you think now is really the best time to get drunk as shit? Now? With all this craziness going on?"

Cooper didn't even break stride.

"I honestly can't think of a better time," he said, with visions of cats and rats and Skinwalkers and Kira Melanson's beautiful face all swirling together. "But not to worry, Miss Wong, I won't be getting drunk as shit. Not yet, anyway. I just need something to put the whole day in perspective."

She grabbed him by the shirt sleeve and spun him around.

"No, Sheriff, what you need is a cake. Putting it off only makes matters worse, or haven't you figured that out yet?" He moved to protest, but she shut him down. "Now, here's what you're going to do, Sheriff. You are going to get in your car, you are going to go to... uh, *Marigold*, and you are going to beg her to come up with something halfway decent. And then you are going to take that halfway decent wedding cake to that godawful reception, and you are going to face the music." She released his sleeve and gave a sideways bob of her head. "As for me, I shall return to my tiny hovel of a supposedly-furnished apartment, go through every scrap of clothing I brought with me, and realize that I have nothing suitable to wear to a dinner with my new boss, Hiram Merriwhether Danvers, and his darling wife, whoever-the-hell."

"Amanda," Cooper offered.

"Who cares?" Emma snarled, then she picked up right where she left off. "And after said search and inevitable conclusion, and with no time left to dash out and peruse Mayberry's dress shops for whatever passes for fashion in these parts, I shall then sink into a soul-numbing depression until I finally grab whatever makes me look least like a penniless hobo, and then I shall suffer through an agonizing evening with a man and woman I don't know at all, well aware the entire time of what a horrible impression I've made on them both. Believe me, Sheriff, if there was enough time for Salmonella to take hold, I'd stop by the grocery store on the way home and lick a raw chicken."

Now, it was Cooper's turn to laugh.

"I don't think you have to worry about Hiram Danvers, Miss Wong. Something tells me the man won't know what hit him. Come on, there's a dress shop just up the block. I'll introduce you to Sam. She'll take good care of you."

"I don't look good in burlap, Sheriff," she cautioned him.

"Try not to be a snob, Miss Wong," he replied.

They hadn't taken a dozen more steps before something splatted to the sidewalk between them. Normally, neither one of them might even have noticed it. It was one of those things that happened a thousand times a day in every square block across every city, every state, and every country on the planet. Somewhere up above, a bird had relieved itself, and its droppings had fallen to the ground as a tiny white glob. In any other city on any other day at any other time, it would have been too inconsequential to even warrant acknowledging. But this was no other day.

Cooper craned his neck, and Emma followed his gaze. Then they both froze to the spot, wide-eyed, slack-jawed, and trying to come to terms with what it was they were seeing.

Birds were hardly a rare sight in the 'Bluff, but this was different. Considering the events of the day, it was different enough to send a ripple of fear up two separate spines.

They were everywhere. Hundreds upon hundreds of birds, roosting in every tree along both sides of the street, piled together atop every telephone pole, and strung along every overhead wire and the eaves of every store and gas station and office building for as far as the eye could see in either direction. Crows. Robins. Starlings. Gulls. Wrens. Every species of bird Cooper had ever seen plying the skies of Keeter's Bluff was represented among the megaflock. As God was his witness, he could even see a hawk high up in the tallest tree, nestled among what would normally be its prey.

"Umm..." Emma fought for words, *any* words, and finally settled on, "This is weird, right?"

It might have been the sound of her voice, or it might have been something else, but a harsh wind suddenly broke down Market Street as a thousand wings took flight. Every bird from every branch and every wire and every rooftop took to the air, turning the sky black. Around and around they flew like a feathery tornado, then the entire flock began to descend, and the tornado touched ground.

Samantha's Boutique just happened to be the eye of the

storm. Starlings and crows and robins by the dozens flew straight into the plate glass windows fronting the shop, and though they held at first, the onslaught was simply too much. The glass gave way, shattering into a million pieces, and the birds poured in. Samantha Abbott came scrambling out with another woman in tow, swatting and waving at a wild riot of beaks and talons, and while Cooper hollered to them and waved them his way, another tornado swept in.

Cooper shoved Emma back and yelled at her, "Get to my car! Go!" but this woman he had only just met surprised him yet again.

"In a pig's eye!" she shouted back, and that tiny woman with the My Little Ponies Band-Aid over one eye and the courage of Alexander the Great led the charge down Market Street.

"Get inside!" she yowled at the top of her lungs, gathering Samantha Abbott and the other woman together and bee-lining it through the next door that presented itself. "Move! Get inside! Now!"

Cooper saw two others in a fight of their own on the other side of the street, so he called to them, "This way! Now! Come on!" and the young couple came charging across the street, narrowly avoiding being crushed under the wheels of a garbage truck careening from one lane to the other with a hundred birds dive-bombing the windows. Cooper wasted no time in shoving the two though the open door, but then he came under direct attack as several crows and one huge raven began pecking furiously at his eyes. Even as he swatted and batted away at the birds, he managed to corral two more fleeing townspeople through the doorway, then he barged in after them and slammed the door shut behind them all.

And at last, there was peace. Of a sort.

Flannagan's Pub was an ugly little hole-in-the-wall, stuck between Samantha Abbott's dress shop and an even uglier hardware store run by the town's resident curmudgeon, Bo Fraser. But this ugly little hole-in-the-wall had one particular advantage. After a particularly cruel storm blew in the front window the year before, it had been replaced with reinforced glass.

With the tornado raging outside, this ugly little sanctuary quite literally held twice as many bodies as it had ever accommodated at any other single point in its entire existence. Samantha and the young lady she'd had pinned to her side were there, as was the couple from across the street, an older pair who had beaten them all over the threshold, and the last two Cooper had managed to corral inside. And sitting at the bar were two others who had come in for a quick hit of lubricant between work and home. He recognized everyone present. Perry and Dottie Longbow. Darren and Margaret Lee. Harvey and Hattie Winfield. The woman clinging to Samantha Abbott was the youngest of the Heywood girls. Trudy, if he remembered right. The boys at the bar were Matt Newcomb's boy, Jim, and Estevan Rodriguez. And way over there behind the far end of the bar sat Ephraim Berkowitz, current owner and proprietor of Flannagan's Pub, completely oblivious to the goings-on around him as he nursed a tall glass of Irish Whiskey.

And there was Emma Wong, as scared as could be but trying not to show it.

"Are you okay?" he mouthed across the room to her. She nodded back, but it was unconvincing.

Outside, one bird after another crashed into the window and dropped to the sidewalk. Despite the fact that the glass was reinforced, Cooper was certain that every strike would be the one that shattered it to bits. He looked around for anything he might use to protect his people should the worst happen, but even as he considered tables and chairs and bottles smashed into stabbing weapons, the onslaught slowed, and then it ceased altogether.

He could hear the tornado cawing and screeing and death-rattling all up and down the street, but it was no longer deafening. In fact, they seemed to be getting more and more distant with every beat of his pounding heart. A minute passed, and then another, and just like that, the skies opened up. Once again, the sun beat down on Market Street, and all beyond that reinforced window was still and silent. Cooper pressed his face against the glass and turned an eye to the sky, but all he could see were fluffy white clouds and the bluest blue he might ever have seen.

Samantha Abbott came up beside him with the Heywood girl still clutched to her side.

"A-Are they gone?"

Emma squeezed in between them to have a look for herself, and Cooper tore his eyes away from the glass long enough to do what he had earlier promised to do with a quick double-nod.

"Samantha Abbott, Emma Wong. Emma, Sam."

"Oh, okay... uhh... hi," Samantha performed the required social nicety, however distractedly.

"Hi," Emma said back, just as distractedly. But then she happened to notice the elegant tunic top the woman was wearing and couldn't help but run a bit of the fabric through her fingers. "Hey, this is cute. Do you have this in a size two?"

The woman grunted some manner of noncommittal response and turned back to Cooper.

"Tom, are they really gone?"

"Looks like," he told her, but as he scanned every inch of sky, he had to add the caveat that only he and he alone would ever hear.

For now...

CHAPTER

XIII

J ermaine Granger was just down the road from the Piedmont Veterinary Diagnostic Clinic when her phone
rang. It was Austin. She answered with a mumbled,
"'Sup, babe," around a mouthful of Tandoori chicken.

"Any word yet?"

She rolled her eyes. This was the third time he'd called
in the last half hour asking the same question.

"You think I'm going to keep it a secret, babe?" she
snarked.

"No, but I think once you tuck yourself into a booth at
Curry in a Hurry, your mind is on one thing and one thing
only."

It was a recurring theme in their relationship. Jermaine
had come to the 'Bluff via New York. Manhattan, to be precise. Upper Manhattan, to be even more precise. Uptown.
The Harlem district. West 139th and Edgecombe, to pin-
point it with absolute precision. Everything a discerning

palate desired could be found within walking distance from that very place. Jewish delicatessens. Italian restaurants. Indian food. Korean. Chinese. Russian. Creole. Hell, there was even a Taco Bell, for when she felt daring.

Then came the move to Keeter's Bluff. It hadn't been planned, but it hadn't been on a whim, either. Austin Granger had come to New York for a cousin's wedding, and her future was sealed. There was a chance meeting and a shared cab ride, and two weeks later, she'd made the move. And though she hadn't suffered a moment's regret in the five years since, there was one crucial element of her old life that would forever be missing in Keeter's Bluff.

"Well, if a girl could find a decent paneer or masala anywhere in the 'Bluff, maybe I'd be more attentive."

"What can I say?" Granger's voice came back. "This is more of a meat and potatoes crowd. How's the car holding up?"

"Good," she said, shoveling in another forkful and savoring the burn. "I guess the new rad hose did the trick. No warning lights the whole way here."

She could hear his relieved sigh through the phone.

"Awesome. I told you, hon, there's plenty of life in that old gal yet."

"Tell me that again, when and *if* I get back," she said, then she waved to the turbaned man behind the counter, and seeing as she was the only customer in the place, she called out, "Parm, could I trouble you for a tea when you have a second?"

"Certainly, Miss Jermaine," the man replied with a smile, turning away from the wall-mounted TV he'd been idly watching. He set about collecting a cup, saucer, cream, and a pot of freshly brewed Darjeeling, but some word or sound from the television grabbed his attention, and he stopped. Naturally, Jermaine's eyes followed his, and she saw it too. A jumble of images. Wolf Blitzer looking anxious. People running. Panic in the streets. Then Blitzer was back again, with the high-res LED video wall behind him declaring in a banner headline, 'Tragedy in NYC'.

"Oh shit, not again," she hushed to herself, and as her stomach tied itself into a knot, she called out, "Parm, turn it up!"

The man complied, but she almost wished he hadn't. No, this was not another mass shooting or another truck bomb or another attack from the sky, but her beloved city was most certainly under attack once again. She didn't know how or by whom, but this time, it appeared to be the Bronx. She listened to Blitzer's commentary, and tried to make sense of the jumble of images from the shaky footage.

"...unclear as yet, but there are now six confirmed dead, and many more injured, four of whom are reported to be in critical condition. All of the injured have been taken to either Bronx-Lebanon or St. Barnabas Hospital, and we are waiting on word." He pressed a finger to his ear. "I've just been told that our own Jason Sinclair is on the scene, so we are going to go live to the Bronx Zoo. Jason, what can you tell us?"

The screen switched to a handsome young man standing before a phalanx of police cars, ambulances, and fire trucks, trying to keep his composure with every light flashing, people running to and fro, and seemingly everyone barking orders all at once.

"Babe, you watching this?" Jermaine said into her phone.

Back at the shop and up to his elbows in paperwork, Granger downed the last of his Pepsi.

"Be a tad more specific, Hon. Watching what?"

"CNN. Something happened in New York."

"Oh shit, not again," Granger hushed, pawing through the deskload of papers. At last, he found the remote control and switched from an old Hogan's Heroes rerun to CNN, then the two of them sat in stunned silence, sixty miles apart, as the handsome young man gave the rest of his report.

"All the authorities know for sure is that the attack began a little over an hour ago when an as-yet unidentified woman was mauled to death in one of the tunnels used by zoo employees to access the various animal habitats. From what I've been told, this particular tunnel is separated from the baboon reserve by a heavy iron gate, so it is uncertain exactly how the animals escaped. But escape, they did."

They ran the shaky footage again. Frightened faces. Running feet. An old woman falling to her knees. Another, barreling over her in a panic. Then came the money shots. A hunched shape coming out of nowhere. A man falling. Wild thrashing as the massive beast tore into him. A quick camera shift to show a woman desperately trying to herd two small children to safety. Another hunched shape suddenly appearing. A gut-wrenching scream. Fangs. Claws. Two small children, frozen in place as they watched their mother come apart. And through it all, the background screams and sobs and pleas to God from a hundred different voices, all punctuated by the ungodly howls of wild animals in a frenzy.

Soon enough, the coverage began to loop back around, so Blitzer returned for the wrap-up.

"Most of the animals have been killed or captured, but five are still unaccounted for. Local residents have been instructed to shelter in place, and of course, anyone who thinks they may have spotted one of these last five animals should call 9-1-1 without delay,"

Granger gave his commentary from sixty miles away, "Fuck."

Suddenly disinterested in the remains of her Tandoori chicken, Jermaine couldn't have agreed more.

"Fuck, indeed."

"That ain't rabies, hon," Granger told her, point blank.

"Nope," she replied, pushing the unfinished plate away and digging through her pockets for a couple of bills as she climbed from the booth. "Give me five minutes to get Snagglepuss's results. If they aren't done with the DFA yet, I'll hold a fork to their throats until they are."

"That's my girl," Granger said, ending the call.

Jermaine dropped a couple of tens on the table, and without even a wave to Parm behind the counter, all but ran for the door.

The Piedmont Veterinary Diagnostic Clinic was only a block up Martin Avenue. On an ordinary day, her trademark Adidas and black yoga pants would have had her sprinting that distance in thirty seconds flat, but no sooner had she thrown open the door of Piedmont's one and only Curry in a Hurry than she came to a screeching halt.

It was as if she had somehow stepped out of reality and straight into that shaky CNN footage. People were running. People were screaming. People were falling to their knees, and others were barreling over them in desperation and panic. But even as her mind struggled to come to terms with why these people should be in such a panic when the drama was being played out so very far away, a German shepherd came charging around the corner dripping saliva from its slavering jaws. And then came another. And then a Pit Bull, and another behind him. Then a collie, and an Irish setter.

Then the rest of the pack showed itself. Bloodhound. Mastiff. Malamute. Doberman. English bulldog. Even a great woolly sheep-like thing she recognized as a Komondor made an appearance. It was a ragtag mix of breeds that should never have come together, but this pack of twenty or more dogs was most certainly together, and they all had one thing in common. Every single one of them was attacking anything that moved.

With a steady flow of traffic in the street, the sidewalk became a killing ground. There was simply no escape. An old woman was taken down by the Mastiff not twenty yards away, and was barely able to put up a fight before a powerful set of jaws ended her struggles. Then a skinny little man was set upon by two of the smaller dogs, and despite their size, he never stood a chance. A tall, leggy woman tripped over her own high heels, and a doberman the size of a pony took full advantage of that brief, off-balanced moment. A big man in a suit and tie rushed to the woman's aid, swinging his briefcase like a battle axe, but then both pit bulls suddenly emerged from out of the maelstrom and bowled him over. One grabbed him by the arm, the other went for his face, and those two snarling dogs tore the big man to pieces.

And it didn't stop there. With their prey trapped in a gauntlet, the pack took down one after another after another. Then the big German shepherd with its muzzle already caked in blood broke away from the pack and charged straight for Jermaine, and there was nowhere left for her to run.

She spun around and threw herself back into the door of Curry in a Hurry, but she was a second too late. The lock clicked, and the door wouldn't budge. Parm's face appeared behind the glass for the briefest of moments, but though she banged on the door and begged him to let her back in, all the turbaned man did was mouth the words, "I am so sorry," before drawing the blinds and cutting her off once and for all from her only means of escape. She hammered and pounded and kicked at the door, but with three other dogs falling in behind the shepherd as it came at her, she at last gave up and ran for her very life.

They were right on her heels. She was dimly aware of people falling all around her, but there was nothing she could do for them. And so, she ran. She ignored the screams and the howls and the dead and the dying, and she ran. She ran as fast as her feet could carry her, but she knew it was only a matter of time. With dogs able to reach speeds nearing thirty miles an hour and a human topping out at half that, this was a race she could never win. Then a trio of dogs came charging out of an alley directly in front of her, and she knew it would be over in seconds.

But this was one ex-New Yorker who refused to give up. She sized up her options in an instant, and took the only path she could. With a pack of snarling dogs coming at her from both directions, she wheeled a sharp left, leaped off of the sidewalk, and hurled herself straight into the oncoming traffic.

Nine times out of ten, she would have been struck and killed in an instant. A soccer mom paying more attention to her kids than the road maybe, or the driver of an eighteen-wheeler finishing a text message. Honestly, she didn't think she'd get across a single lane without being hit, but that brave, desperate act wound up saving her life. When she emerged unscathed on the other side to the sounds of tires squealing, dogs yelping, and an almighty crunch of metal on metal times infinity, she chanced a quick look back, and then she stopped, gasping for breath.

All of those thousands of pounds of steel and glass and rubber had done their work. A dozen or more dogs lay dead or dying in the street, and the rest of the pack was in full retreat, tails tucked between their legs and yowling up a storm. While bewildered drivers and passengers began clambering out of their wrecked vehicles and emerging from store fronts and offices all along Martin Avenue to take pictures and selfies and videos destined for their social media accounts, Jermaine simply stood there, shaking from head to toe. At last, her strength gave out and she dropped to her backside on the sidewalk, and there, sixty miles from home and a million miles away from anything approaching sanity, she put her face in her hands and let the tears consume her.

CHAPTER

XIV

B
ase to KB-One"
Nothing came back but dead air.
"KB-One, come in."

Again, nothing. Grace let it go for as long as her nerves could stand, then she pulled the mike right up to her lips and tried once more. She thumbed the button down and growled, "Base to any car, respond," and finally, a string of voices came through, one nearly on top of each other.

Buck was first. Then Henry. Then Carl. Then Sonny

"KB-Two, copy."

"KB-Three."

"KB-Four copies as well."

"KB-five, copy."

Grace noted all of their call signs on a notepad and jotted down the time. 1615 hours. Four fifteen. Not yet into the evening, and already one of the longest days of her life.

"Any of you dingbats got eyes on the Sheriff?"

"Negative," Henry Greenleaf responded. "You have a twenty?"

"He went out for Aspirin," she advised him, silently kicking herself in the process. "He has an account at the Pharmadeal on Market, and I'm getting calls about something going on downtown."

"I'm close," Carl replied. "On my way," but then another voice broke through.

"KB-One to Base."

It was the sheriff's call sign, but this wasn't the Tom Cooper she knew. This Tom Cooper sounded shaky. Unsteady. If she didn't know any better, she might even have said he sounded scared.

She toggled the button again.

"Is that you, Sheriff?"

"A little worse for wear, but yes, it's me," Cooper replied.

"Glad to hear it," Grace replied without the usual snark. "I'm getting crazy reports from downtown. Something about nuisance birds."

"I'm at that location," Cooper told Grace, then he coolly and calmly gave a brief description of the events. "No major injuries," he tacked on, "but you'd better send an ambulance to take care of some cuts and scrapes. And give the works yard a call. There's broken glass and dead birds all up and down Market."

"Copy that," Grace acknowledged with a barely disguised sigh of relief, then she added, almost reluctantly, "I hate to say it, Sheriff, but I have another 91-Victor at Leeland Farms. 221 Franklin Road."

Henry Greenleaf replied immediately. "KB-three. I'm on the outskirts. Will attend." But Cooper wasn't about to let it go at that.

"Someone go with him!" he all but shouted into the mike. "Buck, Sonny, do *not* let him go alone!"

Buck was the first to reply.

"Copy that, boss. On my way."

Cooper turned his gaze back to the closest thing Keeter's Bluff had to a downtown and shook his head.

It had all happened in the blink of an eye. One minute, Market Street was just another lazy avenue in a quiet little backwater town. The next, it was ground zero for Armageddon. The birds had come out of nowhere. Before he'd even known what was happening, it was happening, and all he could do was try to catch up and keep his people safe. But he did it, and as he sat in his cruiser with Emma Wong beside him with her new tunic top in a bag on her lap and visions of the worst possible scenario playing though his mind, he told both of his deputies responding to the call, "Stay safe, gentlemen. Watch your backs," then he replaced the mike on the hook.

Emma leaned back in the passenger seat and lolled her head his way.

"It's not rabies," she told him as a matter of fact. "It can't be. Birds don't get rabies."

"I know," Cooper replied, not able to lean back in his seat quite so comfortably with the welts under his collar vying for attention with a host of fresh scratches everywhere the bees had missed, but trying nonetheless. "So, we're back to toxins. But no toxin could possibly affect such a wide variety of species. At least, not in the exact same way."

"No toxin we know about," the girl reminded him. "But what if it's something we *don't* know about. I mean, really, new species of plants and animals are being discovered almost as quickly as we can kill them off, right? So, who's to say that something hasn't come out of the blue to affect the brains of dogs and cougars and bees and birds, all at the same time. I mean, it's possible, right?"

"Mammals, sure. Birds, sure. Insects. sure," Cooper grunted his response. "But all three? Not a chance in Hell. Besides, anything coming out of the blue that could do all that would do it to us, too."

Of that, he was certain. He knew he was right, and he knew that Emma knew it too, but this woman new to the 'Bluff wasn't quite willing to give up the fight just yet.

"Then it was something else. City lights can confuse birds."

"In broad daylight?" Cooper scoffed, shooting her down.

"Okay, then. Fracking. Fracking releases all kinds of heavy metals."

"Fracking's not allowed in this state," Cooper countered. "I promise you, no one's fracking for two hundred miles in any direction."

"So, no fracking way?" Emma took a stab at humor, but it went over about as well as she'd expected. "Well then, I have no idea what's going on in your stupid little town," she said at last, the weight of her scowl sinking her deeper in the seat.

"It's *your* stupid little town, too," he reminded her.

"Yeah? Well, I'm starting to rethink my faith in the universe. This isn't Mayberry, Sheriff. This is the Twilight Zone with a little Alfred Hitchcock thrown in for kicks. All that's missing is a kid wishing people into the corn field. Tell you what, Sheriff, you can keep your stupid little town. I'll take LA's shit over *this* shit any day of the week!"

Cooper took one more look at Market Street littered with broken glass and shattered bodies, and he told her frankly, "I can't say that I blame you."

With that, Emma popped open her door, climbed out, and spun back around to deliver the last message she would ever give to this star-breasted stranger she would never see again.

"Nice meeting you, Sheriff," she said, then she slammed the door closed and headed back to her Mazda parked a few spaces farther down the street.

On the way back to her apartment, the tears came again. She cried for the poor, dead thing still occupying the seat beside her under a blanket of Kleenex, she cried for the others strewn across too many blocks of Market Street to count, and because she was too scared and too confused and too distraught to know what else to do, she cried some more.

By the time she pulled back behind her building, the tears had nearly diminished. She sniffled up what she thought was the last of them, but when she collected the poor dead thing from the passenger seat, on they came again. She carried the bundle to the edge of the parking lot and dug a heel into the ground, and as she dropped to her knees and placed the remains in the shallow grave, she cried some more.

Just as she'd finished covering the body with a generous double-handed sweep of dirt, something hit the ground beside her with an all-too familiar splat. She looked to the tiny dollop of white, then she slowly and nervously turned her eyes skyward.

As before, the splat had come from above. And as before, every tree, every rooftop and every overhead wire in sight was alive with birds. They had come as silently as wraiths while she'd had her back turned. Then more, and more still. Even the parking lot was filled to overflowing, as if someone had laid a carpet of feathers across every car and every square inch of asphalt.

She finished pulling dirt over the poor dead creature, then she stood, locked eyes with crows and starlings and every other bird alike, and with her heart pounding in her chest, she began to pick her way through the moving carpet toward the back door of her apartment building.

Surprisingly, they let her pass easily enough. Her sneakered foot would rise, the carpet would separate just enough to open a hole, and the foot would come down again. And every time it happened, she was sure it would be the last. With every step she took, she was certain that the entire flock would suddenly come alive, and once they had her on the ground, they'd have her eyes pecked out and the flesh stripped from her bones before she could let out so much as a whimper. But it was not to be. Before she knew it, she was at the door, slipping her key in the lock. Then she was sidling through, with the door shnicking closed behind her.

She took the stairs two at a time and was soon in her apartment, but instead of setting about filling her suitcase and heading west as fast as her car could carry her, she took a beat, helped herself to the barest sip of vodka from the too-tiny bottle in the fridge, and plunked herself down at her desk before an array of books and a slim binder with a headline she had written herself, still there on the open page.

Gaia.

Newly intrigued, she brought the book down to her lap and started reading. An hour later, she closed the book, clutched it to her heart, and stood at the window, gazing out upon this new home the universe had chosen for her. And as she stood there, numb with disbelief, all she could think was that the horror show wasn't over yet. In fact, it might only just be beginning.

If she was right, and if the words she had just read were true, things in Keeter's Bluff were about to get much, much worse.

CHAPTER

XV

Henry Greenleaf manoeuvred his massive frame out from behind the wheel and had a good look around. From what he could see, all looked in order. And why wouldn't it? Leeland Farms dealt in poultry and eggs. All they had here were chickens. There was a time when he used to feel sorry for the poor dumb birds at Leeland Farms, but he'd since come to the realization that chickens were and always would be the lowly pawns in the chess game of life. Even before the skinny little birds they used to be were fattened up to feed the masses during World War II, they'd been the go-to for every predator around the globe. Foxes, coyotes, wolves, snakes, weasels... there wasn't a predator in the world that wouldn't go for a skinny little bird that could barely get off the ground. So all things considered, a lifetime spent safely behind bars, pooping out eggs, wasn't such a bad deal. Even the birds raised for slaughter didn't have it too bad. They had fresh water, plenty of food, and a big, open field to spend their days scratching around in. What happened to them after that was brutal, but it was their own fault for being so damn tasty.

Which brought him back to the matter at hand. The 10-91 Victor. Something else was after those damn tasty birds. Enough of a something to warrant a call to the Sheriff's Office. The usual culprits were those critters that had already crossed his mind, but it wasn't too much of a stretch to imagine that even a bear might've snuck down from the hills, following the scent of those tasty, tasty chickens.

But Henry Greenleaf did nothing on impulse. While other men might go charging in with fists swinging and guns blazing, Greenleaf used a methodical approach in all things. So, with his cruiser parked at the far end of the dirt road leading up to a cluster of buildings, he stood beside his open door, tucked his sunglasses into the crook of his shirt, and used every one of his senses to check the place out.

Four minutes later, Buck rolled in and found Henry Greenleaf lying in a puddle of blood beside the open door of his cruiser. But Deputy David 'Buck' Rogers didn't live long enough to radio in a report. He died with his pistol still in its holster, blood pouring from a dozen wounds, and not understanding one damn thing about any of it.

CHAPTER

XVI

D unno, Sheriff. They just don't answer. It keeps going to voicemail."

Cooper shot him a look as the two snuck in
through the back door of the Elk's Hall.

"Let me get this straight, Carl. You're telling me that the
State *goddam* Police aren't answering their *fucking* phone?"

"I tried the switchboard, Captain Callahan's private office, and even the emergency line," Deputy Rankin
shrugged. "If anyone's home, Sheriff, they ain't answerin'."

Just then, Cooper's phone beeped. It was a text from
Austin Granger. But where he'd expected it to say yay or nay
to the rabies, all it said was, 'CNN. NOW!'

"All caps?" Rankin scowled, sneaking a peek. "Geez,
dude. That's rude."

"That's just part of the magic and majesty that is him,"
Cooper replied distractedly, stepping into the Elks' lunch
room and flipping on the ancient TV.

Rankin followed along behind, then two elderly Elk's came in to see what had gotten them both oohing and aahing and *omigod*ing, and soon enough, others drifted in. At last, with twenty or more bodies crowded around the tiny TV screen and Fancy's reception set to begin in a few minutes in the main hall, Cooper barked, "Someone shut the goddam door!" and notched the volume just a little bit higher.

Word was coming in from St. Barnabas Hospital in the Bronx. The death toll was up to eight, but more were expected. The injuries ranged from twisted ankles and scratches and bites, all the way up to things that brought horrified gasps and sickened moans from everyone in the room. Like most primates, the specialist on the video wall told Blitzer, baboons in a frenzy went for two targets first. They went for the face, and they went for the genitals, in no particular order. And needless to say, those big canine teeth and Freddy Kruger claws could inflict considerable damage.

"Jesus, Mary and Joseph," Rankin hushed at hearing the descriptions of what the maulings had left behind. "Those poor bastards would be better off dead."

No one argued the point.

Cooper's phone beeped again. It was Granger. Again.

'U watching? Wait for it. They'll cycle back around.'

Cooper wasn't a fast typer with his big fat thumbs, but without a ten-year-old assistant to whip off a text in a blur, he plugged away as best he could.

'wish i wasnt', he replied. Eventually. And poorly.

'It's not rabies,' Granger texted back.

'There or hear?' Cooper typed, realizing the misspelling only after he'd hit the send button, but not caring either way.

Granger's next text took a few seconds longer to come through. Long enough for the scene on the TV to change to what he had obviously wanted him to see. Now, it was showing what Cooper recognized as the Angel of Independence statue in Mexico City. Just like the video from the Bronx Zoo, people were running, people were shouting, and that same *damn* shaky camera shit recorded it all like the Blair Witch Project on Ritalin. But before he could figure out what the hell it was he was watching, his phone beeped again.

'Both. Papio Anubis is as susceptible to rabies as any mammal, but no f'ing way they were ALL infected. And J just called. Snagglepuss was perfectly healthy at TOD. There was an incident in Piedmont while she was there. Sending the link.'

Cooper tapped the link and was taken to a YouTube upload. More *goddam* shaky video. But then the phone recording the video fell to the ground, and he had a steady, worm's eye view of the event from then on. Both he and Rankin looked from the cell phone to the TV and back again as the two tales were told.

In Piedmont, it was dogs. In Mexico City, it was worse. Between the quick flashes of frightened faces and running feet, there were other quick flashes of horns and hooves, and blurs of black and brown and white that could only mean one thing.

Bulls. Not in the Plaza de Toros, but in downtown Mexico City. It was like the running of the bulls as filmed by Quentin Tarantino. Eight million people lived shoulder to shoulder within the confines of that ancient city, with apparently not a single picador or banderillero in the bunch. The result was carnage on an epic scale. Gored, torn asunder or crushed underfoot, the death toll was already in the hundreds. More were expected. Many, *many* more.

There was carnage in Piedmont, too, but it was carnage on a different scale. When another camera pulled back to show the entire scene, it became clear that the drama had been limited to a few city blocks of some nameless street. Cooper counted eight bodies strewn along the sidewalk of this one block alone. Multiplied by three, it still paled in comparison to the carnage in Mexico City. And yet, Piedmont was different. Piedmont wasn't a trainload of Torero fodder breaking loose and wreaking vengeance on the mob they were born to die for. Piedmont was dogs. Dogs! And not even *wild* dogs. These hadn't been abandoned, half-starved mongrels left to fend for themselves and doing what they must to survive. These were just dogs. Peoples' pets. Pampered. Groomed. Taken to the park. Chasing after sticks. Curling up by the fire. Hell, they were just *dogs!*

Cooper took a moment to wonder if the man or woman who had been so obsessed with their social media presence to have set their phone to automatically upload the carnage to YouTube was still so obsessed with their likes from the other side of forever, then he texted back to Granger.

'its getting worse'

'Yup,' Granger replied, and that ended the conversation.

Cooper grabbed Rankin by the collar and pulled him back to the outer room, closing the lunch room door behind them so they could speak in relative privacy.

"Alright, Carl, listen. We don't know that any of what's happening elsewhere has anything to do with what's happening here, but people are going to watch the news and surf the 'net, and they're going to be scared. Our job now is the same as it's always been. We serve, and we protect. You got your shotgun in the trunk?"

"Yessir, Sheriff," Rankin replied with a nod.

"Well, keep it up front until I say otherwise. And swing by the station for another box or two of shells when you get a minute. Better safe than sorry."

"Words I live by, Sheriff," Rankin stiffened his back. "Will do."

The deputy turned to go, but Cooper stopped him in his tracks.

"And Carl, from now on, every call we get is a potential 91-Victor. You got that? Pass it along."

"Uh... okay. Copy that," Rankin replied with a nod.

With that, Cooper let him go, but not without a few last words.

"Stay frosty out there, Carl," he called after him. "Mindy-Lou will have my ass if you so much as skin your knee."

"She most certainly will, Sheriff," Rankin called back over his shoulder, then he disappeared through the door and Cooper was alone again.

But not for long. With the clock chiming six, the parking lot full, and Fancy's reception just ready to start cranking up, there wouldn't be a corner of the entire Elk's Hall to hide in within the next five minutes. Dinner would be served, toasts would be offered, and drinks would flow. And then would come time for the fat little wife and her gawky new husband to cut the wedding cake, so the catering staff would be sent to this very room to collect the symbol of the union of those two souls for all of eternity.

Cooper had no intention of being around when that time came. He threw one last look at the replacement cake he'd brought, muttered, "Better get to it quick," to no one in particular, and followed Rankin out.

Behind him, the cake he had procured for the evening's festivities sat in the precise center of a twenty-foot-long table, covered with the whitest of linen and strewn with the freshest of rose petals. It was a chocolate ice cream log from Dairy Queen, and if they got to it quickly enough, they would even find a tiny broken Fancy and Jerome Harsh-waldt sticking out of the top, already up to their marzipan asses in melting chocolate.

CHAPTER

XVII

I swear, I'm gonna *kill* those bastards!"

Ivan picked his way through a minefield of broken glass and picked up the baseball, turning a snarl loose on the shattered window. A high wooden fence blocked the view beyond his property, but he knew they were there. Sure, they were being quiet now, but he'd heard them. He *always* heard them. All day long, all summer long, the little bastards were over there in that field, cackling and hooting and whooping it up like a pack of wild monkeys.

He dropped the baseball behind the couch with the rest of the balls and Frisbees and toy airplanes he'd collected from his yard this year alone, then he stormed out the back door in a rage.

"I swear, you damn punks, I'm gonna ring your scrawny little necks one at a damn time!"

He howled the words loudly enough that any monkeys hiding behind the fence would be sure to flee in terror. One of these days, he would put the fear of Ivan the Terrible into enough of the punks that the whole damn lot of them would stay the hell away forever! And if not, well wouldn't that be just too damn bad for them.

He formed an image in his mind of his big hands wrapping around a few scrawny little monkey necks, and his sneer deepened.

"I've had it with you punks!" he swore at the fence, crossing the yard in six angry strides to put an eye to a narrow slit between two of the boards. "That window's gonna cost a hundred bucks to fix, and I plan on taking every last penny of it out of your damn hides! You hear me?"

He caught movement on the other side of the fence, but the slit was too narrow to make out any detail. If only he could see a face. Just one clear image of one snotty little monkey face. Keeter's Bluff wasn't a very big town. He knew most of the brats in the 'Bluff by sight, if not by name. If he could just see one face clearly, he'd go to that kid's house and raise holy hell with the parents who should've taken a coat hanger to the little prick before he was born. As God was his witness, he'd get his hundred bucks one way or the other.

More movement. He tried angling his head to get a better view, but it was no use. His entire universe at that point was a tiny sliver of grass below, blue sky above, and an occasional blur of color obscuring both. But wait. That spot where he'd thrown a beer bottle the day one of the little punks had dared to bark back at him through the fence. That full Schlitz had taken a chunk out of one of the boards, hadn't it? Not much, just a dime-sized chunk, but he'd seen it the next morning when he'd gone out in his bare feet to pick up the broken glass. Even with his pinky toe gushing blood, he'd seen it. He hadn't realized it at the time, but that little dime-sized chunk of missing cedar would make a damn-near perfect spy hole, wouldn't it? At last, he might actually be able to catch a few of the punks red-handed. And if he did that, he'd be able to send a message to every other punk in town who thought it would be fun to mess with Ivan the Terrible.

He took three awkward steps to the side and put an eye to the spy hole, but as hard as he strained and as much as he willed his eyeball to conform to that tight little hole, the sliver of sky and grass and blurred colors barely widened by half.

"I see you!" he lied through the spy hole. "I see you there! If you know what's good for you, you'll march your butts right up to my front door and bring all your friends with you! It'll go a lot better for you if you do! If I have to call your parents and tell them you didn't even have the balls to apologize face to face, there'll be hell to pay. You hear me?"

It was a bluff. He couldn't see a damn thing though that tiny dime-sized hole. His frustration growing, he reached up to the top of the fence and tried hoisting himself high enough to peek over, but he was forced to give up before his feet even left the ground. When he was a younger man, he could have *vaulted* over the thing, but that was a lot of beer and pizzas ago. He lowered himself back down as gracefully as he could, with his shirt riding up to his man-boobs and the coarse wood scraping against his bare belly, then he tried the spy hole again.

More movement. *Damn* it! Those little punks were still there, running back and forth too fast for him to see clearly. And there were footsteps now, too. Little monkey feet, scampering back and forth just on the other side of the fence. Then someone giggled, and someone else joined in.

Son of a bitch. They were laughing at him. Those little

monkeys were actually *laughing* at him!

His face grew red as he pounded out his anger and frustration on the fence.

"God *damn* you little punks! I see you Tommy Wilkins! I see you there! And Tracy Coggins, I see you, too! And Harvey Denton's little brat, I see you, too!" He rattled off a few more names at random, hoping to hit a bullseye. "Kyle Pendergrass! Martin Chang! Pardeep....uh, *whatever*-the-fuck! I see you all, and I'm going inside to call your parents right now! The best thing you can do is march your butts right up to my front door this very second and apologize. You hear me?"

All that came back was more giggling, and the occasional flash of color across the spy hole.

"Damn it all too *hell!*" he howled, giving the fence one last punch hard enough to scrape two of his knuckles bare. "God *damn* it!" he shouted, cradling his sore hand against his oversized belly as he stormed back into the house.

"I swear to *God*..." he snarled as he pounded into the kitchen and grabbed a handful of paper towels from the roll to wrap around his wounded wing. As he watched the blood soak through the paper towels, he cursed again and marched back into the livingroom to snatch up the phone. But then he paused with his shirtfront rumpled, his hand wrapped up like a bloody mummy, and his fingers hovering over the buttons.

So, who exactly was he going to call? The cops? Hardly. Sheriff Cooper was a waste of skin, and all of his so-called deputies were even worse. They'd just laugh at him and do sweet bugger all. No no, he had to go right to the heart of the matter. Sam Wilkins? God knows, he'd had a run-in with that punk kid of his more than a few times already. Sure as hell, Tommy Wilkins was one of them. In fact, as one of the bigger kids his age, he was probably the ringleader, getting everyone else to hunker down behind the fence and laugh up a storm. But Tommy Wilkins' old man was a big guy. He had tattoos, and real, actual muscles. Fact was, the guy was a little on the scary side. There were even rumors floating around the 'Bluff about some kind of outstanding warrant back east.

Ivan looked down at his paunch, then at his wounded hand, and he reconsidered.

Okay then. How about Harvey Denton? Denton was a sawed-off little banker with Coke bottle glasses and more often than not a stupid Bluetooth thing clipped to his ear like a damn earring. His kids weren't exactly wild monkeys, but he'd seen them around and they seemed like the kind of kids who could easily fall under the sway of a punk like Tommy Wilkins. So who was to say that those two weren't part of it? Certainly not that little milquetoast banker, that's for sure. Sure, the Denton kids might be halfway across town this very minute watching cartoons, but no one could say for sure that they weren't out there right now, laughing their heads off at a poor old man with blood gushing from his hand, right? Either way, he couldn't imagine sawed-off Harvey Denton putting up much of an argument over a hundred bucks with Ivan the Terrible staring him down.

Okay then, it was settled. Harvey Denton would pony up, or else.

He began to dial information for Denton's number, but then the doorbell rang and something that might have passed for a grin spread across his face.

"Gotcha," he growled, dropping the phone back into its cradle.

As pleased with himself as he'd been that one time he'd finished the TV Guide crossword puzzle all by himself, he marched straight across the livingroom before the monkeys had a chance to rethink the shit storm coming their way and run off before the clouds broke. Whoever it was pushing the buzzer, he'd make him and whatever other poor fools that'd stuck along with him pay. And not just for the window, either. No way. Not now. Not with his bloodied knuckles and scraped belly and wounded pride. *Hell*, no. Now, those monkeys would pay for every summer day ruined by the constant cackling and whooping, and they'd pay for every time they and the other little shits hid behind the fence and laughed at him. And they would sure as *hell* pay for not running their asses over here double-time when he'd first told them to!

"Alright, you little punks," he grumbled to himself. "Prepare to get your scrawny little necks wrung like a goddam chicken."

He threw open the door, and his grin melted away. He tried to slam the door shut, but he was too slow. He even tried to run, but he didn't get far. Less than a minute later, it was all over.

As the last of his blood seeped into the age-old carpet of his livingroom, Ivan the Terrible registered one final sensation as his last experience on Earth.

The sound of giggling.

CHAPTER

XVIII

T he phone rang and rang and rang, then the call went to voicemail.

"We are sorry, but we cannot take your call at the present time. Please leave a message, and we'll get back to you."

Cooper swore under his breath. Then he swore out loud, times four.

"How the *fuck* do the State *goddam* Police not answer their *goddam motherfucking* phone?"

He punched the thing off and dropped it back in his pocket, but he couldn't help feeling cheated by the modern-day equivalent of hanging up a phone. Back in the old days, he could slam a receiver down hard enough to make the phone lines quiver for a mile in every direction. Now, he tapped a little red X and slipped the phone back in his pocket. Given the fact that he was able to make that phone call from a moving car, he knew he probably shouldn't miss such a ridiculous thing like a proper hang-up, but he missed it all the same. And it wasn't the only ridiculous thing he missed from the old days. He missed the snap, crackle and pop of listening to a record on his old turntable. He missed tape decks. He missed getting an actual letter in the actual mail. And despite a PVR loaded with shows he would never get around to watching, he even missed the days of the television event, where a show would be broadcast once and only once, and if you missed it, you were just plain out of luck.

The train of thought naturally led him back to his youth, and he recalled images of him and his friends climbing trees, and stealing crabapples from the neighbor's tree, and jumping their bikes over a ramp made of rocks and dirt and bits of plywood stolen from the lumberyard. He remembered the scraped knees, and the splinters in his hands, and the way old man Pendergast used to chase after him and his buddies with their pockets full of purloined crabapples. And with all of those memories of an impossibly perfect world swirling through his head, there were times when he would have done almost anything to get back there.

But still, modern convenience's did have their upside. His pocket chimed again, and when he answered, he heard Emma Wong's voice at the other end.

"Sheriff? Hi, it's Emma Wong," the voice announced, then it added a completely unnecessary, "Remember me?"

He forced his voice into its lowest register and hoped his reply would sound at least slightly Gary Cooperish.

"Of course, Miss Wong. What can I do for you?"

"Can we meet?" she asked, just that simply.

"Uh, sure," he replied, stumbling over his own tongue. "I'm only a mile from your place. Why don't I drop by?"

Now, it was Emma's turn to stumble.

"Umm... yeah, sure. Why not? Umm... One question. How do you know where I live? I don't remem..."

"You said you lived in a furnished apartment," Cooper said, cutting her off. "There are only two places in the 'Bluff that offer furnished apartments, and no one in their right mind would be caught dead at the other one. I'll be at your door in five minutes."

"Third floor, Sherlock," Emma replied. "Number 317."

"Five minutes," Cooper repeated, then he dropped the phone back in his pocket.

On the way, he unhooked the radio mike and called Deputy Greenleaf.

"KB-One to KB-Three."

No answer.

He tried again.

"KB-One to KB-Three, copy?"

When nothing came back, he changed tack.

"KB-One to KB-Two." He waited twenty seconds and tried again. "KB-One to KB-Two, copy?"

At last, after a full minute of nothing, the dulcet tones of chain smoking, whiskey drinking Grace *goddam* Tolliver came back with a gravelly, "Henry called himself onsite ten minutes ago, Sheriff. Buck radioed the same a few minutes later, but it's been radio silence ever since. I've been radioing and calling their cell phones ever since, but neither one of them answer."

"Alright, Grace," he replied. "It's probably nothing, but keep trying, will you? With everything that's been going on, I'm not afraid to say that I'm a little worried about them both."

"I couldn't agree more, Sheriff," Grace responded, and

now he could pick up Wolf Blitzer's voice in the background, so he knew that she was at least on the same page.

By the time he reached King Albert Apartments, he'd heard Grace try to raise Henry and Buck a dozen times each, and with each of those increasingly frantic calls, he knew that there had been at least as many calls to both of their cell phones. And yet, nothing. For all the good it was doing, Grace might just as well have been hollering into the wind.

He climbed to the third floor and rapped his knuckles under a plate bearing the numbers 317. The door flew open, and Emma Wong unceremoniously grabbed him by the hand, dragging him in.

"Have you heard?" she asked him excitedly. "New York? Mexico? Paris?"

"Yes, yes, and no," he replied, turning his eyes from a blaring TV to the stack of books on a desk ringed with ancient cigarette burns. "What happened in Paris?"

"Believe it or not, *pigs*," she told him, almost daring him to raise a challenge. "*Pigs*, Sheriff. Seven workers on a farm on the outskirts of Paris were severely mauled. Four dead, two more touch and go."

"You didn't get me here to tell me that," Cooper said, stepping up to the old desk and tilting his head to read the spines along the stack of books. UFOs. JFK. Flat Earth. 9-11. Edgar Cayce. Saint Malachy. They were all there. Every lunatic conspiracy and every bit of new age claptrap. He couldn't help but snort his disgust at the lot. "What, nothing about Elvis on Mars? Listen, Miss Wong, if this is..."

"Sheriff," Emma said, cutting him off. "Do yourself a favor. Sit down, shut up, and listen." She grabbed another book from the arm of the couch and flashed him the cover. 'The Gaia Theory', it proclaimed in stark white letters. While

Cooper rolled his eyes, she began reading from a saved page.

"The Gaia Theory, also known as the Gaia Principle or the Gaia Hypothesis, proposes that living organisms interact with their inorganic surroundings on Earth to form a synergistic and self-regulating complex system that helps to maintain and perpetuate the conditions for life on the planet. The hypothesis was formulated by two scientists in the 1970s. They named the idea after Gaia, the primordial goddess who personified the Earth in Greek mythology. "

"Uh, look..." Cooper tried to head her off at the pass, but it didn't work.

"*Shush* now," she snapped, holding up her hand for silence. "This is no crackpot idea, Sheriff. This is actual science by actual scientists, so shut the fuck up and listen." She turned her eyes back to the saved page and read on. "The Gaia Theory was initially criticized for being teleological and against the principles of natural selection, but later refinements aligned the Gaia Theory with ideas from such diverse fields as Earth system science, biogeochemistry, and systems ecology. *Fuck*, dude!" She slammed the book closed around her finger. "Okay, here's the Coles Notes version. Think of this planet not as a ball of rock and magma with a few billion tiny living things scurrying around on the surface. Instead, think of it as one big living organism."

"Sure," Cooper scoffed. "Just as soon as you explain how rocks, magma, and a solid iron core could possibly be considered alive in any way."

"Okay then. Fair enough." She backtracked and started over. "Forget all of that. Instead, let's think of the magnificent biome inhabiting the surface of this ball of inert rock and magma and solid iron core as a single living entity. That's not so absurd, is it?"

"I suppose not," Cooper acquiesced. "At a stretch."

"Okay then. So, while life teems away on its surface, the Earth does what it always does. It throws up volcanic ash, it builds and erodes mountains, and it moves tectonic plates around like bath toys. It shakes, it rattles or it rolls. But life on its surface goes on. It adapts. It changes just as much as it needs to, and it goes on. But when one part of it changes, so do all the others, because all of life is interconnected. It's all one. Every living thing on Earth is woven together in this incredibly complex tapestry that no human being will ever be able to fully comprehend, but you know as well as I do that if you pull on one loose thread in a tapestry, it *all* starts to unravel. It's like they say, a butterfly flaps its wings in Red Square, and Central Park gets rain. Because it's all woven together, you see? Nothing can happen anywhere on the planet without a ripple effect across the entire biome. That's Newton's third law, Sheriff. For every action, there is an equal and opposite *re*action."

As she drew in a deeply needed breath, she took in the look of incredulity etched across Cooper's face and dialed it down a notch.

"Tell me, Sheriff," she said. "What would happen if the Bornean smooth-tailed tree shrew were to suddenly go extinct?"

"Uhh..." Cooper started, but again, Emma raised her hand for silence.

"I'm serious, Sheriff. Let's say that tree shrew soup becomes all the rage, and the Bornean smooth-tailed tree shrew is eventually hunted to extinction to satisfy the demand. What do you think would happen then?"

"Uhh..." Cooper started again, struggling for an answer but coming up empty. "I have no idea."

"Neither do I!" Emma hooted excitedly. "Neither does anyone else! And that is precisely the point. We don't have the slightest clue what would happen if the Bornean smooth-tailed tree shrew died off, but something is *sure* to happen, don't you think? I mean, this world had billions of years of growth and change and evolution to put every single bit of its biome into proper balance, so its not like it'll just shrug its shoulders and say, 'Bornean smooth-tailed tree shrew? Meh...' One and a half *trillion* species of plants and animals have existed on this planet in the last four billion years, Sheriff. Some lived, most died, and life went on. A big motherfucking rock hit the Yucatan, wiping out most of the dinosaurs, and the planet went ticking right along. It absorbed all of those millions of bodies back into itself, it covered up the impact crater and cleaned the dust from the air, and *voilà*, mammals inherited the Earth."

"Sure, but..." Cooper tried. And failed.

Emma held up her hand once more and started anew.

"Okay, think of it this way. The human body is attacked by a virus. What does it do?"

"It fights back," Cooper replied, though he wasn't entirely sure that what he was saying was correct.

"Exactly!" Emma whooped, bringing a smile to Cooper's dour face. "It fights back. It sends out armies of antibodies to attack the enemy, it raises the body's temperature in hopes of burning off the virus, and it tries to make you sneeze and shit and snot the infection out of you. It does everything it possibly can to bring the body back into equilibrium. Back to when all of the bodily functions were working in perfect synchronicity. Back to when everything was A-Okay."

"I thought you taught history," Cooper tried again. And failed. Again.

"Sheriff, the current estimate puts the number of plant and animal species on this planet at somewhere between ten and fourteen million, of which only a little over a million have been catalogued. Out of that million-plus known species, we are only now beginning to understand how a tiny few of them fit together in an incredibly small ecosystem. How they fit into the global picture, nobody knows. Would the demise of the Bornean smooth-tailed tree shrew have an effect on an ecosystem on the other side of the planet? We don't know. We *can't* know. And so, while we lament the future *ex*-polar bear and the future *ex*-giraffe and the future *ex*-elephants with their beautiful, long tusks that some idiots think work better as ornaments, no one bothers to give a single thought to the Bornean smooth-tailed tree shrew. For all we know, the ripple effect from the loss of that tiny little tree shrew could mean more than the elimination of the African elephant or the bald eagle. There's just no way to know. In truth, we know more about the *moon* than we do about our own world."

"Okay," Cooper raised a hand in surrender, "But I still don't..."

"Sheriff, our bodies are made up of around thirty trillion cells," Emma barreled on. "The bacteria we carry along with us amounts to something like thirty-*nine* trillion cells. So, in a very real sense, you and I and everyone we know and love is more bacteria than human. And yet, we call ourselves human. We live, we think, we fear, we love, we plan for the future, and as long as everything remains status quo, hurray for us. Human cells and bacteria cells live on in peace, and we all prosper. But the planet Earth, or *Gaia*, isn't status quo. Not anymore. We humans are a newcomer to this world, but we've had a monumental effect in a very short time. Until a few centuries ago, we numbered in the millions. By 1800, we crossed the billion mark. Now, we're closing in on eight times that number. We're like a virus, reproducing ad infinitum. And just like any other living organism under attack, the Earth occasionally counter-attacks with its own immune system. Influenza. Polio. Rubella. Smallpox. And every time we clever humans find a way to defend against those attacks, she ups the ante. Malaria. Bubonic Plague. Dengue Fever. Ebola. She keeps increasingly deadlier weapons hidden away, deeper and deeper in the darkest jungles, and as the human infection spreads and cuts down those jungles in order to exploit those last few untouched places on Earth, the virulence is unleashed. So, I see two possibilities. One, maybe someone went into one of those deep, dark, hidden places and unleashed a weapon designed by Gaia to turn all of nature against us."

"And two?" Cooper asked, already knowing what was to come.

Emma looked him square in the eye, and her tone turned grim.

"Maybe she couldn't afford to wait."

Cooper said nothing, but the pained expression on his face spoke volumes.

"You don't think it's possible?" Emma asked him at last.

He made no reply. He didn't have to. His grimace did the talking for him.

"Not even remotely?"

Again, nothing. Just the grimace.

Emma let the book close and dropped it to the couch.

"None of it?"

"Frankly, no," Cooper said at last. "Oh, I agree that everything in nature is interconnected, sure. I've seen the effects of imbalance myself. Back in the thirties, sheep and cattle ranchers staked a bounty on wolves in these parts, and every last wolf in this corner of the state was killed off. As a result, the elk and deer population exploded, which was fine for them and made for some good hunting, but without wolf packs to keep the herds on the move, they would all stay in one spot until they stripped the land bare. They grazed every plant right down to its roots, including the willow trees that used to thrive in these parts. When the willows went away, so did the beavers. And with the beavers gone, all the wetlands dried up. That meant no migratory birds. No fish. No frogs. Fewer insects. All those food sources dried up and took every other animal with it. Eventually, even the land itself started to die. It took sixty years and a few brave souls willing to go out a limb and reintroduce wolves back into Yellowstone Park to show us what we'd done wrong. At long last, they did the same thing in this county and in every other county in this part of the state, and all of that diversity is rebounding. But as bad as things got, even with this tiny patch of the Earth dying a slow, agonizing death, at no time did this so-called Gaia of yours unleash a single plague. No Ebola, No Anthrax. Not so much as a locust."

While Emma hemmed and hawed and tried to come up with a valid counterargument, Cooper put the final nail in the coffin.

"I'm sorry, Miss Wong, but that book of yours is a load of one-hundred percent, grade-A bullshit."

CHAPTER

XIX

Bullshit!"

"Jeeter, I told you a week ago that I needed the night off, and you said yes. I'm *going*, Jeeter!" Janice pulled her jacket over her barely-there waitress outfit and grabbed her handbag. "I just have time to go home and change and get to the hall before the party starts. Do you know how many single men will be there? You wouldn't want me to miss out on meeting the man of my dreams, falling desperately in love, and getting married, would you? Jeepers, Jeeter, I'm almost twenty. I'm practically an old maid!"

Not for the first time that day, nor in fact, for the first time in the last ten minutes, Jeeter ran an approving eye over Janice Redman's curvaceous form, but with mousy little Anita Hodges in the back office going over the day's receipts, he did so with one eye glued to the swinging door.

"And who's going to handle the dinner crowd, Janice? Huh? Look around. We're *slammed* tonight."

The girl turned a full circle and took in the extent of the dinner crowd. Namely, Jarod Hall and his son Jim, both of whom were currently doing their best to saw through slabs of meatloaf tough enough to resole a shoe, and with a taste just north of a compost heap.

"I think you can handle it," she said with uncontained animus, and spun about on her tall spiked heels.

"You'd leave me in the lurch, Janice?" Jeeter called after her, but to no avail.

The bell over the door tinged, and she turned back around to fix him with a pair of narrow, hooded eyes.

"In the lurch, in a bind, in a huff, and if I had my way, in a bloody heap on the side of the road," she told him pointedly, then the bell tinged again and she was gone.

"Well, that's gratitude for you," Jeeter Hodges griped to no one in particular. "You give a girl a job, set her up good, and what does she do? She walks out on you, that's what."

He wiped his hands on the stained dishrag hanging over his shoulder, and with a tepid," You boys let me know if you need anything," to the Hall men, he pushed his way back into the kitchen and through it to his little postage stamp of an office.

"Well, she's gone," he grunted, dropping his oversized frame into a chair and spilling out over every side of it. "I think I'm going to have to fire that girl."

Anita Hodges looked up from behind his desk and told him in no uncertain terms, "You will fire no one, Jeeter. Not unless I tell you to."

"But she abandoned me in the middle of the dinner crowd!" Jeeter howled, only to subsequently cower under his wife's withering gaze.

"And without that girl, the only crowd this dump would

ever see would be the cockroaches." She held up a piece of paper for him to see. "Forty dollars for twenty pounds of beef? Where did you get such a good price? The rendering plant? Good Lord, Jeeter, one of these days you're going to kill somebody. Two dollars a pound for beef? I'm surprised you aren't already in jail."

"It was a good deal," Jeeter defended himself while satisfying a particularly irksome itch on one side of his big belly.

Anita returned the receipt to the pile with a sigh that was anything but silent, and sent a scowl across the desk.

"Ptomaine usually is."

She would have added more, but a familiar sound came through the door just then, and she skewered her husband to the spot with a look that bespoke all manner of violence.

"Jeeter, did you leave the water running again? You know that's our money going down the drain, right? I swear to God, Jeeter..."

"I didn't!" he declared, but again his pleas fell upon deaf ears.

Anita lifted her diminutive five-foot frame out of Jeeter's double-wide chair and went to the door with a huff. Then she huffed again and threw the door open. But where she had expected to find the tap running, washing away their life savings in a torrent of hot water, she saw quite something else indeed.

Jarod and Jim Hall were in a pile on the kitchen floor amid a widening pool of blood. And as much as Anita should have been relieved that it hadn't been the meatloaf that had done them in, she took no solace in the fact. A few seconds later, she screamed, but the screams stopped as soon as she joined the pile. Ten seconds after that, a weeping, pleading Jeeter Hodges joined his wife.

After that, the only thing that moved in the kitchen was a single cockroach. It snuck up through the drain, took a single sniff of Jeeter's detached head lying in the middle of the floor, and scurried back down the drain as fast as its little feet could carry it.

CHAPTER

XX

"May I please be excused?"

Tracy Coggins placed her knife and fork diagonally across her plate like a fine young lady, and gave her napkin a few quick folds before placing it daintily upon the table.

"What about dessert, Darling?" her mother reminded her of what they had both always considered to be the best part of any meal. "I made fresh rhubarb pie."

"Oh my," Tracy's father chimed in, patting his rounded paunch. "Rhubarb pie. I don't know where I'll put it, but I'm sure I'll find room somewhere."

"Well, you'd better, my love. My fragile ego simply won't allow for *both* of you turning up your noses."

"Could I have mine later, Mommy?" Tracy cocked her head sweetly. "It's just that my friends and I have been playing a game, and it is *ever* so much fun!"

"Oh, well," her mother tsk-tsked. "A game, you say?

And what game is it that takes you away from a big slice of fresh rhubarb pie?"

"It's called 'grown-ups'. Isn't that fun?"

"Depends on whether or not it's the weekend," her father grumbled through a smirk.

"Oh, Daddy, it's so much fun! Can I go play with my friends, just for a while?"

"And which friends are these," he asked dutifully.

"Jimmy, Tommy, Francine, Mae..." Tracy scrolled through the list of names while both parents checked them off against their own personal records. "Honestly, *everyone* is playing it!"

Man and wife traded looks, and the decision was made, albeit reluctantly.

"Alright then, darling," her mother told her. "But only for an hour. I want you home before dark."

"Oh, thank you, Mommy!" the girl cheered, jumping up from her chair, but an upraised hand held her in place.

"Synchronize watches?" her father said, looking to his own wristwatch.

Despite her enthusiasm to rejoin her friends, Tracy sat back down, pulled back her sleeve, and as the ritual called for, pretended to activate a secret button on the side of her plastic Tigger wristwatch.

"Ready?" her father regarded her over the tops of his glasses, "On my mark, the time will be precisely seven-fifteen. Aaaaand... three, two, one, *mark!*"

Tracy pressed the nonexistent button and chirped back, "Seven-fifteen, on the nose!" which made her father smile proudly.

"Alright then, darling," her mother told her. "You go play grown-ups with your friends. When you get back, we'll have a nice slice of rhubarb pie, and then we'll have movie night. Your choice."

Her father tried to sway the decision by fake-coughing, "Batman..." behind his napkin, but Tracy wrinkled her nose at him.

"Oh, Daddy, that movie is so silly. If it is my choice, then I shall decide." She sat ramrod straight in her chair, raised her chin, and announced, "And I declare, tonight's movie shall be..."

"Not Mary Poppins..." her father muttered under his breath.

"Mary Poppins!" Tracy said, almost at the same time.

"You're excused, darling," her mother said, hiding a grin behind her napkin. And with one last kiss on the cheek, she let the girl go.

"I don't remember ever having that kind of energy," Reginald Coggins sighed, shaking his head. "I swear, sometimes I feel as if I were born an old man."

"My love, you're barely fifty."

"And in another twenty years, you'll know what fifty feels like. Honestly, my sweet, how did I ever convince such a beautiful young woman to marry such a doddering old man?"

She tossed her head to the side, coquettishly.

"I believe you got me drunk, my love," she reminded him. "And then you got me pregnant."

"Ah, the old standbys. God bless alcohol and poor judgement. I just hope I get to see our daughter graduate before snapping a hip. Or worse."

"Oh, don't be maudlin, my love. You'll be all of sixty-one when our daughter graduates." Elizabeth threw him a smile. "Assuming she doesn't fail a grade, that is."

"With *your* DNA floating around in her?" Reginald scoffed. "Hardly. Still, by the time she walks down the aisle, I'll be a wizened old creature in my seventies. 'Who is that old man?' they'll all say. 'Is that pretty young girl walking her great-grandfather down the aisle? Oh, how positively adorable.' And right then and there, I shall clutch my chest and I shall drop down dead. Right there in the church aisle, on our daughter's wedding day."

"Well, it wouldn't hurt to watch your calories," Elizabeth offered, playfully.

"Then you'll have to stop being such an amazing cook," Reginald replied, leaning across the corner of the table to give his wife a kiss.

The kiss lingered and lingered, then Reginald whispered something in his wife's ear that was meant for her and her alone, and she giggled.

"Are you saying that you want to play your own version of grown-ups?"

"Well, we do have an hour," he said, bending his arm awkwardly to get his wristwatch in front of her. "See? We synchronized."

She kissed him again, passionately.

"And what a shame it would be to let all of that hard work go to waste."

They scampered upstairs, hand in hand, like a pair of young lovers. Reginald took the precaution of locking the bedroom door behind them, then his wife was back in his arms, as naked as the day she was born.

Twenty minutes later, the hushed moans and whispers were cut short when a sound came from the outer hallway.

Elizabeth sat up with a startled, "Tracy?"

As it is in every bedroom of every parent with a small

child about to barge in, the man of the house quickly scrambled under the covers and pulled them up to his chin. Then, he listened.

But there was nothing to hear. No knocking on the door by tiny knuckles. No plaintive calls for Mommy coming from the other side. There was nothing. Nothing at all.

"Tracy?" he called out. "It hasn't been an hour yet. Go play some more, honey."

Elizabeth shushed him and called out, "Tracy, darling?"

A full minute later, Reginald sat up beside her and whispered, "Are you sure it's her?"

Another minute passed in silence.

"Tracy, are you there?" Elizabeth called out, and when nothing came back, she shrugged. "I thought I heard her coming up the stairs, but now I'm not so sure."

The emergency gone as quickly as it had arisen, Reginald kissed his wife on her smooth, round shoulder and began tracing a line of kisses down her back, purring, "It must have been the house settling."

"This house has had forty years to settle," Elizabeth scoffed the idea away. "I should think it would be done by now."

"Hey, old things creak and moan," Reginald quipped, unconcerned by it all.

He reached the small of her back and lingered there, inhaling her delicious scent. But just as he was about to go farther south, she shook him off and threw back the feather duvet.

"Or maybe something's happened. Reginald, maybe she's hurt. Tracy? Tracy? Are you alright, my love?"

No answer. Nothing at all. But in the ensuing silence, they could both now hear the subtlest of sounds. Something so faint as to almost be nothing at all, but it was there. A soft rubbing sound. Vaguely metallic. Somehow familiar, but not quite.

Reginald sat bolt upright, gathering the abandoned duvet around his waist, and as they both fixed their gaze on the closed and locked door, they saw a most curious thing.

The doorknob. That ornate glass bauble that had always reminded them both of the world's largest diamond. It was moving. But only just.

"Tracy?" Elizabeth tried one last time, then they both simply sat there in utter confusion, watching that ornate glass bauble move by the barest of degrees.

At last, Elizabeth could take it no longer. As the girl's mother, she had never had a problem with her daughter seeing her naked. They often slept together, and bathed together, and every Wednesday after a swim at the local pool, they would always shower and change together. So, it was with no self-consciousness whatsoever that she climbed naked from the bed and padded across the room. But just as she reached for that ornate glass doorknob, she hesitated.

Yes, she was sure of it now. The doorknob was moving. But not in a normal way. A flick of the wrist was all it would take. A flick of the wrist, a quick half-turn of that chunk of diamond, and Bob's your uncle. Tracy could manage it by herself by the time she could walk. A second was all it took. Half that, maybe. A flick of the wrist, and the door opened. It was such a natural thing that it could be done a hundred times a day without a second thought. And yet, this wasn't what Elizabeth was seeing.

If this was her daughter on the other side, there would be one of two outcomes. Either the door would burst open, and in she would tear like a tiny blonde hurricane, or if the door was locked, there would be a flick of the wrist, a quick turn of the knob, then an exasperated huff, a knock on the door, and a syrupy-sweet, "Mommy, may I come in?"

This was different. This was no quick flick of the wrist, and there would be no plaintive knocking afterward. Where that glass bauble should have spun, it simply turned. Slowly. Almost too slowly to register, even for someone looking down upon it from a matter of inches.

This was no one simply trying to come in. This was someone trying to *sneak* in.

A thousand thoughts raced through Elizabeth's mind as she watched that glass bauble turn. Intruders. Burglars. Rapists. But none of those made sense. Not in Keeter's Bluff. At least, not on this side of town. And anyway, most certainly not at seven o'clock on a Saturday evening.

But even as she dismissed those notions, a new, more horrifying thought took their place. This *had* to be Tracy. It simply *had* to be. But instead of a blonde hurricane or syrupy-sweet, "Mommy, may I come in?' there was neither. So what was quelling the storm?

For a loving mother, there was no need for conjecture. She didn't think, she didn't hesitate, she didn't pause for a moment. She snapped the lock and threw the door open, and when she saw her tiny freckle-faced girl standing on the other side, she dropped to her knees and corraled the girl into her arms.

"Oh, my love," she cooed, holding her daughter as tightly as she ever had. "What's happened, Tracy? Are you alright?"

But again, little Tracy Coggins did something strange. Where Elizabeth expected her daughter to throw her arms around her and hug her back, she simply stood there with the hands tucked neatly behind her back.

"What do you have there, my lo..." Elizabeth started to say, but then a blur suddenly rushed at her from the side. She felt a hard thud against her temple, and with her mind filling with stars, she felt her body give way, and she slumped to the floor.

The last sound she heard on this Earth was a scream. A man's scream. Reginald's scream. It was long, loud, and ended in a wet, sloppy whimper.

After that, everything in Elizabeth's world went black.

Forever.

CHAPTER

XXI

I don't know what to tell you, Tom. Facts don't lie."
Cooper had taken the call from Doc Jenkins at Emma
Wong's apartment. Now, he sat himself down on her
couch that smelled of old tobacco, rubbed his aching temple,
and put the phone on speaker.

"You're sure, Bob? No question about it?"

"Tom, I am sure. The skeleton you found at the old
McIffrin place showed signs of predation on nearly every
bone. Gnaw marks. Scrapes. Scratches. That was to be expected, of course. But several bones showed definite cut
marks. The fourth, sixth and seventh ribs on the dextral-an-
terior side in particular. Tom, Skeletor didn't just die. He was
stabbed to death."

Cooper tried to come up with an appropriate curse
word, but with Emma Wong sitting on the coffee table and
gazing across at him with her big dark eyes, the best he could
manage was, "Balls."

"Sorry to be the bearer of bad news, Tom," Jenkins said back. "But it looks like you got yourself a murderer loose in the 'Bluff. Well, *murderers*, actually."

"Wait, what? What do you mean by that?"

"Well, Einstein, the plural of a noun typically means more than one, i.e. two or more. In this instance, it means precisely that. Two. Or perhaps more than two."

Despite Jenkins' sardonic sense of humor, Cooper already knew what hadn't been said. The only evidence of foul play were cut marks on bone. There could only be one reason for a coroner to suggest multiple assailants.

"Two different blades." Cooper said. It wasn't a question. It was a statement of fact.

"One small and serrated, one larger and straight-edged," Jenkins confirmed. "And that's not all. There were multiple contusions running down the occipital bone as well."

"So he was unconscious before he was stabbed."

Jenkins hedged his bets. "Maybe. Probably, actually. But either way, it was a messy job. A good hard blow to the back of the head will slosh a brain around in the skull, causing it to temporarily short circuit. You'd get the same result with a good uppercut to the chin, or a side impact in a car. It's not the blow that shuts the nervous system down, it's the shaking. I counted seven points of impact on Skeletor's occipital bone, all the way from the lambdoid suture down to the occipital condyle, increasing in intensity from north to south. None fatal, certainly. In fact, the first few were barely enough to dimple the bone. It was only as the assailant worked his way down the back of the skull that bone began to fracture. It was as if someone went into the thing figuring that knocking a man out would be as easy as it is in the movies, and when that man refused to fall, he or she adjusted the severity of the blows accordingly."

"But you said he was knocked out. How..."

"I said *probably*, Tom," Jenkins corrected him.

"Okay," Cooper conceded. "So, why *probably?*"

"Because the blows stopped, genius."

He let it go.

"Any idea on the weapon?"

"The impressions were circular, approximately one inch in diameter."

Cooper did the calculations on his own.

"A hammer," he said with a sickening twist deep down in his stomach.

Now he understood why Doc Jenkins had said he or she. It shouldn't have taken seven hits with a hammer to do the job. One swing from even the least knowledgeable able-bodied man would have caved in the back of Skeletor's head. So what, then? A woman? Hell, women might still be referred to as the weaker sex even in the twenty-first century, but as he flipped through the mental Rolodex of every woman he had ever known, he couldn't imagine a single one of them not being able to take down a man with a goddam hammer in their hands. So, who did that leave? A little old lady?

He had an image of Ruth Buzzi's Gladys Ormphby swapping her old-lady purse for a claw hammer, and dismissed it with a snort.

"Okay. Thanks, Bob. Send me the file, will you?"

"Ya think?" Doc Jenkins replied, and hung up.

Cooper dropped the phone back into his pocket.

"Murder in small town America," Emma remarked. "Sounds like an episode of Dateline."

"So, on top of everything else, I now have a murder to

solve," Cooper grunted back. "Well, isn't that just capital."

Emma's expression ran the gamut from bemused to horrified, and settled on concerned.

"Umm... you've done that before, right?"

"Of course I have." he assured her. "Plenty of times. Well, maybe not plenty, but a few times. Well, twice, anyway."

"Capital," Emma said, patting him on the shoulder. The gesture was meant to be consoling, but it backfired in spectacular fashion. Cooper winced and drew back in pain, and Emma yanked her hand back as if she'd just touched a rattlesnake. "Omigod, I am *so* sorry! I forgot about your bee stings. Are they still bothering you?"

"Not too much," Cooper lied, but apparently Emma saw right through it.

She hurried from the livingroom into the kitchen, calling over her shoulder, "Do you have the Calamine lotion with you?"

Cooper dug through his pockets, and when Emma returned with the age-old bag of frozen peas, he held up the little tube the pharmacist had given him. She laid the peas as gently as she could against one side of his neck and took the tube from his outstretched hand as the rest of him melted into the couch in something akin to pure ecstasy. She squeezed an inch of Hydrocortisone cream onto two slender fingers, pulled back the other side of Cooper's collar, and as gingerly as could be, dabbed a dozen angry red welts as Cooper sighed in relief. That done, she moved the frozen peas to the other side, squeezed out another inch of cream, and tended to the welts she had angered herself. At last, she straightened his collar as best she could and dabbed the last of the cream on the two bee stings perilously close to the man's eyes.

"I don't suppose you have another bag of peas?" Cooper asked, hopefully.

"Sorry. This is the best I could do," she replied, producing the too-tiny bottle of vodka.

He narrowed his eyes at her.

"I'm sorry, ma'am, but we aren't allowed to drink on duty. Maybe you've heard it on all the cop shows."

She allowed one corner of her mouth to curl into a grin, and laid the cold bottle against his neck.

The ecstasy might not have been quite as pure as with the peas, but Cooper uttered a heartfelt, "Thank you," through another relieved sigh as the cold sunk deep. At last, once the itchiness and pain began to subside, he told her, "Small town crime isn't like what you see on TV, Miss Wong. Mostly, it's kids stealing a car for a joy ride, or someone cooking up moonshine in the back shed. We do have a criminal element in the 'Bluff, but it's all small time. Prostitution, gambling, drugs... Certainly nothing to kill over."

"Okay, so it's Mayberry with a hint of Goodfellas. But you *do* have murders here."

"Exactly two since I've been sheriff. Twelve years ago, Myron Copely turned up dead, sprawled across the back seat of his car. The man was a blowhard and a bully and had no end of enemies, but the knife still sticking out of his chest was an exact match for the set in his home. I confronted his wife Inez, and she immediately broke down and gave me a tear-filled confession. Turns out he had bullied her once too often. She plea-bargained down to manslaughter, was sentenced to six years, and got out in two. I think she's up in Jolene now. Then, six years ago, Matt Leland's wife found her dear, departed husband in the driveway beside his car.

Before Doc Jenkins had even determined the cause of death, Phyllis Ragborne came forward to say that she and Leland had been having an affair, and she just so happened to confess it all to her husband in a fit of pique the night before."

"Okay, so Mayberry, Goodfellas and a touch of Melrose Place," Emma quipped. "Gotcha."

"On the bright side," Cooper said, picking up Emma's ball and running with it, "Any murder in Keeter's Bluff isn't likely to need the talents of Cagney and Lacey to solve."

The joke went over like a lead balloon, then it fell from the sky and hit him right where it hurt.

"Cagney and Lacey?" Emma howled, screwing up her face. "Fuck, dude. How old *are* you?"

Cooper winced in pain, but now it had nothing to do with the bee stings.

"I have to go back to the McIffrin place," he said, trying like hell not to give in to another attack of the willies. At least not in front of a female.

Ever the voice of reason, Emma asked him pointedly, "Are you sure that now is the right time to be doing that, Sheriff? I mean..."

I know what you mean," Cooper interjected, "but it's my job. I serve, and I protect. I can't let myself be distracted by..."

Now, it was Emma's turn to interrupt.

"No, Sheriff," she told him in no uncertain terms. Then she repeated the word for emphasis. "No! All of that other shit isn't a distraction. It's the lead story. Bees, cougars, dogs, bulls... Come on!"

"Gaia?" Cooper suggested, already knowing the answer.

"Maybe, maybe not. But one thing's for sure, Sheriff. There's more going on in your freaky little town than a simple case of murder."

"Speaking of things going on," Cooper checked his watch. "Don't you have a dinner to get to?"

Emma looked to the cheap plastic clock on the wall, yelped the single word, "Shit!" and ran off to the bedroom, slamming the door shut behind her.

Once she was gone, Cooper unscrewed the top of the vodka bottle, tipped a goodly amount down his throat, and quickly screwed the top back on. Then he returned the thing to its spot alongside his neck and sighed in something even more akin to pure ecstasy.

CHAPTER

XXII

S on of a *bitch!"*
Conor Brady wasn't a good man. Not by anyone's standards, including his own. Having made that determination early on, he decided that if he couldn't be a good person, he'd be the baddest bad person in all of Keeter's Bluff. Women, numbers, protection... everything was fair game. It was all penny ante of course, but in a backwoods hick town like Keeter's Bluff, those pennies added up to damn-near make him king.

Well, he had to admit as he roused himself from his afternoon nap and fingered aside a bit of curtain to see his kids frolicking in the street, at least he was king *outside* his own castle.

Damn those kids to Hell. Yes, what he felt for Daniel and Colleen might somehow be equated with love, but *damn* them if they weren't going to learn! How many times had he told them to be quiet when Daddy was having his nap? How many times had he given them each a smack on the back of the head, or worse, to drive the point home? And yet, here they were, tramping through the streets like common urchins, howling up a storm and trailing another dozen snivelling, yowling brats behind them. Hell, he spent every night working hard to put bread on the table, and all he asked for was a couple of hours to rest his eyes during the day. Was that too much ask?

He threw open the sash and called out, "Daniel! Colleen!" but neither one of them even bothered to look up. They were simply far too engaged in their silly childish games to hear him. He called out again, "Daniel! Colleen!" but again to no avail. He watched his children lead the dozen others all the way down the street like a marching band, then they rounded the corner, and one by one, every one of them disappeared from sight.

But Conor Brady's fury remained.

"Goddam bastards," he growled through the open window, fully aware that he was speaking of his own children. And why not? Children were supposed to listen to their father and heed his every word. If those unruly brats chose to do the opposite, well, that was just too damn bad, wasn't it? But he knew where the blame really lay. Celine was just too damn easy on those kids. Celine, that devilish, sultry minx. A dumb whore she'd always been, and a dumb whore she still was, though now she gave her body to one man and one man only. Celine was still the hottest woman in the 'Bluff, but that broad couldn't mother worth shit.

A fresh rush of blood flowed to his crotch at the mere thought of the woman, but he willed it away and stood there at the open window in his tighty-whitey briefs and wife-beater tank top, imagining all manner of horrors he'd deliver on those unruly brats the second he got his hands on them.

Damn it, he could still hear them! Somewhere down the street, past the house. A dozen screeching voices, laughing and shouting and doing their level best to drive him crazy and send him off to conquer the world on next to no sleep. And worse, once word got around that he couldn't even control his own bastards, some damn fool was sure to take it as a sign of weakness and try to move in on his territory. After all, a king always had enemies, right? How else could a man ever make it to the top without stepping on a lot of toes and heads and occasional throats along the way?

He had to put a stop to this, and he had to do it now. He bellowed Celine's name at the top of his lungs, but the only reply came from Brutus and Nero. The Dobermans were downstairs where they were supposed to be, but when they should be concentrating every ounce of their canine senses on protecting king and castle, both mutts suddenly started barking their damn fool heads off.

"Jesus *Christ!*" he roared. "Shut the fuck up, *both* of you! Boris! Nero! Shut your goddam mouths, y'hear?"

The barking only grew louder.

He grabbed his jeans from a pile on the floor and slipped them on, roaring one last time, "Jesus, shut the fuck *up!*" and this time, it did the trick. The barking stopped, and the house was silent once again. But that only made things worse. Now, he could hear the caterwauling of a dozen brats coming through the window in exquisite detail, and the return of the racket took his blood straight to the boiling point.

"Goddam unruly sonzabitches," he swore to himself, stepping into his best curb-stomping Daytons and reaching for the bedroom door. "You wanted to piss off Daddy Dearest? Well you've done it. Now get ready for me to rain all over your motherfucking parade."

Those were the last words he would ever utter. The door swung open, and Conor Brady died as he had always lived.

Cruelly.

CHAPTER

XXIII

T he house loomed large in Cooper's windshield. Every bit as large as it had always loomed over the boy he used to be, racing through the thickened air of the Dip as fast as his old Schwinn could carry him.

The McIffrin place. That ugly damned monstrosity that should have been burned to the ground decades ago. If he'd had the power to turn back the hands of time, he would have already gone back and put a match to the place the first time he'd seen it and done himself and the whole town a favor. Sadly, with no time machine at his disposal, there it still stood, as big and as ugly and as creepy as ever. Monstrous. Dark. Forboding. Destined to play a part in every nightmare he was likely to have for the rest of his life.

He parked the cruiser against the curb, popped the trunk, and took as long as he possibly could to unclip his seatbelt and haul himself from the car. He proceeded to the trunk, tucked in his shirt, adjusted his collar ever so gently, hitched up his belt, and even checked to see that his boots were securely tied. Then, after slipping on a pair of rubber gloves and unable to come up with any other ridiculous excuse to avoid the inevitable, he screwed up his courage, grabbed the evidence kit along with one last item he'd stopped for along the way, and padded slowly across a field of century-old weeds as high as wheat.

He pulled up the corner of the rotting step to retrieve Granger's key, but reeled back as a tiny green spider emerged. The thing skittered away as quickly as it had appeared, but Cooper was left once again questioning every decision he had ever made that played a part in putting him outside the door of this place that he should have put a match to a lifetime ago.

There was quite literally nothing he wanted to do less than take a second trip into that house of horrors, but he had no choice. He was the sheriff, after all. In his time in uniform, he had gone up against the worst the 'Bluff could offer. He'd been in bar fights that would have made Muhammed Ali run in terror. He'd had guns pulled on him. Knives. Needles. He even had the dubious honor of having had no fewer than three automatic weapons pointed his way over the years by some of the town's more illustrious losers, and he had taken every single one of them down without a single shot being fired. And yet, even as he slipped the key into the ancient lock, he would have given anything in the world to be facing down a crackhead with a loaded pistol rather than be going back into that godawful place.

The key turned, the lock groaned in protest, and with his testicles threatening to crawl into his abdomen, Cooper pushed his way back into the old McIffrin place.

He clicked on his flashlight and shone it to every corner

of the darkness as he hovered at the threshold. And just as before, there was movement everywhere. The actual beam of light showed little, but wherever he shone the thing, a frenzy of activity exploded just beyond its edges. He shone the thing up the far wall and down another, then he played it across the high, vaulted ceiling now hanging so horribly low. And everywhere the light went, a rolling, undulating wave of black crested before it in a tangle of legs and bodies and ugly little pinpoints of red.

He banged his evidence kit against the door frame and shouted into the house, "Okay, here's the deal! I'm coming in, so as long as you assholes stay hidden away in your dark little corners, we'll have no problems. But be warned, I come armed!" With that, he showed his secret weapon to the room. It was the biggest can of Raid he could find at Bo Fraser's hardware store. He popped off the cap and squeezed the trigger just long enough to send a brief gust of poison into the air, and as it settled to the floor, he hollered, "Okay, do we understand each other? You leave *me* alone, I leave *you* alone. Got it?"

With that bit of insanity to calm his nerves done, he stepped cautiously over the threshold, flashlight in one hand, spray can in the other, and evidence kit tucked squarely in his arm pit.

Instead of sweeping the light from one end of the room to the other and exciting the crowd, he kept it on the floor directly in front of him, and for every step he took forward, the darkest of shadows retreated just quickly enough to stay out of the light. He intentionally kept his eyes on the center of the circle of light and left all movement beyond as a blur, but not seeing the horrible creatures was only half the battle. A thousand pinpoints of red shone back at him from out of the darkness in every direction, and behind it all was a constant rustling and chittering that kept every nerve in his body vibrating like guitar strings.

He took one reluctant step after another through that advancing circle of light, and at last he was out of the horrible entranceway and back in the slightly less horrible room that used to be a kitchen. He began his search at the discolored floorboards and worked his way out in a series of concentric circles, widening the circle with every turn and with one eye nervously fixed on the line where light met darkness. But it was the same everywhere. Rat shit. Dust. Cobwebs. And tromping through it all, Carl Rankin's size twelve horse prints.

He followed Rankin's prints around and around, noting where the deputy had stopped to dust or take a picture, and from what he could tell, Rankin had done his job well. In fact, the man had gone above and beyond the call by extending the search to the rest of the house. Clearly, the kitchen was the crime scene. Whatever happened, it went down right here, right where he was standing. Back door forced. Wood splintered around the lock. Dust and cobwebs disturbed, but only there. A blow to the back of the head, and another and another, and the body fell. Then the stabbing. But not with one knife. *Two* knives. Two different knives, wielded by two different assailants.

No. Correction. *Three* different assailants. Two with knives, and one with a hammer. Skeletor hadn't just been murdered, he'd been mobbed.

"What the hell did you do to piss off that many men?" Cooper hushed aloud, but then he had to add a caveat, at least in his own head.

Or women...

The lightest touch of a single finger against a metal latch had the back door swinging wide open. Besides kicking himself for running the spider gauntlet instead of just popping in the back way, he confirmed what Rankin had already photographed and described. There was an impression on the outer surface of that century-old, weather-worn door. A clean spot amidst a century of grime. Vertical oblong, two feet or so in length. Well defined roundness at the top, tapering off to a general smear down below. Directly beneath the impression, fresh soil trailing over the door jamb, leading to the partial footprint featured in one of Rankin's photographs.

Now that he saw it for himself, he had to agree with Rankin's assessment. This had been no homeless bum looking for a dry place to spend the night. This had been a man on the run. A good kick would have gotten him in, or if he had wanted to be stealthy, there were windows all around the place that could have been easily jimmied. But Skeletor hadn't taken the time to do any of those things. The oblong smear on the door was from a shoulder having been thrown against it. One only did that in a blind panic.

And the print. That partial footprint in the photograph. That partial print spoke volumes, too. No treads. Soft soled. Square toed. A dress shoe, and an expensive one at that. Hardly the footwear of a homeless person. And the attack itself. Brutal. Bloody. Clumsy, but effective. No indigent bum warranted that kind of violence.

He dropped to a crouch at the threshold of the door.

There. Right there in the dirt. Another footprint, complete this time. The same soft soles. The same square toes. A full three feet from the door. Light on the heel, and a little kickback from the toe. Confirmation.

"You were running full-tilt when you threw your shoulder into the door," he said aloud into the darkness. "It was an act of desperation. You were being chased, you saw a door, and you threw yourself into it, hoping to find sanctuary. But you didn't. They were right behind you. You didn't even have time to get the door closed."

The rest of it didn't need conjecture. Hammer to the head. Knives to the ribs. Maybe even a slash across the throat to finish the job. But even as he envisioned this nameless man's last moments on Earth, two glaring questions remained.

"So who the hell *were* you, Skeletor? And who the *fuck* were you running from?"

He took a few careful steps out into the back yard, then he dropped back to a crouch and played his flashlight over what looked to be an imprint in the grass. It was ill-defined, but considering the sequence of events as he'd constructed them in his mind, Cooper saw it for what it was. It was another footprint. But not Skeletor's. This one was nothing like the other. This one was tiny. Barely half the size. And what were those? Tread marks?

He tried to make sense of that one lone print in light of everything Doc Jenkins had said, and he could come to only one conclusion.

"Hell, maybe it really was a little old lady," he muttered to no one in particular. But then another idea occurred to him, and he added, "Either that, or..."

He couldn't speak the rest. Not out loud. He shone his light back to where the body had ended up, and the change in perspective showed him what he hadn't seen before. An air duct, running along the baseboards on the near side of the kitchen. Wrought iron grillwork. Ancient. Ornate. Willow branch motif, or something of the kind. He shone his light through the grillwork and caught a glint of metal. Not wrought iron, though. This other metal was yellow.

His phone buzzed in his pocket, startling him enough to make him jump. He silenced it with a well-practised tap on his shirt pocket, and after one last sweep of the flashlight to make sure the inhabitants of the old McIffrin place were keeping their distance, he dropped to his knees before the ornate, wrought-iron grill. He stuck five fingers through the gaps between willow branches and pulled with all his might, but the grill didn't budge. He put his flashlight right up to the grill to see if he could make out any more detail of the metal thing deep down inside to determine whether or not it was worth his while to keep trying, and now he could see it much better. The yellow metal shone like the midday sun.

Gold. It had to be.

Determined now, he set aside the evidence kit and can of insecticide, positioned his flashlight on the floor facing the duct, and took the grill in both hands. At last the thing moved, but just barely. He reset his footing, took another hold, put his back truly into it, and the thing finally came completely away. And none too soon. He grabbed up his flashlight and threw its beam back into the darkness only to see a thousand furry legs and ugly red eyes disappear in a cresting wave spilling backwards until finally ebbing away to the very limit of the light.

He sent out a cloud of spray, and in those few seconds it took for the mist to settle, he located the yellow metal again in his flashlight beam and reached in all the way to his shoulder.

It was no easy task, and there were times when he very nearly gave up as something skittered through his fingers or came crawling up his forearm, but he stuck with it, and soon enough felt his finger and thumb close around a cold metal loop. He fished it out, held it right up to his face, and shone his flashlight directly at the thing.

It was a ring. A man's ring. Gold, or gold plated. And what was that on top? A signet?

No. It was an initial. A stylized 'J'.

He knew this ring. He'd seen it before. In fact, he'd booked it into evidence more than once. The ring belonged to Jake Peluso, drug dealer, racketeer, sometimes fence, and full-time pain in the ass. Jake the Snake had his hands in every nefarious deal going down in the 'Bluff's backwater swamps, so if someone had done him in, they had also done a service for the Sheriff's Department and for Keeter's Bluff as a whole. But considering the haphazard way they'd gone about it, he couldn't believe that this was a professional hit. So the question remained. If not pros, then who?

He reflected on that pint-sized footprint in the grass and the feeble blows to the back of the skull, but any sense they might have made was simply too horrifying to imagine. And so, he went with his go-to.

"Well, Jake," he spoke to the ring as if it were the man himself. "You picked the shittiest place in the world to die. Congratulations, dumbass."

A gentle tickling at the back of his neck had him jumping to his feet with a start, brushing frantically at what may or may not have been his imagination. Then a writhing black mass dropped to the floor inches away from his feet, and he jumped a foot in the air.

For the briefest of moments, he might have been able to raise a boot and stomp the thing to dust, but the moment passed as the thing sprang to life and came skittering towards him. And in the flurry of activity that followed, he made an even more horrifying discovery. As he backed away from the thing, flailing away at his neck and at his scalp and at every other body part within reach, the crazy dance had the beam of his flashlight bouncing around in every direction, and he just so happened to look up as the light flashed across the ceiling, freezing his breath in his throat.

There, not more than two feet above his head, the ceiling was alive.

A great roiling mass of fur and legs and horrible stalked eyes bubbled and churned across the ceiling from one end of the kitchen to the other. They crawled and skittered over one another in such tangled confusion that they appeared almost to be a single entity. But wherever they came together in a heavy enough bunch, the clot would inevitably break free, drop to the floor, and shatter into a million moving pieces. And even as he danced away from all of those skittering pieces coming straight at him, another clot would break free. And then another. And another.

As anxiety turned to fear, Cooper's flashlight beam was suddenly everywhere at once. The ceiling. The floor. The walls. And everywhere that beam of light went, it was the same. They were everywhere. Literally, everywhere. Then the light fell upon the big can of Raid, twenty feet away and disappearing under an advancing wave of chittering, scrambling rats, and fear turned instantly to panic. Whether through design or random chance, rats and spiders were working together to back him further and further into the darkest reaches of that awful room. But even as the cold tentacles of fear closed around his heart, squeezing it to ice, his last clear thought saved him.

A faint rectangle of reflected moonlight, receding in the

distance. The back door!

It was a one man race like no other. In full flight and full panic, still flailing his arms about like a madman and surrounded by a kaleidoscope of dancing flashlight beams, Cooper ran for the open door. Every footfall was met with a crunching of tiny bones and a skidding as if running on ice, but then the door grew as large as life, and he all but launched himself through it.

He landed in a pile amid the tall grass, but he didn't stay down for long. As the first hairy sausage of a leg probed the unknown world beyond the threshold, he jumped to his feet and ran. He ran, and he ran, and he didn't stop until he had gone completely around the house and was back at his cruiser. And even then, he stopped only long enough to fumble the fob out of his pocket and click the doors open. Then he was in his car with the door slammed shut behind him, wheezing like an asthmatic.

He folded his arms across the steering wheel, lowered his head onto them, and with his breath coming in ragged pants and his rash of bee stings freshly aflame, he spared one last thought for the late Jake 'The Snake' Peluso.

Fuck you, asshole. Fuck you all the way to Hell.

CHAPTER

XXIV

S he did the best she could, considering. Black tights, new tunic top, and a black double-breasted dress jacket overtop. Casual but professional. But maybe too casual. Shit! At the last moment, she stripped off the tights and replaced them with a clean pair of jeans, and now she was ready. Or almost, at any rate. She pasted a fresh, bright blue My Little Ponies Band-Aid over the robin's egg, slipped on her tattered old sneakers, and now she really was ready.

"You look great," Cooper told her as she relieved him of vodka and peas and shoved him through the door.

"I look like a schlemiel," she scoffed. "But as bad as my night's bound to be, I'm afraid yours is going to be even worse." She locked the door behind them and laid a hand on Cooper's arm, nowhere near his collar. "Do yourself a favor, Sheriff. Stop along the way and grab yourself the biggest can of insecticide you can find. If nothing else, it might give you some peace of mind."

"A flame-thrower would be better," Cooper harumphed.

They took the stairs together, wished each other good luck at the bottom, and with that, the two parted ways.

Cooper went out the front door, and Emma went out the back where her car was parked. Naturally, her eyes were drawn upward, but the trees were bare. There was no sign of birds anywhere. She paused just long enough to throw a silent prayer toward the tomb of the unknown starling, then she slid behind the wheel of her Mazda and started it up.

Music. She needed music. She stabbed the radio on, but with every button locked to a radio station a thousand miles away, all that came through was static. She hit the scan button to let the fates decide what she would be listening to, and once again the universe had her back. She couldn't imagine exactly who in all of Keeter's Bluff would be listening to this kind of music, but she drank up every bit of the heavy beat as Wild Cherry told the DJ in no uncertain terms to 'play that funky music, white boy'.

No sooner had she pulled onto the main road when the tunes ended, and a male voice announced, "And now, a WJOQ news update..."

She turned up the volume and listened intently.

"Authorities are still uncertain whether or not the strange incidents seen around the world today are connected, but reports are still coming in. In Bandipur, it's tigers. In Bangladesh, leopards. In Gibraltar, hundreds of macaques have been shot by police or clubbed to death by local citizens, but the carnage continues. In China and South Korea, packs of dogs are responsible for at least a thousand dead and injured, and those numbers are expected to climb. Many

African countries have gone dark after reports of strange behavior among hippo, crocodile and elephant populations. Zimbabwe. Senegal. Burkina Faso. Closer to home, we have reports of bear attacks in Alaska, wolf attacks in Wyoming, and herds of cattle running amok in Texas. The official word is still that there is no connection whatsoever between these far-flung events, but some are now suggesting the possibility that an airborne toxin might be at work. How else, they say, could so many animals be affected over such great distances? In Washington State, Governor Forsyth has just declared a national emergency. In Florida, many parts of the state are now under martial law. Citizens there are being told to stay indoors and avoid all unnecessary travel." Then came the usual sign-off. "This has been a WJOQ news update. Next news, when it happens. Next scheduled news break at the top of the hour."

As a commercial for Jolene's hottest nightspot, 'The Barn' played, Emma checked her watch.

Shit!

Nearly seven-thirty. She was already half an hour late.

She blew through a yellow light, checked the map she had quickly scrawled on a scrap piece of paper, and picked up speed. Four more miles. Five, tops. But the damage had been done. In LA, thirty-five minutes late to a dinner party was practically jumping the gun, but here in Keeter's Bluff, it was undoubtedly tantamount to a spit in the eye. Hiram Merriwhether Danvers was probably standing there right now, trading glances at his wristwatch with scowls through his front window. And there she would be, tearing up his driveway, thirty-five minutes late and climbing out of her rattle-trap of a Mazda looking like a hobo.

Awesome... she said to herself, swerving around a pair of

children dashing recklessly across the road. *It just can't get any better than this...*

She put her foot to the floor to get around a slow-moving pickup, but then she found herself in a quiet residential area with swings and bicycles and trikes on nearly every front lawn, and she forced herself to slow down. At least a little.

Putt-putting along at a mere forty miles an hour, she be-came aware of children playing on both sides of the street, and with an image forming in her mind's eye of how a big-city newcomer might fare after running down one or two of the 'Bluff's children, she slowed even more. And now that she was going nearly slowly enough to watch the grass grow, her attention went from the road in front and the map clutched in her hand to the action playing out on both sides of the street.

Children playing. Random children, running, squealing, chasing. No real game plan as far as she could see, but that was how kids played, wasn't it? The need to play was as nat-ural to kids as breathing. No one cared what the game was, just as long as it was a game. Rules, no rules, it didn't matter. It was all about the play. Flash-forward a dozen years, and a switch got thrown. After that, it was a world of work, car payments, and electric bills. The playing that used to come as naturally as breathing was now a foreign thing. Unfath-omable. Alien. Even removed from that other reality by a mere handful of years, all Emma saw now was just a bunch of kids running around in their own little world. And all she could think was what a wonderfully chaotic world it must be.

For one moment, just one quick moment as the radio commercials ended and the unmistakable opening riff of George Thorogood's Bad to the Bone blasted through her speakers, she considered stopping and joining in on the fun. But it was a ridiculous notion. Even if these kids romping and frolicking from yard to yard accepted her as a playmate, real life would never be so accepting. As much as she regretted it, that other, simpler world was gone from her forevermore. So, she drove on. But now she watched the children on front lawns and sidewalks and green belts all along both sides of the road, and the memories of her own youth brought a smile to her face.

Do you guys still play tag? she wondered. *Hopscotch? Hide and seek?*

Releasing a sigh, she realized that she was too far removed from that perfect, idyllic world to even know what children played anymore. A lifetime-times-four for some of the kids she was seeing. She was a dinosaur now. Too old to understand even a bit of it. While the children of the world kept on playing and running and making nonsensical fun out of nothing, her world had gone from Simon Says and monkey bars to SATs and resumes. Somehow, she had gone from all play to all work without even realizing the transition.

She turned up the radio and tried losing herself in the song.

On the day I was born, the nurses all gathered 'round. And they gazed in wide wonder at the joy they had found...

A tiny girl suddenly stopped cavorting across someone's lawn and stared at her as she rolled by. She had bright red hair, a nose full of freckles, and a red ribbon in her hair. She was adorable, in the way that all children were adorable. But that look. Those eyes. That tight little scowl. Holy Hell.

I'm here to tell ya honey, that I'm bad to the bone...

She eased past at little more than walking speed, and the

girl's eyes followed her every inch of the way. And with every turn of the tires, more of the children stopped and stared. Then more, and more still. Soon enough, every child along both sides of the street was frozen in their tracks like mannequins, watching her go by with the same tight little scowl as the adorable little red-haired girl with the nose full of freckles. And just like the birds in the parking lot, not a single one of them made a sound. Not one. They lined up along both sides of the road and watched her drive slowly by, and not a single one of them made a single, solitary sound.

As her perspective changed, a dog became visible in their midst. A big, black German shepherd. The sight of such a huge animal among so many tiny children sent her nerves into overdrive, but she quickly realized that they were in no danger. Unlike the rest of the dogs in the rest of the world, it seemed that this particular German shepherd was immune to whatever toxin might or might not be wafting through the air. The dog was sitting calmly on its haunches amidst a dozen or more children, and it was only as she passed close by that it uttered a low, menacing growl.

But the presence of the dog wasn't the only thing setting her teeth on edge on this street full of children in this strange little town in the middle of nowhere. Suddenly, she realized that there were no adults anywhere. Where a summer's day in every town and every city across the continent would have people running smoke-belching lawnmowers across the yard, or poking through their garden, or simply sitting on the porch to drink in the cool evening air, here there were none. None at all. Not anywhere. The only living things on this street were Emma, a dozen or more kids, and a big black dog sitting on its haunches, watching her go by.

She felt her foot grow heavy on the gas pedal, and soon enough the strange mannequins receded to pinpoints in her mirror. Then she took a hard left turn onto Dansey and they disappeared completely. Even better, there were adults on this street. Not many, just an elderly couple on their front porch and a young man washing his car, but the sheer normalcy of the sight shook most of her unease away.

She squealed to a stop in front of a wide, white, split-level house and climbed out. She tugged down the hem of her new tunic top and started up the driveway, but a familiar tingling up her spine brought her to a stop.

A movement of the curtains drew her eyes up to the front window. Was this the inestimable Mr. Hiram Merriwhether Danvers peeking out in disgust? Possibly, but Emma didn't think so. A man like Danvers would have had the edge of the drape resting aside his finger by the barest of degrees, and would have let it drop into its natural folds as softly as a feather so no one would know he'd been watching. This was different. It was too clumsy. Too obvious.

She stood in the precise center of the driveway, gazing up at the front window of that wide, white house, and felt every bit of the nervousness return.

A dog barked from somewhere down the street, making her flinch. Then a death rattle drifted down from above, and she looked up to see a dozen crows lining the roof. Then some other sound attracted her attention back to the window, and she put aside all of the distractions to focus every bit of her attention precisely there.

The window was six feet off the ground and the sun was setting over the roof, so she couldn't see much. But wait. Was that pale blur almost lost among the shadows a face? Was it Danvers maybe, trying to hide himself from this big-city woman who hadn't thought enough of him or her new position to even bother showing up for dinner on time?

On second thought, no. It couldn't have been Danvers. In fact, it couldn't have been anything even approaching human. It was a mask, was all. A vaguely flesh-colored mask of something only nominally resembling a man. But no sooner had she made that determination than the thing sank from sight, and a sudden spray of crimson spattered across the glass, all the way from one side of the picture window to the other.

Blood? No, it couldn't be. But it *had* to be.

There was that one quick spray of droplets, then nothing more. Nothing to indicate what it might have been, or what might come next. And so, Emma waited. She stood at the precise center of the driveway and waited for someone to show themselves, hopefully to declare the whole thing as one colossal joke. When two minutes passed with no one jumping out and having a laugh at her expense, she did the unthinkable. She padded slowly up to the front door and put an eye to the rectangle of opaque glass running down its side. Then, she rang the doorbell.

In the quiet of this backwater street, the doorbell gonged like a death knell in a mausoleum. And yet, it went entirely unanswered. Certain now that something dreadful had gone on inside that house, she simply had to do what she could to help. But what dreadful thing had happened? A fall, perhaps? It was the most likely scenario. The Danvers were no spring chickens, and old bones broke easily. Had one of them taken a tumble, then? An aged head striking an end table or lamp on the way down would account for the spray of blood, and it would also account for no one answering the door. After all, calling for an ambulance or holding a cold compress to the lacerated skull of a loved one took considerable precedence over a tardy dinner guest. Hell, maybe the old coots had even managed to smack their delicate little coconut heads together on the way down, Three Stooges-like, incapacitating them both.

More convinced than ever that something was wrong in the house, Emma tried the door. It was locked of course, and if she'd all the time in the world to ponder the question, even she wouldn't have been able to say whether she felt disappointed or thankful.

She rapped on the rectangle of frosted glass and shouted into it, "Mr. Danvers? *Mrs.* Danvers? It's Emma Wong! Are you okay?" When thirty seconds passed by without a peep from the other side, she rapped on the window again and shouted even louder. "Mr. Danvers, if this is a joke, please tell me now because I'm afraid you've been hurt, and I'm about to call 9-1-1!" She let another thirty second crawl by in an almost palpable silence, then she banged on the window and called into it, "Okay, I'm calling 9-1-1! Don't worry, Mr. Danvers. Help is on the way!"

She punched in the numbers, but where she'd expected a stern-voiced operator to immediately pick up, the phone rang and rang and rang.

"Goddam Mayberry bullshit," she hushed to herself.

She dialed Sheriff Cooper's phone, but the call went immediately to voicemail. She left her message in a blur of words.

"Sheriff, this is Emma Wong. I'm at Hiram Danvers' home. Listen, something's happened. I think one of them took a fall and hit his head. Or *her* head. I don't know. I'm outside. I don't know exactly what happened, but no one's answering the door, so I'm getting fairly worried. I tried calling

9-1-1, but there's no answer. Sheriff, *please* get someone over here. I don't know what to do. I need your help."

She punched off the call just as a shadow moved behind the vertical rectangle of opaque glass. No definable shape, just a shadow. Was it Danvers? His wife? Someone else?

Whoever it was, she pounded on the door and called into the house, "Mr. Danvers? It's Emma! Emma Wong!"

No reply. And more ominously, the shadowy shape suddenly froze at the sound of her voice. But had it? She could almost imagine it as a trick of the light, but she could almost swear that it was growing ever larger by the narrowest of degrees. It was as if someone within was descending the stairs like a ninja, one agonizingly slow step at a time.

"Mr. Danvers? Umm, *Mrs.* Danvers? Listen, help is on the way, but it might take them a while. My call went to *godda...* uh, my call went to voicemail. But I do know a thing or two about first aid, so if one of you can make it to the door, I might be able to help!"

Again, no reply. Just that amorphous, undefined shadow that might have been a person, or might just as easily have been a trick of the light.

She pressed her nose right up to the glass as though she'd be able to lift the veil away by sheer force of will, but it was no use. The shadow remained a shadow that might or not have been moving. Determined to have an answer one way or the other, she cupped her hands on either side of her eyes and aimed all of her senses on that ill-defined shadow.

At first, she put it off as pure imagination. The change was so subtle that it might not have been a change at all. Then she became almost certain that she had seen the shadow grow, but after allowing for her agitated state, she again dismissed it. At last, she picked some random spot on the glass, and when the shadow behind that spot shifted by the barest of degrees in relation to that spot, there was no more room for doubt. The shadow *was* moving. And it was growing larger, which could only mean one thing. She'd been right all along. Something awful had happened inside, and either Mr. or Mrs. Danvers was crawling slowly down the stairs to get help.

But just as she came to that realization, she knew how wrong she was.

This wasn't Danvers or the missus crawling their wounded selves down the stairs. This wasn't crawling at all. This was *creeping*. Someone or some*thing* was creeping down those front stairs as stealthily as a jungle cat, and that someone or something was coming directly toward *her*.

Feeling suddenly exposed and completely vulnerable, she jumped back from the glass and retreated several steps. Then she pulled out her phone, held her thumb over the re-dial button in case she needed to leave a last, frantic message for Sheriff Cooper, and just as before, she waited.

The shadow finally grew large enough to nearly fill the rectangular window, but just as Emma became certain that whatever was behind it was about to burst through the door and tear her limb from limb, the shadow crested, ebbed to the left, and then it disappeared from view.

Cautiously, she crept back up to the glass and put her eye to it, just in time to see the shadow recede away to nothing.

A cold chill shivered up and down her spine. This was bad. This might even be as bad as bad could get.

Another shadow appeared at the top of the stairs, but this one didn't waste time creeping down like the other. This one virtually threw itself down the stairs, rounding the corner after the other, and quickly dwindling away to nothing. And then came a third. But as this one came down, Emma made a mistake. With a fresh rush of adrenalin charging up her nervous system, she became too eager, and there came a moment when a bright blue My Little Ponies Band-Aid thudded against the window nearly hard enough to crack the glass.

Emma reeled back in pain, but even as she pressed a palm against her freshly bleeding robin's egg and cursed a blue streak, she kept both eyes squarely on the front door and on that ridiculous little rectangle of glass.

The shadow grew until she could almost imagine that she could make out a shape, but after hovering there for the scantest of seconds, the thing flitted off after the others, and nothing else moved in the Danvers house. At least, not as far as she could see.

In the still night air, she heard what might have been a window sliding open at the back of the house, but there was no way to be sure. There might even have been a sound like distant giggling, but she couldn't trust her senses even for that.

So, she stood where she was. She kept a hand pressed to her reopened wound, she kept a thumb cocked and ready over the redial button on her phone, and she waited. But for what, she couldn't even begin to guess.

Then her phone rang, and every resident along that block of Dansey Street was treated to the sound of a sudden shrill shriek.

CHAPTER

XXV

H ello? Miss Wong? Hello?"
Cooper heard only an unintelligible scramble of sounds, then the call dropped. He tried again, but now no one answered at all.

He hadn't listened to her message. Once he was out of that damnable McIffrin place, he'd seen Emma's number on the screen, and rather than waste time with voicemail, he had called her direct. But now, with either the phone system turning to crap, or Emma unwilling or unable to answer, he thumbed open his voicemail and had a listen.

It was her last words that got to him.

"Sheriff, *please* get someone over here. I don't know what to do. I need your help."

And there it ended. She sounded scared. Desperate, even. And those last words. A plea left hanging in the air.

He cranked the cruiser to life, and after tucking a particularly gaudy ring into his shirt pocket and carefully buttoning it closed, he brought up Hiram Merriwhether Danvers' address from memory and hit the gas.

The Danvers place was only ten minutes away, but even with lights flashing and siren wailing and him weaving through the maze of streets like a madman, it seemed to take forever. Finally though, his headlights caught Emma, pinning her to the front door of Danvers' house, and he skidded the cruiser to a stop.

She was hunched over. Nearly on her knees. She looked as white as a ghost.

Cooper launched himself from the car and gathered the woman in his arms.

"Miss Wong? I'm here. I got your message. Tell me what happened."

Fighting for words and gasping for breath, she tried to do just that.

"Up there," she pointed, "Window. Blood. I thought one of them had fallen, but then there were shadows."

"Huh?" Cooper's brow furrowed. "Shadows? *What* shadows?"

"Dunno. Not human, though. Too small for that. Dogs, maybe. Dunno."

Slowly but surely, Cooper made sense of it. Big picture window, spattered with red droplets. Milky little window beside the door with a tell-tale spot of blood on this side of the glass. Emma, with her My Little Ponies Band-aid soaked freshly through.

"It would take hours to get a search warrant, and that's assuming I can get through to Judge Whittacker, and *if* he'll take my call," Cooper informed her with a snort. He narrowed his gaze directly upon Emma and asked her directly, "Miss Wong, is it your considered opinion that someone inside this house is in danger? Do you believe that it is a matter of life and death that I break down this door?"

Emma was a quick study. She looked up at Cooper and gave him the single word, "Yes."

Cooper did the rest. Legal and ethical requirements met, he turned his back to the door and gave it a swift donkey-kick, bursting it open at the seams.

Emma was all for rushing in, but Cooper stopped her. And thankfully so. He found Hiram and Amanda Danvers crumpled together on the floor at the top of the stairs, just this side of the picture window. Hiram had suffered multiple stab wounds to the belly and chest. Amanda had fared worse. Defensive wounds to her hands and arms. Her face, a bloody mess. Then the coupe de grâce, times two. A whack to the back of the head, and a knife dragged across her throat.

"They're getting better," he hushed to himself, then he went back to the top of the stairs and called down to Emma, "It wasn't dogs, Miss Wong. Not even close."

Trying to hold her back was like fighting the tide. Emma Wong stormed up the stairs, pushed him aside, and had a look for herself. Cooper expected the customary civilian response of turning away, possibly gagging, and most certainly followed by a dash back down the stairs, but again, this young woman showed her mettle. She analyzed ever bit of the crime scene at a glance, and whether or not she'd gathered all of the inferences, of one thing she was most adamant.

"Not dogs," she replied in a hush. "Not even close. I saw them. Or at least I *think* I saw them. Just shadows. Nothing more. They kept low, and went out the back."

Cooper knew better than to chase after ghosts.

"Alright. I'll get Carl to work the crime scene and have Henry check out back. He's a first-class tracker. If they left so much as a bent blade of grass, those bastards are done."

He pulled out his phone and hit Carl Rankin's number, but the phone went dead in his hand. He tried Henry next, but with the same result. In desperation, he even tried Grace *goddam* Tolliver's number back at the station, but his expensive smartphone had suddenly become a brick. As he led Emma back down the stairs and closed the door behind them both, he asked her casually, "Is your phone working," and with one shake of her head, he knew that things had suddenly gone from bad to worse.

He hurried back to his cruiser and yanked the microphone out by its cord.

"KB-One to base."

Nothing.

"KB-One to base, over."

Still, nothing.

"KB-One to anyone with ears on. Copy?"

In the maelstrom of a world apparently coming apart at the seams, all that came back was an awesome and deafening silence.

Cooper dropped the mike back through the window as Emma came up behind him.

"Not working?"

"Not working," he growled. "I don't suppose you happen to have a carrier pigeon on you?"

"Sorry," she said, splaying out the flaps of her jacket. "This is Calvin Klein, not Mandrake the Magician."

"Landlines might still be working, but the station's only a few minutes away. Hopefully my men are there, choking down some seriously bad coffee." He looked back to the front window spattered with blood and shook his head. "Three murders in two days. That's quite a new record for the 'Bluff."

"Congratulations on making the big leagues," Emma grimaced. "Same people who killed Skeletor, you think?"

"Similar MO, but I can't see a connection. Hiram and Amanda Danvers were good people. Pillars of the community and all that. Hard to imagine what they would have had in common with a dirtbag like Jake 'the Snake' Peluso."

"Besides being dead," Emma reminded him.

"Yes," Cooper breathed. "Besides being dead."

"So, you identified your victim?"

"I got lucky and found a ring. It'll be a thousand times more difficult finding out who did him in, though. Jake the Snake had a lot of enemies."

"Hey, speaking of enemies, maybe someone is taking advantage of this whole 'animals attacking people' confusion to settle some old scores. You know, like maybe Danvers expelled a guy from school, so he fell into a life of crime, and ultimately had a run-in with this Jake the Snake fella. It's possible, right?"

Cooper considered the notion, however briefly.

"Do you watch a lot of movies, Miss Wong?" he asked her, almost sweetly.

"Do you really want to piss me off, Sheriff Cooper?" she countered, every bit as sweetly.

He let it go.

"This attack wasn't personal. No anger. No impulse. This was a hit, just like Jake the Snake. And just like Jake the Snake, this hit was sloppy. Not *quite* as sloppy, but still sloppy. Unprofessional. Clumsy, even." He looked up and down the street and saw a few townspeople taking advantage of the cool of the evening. Half a block away, elderly Jim and Mary Johanssen were sitting on their front porch, drinking in the last of the sun. Further down, the Jeffries boy had his brand new Mustang all lathered up against the curb. On the other side, a handful of kids were happily laughing and playing on the Stewarts' front lawn. He swung back to Emma and asked her, point blank, "Tell me, Miss Wong. Who the hell carries out a hit at seven-thirty on a Saturday night?"

"Someone who had to get to bed early?" Emma quipped, humorlessly.

Hell, maybe it really was a little old lady... Cooper thought again, but he kept the words locked tightly away in his head.

A teenaged boy went flying past on his bike, pedaling like crazy. It was one of the Radcliffe boys. Trent, he thought. Or maybe Trevor. The kid was driving age, but cars cost money, so he was still on his bike. The family mutt was with him, charging along in his wake like a missile. The boy spared one quick glance at the town's sheriff and this strange woman standing in the Danvers' driveway, then he flew on as if the devil himself was at his heels. Cooper watched until both boy and dog disappeared around the next corner, then his eyes returned to those others taking in the cool evening air, and he happened to notice something that even he couldn't decide whether or not to consider strange.

It started with old Mary Johanssen. Like Cooper, she had watched the boy and his dog fly past and disappear around the corner. But unlike Cooper, the sight seemed to cause her unease. She sat up in her chair and gripped her husband's hand, and without a word passing between them, the two stood, snuck back into the house, and shut the door quietly behind them.

The Jeffries kid was next. With half of his brand new Mustang still dripping with suds, he turned a nervous eye up one side of the street and down the other, then he slowly lowered the hose to the ground and backed himself all the way up the driveway. He didn't stop until he was inside the house with the door closed and locked behind him.

Cooper looked to the other end of the street where the gaggle of kids had been frolicking on the Stewarts' front lawn, but they were gone, too. He thought he might have heard one or more of them laughing in the distance, but he couldn't be sure. Then the sounds drifted away, and he and Emma were left all alone on that deserted street as the sun dipped slowly towards the horizon.

Emma pulled her jacket tightly around herself and folded her arms across her chest.

"Okay, so what do we do now?"

There was really no choice. Leaving an open crime scene was a clear dereliction of duty, but he could see no other way.

"I have to get back to the station. Are you okay to get yourself home?"

She unfolded her arms just long enough to gather her jacket even more tightly around her body, then she recrossed them with a shrug.

"Umm, I guess..." she began, but then one corner of the bottom lip went nervously into her mouth and she admitted, "Honestly, Sheriff, I'm a little freaked out right now. Couldn't I just come with you?"

On any other day, the answer would have been a courteous but stern "No." But since this was a day like no other Cooper had ever seen in his life, he simply flipped his head towards the cruiser.

Once they were both buckled in, Cooper cranked the car to life and hushed into his chest, "Three murders in two days. The voters are gonna hand me my ass next fall."

"Well, you can worry about that next fall," Emma turned a determined eye his way. "For now, let's just try to keep your weird little town from tearing itself apart."

CHAPTER

XXVI

K B-Three, come in."

"KB-Three. Henry, you copy?"

"KB-*Two*, copy"

"KB-Two. Buck, come in *goddamit!*"

Grace slid the microphone back and tried both of the deputies' cell phones for what must have been the hundredth time, but now the calls didn't even go through. She went back to the radio and pressed down on the button hard enough to turn her finger white..

"KB-Three. Henry Greenleaf. Answer me Henry, you goddam son of a *bitch!* KB-Three! KB-Two! For the love of *Christ*, one of you boys please respond!"

She kept trying and trying, but all that came through was the hiss of dead air. At last, she tried calling Cooper's phone for the twentieth time, only to end up throwing the receiver halfway across the room in frustration.

She stabbed out a cigarette in an ashtray already

over-

flowing, and with a thousand horrible thoughts taking turns conjuring up nightmares in her brain, she tried again.

"KB-Two, come in."

"KB-Three, do you copy?"

Dammit! Forty years she'd been on this job. Forty long years. Long enough to see the old guard retire and watch a new batch of wet-behind-the-ears recruits take their place. Some of those recruits had even been acceptable by her standards. Damn few, to tell the truth, but they were there. A few good men, just a bit better than the others.

"KB-Two, come in!"

"KB-Three, answer me for *fuck* sakes!"

Forty years. Damn near a lifetime. Long enough to watch little Tommy Cooper grow from a snot-nosed schoolyard brawler into the honorable man he was today. Long enough to know that the man he was today was one of the finest men she would ever know. Long enough, too, to remember at least three of his deputies as baggy-pantsed little brats stirring up trouble wherever they went. Dave Rogers, the prissy little mama's boy. Sonny Garcia, the hard-ass punk. Dumb little Carl Rankin, with his shoelaces always undone and dragging through the mud. Henry Greenleaf was a relative newcomer to the 'Bluff, but she felt the same way about him as she did the rest of her boys. She would never tell any of them to their faces, but she loved them all. She loved each and every one of them, truly and deeply. She loved those incredible men as if they were her own sons.

Something had happened to Henry and Buck. Something bad. She felt it right down to her bones. But this was no psychic flash or gut feeling. She knew Henry, and she knew Buck, and she knew for a fact that neither man would leave her hanging like this. Nearly two hours had gone by since the call to Leeland Farms, and not a word from either of them. Two goddam hours! It wasn't just unlike them, it was a sheer impossibility. They were both good cops, and good cops followed the rules. Call onsite, deal with the situation, and report back. And yet, nothing. Not a peep. Not a goddam peep in nearly two *goddam* hours.

The desk phone suddenly rang, startling her nearly out of her chair. But it wasn't Henry, and it wasn't Buck. It was Fancy's number showing on the screen. She reeled in the receiver by its cord, clicked the flashing button, and listened to Fancy's tirade for as long as she could stand it. As it happened, she could only stand it for somewhere south of five seconds.

"God *damn* it, Fancy! What the flying *fuck* do I care about your *fucking* wedding cake? Clear this line for official police business, God *damn* it!"

She slammed the phone down in its cradle and tried the radio again. When that failed, she tried calling the deputies' cell phones again. And when that failed, she hung up the phone, shoved both it and the radio mike as far away as she could, folded her arms on the desk, and laid her face into her arms. Then Grace *goddam* Tolliver did what no one in the world had ever seen her do before.

She prayed.

She prayed for all of her boys.

CHAPTER

XXVII

A mber Gleason was a sweet little thing. With the face of an angel and an attitude to match, the only child of Martin and Gwen Gleason quickly became the darling of Jesper Street. Not a single soul living on that long block had failed to come under her rosy-cheeked spell. The girl was a social butterfly, flitting about the neighborhood, spreading joy wherever she went. So it came as no surprise to Agnes Smithers when there came a gentle *tap tap tap* at her kitchen door, and she opened it to see Amber Gleason's fresh, beaming face.

"Well, hello sweetie-pie!" Agnes beamed back, wiping her hands on her flowery apron. "I must say, you have impeccable timing. I just made a big batch of cookies. Have you had your dinner yet?"

"Yes, Ma'am," the girl said, ever so sweetly, and let herself be ushered into a toasty-warm kitchen that smelled of all manner of wonderful things.

"But I bet you have just enough room left over in your tummy for a cookie or two. Am I right?"

"I s'ppose," the girl smiled back, shyly.

Agnes led her to a tall stool alongside a wide island in the middle of the kitchen, and helped her up.

"Seems to me, chocolate chip is your favorite. Am I right, sweetie-pie?"

Amber giggled, hiding her face in the nonexistent collar of her Care Bears t-shirt.

"Yes, Ma'am," she cooed back.

The elderly woman slid a plate of cookies across the island. "Well that's good, 'cause I made a special batch with extra chocolate chips, just for you." She poured a tall glass of ice-cold milk and set it beside the plate. "I sure hope you like them."

Amber wasted no time in dunking one of the cookies and taking a big bite, then she beamed a smile up at Agnes and blessed her with the sweetest of smiles and a delightful, little-girl, "*Mmmm...*"

"Oh, thank you, sweetie-pie. That might just be the best compliment I've ever been paid. And don't you worry, there's plenty more where those came from." She rapped a knuckle on the side of a stack of Tupperware containers piled on one corner of the counter. "My goodness, I think I might have made enough for all of Keeter's Bluff!"

The girl's eyes widened as she managed an excited, "Wow, that's a lot!" around her mouthful of cookie.

As she dunked and ate and dunked and ate, Agnes busied herself with puttering about the kitchen, straightening, tidying, and running a wet cloth over every inch of every countertop.

"Well, when I'm nervous, I either clean or I bake. I spent

all yesterday cleaning, so today, I bake."

"What are you nervous about?" Amber asked, sweetly. "All that stuff on TV?"

"Hmm? What? TV? Oh, I'm not really one for television, sweetie-pie. Except for Matlock. I do love me some Matlock. No, sweetie-pie. I'm nervous because Mr. Smithers was supposed to be home from his hunting trip three days ago, and it's not like him to be so late. But don't you worry your pretty little head about it. I'm sure everything's just fine. The old goat's probably just starved for attention, so he's letting me get all worked up before he finally drags his sorry old backside home."

The girl quietly finished one cookie and started on the next as the old lady puttered about. When the last of this second cookie had been dunked and swallowed, she wiped her mouth on a napkin and asked distractedly, "He hunts a lot, doesn't he?"

"Oh my, yes," Agnes harumphed. "Every year, it's the same thing. First week of summer, he's after deer. Come fall, it's wild turkeys. Next spring, it'll be ducks. It's been the same for forty years now. Forty *da...*" she caught herself in time, and angrily swatted an errant crumb into the sink.

"You don't like him to go?"

"Oh, I reckon I knew what I was getting myself into," Agnes said, returning to her puttering. "I even went with him once, back when we were first married. After that, I let him go alone, and I'd stay home, worrying the whole time that he'd fallen in a creek or broken an ankle chasing after some critter or another. Then one day I stopped fretting, and it got so I enjoyed that time alone. But Jedediah ain't no spring chicken anymore, so now I'm back to worrying."

Amber took a sip of milk, then proceeded to dunk cookie

number three.

"You think he fell in a creek?"

This made Agnes laugh, but it didn't last long.

"It wouldn't surprise me one little bit," she snorted. "That old fool thinks he can leap tall buildings in a single bound, but between you and me, there are times when he gets winded taking out the garbage."

Now, it was little Amber Gleason's turn to laugh. It came out as a giggle, shy and sweet, with her face half hidden in a collar that wasn't there.

Agnes used the time to refill her glass to the very top.

"There you go, sweetie-pie. That'll make dunking all the easier."

"Thank you, Mrs. Smithers," the girl said politely, then she immediately proved the theory, much to their mutual delight. She bit off as much of the cookie as her little mouth would allow, then she mumbled around the mouthful, "If you don't like him going, why don't you just tell him not to?"

Agnes didn't have to think it over. She propped her generous backside against the sink and harumphed across the island to the sweet little girl expertly catching an errant drop of milk with a flick of her wrist.

"I wish it was that easy, sweetie-pie, but it ain't. Men get stuck in their ways, and the older they get, the more stuck they get. After forty years of Jedediah going hunting, me telling him not to go would be like telling him not to breathe no more."

"But he kills animals," Amber said between bites, and for the first time since Jesper Street had been graced with the singular presence of precious little Amber Gleason, the smile vanished from her face. She sat there dunking and eating and dunking and eating, but now her pretty little face was all screwed up in a kind of glower. With one last dunk to finish off the cookie, she shook her head and announced, "Killing animals is bad. You should have told him so."

In that toasty-warm kitchen that smelled of all manner of wonderful things, a sudden chill gripped the old woman's heart. But it had nothing at all to do with *damn* Jedediah and forty years of his *damn* fool notions. No, it was the look on little Amber Gleason's face that had dropped the temperature in the room from the height of summer to the depths of winter. For the first time in her nearly eight years of life, the darling of Jesper Street was showing disapproval. That adorable face with its permanent smile as bright as the sun now wore the half-lidded semi-scowl of someone who had just caught their first faint whiff of the stink of humanity.

"Yes, I should have. You are absolutely right, sweetie-pie. But it ain't really about the killing now, is it? After all, you go to McDonalds from time to time, don't'cha? You like a good burger? You like bacon? You like them chicken nuggets? Well, all those things come from animals dying, sweetie-pie. Fact is, something on this good Earth always has to die when something else needs a meal. You've seen the Lion King, right? I know you have, 'cause I gave it to you myself. Now, don't go making me sing Circle of Life, girl!"

Little Amber Gleason went right on dunking and right on eating, but she found time between bites to say, "My dog died last year. It was sad. I cried a lot. So did my mom. But something dying isn't the same as something getting killed." She took one last bite of her cookie, and having had enough, she laid the leftovers back on the plate.

"I remember your dog, sweetie-pie." Agnes leaned across the island and patted the girl's hand gently. "I was there at his funeral, remember? Why, Rufus used to come scratching at my door every morning, looking for a treat. And he did that 'cause he knew I kept a box of them Beggin' Strips under the counter, just for him. He was a sweet boy. A sweet, sweet boy."

"He's dead now," the girl said, betraying no emotion whatsoever. "I was sad that he died, but I'd have been a lot sadder if he'd been killed. Your husband kills animals for fun, and you let him. That's just wrong. Anyway you say it, it's wrong."

Agnes fumbled for words, but she could find none. With those half-lidded, disapproving eyes nailing her to the spot, the best she could manage was a weak, "I know, but Jedediah loves nature so."

Amber drained the last of her milk and shrugged.

"Strange to show love by killing," she said, then she folded her hands politely in her lap and smiled sweetly. "Thank you very much for the cookies, Mrs. Smithers. They were delicious!"

Uncertain exactly what had gone on between them but relieved that it was over, Agnes began fumbling a few Tupperware containers together, saying, "Shall we take these along?"

"Oh yes, *please!*" Amber chirruped, and with that, the smile returned in full and Agnes Smithers was back under Amber Gleason's spell.

"It would be my honor and my privilege," the old woman replied in kind. Then she helped Amber down from her stool and led her back to the door.

But Amber took only one step outside before spinning around and stopping Agnes in her tracks.

"You don't have to come. I can carry those."

"No, it's okay," Agnes insisted. "I've got them."

Little Amber Gleason held her ground.

"No. *I'll* take them, thank you very much," she said, and after standing there for far too long with her tiny arms outstretched and her face curled into a pucker, Agnes finally acquiesced.

"Alright, sweetie-pie," she said, passing over the plastic containers and for some reason choosing not to ruffle the girl's hair as she always did whenever they parted. "Tell your momma and daddy 'hi' for me. I ain't seen your momma in a month of Sundays, so tell her to get over here for coffee some morning so we can catch up."

"I will," Amber replied, smiling as sweetly as she ever had. Then she made her way across the front lawn, back to her own house next door.

Agnes closed the door behind her, and with no real understanding of why she would ever do such a thing, she flipped the bolt to lock the door tight. Then she went through every room in the house and bolted every door, locked every window, and drew every drape. Then and only then did she return to her kitchen, but even as she collected Amber's used plate and glass and began rinsing them off in the sink, there came again a gentle *tap tap tap* on the door.

Wholly against nature, Agnes peeked through the window before reaching for the latch. It was Amber Gleason again, her tiny arms still piled high with Tupperware, and a sweet smile etched across her rosy little lips.

Just that suddenly, Agnes felt like a complete and utter fool. Without a moment's hesitation, she unbolted the door and swung it wide.

"Did you forget something, sweetie-pie?"

Little Amber Gleason shook her pretty blonde head and said, ever so sweetly, "No, ma'am. I just wanted to tell you that you shouldn't be nervous anymore."

Agnes put a hand to her chest and beamed a smile down at the girl.

"Well, aren't you just the sweetest thing. Thank you, sweetie-pie. I appreciate you saying that."

Amber shrugged her tiny shoulders and tossed her head to the side.

"I figured you should know," she said, the bright, sunny smile not fading for an instant. "Your husband's dead, and so is everyone they sent looking for him, so there's no reason to be nervous anymore. 'Kay, thanks again for the cookies!"

With that, the darling of Jesper Street spun around and marched off across the lawn, leaving Agnes Smithers standing in her open doorway, shaking like a leaf.

CHAPTER

XXVIII

W e warn you that what you are about to see is graphic in nature. Viewer discretion is strongly advised."

The talking head wasn't lying. Hermione had seen most of the videos already, but there was new footage from Lisbon, Krakow, Saint Petersburg, and some place called Moose Jaw up in Canada. It was the same all over. Blood. Carnage. People running. People screaming. Then the gory shit. Endless footage of the dead and dying, up close and personal.

Most of it showed only the aftermath, but several attacks had been caught on camera. Horses on a farm in Idaho. Chimpanzees in some reserve in Nairobi. Snakes in Myanmar. Wolves in Colorado. Legions of rats pouring out of the subways in Chicago, Moscow, and Montreal. An honest-to-God herd of bison tearing through a prairie town. And perhaps the most shocking footage of all, a pod of beautiful humpback whales causing utter destruction in a yacht race off Anguilla.

Nowhere was immune. From polar bears in remote Inuit villages to scorpions in Cairo to a mounted cop in downtown Manhattan being thrown from his horse and trampled to death, it seemed that all of nature had chosen this one day in all of history to turn against man.

"Top of the food chain, my ass," Hermione huffed, loudly enough to wake the miniature poodle curled up in her lap. She petted the dog until it settled back down, and since the carefully maintained social convention within the family obliged her to give every other dog the exact same amount of attention, she scratched the boxer curled up on one side of her between the ears, patted the rump of the big black labrador splayed out on her other side, and leaned forward to ruffle Samson's ears. The Great Dane raised a lazy head, yawned, and laid back down over her slippered feet, and all went back to what it should be on a Saturday night in Hermione Alcourt's little house at the end of Clinton Drive.

The talking head returned, and in typical Fox fashion, played up the fear angle for all it was worth.

"With so many states now under martial law and the President declaring a state of national emergency, many are wondering if that might have been the plan all along. American troops have been sent into the worst-hit areas, supposedly to protect the populace, but several firefights have already broken out between those soldiers and the people they are sworn to protect. In Colorado, seventeen civilians dead. In Alabama, twenty-three confirmed killed by the National Guard. In Montana, the numbers are even worse. There, members of the 101st Airborne came under fire when they strayed too close to a camp belonging to the so-called Montana

Free Militia in Missoula County. Result? One hundred and thirty-seven dead, and helicopter gunships now patroling American skies."

Hermione took a swig of Jack Daniels and cursed not quite under her breath, "God *damn* it. It's not enough that the whole world wants us dead, now we're killing our own?"

The poodle raised its head and regarded her sleepily, so she spread affectionate pats and head-scratches all around once again. But Hermione Alcourt was no fool. Once the brood settled back down, she cast an eye to the revolver on the end table, well within reach. The thing looked like something Wyatt Earp might have carried back in the day, but this was no relic from a bygone age. This was her latest acquisition, and what she'd used outside the S&J not four hours ago. It was a Linebaugh .500, loaded with five fifty-calibre hollow-point rounds, each one capable of bringing down a Cape Buffalo. Maybe even two, if they were standing the right way 'round.

Hermione loved her dogs. They were her best friends, her confidantes, her security blanket, and so much more than that. There was nothing in the world Hermione Alcourt wouldn't do for them. But the incident at the S&J had given her a close-up look at what was happening all over the world, and if lightning happened to strike Keeter's Bluff twice, she was determined to do what she must. She owed her boys that much, and more. Should John, Paul, George or Samson show any signs of aggression, she wouldn't hesitate. She would put a bullet into each of their heads, and once that horror show was over, maybe she'd use the fifth one on herself.

But for now, all was as it should be in that little house at the end of Clinton Drive.

"Strange reports coming out of Russia, now," the talking head brought her attention back to the TV, but it was just trading one horror show for another. "This video comes from the city of Orsk, just north of the Kazakh border, and it purports to show members of the city police and Russian military shooting into a crowd of unarmed civilians, many of whom appear to be children. Now, this video has yet to be authenticated, but if true, it might just be a glimpse into our own future. One has to wonder, how long will it be before the same thing happens here?"

Hermione had seen enough. With one last swallow of Jack to finish the glass, she muted the talking head, lifted John as a bundle from her lap, laid him down beside his big brother Paul, and carried her empty glass to the kitchen. She poured herself another three fingers, then she stood at the kitchen sink and looked out the window at the world beyond.

The sun was still cresting toward the western horizon, but as it never was in small-town America on a summer evening, no one was out walking their dog, or barbecuing in their back yard, or simply sitting on the front porch with a cold can of Bud. The only people out and about this evening were children, playing as they always did. Time was, Hermione could keep up with the best of them, Hell, as the toughest kid on Clinton Drive, she'd *owned* their asses back then, girls and boys alike. But that was a lifetime ago. Now, she didn't even know the rules anymore.

A gaggle of girls came sprinting out of Henry Lee's house across the street, laughing and giggling and chasing one another through the street, but she had no idea at all what game it was they were playing. This wasn't tag, or kick the can, or even cops and robbers. The gaggle of girls met up with the Chadwick sisters just emerging from the side door of Leon Chapelle's little bungalow, then Timmy Doogan and little Raoul Jimenez came out from behind Trish and Mary's place a little farther down the block, and they all met up, only to disperse once again in every different direction.

Hermione did her best to reason out the objective of whatever game they were playing, but it seemed to make no sense at all. The Chadwick sisters followed Timmy Doogan to the Marcello's house a few doors down, and the rest headed straight for Big Max Hembroff's front door. Then the mystery deepened. One of the gaggle rang Max's bell, and though she was certain they would all scatter like chaff in the wind and have a laugh at the big man's expense when he came to the door to find no one there, they did nothing of the kind. They waited there on the front stoop until Big Max answered the door, they spoke a few words, and when Max shrugged, the entire gaggle filed in.

If the kids had all had their phones out, she might have imagined that they were chasing imaginary creatures around the neighborhood, eager to best one another on some virtual scoreboard. But that wasn't it either. Well, okay then. Maybe this wasn't a game after all. Maybe they were selling Girl Guide cookies, or hitting the neighbors up for a few bucks to buy themselves new baseball gloves or whatever. Well, if that's what it was, she'd even pony up a few bucks herself. It was well worth it if it kept kids in the real world instead of with their noses stuck in a phone.

By the time she poured another three fingers, a fresh gaggle of kids was heading across her front lawn.

She leaned across the sink to have a good look at who was in the gaggle. Was that the Beaudrell girl from the next block over? The one with the striking green eyes? What was her name? Kylie? Kaylie? Kristian? Ah, whatever. And the boy. Wasn't that Ian Tompkins from up the road? Hell, they were both good kids in her book. Many's the time one or both of them would come wandering by, just on the off chance her boys were out running loose in the yard. And if they were, how those kids would spoil those dogs with affection.

Yup, Ian Tompkins and the little green-eyed Beaudrell girl were good kids, all right. Never a fuss, never a problem, and if they loved dogs that much, she had to give them extra credit for having their heads screwed on straight.

But now, even as her eyes focused in the waning sun and she got a proper look at the rest of the approaching gaggle, one tiny freckle-faced girl with a bright red ribbon in her hair pointed up at the window over the kitchen sink, and they all stopped as one. Then they just stood there, each and every of them staring up at Hermione Alcourt through that narrow kitchen window.

Suddenly, the room grew chilly. Hermione lowered her last finger of Jack to the counter and took a step back from the window. Then, for reasons she wouldn't have been able to explain in a thousand years, she reached for the switch on the wall and plunged the kitchen into semi-darkness.

A tight little yip from the livingroom grabbed her attention. It was Johnny's yip. Was one of his brothers trying to bully the poor boy? Were they ganging up on him again for being so tiny? But no. Even with the lights out, the flickering TV showed all four of her boys right where she'd left them.

This was no bullying. No ganging up. This was just four dogs confused by the sudden darkness, and looking to their momma for reassurance.

"It's okay, boys," she cooed to them as best she could

with a voice laden with gravel. "I just turned the lights off, is all."

She turned a wary eye back to the window, but just like that, the gaggle was gone. Breathing a sigh of relief for she knew not what, she downed the last finger of Jack and returned to her boys.

"Now, where were we?" she said, tucking herself back between Paul and George, and hoisting little Johnny back onto her lap. She tucked her slippered toes back under Samson, gave head scratches and butt pats all around, and all was once again right in that little house at the end of Clinton Drive.

Little Johnny yipped again, and Hermione petted the dog as tenderly as her calloused hands would allow.

"Are you okay, my boy? Has the TV got you all scared? Well, as long as momma's here, ain't nothing gonna hurt my boy. Ain't nothing gonna hurt *none* of my boys," she added with no small amount of resolution as she patted each of them in turn.

She gave little Johnny one more pat on his head, and turned her eye to the Linebaugh .500 on the end table.

She unmuted the TV when the old talking head left and the blonde girl came on. Yes, this young tartlet was just as much a douchebag as the rest of them, but she was a beautiful douchebag with the hair of a Greek goddess, a face to die for, and a voice that could melt butter, so Hermione listened intently as the beautiful blonde douchebag explained in exquisite detail just how deep a shithole the world was in.

"Portland. Phoenix. Los Angeles. Detroit. New York City. We've all seen the footage, and we've heard the eyewitnesses. In every city in every country around the globe, it's the same story." All of the images Hermione had seen throughout the day started to play over again, this time with the beautiful blonde douchebag melting butter over it all. "For us, it began at the Bronx Zoo, but reports soon started coming in from Budapest, London and Madrid. Animals going crazy. Attacking. Killing. And even as the world struggled to understand what was happening, the game changed again. The first report was out of Australia. In Melbourne, a family murdered in their sleep. Mother, father, and oldest son found dead in their beds. Two younger children yet to be located. Then the Philippines. A family dead, and the youngest child missing. Then China. Then, everywhere else. Entire families dead, and children missing. Is this the work of terrorists? Human traffickers? Or maybe, just maybe, might all of these things be related in some way..."

Little Johnny gave another yip and jumped awake in Hermione's lap. She made as if to pet him back to sleep, but he snapped at her fingers as they came close, and she instinctively drew her hand back. Then she looked the dog closely in the eyes. She looked into that dog's eyes more closely than she'd ever looked at anything in her life. But, contrary to her fears, there was nothing there to see. No wildness. No bloodlust. Nothing out of the ordinary at all. But then again, if she'd been forced to swear on a stack of Bibles, she might've had to admit that for one second, just one quick second mind you, that she might have seen something like a shadow flit behind those brilliant brown eyes.

"No one has seen the President since this afternoon's press conference," the blonde douchebag went on melting butter in the background. "Some sources say he's in the White House bunker. Others that he's aboard Air Force One, high above the fray. All we know for sure is that America wants answers."

Paul the boxer suddenly jumped to his feet and yapped at nothing in particular. Hermione tried her best to quiet the dog, but then George jumped up on her other side, matching each of Paul's yaps with a throaty bark of his own.

Hermione tucked both of her hands carefully into her sides and crawled gently out from under little Johnny, and as Samson raised his huge head and regarded her departure with a growl, she retrieved the Linebaugh .500 and retreated with it back into the kitchen.

The sun was just beginning to set, but it was still light enough to make out little Ian Tompkins and the Beaudrell girl back on her lawn. And once her eyes adjusted, she began to recognize the others that were with them. The Slattery boy from up the block. Cindy Gamble's girl, Wanda. Four or five others she knew from around the neighborhood, but wouldn't be able to put a name to if her life depended on it. They were all standing there on her front lawn, staring up at that little window over the sink.

The scratching of nails on linoleum signaled the beginning of the end. Only one dog in the world made a sound like that. Those were Samson's big snowshoe paws, coming out from the livingroom. And behind him were the others, all with their own distinctive clicks. George was right behind Samson, just like always. And beside him was Paul, smart as a whip, sweet as an angel, but with jaws powerful enough to crush bone. And behind Paul came Johnny. Her youngest. Her little Johnny Minipoo.

She didn't turn around. She didn't have to. Even if she didn't know her boys like the back of hand, the sun was low enough now to let her make out their reflections in the window. All four were lined up on the other side of the kitchen, backlit by the flickering light from the TV. She couldn't quite make out their body language, but again, she didn't have to. A low, guttural growl emanating from Samson told her everything she needed to know. She took a second to pour one more finger of Jack and down it in a swallow, then she cocked her massive handgun, pivoted about on her heels, and leveled the cannon at a spot just over their collective heads.

"Please, boys," she pleaded to one and all as they padded slowly toward her. "Please don't make me." But she might as well have been whistling Dixie.

George moved first. The big lab came at her with lips peeled and teeth bared, and Hermione squeezed the trigger without hesitation. Then came Paul, then little Johnny, and with tears streaming down her face, she dispatched both of them with two more pulls of the trigger. Then big old Samson snarled up at her, and she felt her heart break into a million pieces.

Samson had been with her the longest. Damn-near twenty years, now. He'd been a pup when she'd taken him in, and she, just another broken ex-WAC. She'd lost count of how many times she'd cried into his back, but each and every time, he had given her a lick on the cheek to let her know that everything would be okay. But looking at Samson now, Hermione knew that nothing would ever be okay again. That big, beautiful dog was a stranger now. That warm friend of thousands of nights was gone. In his place was only madness.

Samson growled once, and Hermione didn't hesitate. She pulled the trigger that sent a fifty-caliber slug downrange at fourteen-hundred-plus miles per hour, vaporizing the vast majority of the big dog's massive cranium. As the animal crumpled to the floor, she threw the revolver to the farthest corner of the room with a wail, then she fell to her knees, put her face in her hands, and she cried. She cried for all of them. She cried for John. She cried for Paul. She cried for George. But she cried most for big, beautiful Samson.

Good *God*, where would she be if that gorgeous hound hadn't looked up at her with his big cow eyes all those years ago? He'd been the oversized puppy no one else wanted, but he had proven his loyalty and affection over and over, every single day of his life. And now, there he was, dead on her kitchen floor. He'd gone mad, and she'd put him out of his misery. And there he was, dead. There they *all* were. Dead on her kitchen floor. Her brood. Her boys. Her children. Dead. All of them. Dead.

She cried until her eyes ran dry, then she hauled herself to her feet and made for the front door. Surely, the neighbors would have heard the shots. They would have ducked for cover, grabbed their phones, and called the cops. She should be hearing the sirens any second now. But what of it? Let them come. Let them come and take her away. Let them take her away, let them toss her in a cell, and let them throw away the key. What did she care? And yet, even as she threw the door open and stepped over the threshold, ready to face the music, all she saw were those same neighborhood children still standing in a knot in the middle of her front lawn.

The little Beaudrell girl broke the silence as she peeled away from the gaggle and padded the rest of the way across the lawn. Her rosy lips spread out into the widest of smiles, and she looked up at Hermione with her striking green eyes. Green, with just a hint of a shadow flitting behind them.

"We're playing a game," she told Hermione, sweetly. "It's called 'grown-ups'. Wanna play?"

CHAPTER

XXIX

T he music died with a turn of the key, but neither Cooper nor his passenger made any move to climb out of the cruiser just yet. They sat on State Street in front of a flat little building bearing the sign 'Keeter's Bluff Sheriff's Department', and continued the debate that had raged for the entire drive.

"If it were a toxin or a virus, the CDC would've found it by now," Emma said emphatically, but the statement only raised Cooper's hackles.

"Clearly, you don't know how government entities work," he informed her with a sigh. "Look, I'm sure the fine folks at the Center for Disease Control are doing their best, but they're working at the same cross-purposes as everyone else paid by tax dollars. They have to do their job, but they also have to protect next year's budget. That means getting results, but not getting them too quickly."

"Is this the government entity speaking, or just a jaded

old man?" Emma shot back.

"Both," Cooper replied without a doubt.

"So you still don't believe any of it?"

"Not a word, Miss Wong. A living Earth, trying it's best to wipe out all of humanity? Give me a break."

"*I* didn't come up with the Gaia theory, Sheriff Cooper. Scientists did that. Actual *smart* scientists."

"And I'm sure they sold a lot of books," Cooper harumphed. "If that pile of new age nonsense was even halfway right, Gaia wouldn't have to kill us off with dogs and rats and cougars. All this living Earth of yours would have to do is shrug her shoulders. Hurricanes. Droughts. Earthquakes. Tsunamis. A lot of people died today, Miss Wong, but I'm betting more people died in a single morning in 2004 when the ocean spilled its banks."

"Okay," Emma conceded, clearly struggling with the obvious logic. "Well then, maybe it isn't about killing us all. Maybe it's about killing just enough of us to put the world in balance."

"Balance? More animals than humans died today, Miss Wong. What, Gaia didn't know we had guns?"

"Well," Emma struggled on, "maybe it's to send a message, then. You know, letting us know that we have to be better stewards of this world."

Cooper shot this idea down, too.

"If that's the case, then I'm afraid it's backfired in rather spectacular fashion. Do you really think anyone's going to give a damn about global warming after watching polar bears eat their way through a tour bus, live on TV?"

Argued into a corner, Emma took the only path still open to her.

"You're pissing me off again, Sheriff," she grumbled,

crossing her arms and sinking into the seat.

"Welcome to Keeter's Bluff, Miss Wong," he replied. "Hey, you know what? You should tell Grace all about this Gaia theory of yours. She'll probably lap it up. She has a *very* open mind."

"Really? Okay, then. Umm... who is Grace? Exactly?"

"Just the sweetest woman in the whole 'Bluff!" Cooper hid a smirk as he climbed from the car. "You'll love her. Trust me."

One look at the parking lot dashed Cooper's hopes. It was too empty. Just Grace's Buick, and an impound waiting for a tow. No Deputies' cruisers. No State cops. No one at all. No one else coming to help.

With the sun dipping low over the trees, the street was in twilight, but a few people were still out and about. Old Gerald Mooney on his evening stroll. Maria Gonzales pushing her new baby along in a stroller. On the far side of the street, pretty Adriana Myles, arm in arm with her latest beau, Jim something-or-other. And there, tearing down the sidewalk in whatever incomprehensible game children were playing these days came the Washington twins, little Jorge Hernández, and one of the White Owl boys. Chaytan, if memory served.

As he and Emma climbed the steps to the station, a single crow cawed from somewhere behind, making them both swing around and turn an anxious eye to the trees. But there was no repeat of the avian tornado. The caw had come from a single crow, sitting on an upper branch of the closest elm and staring down at the humans below. The bird switched tunes and uttered a long, low death rattle, then it simply sat there and watched the two of them mount the rest of the steps.

Grace Tolliver nearly came out of her skin when Cooper banged through the door. She jumped up behind her desk, and against all reason, there was one fleeting second when Cooper was certain that the old gal was actually going to run out and throw her arms around him. Thankfully, she stood just long enough to brush a few nonexistent crumbs from her dress, then she sat back down and scowled over her glasses at her wayward idiot Sheriff and the unfamiliar stray who'd followed him home.

"So you're still alive," she snarked. "Good. I'd hate to see you get out of this shit so easily."

"Good to see you're still breathing too, Grace," Cooper snarked back. "Where would the world be without your shining beacon of joy."

"And who is this?" Grace harumphed. "You been cruising the junior miss department at Walmart, Sheriff?"

Cooper didn't take the bait, but he allowed a second to make the introductions as he stormed past.

"Grace Tolliver, Emma Wong."

As Cooper barged through the door of his office, Emma hung back and extended a hand over Grace Tolliver's desk.

"Hi, Grace!" She beamed a smile. "It is *so* good to meet you."

"Yeah? Why's that?" the woman answered back, one eye fixed on the bright blue Band-Aid on the girl's forehead. "You need your training wheels tightened?"

Emma withdrew her hand.

"Never mind," she said courteously enough, but with a tell-tale curl of her lip. "I thought you were someone else."

"Any word from the Staties," Cooper asked Grace from the safety of his doorway.

"Not a one," Grace huffed, putting a lighter to a fresh

cigarette. "The landlines still work, but only in town. As far as I can tell, we are officially cut off from the rest of world. Ma Bell must be going through menopause."

"*Damn* it," Cooper cursed. "Where are the men?"

"Sonny's on his way in as we speak, and Carl took a call up Whatcom way. Possible 10-16. The neighbors called it in."

"Umm... 10-16?" Emma had to ask.

"Domestic violence," Cooper translated with a scowl. "I wish I could say it was a rarity."

"Fucking rubes," Grace grumbled, blowing a double stream of smoke through her nostrils.

"What about Henry and Buck?"

"Not a peep," came the reply, and for the first time since he'd known her, Cooper detected an actual trace of human emotions behind the substantial armor of Grace *goddam* Tolliver. He wouldn't bet his life on it, but he could almost swear the woman was actually worried. "Cell phones are out, and the radio's been spotty as hell," she said, swinging her chair around to turn her back on the Sheriff. She deposited her smoldering cigarette in the overflowing ashtray and reached for a box of tissues. Cooper noted that the wastebasket was already nearly full of crumpled tissues, but he said nothing. "I've tried calling the Leelands and the farms on either side of them more times than I can count, but so far, nothing."

It was her tone more than her words that set Cooper's nerves on edge.

"I'd better get out there," he said, but before he could take a single step, Grace *goddam* Tolliver jumped to her feet and positioned her considerable form between him and the door.

"The *hell* you will!" she snarled up at him, aiming a

locked and loaded finger directly between his eyes. "Listen to me, Sheriff. Your place is here. Right *fucking* here. Either your deputies can take care of themselves, in which case they should be tromping their muddy boots all over my clean floor any minute now, or they ran into something they couldn't take care of themselves, in which case there is nothing you can do about it. Either way, your place is here, Sheriff. Here. Right fucking *here!*"

He watched as a single tear formed in the corner of Grace's eye, but before he could even begin to come to terms with that particular anomaly, all of the lights in the station suddenly flickered, and all three occupants looked ceilingward, holding their collective breath. Several long seconds passed as the lights flickered off and on and off and on, then they finally flickered back on and stayed that way. At least for now.

Emma bit at the corner of her lip. "Umm... that's not good, is it?"

"Not in the least," Cooper admitted. "Everything in the 'Bluff comes through Jolene. Phones, power, water... That means that as bad as things are here, they're even worse up there."

"And things are likely to get a whole lot worse here, too," Grace picked up the narrative and ran with it. "We already lost the cell towers, which means the power grid's been compromised, same as when we get hit by a big lightning storm. Unless they get it fixed fast, I'd say we have less than an hour before we're all groping around in the dark."

Emma retrieved the bottle of Tylenol from her jacket pocket, popped it open, and dry-swallowed two at once.

"Yup, not good at all."

A shout from outside drew Cooper's attention back to

the street. The gathering dark was already reflecting the room back through the windows out front, but the lights were still off in his office, giving him a clear view through the corner window. Pretty Adriana Myles and Jim something-or-other were still arm in arm and in no hurry as they strolled slowly up the street. And there was Maria Gonzales, just now making her way across State Street towards her apartment a few blocks over. A car passed by. Then another. Then a big ugly tow truck rattled by in the opposite direction, and Harlon Abrams threw pretty Adriana Myles his usual wolf whistle.

It was wrong. Every bit of it. It was right, but it was so very, very wrong. In fact, it was wrong precisely because it looked so *damned* right.

On an ordinary small-town summer night, people should be out and about in droves. He had figured as much himself, not too long ago. But he'd since had cause to change his mind. On this night, this one summer night like no other, the streets should be entirely empty. Anyone with half a brain would have heard the news from around the world by now and hunkered down. Hell, even those *without* half a brain would have seen the lights flicker and known what was coming. And yet, here these people were, treating this like it was any other small-town summer night.

A random movement drew his attention skyward, and he put a finger to the blinds.

High above, a flock of crows was descending from the sky in a whorl, directly over Maria Gonzalez and her baby stroller. But no. Not a *flock* of crows. This was a *murder* of crows, coming back for a rematch. He ran out of his office, tore across the lobby, and threw the front door open with a crash, but just as he was about to race to the woman's aid, the crows used the very last of the suns rays to settle into a tree over Maria Gonzalez's head... and that was it. No running. No screaming. No blood. The birds simply took roost in the tree, and Maria Gonzalez idly pushed her new baby around the corner and out of sight.

Cooper stood there for some time, watching the birds and waiting anxiously for a return of the tornado, but it was not to be. A full minute passed before he allowed himself to believe what his eyes were telling him, but apparently this was just an ordinary flock of ordinary birds doing what they ordinarily did every ordinary night.

So, was that it then? Was the craziness over? Like waking from a bad dream, it seemed that everything in Keeter's Bluff was suddenly, wonderfully, *impossibly* right. But then Cooper happened to look back to pretty Adriana Myles and her new beau, and something just beyond the happy couple caught his eye. It wasn't much, and he couldn't tell for the life of him what it was, but as Adriana and Jim something-or-other were swallowed up by the shadows at the far end of State Street, he could just make out a quick little flurry of activity. Then a high, shrill shriek ripped through the air.

Cooper didn't hesitate. He threw himself down the steps, considered his squad car for a fraction of a second, then dismissed it and made ready to run those two blocks faster than any man had even run before. But he hadn't even reached the far side of the parking lot before he pulled to an awkward stop and cocked his head curiously.

The scream dissolved into gales of laughter as a cluster of children came running out of the shadows. The Coggins girl. And the cute little Lee kid. What was her name? Lily? Rose? Petunia? Some damn flower, anyway. Then the Denton boy. Jeremiah, like the guy with the bullfrog. And following up, sweet little Amber Gleason, the darling of Jesper Street.

They all waved as they tore past, and Cooper did his best to approximate something like a wave back. And once again, that was it. The scream hadn't been a scream at all. No one needed rescuing. It was all just a trick of the night, and a cross-firing bundle of rattled nerves.

By then, Grace and Emma were both on the stoop, but he waved them back in and followed along behind. Then they all stood there in a rough triangle in the reception area, looking from one to the other and back again.

But even as right as everything seemed outside, an ugly thought was beginning to brew away in Cooper's mind. A dark thought that twisted his stomach into knots and brought up the rancid taste of bile. It was a brooding thought. A horrible thought. An *insane* thought. Every rational part of his being fought against it, and yet, as hard as he tried, he couldn't quite keep that awful, dark, insane thought from rolling over and over and over in his mind.

"Tell me, Miss Wong," he said at last. "What does an army do when it comes upon withering fire from an enemy armed with far superior weaponry?"

Emma shrugged. "Umm... I dunno. Keep on fighting? Go, go, go?"

Before he could gently shoot her down, Grace *goddam* Tolliver unleashed the howitzer.

"Bullshit!" she boomed away. "Every second you spend in the line of fire costs lives, so you retreat. You retreat, you regroup, and you come up with a way to get around their defenses. And once you figure out how to do that, you kill every last one of the bastards."

Cooper had one last look through the window as sweet

little Amber Gleason bounced down State Street, giggling gaily at forever being the one needing to catch up to the other kids. Then she and the others were gone, the street was quiet again, and Cooper was left alone with that ugly, dark, utterly insane thought.

Was it possible? he wondered to himself, feeling the very blood in his veins growing colder by the second. *Dear God in Heaven, was it really possible?*

CHAPTER

XXX

You cannot be saying what I hear you saying, Princess Barbie. Are you *nuts?"*

This was the inimitable Grace *goddam* Tolliver, explaining her reticence to accept new ideas in her usual erudite fashion.

Emma paid it no mind. She simply asked, "Do you have a better idea?"

"Oh, hell, I don't know," Grace scoffed, folding her arms across her ample bosom and pretending to ponder the notion. "Uh, how about anything in the whole goddam world other than that?"

Emma looked from Grace to Cooper and back again, then she turned her eyes to the sky.

"I swear, you two are just like every other close-minded country bumpkin I've met since pulling into Mayberry. And believe me, since coming to your quaint version of Little House of Horrors on the Prairie two short days ago, I've met more close-minded, boot-wearing, straw-chewing, cowshit-smelling country bumpkins than I'd ever want to meet in a thousand lifetimes! Now, how about this? How about you both get the God damn cotton out of your cotton-pickin' ears and consider for one second, just one *fucking* second, that maybe you're wrong. I mean, there has to be a first time for everything, right? So, maybe you're both wrong, and maybe I'm right. And if I'm right, it means that every single one of us is fucked six ways to Sunday!"

Once the tirade wound down, Grace regarded the woman over the tops of her glasses and asked, "What is it you do again?"

"I'm a school teacher," Emma told her.

Grace nodded knowingly and let her scowl melt away.

"Alright, Miss Wong. Tell me that pile of crap again, and I'll do my best to not act like it isn't the stupidest damn thing I've ever heard in my entire life."

"Yeah, that's the spirit," the girl harumphed. "Look, I'm not saying that you have to believe it. Hey, I'm not even sure that I believe it. But it has to be possible, right? Right?"

Grace turned to Cooper.

"And how does Keeter's Bluff's senior law enforcement officer feel about all this hippie-dippy bullshit?"

Cooper didn't answer. Not at first. So consumed was he with his dark thoughts as he gazed out at the town he was sworn to protect that he was barely even aware of the conversation going on behind.

To his well-trained eyes, something had changed with the setting of the sun. Where just minutes ago, everything had seemed to be wonderfully, pleasingly right, the growing darkness came like a funeral shroud dropped over their little slice of the world. Now, instead of ordinary citizens out for a stroll or heading home from work or popping around the corner to drop in on a neighbor, all he could see moving on State Street and beyond were brief glimpses of movement dashing through flickering circles of light thrown down by the street lamps above.

Children. They were all children. He watched and he waited, but not a single adult appeared. No one coming to call their kids home for the night. No one chasing after a little one who was already out too late. No one worried about what little Bobby or Suzy or Daisy-Mae was up to. The children came rushing by in pairs, and in straggled little clumps of three or four, and in larger groups of ten or more, and not a single solitary adult so much as made an appearance.

"Did Carl call himself onsite at the 10-16?" he asked Grace over his shoulder.

"Like I said, the radio's been spotty as hell," she replied with a tightening of her lips. "There was a burst of static around the time he would've got there, so I figured it was him trying to get through, but there's been nothing since. I called the residence a few times, but no answer."

"What's the twenty?"

Grace gave him the address from memory, then she reminded him, "Your place is still here, Sheriff."

"To do what? Twiddle my thumbs?"

"You're in command, Sheriff. Your job now is to coordinate your forces for maximum effectiveness."

"With what?" Cooper scoffed. "Smoke signals?"

Grace relented without a word. She merely dropped her glasses to the end of their chain, clasped her hands before her, and tried her best not to look frightened to death by the very idea.

"I'm going with you," Emma said, but Cooper stopped

her in her tracks.

"No you're not. You're staying right here."

The My Little Ponies rode high up on her forehead.

"Excuse me? Umm... I hate to break it to you, Sheriff, but you are not the boss of me."

"No, that would be Hiram Danvers, currently lying in a pool of blood beside his dead wife," Cooper reminded her, perhaps more bluntly than he should have. He dutifully softened his tone and told her honestly, "Miss Wong, I just want you to be safe."

The Ponies went even higher.

"Safe? Are you kidding me?"

"You have objections to being safe?"

"No, Sheriff, I have objections to you thinking I can't keep *myself* safe." She stabbed a finger into his chest. "Look, I may not be big and strong and have a gun strapped to my hip, but I assure you, Sheriff Buckwheat, I am no damsel in distress. I have been looking after my own shit my entire life. I've never needed help, and I sure as *hell* never needed a man. The last thing I need now is some sanctimonious bumpkin in shining armor and shit-stompin' boots riding to my supposed rescue."

"Miss Wong, it is my job to..." Cooper tried, but there was no point.

"Your job, my ass!" Emma howled. "Would you be so insistent if I was a foot taller and could piss out of a moving car?"

"Of course," Cooper answered, more or less honestly.

"Bullshit," Emma replied, even more honestly.

Cooper ran through every possible argument he could make, and found each and every one of them lacking. And so, he said the only thing he could.

"Alright, then."

With that, he passed around behind the counter, unlocked the weapons cabinet, and helped himself to two full boxes of double-ought buckshot shells. Then he brought out a device that looked a little like an electric razor and placed it on the counter.

"Do you know how to operate one of these, Miss Wong?"

"A Lady Schick?"

"Not quite. Shave your legs with this and you'll light up like a Hanukkah candle. This is a stun gun, Miss Wong. It delivers a pulse of over nine hundred thousand volts. Safety here, 'on' switch here. See? A one second jolt will drop a two-hundred-pound man to his knees. A three second zap would be enough to take down a rhinoceros. Any questions?"

She picked up the device, tested it, appeared suitably impressed with the lightning bolt flying between the contacts, and slipped it casually away in her jacket pocket.

"Just one," she said. "Are we expecting a rhinoceros?"

This time, Cooper answered her with the absolutely truth.

"Miss Wong, I wouldn't be at all surprised."

He left the door to the gun locker wide open and threw Grace the barest of nods. Grace eyed the array of shotguns, pistols and high-caliber rifles, and nodded back.

"Grace, keep trying to get a line out of town. If you can, get in touch with all the TV and radio stations up in Jolene and have them broadcast warnings to every town their signals can reach."

"Will do," she assured him. "And you be careful out there, Sheriff."

Taken aback by her apparent concern and complete lack

of snark, he told her simply, "I will," and moved to step around her.

Unfortunately, the woman made a formidable roadblock.

"I mean it, Sheriff. I don't like this. I don't like this one damn bit. So I say again, you be careful out there. Copy?"

Better, but still off the mark.

He managed a strangled, "Copy that," and maneuvered past her impressive bulk.

She let him go, but even as he reached the door, she called out one last thing.

"I'm too old to train another snot-nosed dumbass with a badge, Sheriff. Watch your skinny ass out there, or you'll have to answer to me!"

Ah, at last. Grace *goddam* Tolliver was back, and everything was right with the world once again.

Cooper forced a growing smile into a scowl.

"And you make sure to lock the door behind me, Grace. I'm sure any high school dropout could answer a phone, but I don't have the time or patience to find someone to take your place." He dropped the pretense and told her honestly, "Don't let anyone in but Sonny, y'hear? When he gets here, you lock the door after him and keep him here, no matter what. I'm sick and tired of having all my sticks in the wind."

With Cooper already out the door and Emma hurrying after him, Grace called out a last jeering, "You think you can replace *me?* Ha! You wouldn't be able to wipe your own *ass* without my help!"

Emma stopped at the threshold and swung back around, grinning sheepishly.

"You're not fooling anyone, Grace. Even *he* can see how much you care about him."

Grace merely harumphed.

"That man can't see shit," she sneered. "He's an idiot. Hell, they're *all* idiots!" But then her tone and sneer both melted away, and she told Emma plainly, "But they're *my* idiots, so do me a favor, young lady. Watch out for that idiot's skinny ass. And watch your own while you're at it." Then she added with an unconvincing scowl, "I don't need the paperwork."

"Copy that," Emma smiled, throwing the woman a wink.

And with that, they were gone.

CHAPTER

XXXI

"Hey, rhinos are near-sighted aren't they?"

"I have no idea," Cooper shrugged, keying the cruiser to life.

"I'm sure I read it somewhere," Emma mused from the passenger seat. "Or maybe I saw it on National Geographic. I bet I could sneak up behind one of those big, beautiful, near-sighted wonders of nature and zap that motherfucker right in the ass!"

"I have no doubt," was all Cooper could think to say as he shifted into gear and pulled out onto State Street.

Whatcom Road wasn't far. In normal traffic, maybe five minutes. With the roads empty and his foot heavy on the gas, Cooper could cut it down to three. But even as he wheeled south on Harriman and blew the red light at Main, he was forced to slow down when he saw children out and about, running back and forth from yard to yard as if every kid in town was playing one all-encompassing, town-wide game of tag.

He knew all of these kids by sight. Ben Lowe's kid, Jarod. Kyle Pendergrass, from a few streets over. The younger Sumner boy, Frankie. Martin Chang. Pardeep Singh. Tracy Coggins. Mae Chappelle. The Welles girls, Harmony and Gloria. Both of the Daniels boys were there, too. He thought he'd even spotted fat Conor Brady's kids in the mix as well, but what the hell would they be doing all the way across town?

One group of kids broke off from the general whirlwind and tore across the road directly in front of the cruiser, causing Cooper to slam on the brakes. He laid out twenty feet of rubber and managed to stop the car with only inches to spare, yet every kid simply stood there and stared at him, almost daring him to run them over.

Tommy Wilkins. Jimmy Stafford. And the cute little girl who looked like she just fell off of a charm bracelet. Little Wanda Gamble.

He knew these kids, too. The Wilkins boy collected comic books and dreamed of becoming an astronaut. Jimmy Stafford was a straight-A student and worked at his parents' store on the weekends. Little Wanda Gamble was only five years old, but she was already helping her mother take care of her new baby brother. They were all good kids. He knew them well. He knew their parents, he knew their teachers, and he knew most of their friends. And yet, as he met each child's eye through a hazy windshield on that darkened street, he could have sworn that something about these kids was different. Something about them had changed. He couldn't put a finger on it, but something about every one of those children was most decidedly... off.

He reached for the button to roll down his window, but

something stayed his hand. Maybe it was a look from one of the boys. Or maybe it was the way Jimmy Stafford took an excited step towards the door when he thought the window was coming down. But whatever it was that kept his finger off the button, Cooper simply sat there, clutching the wheel with both hands and staring out at three perfectly good kids who just happened to be setting his nerves on fire.

At last, the two boys shared an elbow jab and moved slowly out of the way, but not once did they take their eyes off of Cooper behind the wheel. Now, the only one left was little Wanda Gamble, with her tiny little pig-tailed head only a few inches higher than the cruiser's hood. She stood in the precise center of the road for a few more seconds, then one of the other kids called to her, and as if a switch had been thrown, back was Terri Gamble's sweet little girl. Wanda waved to Cooper, beamed a big, toothy smile at Emma beside him, and skipped off to join her friends.

"What the flying fuck was *that*?" Emma gasped.

Cooper had no answer. He breathed a heavy sigh and continued down Harriman Avenue as fast as he dared and as slowly as he must. Two minutes later, he pulled in behind Carl Rankin's cruiser parked against the curb at 215 Whatcom Road, and piled out with his shotgun in hand and Emma Wong at his side.

He hadn't recognized the address, but he knew this bungalow. It belonged to Ben and Margaret Lowe. Ben was a councilman. Had been for three terms. Margaret worked at First Financial. Assistant Manager, last he'd heard. Their son, Jarod, had been one of the kids running around Harriman Street like a nutcase.

He tucked the butt of the shotgun under his arm and clicked off the safety, but he didn't go so far as to pump a round into the chamber. Not on this quiet suburban street, not without a clear and present danger, and sure as *shit*, not with two of the neighbor kids tearing past, laughing and chirping as they went.

"Hi, Sheriff!" the Bartholomew girls called out in unison as they ran by.

Emma threw them a half-hearted wave, but Cooper only watched them go until they disappeared between a couple of houses farther up the street.

The bungalow was dark, as were most houses along this block of Whatcom Road. Evidently, either this particular neighborhood went to bed *far* too early on a Saturday night, or they'd all gone out for the evening.

Of course. Fancy's wedding. He'd actually forgotten about that damned wedding. It was the social event of the year. Of *course* the entire town council would be there, as would anyone of importance in the whole 'Bluff. But the 10-16 only came in a short while ago, so if the Lowe's were supposed to be at a reception that started two hours ago...

He rushed the last few yards and found the front door hanging slightly ajar. Not much. Just an inch or two. Not enough to see inside, but enough to know that Rankin had entered the premises. Which meant one of two things. Either someone had invited the Deputy in, or he'd had just cause to break it in.

Cooper clicked on his flashlight and checked the door. No splintering on either door or frame. No size-12 boot print. No signs of forced entry at all. He put a finger to the edge of the door to push it open wider, but it suddenly flew all the way open all on its own, and there on the other side stood the startled face of Deputy Carl Rankin,

"Fuck *me!*" Rankin howled, taking the very words from

Cooper's mouth and putting a hand to his chest. "Jesus, Mary and Joseph, you scared the *bejeezers* out'a me, Sheriff!"

Cooper felt his own heart about to explode from his chest, but he hid it slightly better than the others.

"I'm not sure any of us has any bejeezers left, Carl," he said, hearing a chorus of childish laughter from somewhere down the street and doing his best to ignore it. He tossed a finger at Rankin and a thumb back over his shoulder. "Carl Rankin, Emma Wong."

"Oh yeah? Ride-along?"

"Of a sort," Cooper said, stepping into the foyer.

"I'm on rhino patrol," Emma quipped, following at his heels.

Rankin screwed up his face. "Huh?"

"Whatcha got, Carl?" Cooper asked, getting him back on track.

"Uh, right." Rankin aimed a flashlight into the house. "Back bedroom. But it's pretty ugly. You might want to stay here, Miss Wong."

"Wanna bet?" she and Cooper said as one.

"Alrighty, then," Rankin raised his hands in surrender and took a step back. "Just watch where you step."

A long hallway split the bungalow in two. Directly inside the door was the livingroom on one side and a parlour on the other. Farther down was the kitchen and dining room. Then came the rest of it. A bedroom with bright blue walls covered with superhero posters. Across from it, a bathroom. After that, a sewing room across from a home office. Then they were at the end of the hallway, and there was only one more door.

Cooper followed his light around the corner and heard a horrified gasp from Emma close behind.

Margaret Lowe lay in her underwear across the four-poster bed as if she'd fallen asleep in the middle of changing her clothes. The black skirt and business jacket of an assistant manager were in a pile on the floor, and the brilliant green dress of a wedding guest was laid out carefully beside her. But the dress was speckled with red, as was the bedspread, the carpet, and the wall several feet away. He found the reason why under Margaret Lowe's left ear. Someone had carved a ragged slice straight through her carotid artery.

Deputy Rankin leaned in and shone his light at a door on the far side of the room.

"In there," he said, looking decidedly ill.

Ben Lowe had suffered more. He was in the bathtub, naked. Defensive wounds on his hands and arms. One of the slashes had opened a vein in his wrist, turning the bathwater a brilliant shade of crimson. Then the final insult. A stab wound straight through the throat.

Some of the water had spilled over the edge, wetting the carpet. And there, right in the middle of the puddle, was a footprint frozen in time. A small footprint. Far too small. Just like the one behind the old McIffrin place.

"The Garridebs next door called it in," Rankin reported, hitching his thumb south. "They didn't see or hear anything, but they noticed the Lowe's Volvo still in the driveway when they were heading out to Fancy's reception, so they came over and knocked, and when no one answered, they used their spare key and found Mrs. Lowe just like you see her. They don't know about the husband yet. They stuck around just long enough to tell me what's what, then they tore off back home, locked their doors and killed all the lights. I figured I'd just keep them in the dark 'til you told me otherwise."

"You did the right thing, Carl," Cooper said, but then a darker thought invaded his mind and he had to ask, "Say, Carl, is Mindy-Lou home tonight?"

Rankin's eyes pinched nearly closed.

"S'far as I know, Sheriff. Why?"

Cooper chose his words carefully before he replied.

"Tell you what, Carl. Why don't you swing back around your place, pick up Mindy-Lou, and bring her down to the station. We're having a kind of... gathering. You know, just hanging out and chewing the fat."

Rankin tried to hide a sheepish grin, but he failed miserably.

"Sheriff, you can't fool me. You figured out that tomorrow's Mindy-Lou's birthday, didn't you? I don't know how you did it when I never said a word, but she's gonna *love* it!" He dropped to a conspiratorial sort of hush and asked excitedly, "Hey, Sheriff, did'ja get her a cake?"

Cooper was perfectly happy to take the lie and run with it.

"Of course! An ice cream log from Dairy Queen, just like you said."

"Oh man, oh man," Rankin fairly bubbled over with glee. "I tell you what, Sheriff, you can *never* go wrong with a DQ ice cream log. Not never! Mindy-Lou's just gonna *die!*"

Cooper regarded the last mortal remains of Ben Lowe swimming in a soup of his own gore and wondered what other horrors the darkened houses all up and down Whatcom Road might contain. He turned his light back to the impossibly small footprint, frozen in time beside the corpse steeping in its own juices, and his mind went back to the children running feral through the streets. And as he descended further into the depths of madness, he had to say, if only to himself,

Let's hope not, Carl. Let's damn well hope not.

CHAPTER

XXXII

With the squat towers of Piedmont receding in her mirror, Jermaine finally began to feel something akin to normal. This day had been a day like no other. By far, it was the most exhausting, exciting, *harrowing* day she had ever experience. And this, coming from a girl born and raised in Harlem.

Once everyone with a uniform had descended on Martin Street with badges and guns and stethoscopes and stretchers, she gave a quick statement to a cute cop with even cuter dimples and made her escape. But not before attending to one last order of business. She stopped by Curry in a Hurry on her way back to her car, and knocked politely on the door. After a brief ruffling of window blinds, the turbaned man appeared and looked both ways up and down the street before carefully and cautiously unbolting the door.

"It is over, Miss Jermaine?" the man asked nervously as he swung the door open.

"It is," she told him, plainly. "But in all the confusion, I forgot to give you something, Parm."

The man shook his head.

"No, no, miss. You paid your bill. I am sure of it."

"Sure, but I forgot the tip," she said, then she wound up and drove her fist into the man's chin, dropping him to the floor like a sack of laundry.

That last order of business seen to, she swung past the Veterinary Center, scooped up Snagglepuss's file, and drove out of Piedmont as fast as her aged Honda could carry her. She punched button after button on the radio, hoping to find some tunes to wash away the dread, but every station was the same. Any and all music was gone. It was all news now, and all of it bad. Caracas. Mumbai. Sao Paolo. Oslo. Tokyo. Venice. Athens. The names fell like dominoes, and the stories coming out of those places were the stuff of nightmares.

She tried the AM band, but it was even worse. This was the home of talk shows, and every host and every caller to every station had his or her own pet theory. Insecticides in the grain. Hormones in the beef. Antibiotics in the chicken. Heavy metals in the water. Global warming. Fluoride. Vaccines. Ergots. Chem trails. Some were adamant that it was all a hoax, and others were just as convinced that it was either the second coming or an attack by aliens. But then she discovered one lone station at the far end of the dial still playing music, and she locked it in, cranking the volume up as high as it would go.

I don't miiind, other guys dancing with my giiirl...

The Who. Now, that was more like it. She started singing along, and that wonderful, familiar tune soon began to take her back to a time before Piedmont, before Snagglepuss, and even before Austin Granger. Music had always been her sanc-ttuary, even as a child. If she had a bad day at school, she'd find her favorite station on the stereo in her room, crank it to the limit, and let her headphones carry her away to another world. Later on, whenever her heart was broken or her job wasn't going exactly as planned, she'd plug in her earbuds, turn the MP3 player to max, and sing her heart out, however off-key. And when her parents died, she slipped in the earpods, thumbed her iPhone as high as it would go, and lost herself in music that would forever be unchanged.

That's fiiine, I know 'em all pretty weeell...

She sang along at the top of her lungs and just started to feel halfway normal when a tiny figure suddenly appeared from out of the gloom directly in front of the car. She barely had time to howl a quick, *"Fuck!"* before the Honda's wheels locked up, and the ugly little car skidded to a sideways stop mere yards away from that tiny figure.

"Oh my God..." she panted, her knuckles white against the wheel.

It was a child, standing in the middle of the road. A girl, no more than four or five years old. She thought she might even recognize her, but she couldn't be sure.

"Maizie?"

It was. It had to be. And yet, it couldn't be. Not way. Not out here, not in the middle of the road, and most certainly not alone.

"Maizie?" she called out through the open window. "Maizie Pritchard, is that you?"

But to no avail. The tiny figure said nothing. The girl merely held herself at just the right angle in the Honda's headlights to remain in half shadows.

"Maizie?" she tried again. "Maizie Pritchard?" but even as she called out the name one last time, she couldn't imagine how it could possibly be her. Sure, the Pritchards lived on this block, but they were good people and good parents. Austin had known them since forever, and Austin only made friends with good people. Tom was a business bigwig, and Susan was on the Piedmont school board. And Maizie was only four, for Christ's sake. No way would they have let their four-year-old girl out alone, especially after dark. And no *fucking* way would they have let her run wild in the streets with the whole world gone batshit crazy.

And yet, there she was. Jermaine was sure of it now. This was little Maizie Prichard, standing all alone in the middle of the street in her bare feet, wearing only a long pink nightie and a big, bright smile on a face caked with dirt.

"Maizie?" she howled as she leapt from the car. "Maizie, what happened? What are you doing out here?"

The girl said nothing. She merely put a tiny finger to her little-girl lips and giggled.

"Maizie, why are you out here alone? Where are your mom and dad?"

"Back there," the girl giggled, pointing somewhere over her shoulder.

"Back there?" Jermaine fought to keep her temper from boiling over. "What the *hell* are they doing back there? Oh, we're gonna see about this!"

She held out her hand, the girl took it, and Jermaine led her farther down the road.

"John?" she called out, "Mary?" but there was no answer. She turned up the volume and tried again. "John Pritchard! Mary Pritchard! Where the *hell* are you?"

The girl giggled and pointed a few degrees to the right.

"They're over there, silly!"

And indeed, there they were. John and Mary Pritchard,

at the very end of their long, winding driveway and the very limits of the old Honda's headlights. Both were face down and unmoving. They were laying several feet apart, but their bodies were connected by a veritable lake of blood.

"Christ on a cracker..." Jermaine hushed, but then the reality of the situation hit her and she spun Maizie around, turning the girl's back to the horrific scene.

"Maizie," she said, dropping to a knee and taking the girl by the shoulders. "What happened? Who did this?"

The girl giggled and said nothing.

Jermaine reeled her in, intending to bundle her back to the car and rush her to the hospital or the police station or who-the-*fuck*-knows-where, and that was when she saw it. Just then. Just as their positions changed by a fraction of a degree, and some odd bit of headlight happened to fall across the girl's face.

It wasn't dirt that caked the girl's face after all. It was blood. Spatters, splashes and horrible streaks of blood. More of it painted the front of her nightie from neckline to hem, and both of her hands were solid red up to the elbows.

"Maizie, are you hurt? Where are you hurt, sweetie. Show me."

She pulled up the girl's sleeves and looked down her neckline and pulled the nightie almost over the girl's head, but there was nothing to see. No cuts. No lacerations. Nothing at all. It was only then that she realized the truth. The blood wasn't hers, it was theirs. The poor girl was wearing the blood of her own dead parents.

"Oh, Maizie," Jermaine cooed, and now she did gather the girl in her arms and start back to the car.

Up ahead, the song reached its final chorus.

And I know if I don't, I'll go out of my mind. Better leave her

behind, the kids are alriiight!
The kids are alriiight!
The kids are alriiight!

Little Maizie looked over Jermaine's shoulder to her parents lying in a heap, and she put a bloody little finger to her little-girl lips.

"I know a fun game," she giggled sweetly in Jermaine's ear. "Would you like to play it with me?"

CHAPTER

XXXIII

C ooper was on his way back to the Sheriff's Station
with his passenger flipping between radio stations
for that elusive announcement from Jolene when it
hit him.

"Doc!" he shouted, putting the cruiser into a full one-
eighty that threw Emma hard against her door.

"*Fuck*, dude!" she howled. "Whatever 'Doc' means in
cop talk, a simple 'hang on' would have been great."

"Okay, hang on," he said, then he took the next right
hard enough to throw Emma back the other way.

Keeter's Bluff General was a dozen miles away. They
made the trip in three minutes. Three long, interminable
minutes. And for every second of every one of those
minutes, Cooper imagined the worst. Then he saw all three
of KBG's ambulances lined up outside the Emergency doors,
and he imagined far worse than the worst.

The cruiser skidded to a stop, and Cooper all but launched

himself at the hospital doors. He barreled through and tore straight into the Emergency Room with Emma racing to catch up.

"Doc!" he howled at the top of his lungs, pulling aside one curtain after another, eliciting angry shouts and curses from patients, nurses and doctors alike. "Kira! Where are you? Doc!"

At last, Doctor Kira Melanson appeared from behind a thick plastic curtain, and he all but grabbed her into his arms.

"What the... Tom?" she roared, shoving him back on his heels. "What the hell's gotten into you?"

He said nothing. At this point in the craziest day that any man had lived since the whole crazy world began, he simply reveled in this woman's continued existence.

"Tom?" She took him by the hand and led him back into a gleaming white corridor behind the ER where they would be away from prying eyes, then she asked him with genuine concern, "Tom, are you alright?"

"I'm fine," he lied. Then he composed himself enough to tack on what he considered a reasonable request. "Listen, Doc. You have to come with me. Right now."

The woman shook her hand loose and took a quick step back.

"What? Tom, I have a job. And I have patients. Are you insane? Look, if this is supposed to be some kind of bold, romantic move to sweep me off my feet, you've missed the mark by about a mile and a half. Now I'm sorry I ever made you watch that *stupid* movie."

"Not as much as I am," Cooper muttered, more or less to himself.

Just then, a panting Emma burst into the corridor, but with one look at the situation, she hooked a thumb over her shoulder and began backing away with a meek, "Umm... I'll just wait out here. Pretty sure I saw Cheetohs in the vending machine."

Before she had taken three steps, Kira froze her in place.

"I'm sorry," she said, narrowing her eyes. "You are...?"

Consigned to her fate, Emma leaned awkwardly forward and stuck out her hand.

"Emma Wong, Rhinoceros Hunter."

"Sure, why not," Kira said back without batting an eye. "It's good to know that Tom will have a friend in the next padded cell over."

"Haven't you heard, Doc?" Cooper stepped in. "It's not *us* who've gone insane, it's the whole damn world!"

The good doctor hung her head.

"Yes, Tom. I am well aware of what's going on. I work in a hospital, remember?"

Of course. Idiot! Here he was, trying to explain a baking soda volcano to a nuclear physicist. Somehow, when it came to Kira Melanson, he always managed to find new depths of stupid to plumb.

"How many?" he asked, plainly.

"Seventy-two and counting," she told him just as plainly. "The good news is, the calls have tapered off in the last hour or so, so maybe the war is over at last."

Cooper imagined another reason entirely, but he kept it to himself.

"Anything serious?"

"Some."

"Any fatal?"

To that, the doctor let out a long, beleagured sigh.

"Two. Ned Banks took a kick to the head from one of his horses, and Jim D'Agostino was under his pickup when

some-
thing knocked the jack loose and dropped the whole thing on top of him. A few others were touch-and-go for a while, but I think they're all out of the woods. We've been lucky so far."

"That wasn't luck, Doc, that was you," Cooper said. Then he took her by the hand, led her a few steps away from Emma, and lowered his voice to a whisper as he asked the question he absolutely did not want to ask.

"Doc, have any children been brought in?"

She looked to the heavens.

"No, thank God! That's actually been the one saving grace. Most of the injuries have been bites and cuts and scratches, but some of what I've seen could easily have been life-threatening to a child."

Cooper had his doubts as to who to thank, but he kept that to himself, too.

"So, no kids at all?"

"The youngest was Theresa Russo. She just had her *quinceañera* a week ago. Apparently, the family cat tried to scratch her eyes out. Damn near succeeded, too."

"No one younger? No one at all?"

She regarded him suspiciously.

"You sound disappointed."

"No, no, of course not. It's just... I dunno. Isn't that a little weird?"

"You say weird, I say extremely fortunate." Kira put a hand to her chest. "Believe me, nothing does my heart quite as much good as seeing empty beds in the pediatric ward." But then she looked past Cooper and gasped, "Damn! Speaking of which..."

She all but shoved him aside and rushed toward a young

boy struggling down the hallway on a tiny pair of crutches. Cooper recognized the boy. It was Bob and Carol Hutchison's kid. Since gossip spread like wildfire in small town America, he also knew the reason for the crutches. The kid had taken a tumble off his bike a few days ago. The broken leg was easily fixed, as evidenced by the bright blue cast replacing one leg of his cowboy pajamas, but he had also suffered a pretty good whack to the head, so he'd be in KBG for a while longer.

"Denny!" Kira dropped to a knee and steadied the boy with a hand on either side of his skinny waist. "What do you think you're doing? You're supposed to be in bed."

"Cecie and I were playing," the boy chirped, happily.

"What? Cecie's running around this cold hospital, too? Oh, that's just great." She looked back to Cooper with a worried grimace. "Tom, it's Cecie Tyler."

She didn't have to say another word. Everyone in town knew the Tyler family's sad story. Only four years old, and Cecie's kidneys were already shutting down. Until a new one could be found, the poor girl had to spend every other day hooked up to a machine.

"On it," he said, but before he could take a single step, a shrill scream came echoing down the gleaming white corridor, and the cop in him took over. By the time Kira corraled the boy into her arms and called out a frightened, "Tom?" he was already halfway down the hall.

"Stay there!" he hollered back, and as doctors and nurses and curious patients and visitors alike appeared from out of nowhere to see what all the commotion was about, he swung around the corner and kicked into high gear.

Then he saw her. There, at the end of the gleaming white corridor, just staggering out of the staff breakroom. Ivy

Christian. Bev Christian's youngest, and one of KBG's newest nurses. The girl was slim, pretty, and currently pressing a hand to her side atop a widening circle of red. Tears streamed down her cheeks as she reached a trembling hand out to Cooper, then the breakroom door began to swing open again, and the girl fell to her backside, quite literally shrieking in fear.

Cooper drew his pistol and flew the rest of the way down the hall. He positioned himself directly between Ivy Christian and the breakroom door, then he drew a bead on the widening gap at the approximate height of a man's chest, and his finger whitened on the trigger. But nothing could have prepared him for what was coming.

It was insanity. Pure, unadulterated insanity.

The door opened a few more inches, and out sidled little Cecie Tyler, one arm dripping red all the way to the wrist, and a bloody scalpel held tightly in one tiny little hand.

The girl looked up at Cooper with the sweetest of smiles and chirped happily, "Hi! Would you like to play a game with me?"

Cooper quickly reholstered his weapon, but then he held up his hand, palm out, and told the girl in no uncertain terms, "Stop right there, Cecie. "

Her little bare feet took another step, and the sweet smile diminished by less than half.

"Won't you play with me? It's such a *fun* game."

Cooper took a cautious step to the side and told her as calmly as he possibly could, "Cecie, I want you to drop what's in your hand, okay? It's very sharp, and you could hurt yourself."

"You'll really like this game," the girl fairly squealed with excitement. "It's so much fun!"

"This isn't a game, Cecie. Look at Ivy. You hurt her. Now I'm telling you, Cecie, I want you to drop that thing in your hand right now. Just drop it to the floor, and we'll play a *real* game, okay? Hey, how about Hide and Seek? Do you like Hide and Seek?"

"Aw, that's for babies," she said, rolling her big brown eyes. But there was something else there. Something behind her eyes. A fleeting shadow that came and went almost too quickly to be seen. Before Cooper could even begin to put a name to any of it, the smile returned in full force and Cecie squealed, "I like *this* game. Ivy will play with me some more. Won't you, Ivy?"

The girl took a single step toward the nurse already scuttling backwards as best she could on ass and elbows, and Cooper acted without thinking. He dashed forward, grabbed Cecie Tyler by the wrist, and shook that tiny little wrist as hard as he could until the scalpel clattered to the floor.

"Oww! You're hurting me!" Cecie screeched, and as tears pooled in those big brown eyes, Cooper let his guard down for the briefest of seconds. The briefest of seconds that very nearly cost him his life. No sooner had he released the girl's wrist than she retrieved the scalpel from the floor and threw herself at him, blade first.

It was only instinct and adrenalin that saved him this time. With no time for conscious thought, Cooper lashed out and caught the girl's cheek with the back of his hand, dropping her like a sack of potatoes and sending the bloody scalpel skittering down the hallway.

"Tom! What the *hell?*"

Of course, Kira Melanson chose just that moment to come charging around the corner with Denny Hutchinson in her arms, Emma Wong at her side, and a phalanx of the curious and concerned following in their wake, all full of fire and indignation. The only thing missing was someone with a smart phone and an automatic upload to YouTube to catch this dirty cop brutalizing a sick child.

Everyone in a white coat or scrubs ran to the bleeding Ivy, but chief resident Doctor Kira Melanson ran past them all with Denny in her arms and dropped to a knee before the little girl lying in a heap on the floor.

"Jesus Christ, Tom!" she howled as she planted Denny on his feet and reached for the poor crumpled girl. "Cecie, are you alright?" She helped the girl up and cradled her against her chest. "Are you alright, sweetheart? Are you hurt?"

"Wow, dude. Talk about tough love," Emma hushed Cooper's way, then she pulled the stun gun from her pocket and offered it to him. "Hey, Sheriff Andy, want to finish her off with a quick million volts?"

Cooper only scowled.

"I was playing a game!" Cecie squealed, tears pouring down a cheek already beginning to swell. "I just wanted the mean man to play with me!"

Kira held the girl all that much tighter and stared hateful daggers up at Cooper.

"Don't worry, sweetheart. The *mean man* isn't going to hurt you anymore. Tom, how *could* you?"

"It's not what you think..." Cooper started to say, but those daggers sent up from the only woman he had ever loved cut deep, straight through his heart.

"Oh, you want to know what I'm thinking, *Sheriff?*" Kira snarled. "I'm thinking that you're not right in the head, that's what I'm thinking. And I'm thinking that you need to seek professional help. Like, *serious* professional help. But, you know what? Most of all, I'm just wondering what the hell *I* was thinking."

The daggers sunk even deeper, piercing his very soul and silencing his tongue.

But even then, he could see the keen mind of Doctor Kira Melanson at work. Emma's, too. With the drama played out and nothing to do but assess the damage, both women looked to the evidence and began slowly putting the pieces together, each in their own way. First, Kira took the girl's bloodied hand in hers and inspected it closely, turning it first one way, then the other, then back again. Then she and Emma both turned an eye to the skittering trail of red running up the corridor, ending at a bloody scalpel lying thirty feet away. And as a certain numbness dropped over both women's features, Cooper began to suspect that for better or worse, he might no longer be entirely alone in his darkest of dark thoughts.

They hadn't seen it. No one had. But these two intelligent women had to at least begin to see the truth by now. The blood wasn't Cecie's. None of it. Every drop of it was Ivy's, from the red snake slithering up the hallway to the goo dripping from that tiny little hand.

"No fucking way..." Emma hushed to no one.

With Cecie still clutched to her breast and Denny Hutchison tottering beside her with a steadying hand on her shoulder, Kira looked up at Cooper once again. But now the daggers were gone. In their place was a look of utter and absolute confusion.

"Tom?" she asked, almost pleadingly.

He said nothing back. There was no point. Either she'd see it for herself and vindicate his darkest of dark thoughts, or she'd hate him forever and rue the very moment their paths had ever crossed. And if he'd had an eternity of eternities to ponder the question, even he wouldn't have been able to say which one he'd rather it be.

"Cecie?" Kira cooed, holding the girl as gently as a newborn kitten. "Sweetheart? Can you tell me what happened?"

No longer completely alone and utterly lost in his insanity, Cooper looked from Emma, to Kira, to the little broken boy with the swirly, spiky hair, and finally to the little sobbing girl with the face of an angel. Then he began to ponder just how mad a man would have to be before he no longer thought himself mad.

It didn't take long to get an answer.

It wasn't much. Just a subtle shift of movement. But he'd caught it, and he reacted without thinking. With one quick strike, he snatched Denny Hutchinson's arm out of the air, and now there could be no doubt. Not for brilliant Emma Wong, not for big-hearted Doctor Kira Melanson, and not even for the man who would have given anything to know that his delusional mind had created it all.

The boy had a scalpel in his hand. A scalpel just like Cecie's that he'd kept hidden away until just now. It was only by the sheerest of luck that he'd managed to stop the blade mere inches from Kira's neck.

"Aww, don't you wanna play?" Denny tried to pull his arm loose, but Cooper held him in a rock-solid grip.

Kira gently pried the scalpel from the boy's hand and stared goggle-eyed at it.

"He tried to stab me," she gasped, the words nearly catching in her throat. "This sweet little boy actually wanted to *kill* me."

Most of the white coats and scrubs were busy hustling

Ivy Christian away toward a waiting gurney, but a single shout from Emma got the attention of the rest of them. She waved them in, and Cooper barked them their instructions.

"Take these kids back to the pediatric ward and tie them to their beds. I mean it! Tie them to their goddam beds! And no one goes near them, y'hear? No doctors, no nurses, and no visitors. If any of their parents give you any shit, you tell them to come talk to *me!*"

A junior resident swooped in for the boy, an elderly nurse gathered up the girl, and with the others all gathered around in a cooing, clucking nest, the whole lot disappeared around the corner and out of sight. Then it was just the three of them, all alone in that corridor that was no longer quite so white nor quite so gleaming.

"It can't be," Kira hushed, looking at her own hand, stained with another woman's blood. "It just can't."

"It is," Cooper answered back, plainly enough.

"The shadows in the glass, back at Danvers house," Emma said, shakily. "Was it...?"

He answered her with a look.

"He's only eight years old, Tom." Kira aimed a shaking hand down the hallway. "Cecie's only five. And they tried to kill us. They wanted us dead!"

Cooper helped her to her feet and wrapped his arms around her while Emma looked at the floor and at the ceiling and at everywhere and anywhere but directly at them.

"How, Tom?" Kira pleaded into his chest. "Why?"

"I have no idea," he said, but then something Emma had proposed earlier popped into his mind and he had to try it on for size. "Who knows. Maybe it was in them along."

He knew what was coming, and it came soon enough. Kira Melanson shoved him back, aimed an accusing finger his way, and fixed him to the spot with a look he knew only all too well.

"What do you know, Tom? What do you know that you aren't telling me?"

It wasn't a question. It was demand.

"Not a thing, Doc. Believe me, I don't know a damn thing." But he had to tack on, however grudgingly, "Miss Wong does have a theory, though."

Kira turned her glare on Emma.

"Oh?"

At first, Emma hesitated, but then she shrugged and said, "I think Gaia might've just upped the ante."

"What?" Kira screwed up her face and hit Emma with both emerald-green barrels. "What the hell does *that* mean?" She traded glares between Emma and Cooper and threw up her hands. "What does *any* of it mean?"

Cooper looked Senior Resident Doctor Kira Melanson squarely in the eyes and confirmed the madness in eight simple words.

"It means the war ain't over yet, Doc."

CHAPTER

XXXIV

N o, I don't want to play your stupid game!"
Charlie Sumner sneered as he checked the shine
on his pickup truck under the streetlight. He
wiped away one last trace of wax from the edge of the hood,
and used the rag to shoo his little brother away. "Buzz off,
will ya? I've got a date tonight. You go play grown-ups your
way, I'll play mine."

Frankie Sumner regarded his brother closely. At nine
years apart, the two had little in common, but he still looked
up to his big brother. Mike was big and strong, and he even
had the beginnings of an actual moustache as long as you
checked his upper lip from just the right angle. But his
brother had changed in other ways, too. With the end of high
school, it was as if he had dumped all of his childhood in a
pile on the school steps. Gone were the play fights and the
comic books and the scary movies on Saturday nights. Now,
it was all about cars and girls and learning the tricks of the

trade at Big Dave's Used Car Bonanza.

"Told'ja," Jarod Lowe scoffed. "He's too old. He's practically a grown-up already."

"I *am* a grown-up!" Charlie scowled at the Lowe boy, then he meted out the same amount of derision on the other two, Lawrence Denton and his little sister Tabitha. "I'm *eighteen*, for Christ's sake!"

That was enough proof for Frankie. After all, only grown-ups could cuss so openly like that. But still, he had to try one last time.

"Are you sure? It's such a *fun* game!"

"Yeah? Well guess what, Frank 'n' beans. You and I have very different definitions of the word 'fun'."

He took a few steps back from the pickup to admire his handiwork, and with every inch of metal not being eaten away by rust gleaming like new, he pronounced the job finished with one final snap of the rag.

"Let's go, Frankie," the Denton kid harumphed, a sentiment immediately seconded by his little sister.

"Yeah, this is boring. Come on, Frankie. Let's go play."

Frankie Sumner looked to his brother one last time, but all he saw was a widening of the sneer under what might have been the milkiest of baby caterpillars riding that curled upper lip.

"Yeah, Frankie," Charlie told him, and this time he made no bones about it. "Go *fucking* play."

That did it. Frankie Sumner shrugged, then he and his trio of friends went running off together down the road. Charlie took one last curious look as they rounded the bend, and though one tiny echo of the child that was longed for those simple pleasures of a youth gone forever, the freshly minted adult scoffed aloud, "Damn kids," as he gathered up his rags and bottle of Turtle Wax and headed back inside.

He didn't have to check the clock on the wall to know the time. Final Jeopardy was booming out of the livingroom, which put it at a few minutes before nine. He didn't know why his parents watched that stupid show, but it had been part of their nightly routine for as long as he remembered. Dinner at seven, then Wheel of Fortune, Jeopardy, and on to whichever reality show was the current rage. Lately, it was some dancing shit. What those two old farts got out of has-been celebrities prancing around in leotards was beyond him, but whatever. As long as they were pinned to the TV in that dark room with its ugly wood paneling and ratty shag carpeting, he could almost fool himself into believing that he lived all alone in that big old house.

Nine o'clock. His text to Trudy said he'd pick her up at nine-thirty, and she just lived around the block, two minutes away. That gave him plenty of time for a shit, shower and shave. *Minus the shave...* he said to the mirror as he ran a finger over the fine moustache that was sure to make Trudy Heywood swoon. One quick check of his bowels later and he eliminated another third of the equation, leaving him a full twenty minutes to primp and preen and make himself irresistible.

"Ha! I told you, Meg. Elwood Haynes. Didn't I say, 'Who was Elwood Haynes?'"

That was his old man blustering away, one floor down. He didn't hear his mother's response, but it would have been the usual. A gentle pat on the arm, a half-smile, and a trite, "Yes you did, dear. Aren't you clever?"

Charlie cranked the faucet as high as it would go and stepped into the shower.

The bar of soap was little more than a sliver, but he made

it work. Then he grabbed up the shampoo, exposing that little patch of porcelain that had chipped away years ago and been hidden by one shampoo bottle or another ever since, and he scoffed to himself. Then the water started to turn cold, and he scoffed again as he quickened the pace.

Man, he couldn't wait to move out. The old farts were all right as far as parents went, but they were still his parents, and what self-respecting eighteen-year-old wants to hang around with his parents for one second longer than necessary? A man needed his own place in this world. A place where he could sleep in the raw, and not have to worry about running into Mom or Dad as he snuck down the hall for a squirt in the middle of the night. A place where he could crank the music as high as he wanted, and have friends over without having to ask permission. A place where he could entertain pretty young things like Trudy Heywood without anyone banging on the door with second base almost in sight.

One thought of pretty Trudy Heywood was enough to get the juices flowing. The image of that gorgeous face and those gravity-defying titties flowed down from his brain in a cascade that ended directly at his crotch. Any other time, he might have taken a minute or two to spill that image all over the flowery tiles surrounding the tub, but now, he didn't dare. The real Trudy Heywood was only a block away, and if everything went according to plan, this might even be the night when he saw those perfect little titties for real. And if he got that far, he might just be able to parlay the base hit into a grand slam home run.

A fresh shudder ran through his loins, but he fought against the urge to take the matter into his own hands. Instead, he cranked the water to full cold and held himself there just long enough to dampen the fire.

As he stood there, steadfastly refusing to lend a hand to the predicament, he heard sounds coming through the bathroom door. Not the TV, though. By now, the dancing shit would be on. All he should be hearing at this point was some lame 90's crap, and the fake oohs and aahs of a fake studio crowd. But that wasn't what he'd heard. What he'd heard had sounded like a scream. A wild scream cut suddenly short.

He turned the water off and listened through the drips and dribbles beating out an off-tempo beat on the porcelain.

Wait, *had* that been a scream? And that other sound. What the hell was that? A growl?

Then he had it. It was the TV, all right, but instead of turning straight to the dancing shit immediately after Jeopardy, his father had swung past the news channel. He'd been hearing the same stuff himself, all day long. On TV, on the radio, on Twitter and on Facebook, all anyone could talk about was the weird shit going on all around the world. Animals attacking people. Animals killing people. Animals subsequently being turned into hamburger. It was weird shit, sure enough, but big whoop. The last report had come out of China two hours ago, and there'd been nothing since. The crisis was over, if that's what it ever was. Chances are, it was all just fake news anyway. Just another bullshit story to keep people so scared, they wouldn't notice Uncle Sam stripping away a few more of their inalienable rights.

"Fucking pricks," Charlie grumbled as he dripped away the last of the suds and the last guttering embers of a tempered fire.

He threw back the curtain and grabbed a towel, but just as he started to dry himself, he heard a familiar clicking of the doorknob and quickly wrapped the towel around his more intimate areas.

"*Jeez*, Mom!" he cried out at the usual suspect.

But it wasn't she. The doorknob turned, the door creaked open, and little Frankie's face appeared around the corner.

"Frankie?" Charlie howled, "Jeez, dude. Can't a guy have a little privacy around here?"

With the opening of the door, the sounds from downstairs trebled in volume. But now, there was no more screaming, no more howls, and no more fake newsman telling the dim-witted viewers how scared they should be. Now, there was only music. Swish Swish, by Katy Perry.

Frankie said nothing. He merely opened the door wider and stepped fully into the bathroom.

"Jeez, dude! If you have to take a piss, come in and do it. Just shut the damn door, will ya?"

Frankie made no move to shut the door. He took two steps closer to the edge of the tub, looked up at his big brother, and said simply, "I don't have to pee."

"Well then, get the hell out!" Charlie screeched, but to no avail.

The boy took one step closer as his brother fought to get the towel wrapped properly around his waist.

"I'm playing," Frankie explained, as though this used-to-be-boy before him might just be the dumbest human being on the planet.

The tone rankled Charlie more than the intrusion ever could. It was one thing for a kid brother to want to check out what the future had in store for him pecker-wise, but it was quite another for him to not do precisely what his big brother told him to.

"Frankie, you have exactly one second to get the fuck out

of here. One second after that, I will beat you into the ground like a railroad spike. "

Frankie didn't move. He stood there on the far side of a knee-high wall of porcelain with his hands tucked behind his back, and tilted his head to the side as if he was seeing his older brother for the very first time.

Charlie Sumner could put up with many things, but none of them would ever come from his peewee kid brother. He proclaimed, "One," as ominously as he could, then he gathered the towel around his waist and stepped from the tub.

He could never have expected what came next. Even as his kid brother brought a knife out from behind his back, he refused to believe it. This was a scene from a slasher movie, not real life. And yet, there was his ten-year-old brother, holding their mother's prized Henkel butcher knife like a pint-sized Michael Meyers.

"*Jeez*, dude," he hushed, watching how the cold metal glinted in the light. "If Mom or Dad saw you with that, they would literally skin you alive. Go put that stupid thing back where you found it before you hurt yourself, dumbass!"

Frankie didn't move. He stood right where he was as Jarod Lowe and the Denton kids came around the corner to join him.

Charlie frantically tightened the towel around his waist, making sure that everything of value was tucked well away.

"*Jeez*! Alright, guys, this just made the jump from weird to borderline criminal. If that little girl so much as sees my junk, I'll go to jail. Frankie, what the fuck are you thinking? Get her out of here!"

None of them moved. Not a one.

"...We interrupt this program for a special new bulletin..."

the sexy girl on Fox blared up from down below. "Strange reports coming out of Moscow, now. This video comes from the city of Orsk, just north of the Kazakh border, and it purports to show members of the city police and Russian military shooting into a group of unarmed civilians, most of whom appear to be children. I say this again. They are shooting at children. Children!"

"Alright, fun's over, Frankie. Get the fuck out," Charlie said in a huff, but barely had the words left his mouth before the first strike came. It was Frankie, his own kid brother. The knife came down just above the towel line, and it went deep. Then it was Jarod Lowe's turn. But instead of a butcher knife, this bigger kid had a hunting knife, eight inches long and curved like a scimitar, and he didn't hesitate in driving that blade up into Charlie Sumner's exposed abdomen, right to the hilt. Charlie managed to grab the boy's hand before he could drag the blade across his belly and gut him like a fish, but then Lawrence Denton rushed in with the business end of a screwdriver, and it was all Charlie could do to deflect the blow from his chest to somewhere over his left armpit.

With a wild screech, he backhanded the Denton boy away in a tumble and drove his fist smack into the Lowe kid's solar plexus, dropping him to his knees, gasping for breath. Then he turned on his own brother, still holding the butcher knife and paying no attention whatsoever to the blood pooling at his feet. Charlie raised a hand that would drive his punk-ass brother clear into the ground like a railroad spike, but then little Tabitha Denton rushed up and punched him on the side of the head.

But no, not just a punch. His head rang too much for it to be a punch from a little girl's fist. She'd had something in her hands. What was it? A knife? A screwdriver? No, too long for that. Something brass, with a kind of a hook at the end. Damn! He knew what it was. It was a fireplace poker. But not from here. This house had no fireplace. She'd brought it from home, then. She had brought a fireplace poker all the way from home in order to cave in the side of his head.

Bleeding from three separate wounds and his head ringing like a bell from a fourth, Charlie Sumner's entire world was now all about survival. Gone was the notion that these children were children. Gone was even his recognition of one of those children as his own brother. From that point on, it was a rush of pure adrenalin that guided him. In one swift motion, he hammered the butcher knife out of Frankie's hand and punched Jarod Lowe hard enough to send him reeling, then he sent little Tabitha Denton flying into the far wall with the back of his hand. But just as he ran for the open door, a sharp sting caught him in the back of the head, and everything turned a surreal shade of red.

He collapsed to the floor, and at last his towel betrayed him. And as he lay there completely exposed and fighting for consciousness, he was afforded one last image to carry with him all the way to the end of time.

Little Frankie stood over him, grinning from ear to ear. It was his Christmas morning smile. The smile he reserved for only the brightest of occasions. And what was that in his hand? The knife again? No, he had swatted that bloody thing away. So what, then?

The boy raised both of his hands above his head, and Charlie could finally see what he was holding. It was from his dad's tool box downstairs. He had wielded it himself not one summer ago when he'd helped his old man nail down some loose roof tiles. It was his dad's hammer, and it was already red with blood. But not his. The hammer hadn't touched him yet, and there was just so damn much red.

"Mom?" he managed, but it came out as little more than a squeak, "Dad?"

"You should have played with us," Frankie Sumner said in a pout, then the hammer came down and another scream was cut suddenly short.

CHAPTER

XXXV

G aa... Fe... erl... ign... sa..."

Cooper keyed the mike. "10-9?"

"...sai... wen... boa... pen..."

"Say again, Grace? You're breaking up."

After that last cryptic jumble of sounds, the only thing that came back was silence.

"Grace? Grace?"

In abject frustration, Cooper slammed the radio mike against the dashboard again and again and again, coming up with more inventive and ridiculous curses with every beat of the drum.

"*Fuck* this goddam son of a motherfucking, douche-sucking piece of *ass-fuck!*"

On the tenth blow, the microphone came apart, raining bits of plastic and metal across the floor.

He bowed his head briefly at his passenger and offered a muttered, "Sorry about that."

"Yes," Emma replied, deadpan. "You offend me greatly. As a school teacher, I am unaccustomed to hearing harsh language."

Cooper's scowl deepened, but absolutely none of it had to do with Emma Wong.

She had refused to come. Doc. Kira. She had steadfastly refused to come. And when he told her that he would stay right where he was and keep her safe, she refused that, too.

It was as she'd come down from the pediatric ward after making sure that Denny and Cecie were both settled in, comfortable, hooked into every monitor possible, and most assuredly tied to their bed rails that the landlines died. Then had come the argument, the rebuttal, the anguished tears, and Kira's final decision.

"I'll take care of these people, Tom," she'd said through a warm kiss on his lips. "You take care of everyone else."

"And how do you propose I do that? I can't exactly tie every kid in town to their beds."

"I have no idea, Tom. But even if you can corral and hogtie a few of them, that's got to mean something. I've sedated Denny and Cecie, so they'll sleep through the night, and that's good enough for me. At least for now. We'll deal with tomorrow, tomorrow. Let's just hope this is a temporary thing. Like a twenty-four-hour flu bug from Hell."

"Hope? That's all you got?"

"Sometimes hope is all any of us *ever* have, Tom," she'd said, and kissed him again.

And that was it. As much as his heart ached at leaving her there, she was right. He had to go. He had to go and try to save his godforsaken town. And she was right about the other thing, too. She had to stay. She had to stay and try to keep her people safe. And she would, too. She would do exactly that. She would try. Her heart was just too big to let her abandon her friends, her comrades, and her patients. All he could do was hope that that big caring heart of hers wouldn't be the death of Doctor Kira Melanson.

He turned onto Main Street, but this was no longer a Main Street he knew in the slightest. On any other night, there would be people and cars everywhere, especially on a warm summer Saturday night. On a warm summer Saturday night, he would be seeing teenagers out for a cruise, and elderly couples strolling along, arm in arm. He'd see families and friends heading to the Bijou or the Big Strike Bowling Alley, and others still, popping around to any one of a dozen restaurants, bars and pizza joints in the neighborhood. But not tonight. On this particular warm summer Saturday night, there was no one.

No one, that is, but children.

Everywhere he looked, endless bunches of children were running to and fro, laughing, squealing, playing. They tore through the streets, down alleyways, and across carparks in wild confusion. They gamboled about from one street to another, from one yard to another, and from one house to another, and as he watched them dash to and fro through the dirty glass of the Sheriff's cruiser, Emma Wong posed the question he couldn't even find words enough to ask himself.

"Did they ask you to play a game?" she spoke aloud as they cruised past block after block of houses sitting strangely dark and quiet on this warm summer Saturday night. "How many of you let them in, and how many of you barred the doors, turned off the lights, and hunkered down in the deepest, darkest corner of the basement? Jesus Christ, how many of you played the game the *right* way?"

And still, Cooper couldn't quite make himself believe it. At least, not entirely. Even with two of the sharpest minds he had ever known now on his side of insanity, a crystal clear image of both Cecie Tyler and Denny Hutchison ready, willing and able to carve the lives out of two women who had shown them nothing but love, and many of the children they now passed by stopping their play to stand and watch the cruiser rumble by with blank, expressionless masks in place of their normal, bubbling faces, he still wasn't quite able to choke down those last few bitter drops of Kool-Aid.

He knew these kids. He knew most by name, and the rest of them by sight. He had spoken at their schools. He had dropped a few coins in the can whenever any of them were out for a fundraiser. He had been to their homes for dinner, and drinks, and backyard barbecues. He had bought cookies from every Girl Guide, and apples from every Boy Scout among them. He knew their parents. He knew their teachers. He knew their doctors and he knew their neighbors. He knew them all, just like he knew everyone else in Keeter's Bluff. He knew them precisely because this *was* Keeter's Bluff.

He wheeled north onto Taylor and slowed to a crawl to maneuver the cruiser around Harlan Abrams' tow truck abandoned in the middle of the road. As he passed, he noted the driver's door open, dark splotches staining the pavement below, and smaller splotches blazing a spotty trail all the way to the mouth of the alley, half a block up.

As he neared the alley at a crawl, Tommy Doogan and the Jepson twins came bursting out, laughing and squealing with delight. The laughter stopped as they turned the cruiser's way, then they just stood there and watched the car go by with their horrible, expressionless eyes. As soon as the cruiser was past, the laughter picked up precisely where it left off, and the boys all went racing off across the road.

"*Jesus...*" Emma hushed for both of them.

Cooper took a moment to flick the master door lock, then he drove on.

Harrow Street was still a few blocks away when they came across the first of them. A big man in a suit was lying face down in the gutter. Beside him, a buxom woman in a low-cut dress and spiked heels lay sprawled across the sidewalk. Carl and Sonya Radcliffe. Between the two of them, they'd earned commissions on just about every sale of every property in town for the past ten years. Just beyond them, a dozen or more children were happily chasing each other around and around in circles and having the time of their lives. The boys were dressed in their Sunday best. The girls were all frilly and lacy in their little princess dresses. All of them wore the spatters of someone else's blood.

He drove on.

A quick cut up Fleming, a left on Harrow, and they were there. Cooper slowed the car to a stop, and they both looked out at a brightly lit Elk's Hall behind a parking lot full of cars. And while Emma cursed to high heaven, Cooper felt his heart sink into his belly.

There should have been music, but there was none. There should have been someone on a loudspeaker, raising a toast to the bride or the groom or God Almighty or sweet Aunt Fanny, but there was none of that either. Two hours into it, there should even have been little clusters of guests hanging out in the parking lot, sneaking a smoke or trying not to puke on their shoes, but the only people he could see in the parking lot were children.

"Mother of Christ..." Emma hushed, again for both of them.

There'll be lots of kids there. That's what Doyle Brannigan had said. And indeed, there must have been. Besides the plus-threes, plus-fours and plus-whatevers, there would have been others brought along for lack of babysitters. Cooper had no idea what that number might have been, but he counted over a dozen in the parking lot alone. Over a dozen children, running and laughing and carrying on as if this was their own personal playground. But one close look at the children themselves was enough to turn that ersatz playground into a circle of Hell unimaginable by even Dante himself.

There was Daryl Brannigan in his tight little suit and tie, running circles around his kid sister Maggie as she giggled and squealed and bubbled over with glee. Maggie's puffy green dress was painted crimson all down the front. Daryl's tight little suit pants were soaked through at the cuffs as if he'd been wading through a river of blood. And in each of their hands was a knife. A steak knife, snatched from any one of a hundred tables in an overcrowded reception hall.

And there were bodies there, too. Too many to count, both in the parking lot itself and scattered in either direction along Harrow Street. Some showed multiple wounds, some showed a few, and some showed none, but he could tell at a glance that every last one of them was dead. Some of the guests had made it to their cars before the shit hit the fan, as evidenced by several twin tracks of rubber left behind by the desperate, but the parking lot was still nearly full, so clearly, most hadn't. These others had left their cars where they were and fled on foot, but the old or portly or drunk didn't stand much of a chance. One daring soul had even tried to escape by climbing the big Elm tree across the way, but they had either followed him up or had kept him trapped up there until he bled out. Either way, Doc Jenkins was now hanging from a branch halfway up the tree like an oversized rag doll, his dead, unblinking eyes reflecting the terror of his last moments on Earth.

"Should we...?" Emma started to say, but Cooper quickly shut her down.

"No point," he huffed, watching his best friend's children laugh and run and play through the minefield of scattered corpses as if they were the funniest things they'd ever seen.

Cooper tried to imagine what must have gone inside that brightly lit hall, but it was impossible. Five hundred guests, all packed together like sardines, and most of them half-corked, thanks to a free bar. Had it begun with a single child, he wondered, or had they all acted at once? After some consideration, he reckoned that it had to have been the latter, otherwise more of the cars would have been gone. After all, nothing breaks up a party faster than little Suzy plunging a steak knife into dear Mommy's throat.

Yes, it had to be the latter. All of those countless children had chosen the exact same moment to act, and what followed had been a slaughter. But had they planned it? *Could* they have? Was it possible that all of those children had gotten together to map out the wholesale murder of their own parents? It didn't seem likely. After all, these kids were from all over town. They didn't know each other, they didn't go to the same schools, and they sure as hell didn't hang out at the same 7-11s. Was it a social media thing, then? But again, he couldn't see how. Even if they had all texted and Tweeted and Facebooked their asses off, getting a bunch of kids to agree on anything at *all* was like trying to herd cats.

And so, unable to wrap his mind around the unwrappable, he turned his cop's mind to knowing the knowable.

Doyle Brannigan was dead. Mary-Ellen, too. There was simply no way on Earth that either one of them would have abandoned their kids, no matter the cost. But had there been survivors among the guests? Yes, there had to have been. Some well-meaning folks would have tried to restrain those first few kids, and as things quickly spiraled out of control, others would have fought, and others would have run. And some of those who ran would have made it. Which told him something else.

This carnage was a recent thing. The phones had been out for less than an hour, and there was simply no scenario Cooper could conjure up in his mind's eye that would account for not a single partygoer thinking to call 9-1-1.

He drove on. Carefully.

Four minutes later, the cruiser pulled back into the station's parking lot. Aside from Grace's Buick and Kelly Andruchuk's Challenger waiting for impound, there were now two other vehicles angled close to the building. He was glad to see that one of them was Carl Rankin's cruiser. The other was Jermaine Granger's old wreck of a Honda, currently parked at the business end of a river of spilled coolant.

Cooper keyed off the ignition, and he and Emma both sat there, looking out at State Street and imagining how much worse it could get. Two seconds later, they had their first inkling. The streetlights above flickered once, twice, and then they went out.

This time, for good.

But it wasn't all darkness. Not completely. In the distance, Cooper could just make out a pair of headlights weaving drunkenly from lane to lane as they crawled down State Street toward the station. The lights grew larger and brighter as they approached, and at last there could be no doubt as to whose car it was.

Cooper launched himself into the street and met Henry Greenleaf's cruiser as it beached itself on the median, half a block away. He wrenched the door open, and he and Emma together caught the falling man before he hit the ground.

"Henry?" Cooper howled, "Henry?"

It was he, but it wouldn't be for much longer. The man's uniform ran red from the collar of his shirt all the way down to the hem of his pants. Cooper counted eighteen holes in the deputy's body before he gave up. But Henry Greenleaf was a man like no other. As damaged and destroyed as that massive body was, the faithful man inside still groped frantically at Cooper, desperate to say what needed to be said.

Sadly, he didn't get the chance. Before a single word came out, the man died in one last convulsive fit, and Cooper held him until he was well and truly gone. He held him like a child. He held him like a friend. He held him like the beloved man he had become, and he held him until he was no more. But still, Cooper understood the message his faithful deputy hadn't lived long enough to deliver.

"No man or group of men could ever have gotten close enough to Henry Greenleaf to do this," he said aloud, whether for Emma's benefit or his own. "No way, no how. If he'd faced off against a hundred armed men, there could have been only one of two possible outcomes. Either Henry Greenleaf would leave them all in a pile and emerge unscathed, or there wouldn't be enough of him left to bury."

The rest needn't be said. Change those hundred armed men to a hundred children. Or fifty. Or a handful. What then would this big powerful man with a heart of gold have done? What would *anyone* do? At what point did a man become desperate enough to take a child's life in order to save his own? And once he got to that point, would he really consider it a life worth saving anymore?

"Is he..." Emma asked, softly.

Cooper turned the car off, bade his friend one last silent goodbye as he laid him out across the seat, and eased the door shut again.

"Yes. So is Buck, or he'd be here too."

From somewhere in the darkness beyond came a chorus of children's laughter.

Inside the station, he found Carl Rankin and his pretty wife with her delightful overbite huddled around a battery-operated lantern. And he was glad to see Austin Granger there too, perched on the end of the bench, nursing a styrofoam cup of Grace's famously bad coffee. And there was Jermaine, just coming out of the back room with a flashlight in hand.

"Well, the good news is, I found the breakers and they're fine, so it's not just us, it's the whole town. The bad news is, I found the breakers and they're fine, so it's not just us, it's the whole town." She spotted Cooper in the shadows and stabbed her light at him. "Hey, Tom, shouldn't every police station have a generator? You know, in case of power outages or, I dunno, Arma-*fucking*-geddon?"

"It's on next year's budget," he answered her coolly, then he offered a hand to Granger. "Good to see you, Austin, but why aren't you in your Ratmobile?"

Granger shook his hand.

"Good to see you too, Coop. Hell, at this point, it's good to see anyone with a five o'clock shadow." Every female in the place harumphed as one, but Granger ignored it. "If you must know, my company vehicle is presently in a state of disrepair."

"Disrepair?"

Jermaine sold him out from across the room.

"He crashed it. Into a bus. A *parked* bus, I hasten to add."

"You didn't have to hasten," Granger informed her pointedly. Then, in his own defense, he told Cooper, "I was somewhat... preoccupied."

"It was just pure luck that I happened across him." Jermaine fixed her man in place with the flashlight. "Damn-near ran him over, actually."

"But you didn't, hon," Granger called back, shielding his eyes from the glare of the light with his styrofoam cup. "And once Hallmark comes up with a thank you card for not crushing one's beloved husband under one's wheels, you can expect a little something in the mail. If you're lucky, I might even throw in an Arby's gift card."

"Oh, I do like Arby's," came the wistful reply.

"You know your Honda's sprung a leak, right?" Cooper advised them both.

"Believe me, I am well aware." Jermaine sneered at her husband. "Plenty of life in that old gal yet, my anal sphincter."

While Granger did his best to hide behind his cup, Cooper shook hands with Deputy Rankin and gave his pretty wife a quick peck on the cheek.

"I'm glad you guys are here. Happy birthday, Mindy-Lou."

"See, I told'ja, Min!" Rankin hooted. "I told'ja it was a birthday party!"

But, as always, the smarter half of the Rankin clan was

already a few steps ahead. Mindy-Lou shone her adorable overbite up at Cooper and, as always, Cooper's heart skipped the tiniest of beats.

"It ain't, is it?"

Cooper shook his head.

"Nope."

"It's all the crazy shit, ain't it?"

"Yes, it's all the crazy shit."

"You were looking after your deputy."

Cooper shrugged.

"He wouldn't be much use to me if he was worried about you."

She took him by the hands, stretched up on the tips of her toes, and kissed him warmly on the cheek.

"That is one colossal pile of moose pucky, but thank you."

He felt his cheeks redden, and hoped no one would notice in the bad lighting.

Now came the hard part. He approached Grace Tolliver's desk, but rather than speak to her across that great expanse, he came around to the side and stood inches away from the woman. And though the words were sure to catch in his throat, he included Rankin in the conversation as he said aloud the last thing any of them would ever want to hear.

"Guys, it's Henry. And Buck. I'm afraid they're..."

That was as far as he got. Grace slammed a fist down on her desk and cursed like a sailor, and then she did what Cooper couldn't have imagined her doing in a million years. Grace *goddam* Tolliver dropped her face into her hands, and she cried.

"I knew it," she managed between the tears. "I knew it.

I God damn fucking *knew* it."

There was nothing Cooper could say, and nothing he could do. He thought about a pat on the back or a comforting arm around the shoulder, but he could only see either of those ending with him on his ass and Grace Tolliver nursing a set of bruised knuckles. So he did nothing. And he said nothing. But then Emma Wong threw herself into Grace, and that wonderful woman who had only known any of them for a few hours matched that *goddam* woman tear for tear.

"They were such good men," Grace poured into Emma's shoulder. "Both of them. They were fine, fine men."

"I know," Emma poured back. "They were your boys. Oh, Grace, I am so sorry."

As they hugged and clutched and wept, a decidedly misty-eyed Carl Rankin sidled up beside Cooper and hitched a thumb towards his office.

"By the way, Sheriff, you got company."

Cooper popped his head around the corner and squinted into the darkness. Sure enough, there was someone in his chair. Or some*thing,* at any rate. It was too small to be a person. Too still. Too inanimate. But just as he'd made up his mind that his deputy must be playing some kind of joke on him, his eyes adjusted enough that he could just make out the silhouette of a tiny human form among the shadows.

Jermaine swung in, aiming her flashlight directly at the thing, and now he could see it clearly.

It was a girl. Four years old. Five, at the outside. Cute, in a porcelain doll kind of way. Adorable little hair bob. Rosy cheeks. Big blue eyes. But when he looked closer, he saw that the cheeks weren't rosy at all. The red came from blood. Her nightie was red too, from what he could make out through the several layers of duct tape holding her securely to the chair.

"Tom Cooper, meet Maizie Pritchard," Jermaine huffed. "Little bitch tried to shoot me in the throat."

Cooper squinted into the semi-dark.

"Are those bungee cords?"

"I improvised," she replied, deadpan. "Sue me."

"Dean must have dug his old .32 out of the lock box in the closet after seeing the news on TV," Granger posited from the doorway. "Or maybe he had a more, shall we say *pressing* reason. But either way, it looks like dear little Maizie got her hands on it somehow."

"Happens all the time," Rankin said, sourly. "Kid finds a gun lyin' around and thinks it's a toy."

"It wasn't like that," Jermaine cut in, setting the record straight. "Little bitch knew exactly what she was doing. She killed both her parents, then she tried to kill me. "She gave Rankin and Cooper a quick glimpse of a .32 revolver before slipping it back in her pocket. "It must have been lying on the ground right beside her, but I didn't see it in the dark."

"Jermaine, that's evidence," Cooper reminded her, holding out his hand.

She left it right where it was.

"And when I'm sure I won't be needing it, you can have it. Or I suppose you could try to take it from me."

Rankin took a step toward her, but Cooper waved him off.

"It's not just Dean and Carol," Granger piped up from behind his coffee. "There are others, Coop. I've seen them. Out there. *Lots* of others."

"I know," Cooper said, and left it at that.

"And the children..." Granger started to add, but Cooper cut him off.

"I know," he repeated, and that was it.

Cooper looked to the tiny girl trussed up in his chair, and she smiled up at him. She actually *smiled* at him. From beneath all of those layers of duct tape and bungee cords, the girl beamed a smile as bright as all outdoors, sending Cooper's skin crawling across his back and bringing back the words he might have heard a lifetime ago.

Maybe it was in them all along...

He shook the words from his mind and propped himself on the desk, three full feet away from the adorable little girl with the big bright eyes and the cheeks spattered with her parents' blood.

"Maizie, I'm Sheriff Cooper," he told the girl as properly as could be, but she took little notice.

"Do you want to play a game with me?" she chirped, her smile only brightening. "It's *so* much fun! Will you play with me?"

"Not today," he told her, point blank.

"But it's such a *fun* game!" the girl squealed. "I want to play!"

As his skin crawled and the welts under his collar burned, Cooper focused on the girl's eyes. They were big, they were blue, and they were filled to the brim with excitement. But there was something else there, too. Just like with Cecie Taylor, for one second, just one single, solitary second, he thought he saw something dark pass behind those big, blue eyes.

"Tell me about your game, Maizie. Who taught you to play this... this *game*? What are the rules? What is the ultimate goal?"

She said nothing, but the smile remained.

"Maizie?" another voice spoke up from behind Cooper.

It was Emma Wong, wiping away the last of her tears with the back of her hand. She stepped around the Sheriff, dropped to a knee, and brushed an errant lock of hair from the girl's face. "Maizie, my name is Emma. I would *love* to know about your game. Is it really fun?"

The smile beamed as bright as ever. "Oh, it is! It is *so* much fun!"

Against Jermaine's rather vocal protests, Emma unclipped the bungee cords and tossed them aside. Then she set about peeling away most of the duct tape, leaving only enough around the girl's chest and wrists to keep her stuck to the chair like an insect in amber.

"Why is it fun, Maizie? What makes the game so much fun to play?"

The girl ignored the question as she bounced excitedly in her seat. "I want to play! Will you play with me?"

"But you're hurting people, Maizie. You hurt your mom and dad, and you tried to hurt Jermaine. How can hurting people be fun?"

The girl stopped bouncing and told her squarely, "Because it's a *game*, silly!"

It was Cooper's turn again, but this time he spoke to his tiny prisoner as gently as he could. Almost as gently as if he'd never known that this sweet little girl had just butchered her own parents.

"Who was it that taught you the game, Maizie?"

"Dunno," she shrugged. "No one, I guess."

"But it's a *new* game. How could you know how to play a brand new game unless someone showed you?"

There came back only silence.

"She doesn't understand," Mindy-Lou threw in her two cents from the doorway. "She has no idea why she plays the game, and she doesn't realize that people are getting killed."

"Or she doesn't care." Austin Granger snuck in beside her. "Classic psychopathy. Some people are just bad seeds, born with a complete and total lack of empathy."

"Every kid in town?" Cooper scoffed.

"Not just in town," Emma reminded him, grimly.

"That's a whole lot of bad seeds," Grace said from the back row, her tears gone for good and the perma-scowl back in place where it belonged. "No wonder the garden's gone to shit."

Cooper searched little Maizie's eyes for anything out of the ordinary, but with the dark shadow gone, Maizie Pritchard appeared to be nothing more than what she was. A child. A sweet, innocent, fresh-faced child. But she was really only one of those things. The sweetness and innocence had been blown to bits with a couple of pulls of a trigger, and the face was stained with the blood of others. Now, all that remained was the child. A child that desperately wanted to play her brand new game.

"So what do we do with her?" he asked no one and everyone. "What we do with *all* of them?"

Just then, a shadow loomed up behind Grace and a new voice entered the debate.

"I say we blow them all to Hell and let God decide."

CHAPTER

XXXVI

E very head turned to see Deputy Santino Garcia, bloodied, battered, and looking every inch ready to act on his threat.

"Sonny!" Grace howled, spinning on her heels and throwing her big arms around the man, but he barely even noticed.

"Henry's dead, Grace," he told her flat out.

"I know," came the solemn reply. "Buck, too."

He accepted the news with a grunt. "And so are a whole lot of others. Dozens. Hundreds. Thousands! *Fuck*, who knows?"

"And your solution to all of that death and destruction is *more* death and destruction?" This, from an incredulous Emma Wong. "I'm sorry, but are you seriously suggesting the wholesale murder of every child in Keeter's Bluff?"

Garcia narrowed his eyes at little Maizie Pritchard and growled, "Why the fuck not?"

"Yes. Why the fuck not, indeed. But why stop there, Deputy Dawg? There's a whole *world* of children out there. Let's gun the whole damn *lot* of 'em down."

"Sounds like a plan," Jermaine hushed, not quite under her breath.

"You'll have to excuse my darling wife," Granger spoke to the group as a whole. "She's not exactly big on children. But in her defense, there was never a time when she *didn't* want to murder them all, so..."

"Not all," she corrected him. "Just most."

"Beg pardon, hon."

"S'alright, babe."

Garcia aimed an accusing finger at Emma. "You were the girl on the phone. Wong, wasn't it?"

"Still is," she said through a scowl.

"Well, Miss Wong, I hate to break it to you, but we are at war. And I, for one, do not intend to go down without a fight."

"Fighting children," she snorted. "How manly."

Garcia took a threatening step closer, but Emma held her ground.

"And what would *you* do? Give them a time out? Sing 'Soft Kitty' while you tuck them into their little beds? I'm telling you, Miss Wong, this enemy will not be placated with lollipops and sugar cookies."

The man's tone was rankling, but Emma Wong was clearly made of sterner stuff. She nodded, stepped back, and made a grand gesture toward the tiny girl still beaming a bright, sunny smile from way down in Cooper's chair.

"Alright then, let's do it your way. This child brutally murdered her parents, Deputy Garcia. She shot them both to death, and then she tried to kill Jermaine. So have at it, tough guy. Wrap those big manly hands of yours around Maizie's throat and squeeze the life out of her. You don't even have to look her in the eyes. You can turn away and sing Nearer My God To Thee if that's what does it for you. Just come over here, grab that skinny little neck, and listen to it pop and crackle as you strangle this tiny child to death. I promise you, if anyone tries to interfere, I'll drop them like a rhino."

Garcia looked to Cooper, but Cooper merely shrugged.

"It's your call, Sonny. I won't raise a finger either way. Miss Wong is right, but so are you. There *is* a war going on, and I don't have the vaguest idea how to fight it. So if you want to take the initiative and eliminate an enemy combatant who has already killed twice and wouldn't hesitate to murder every single one of us where we stand... Well, hell, go for it, brother! If you like, we'll even leave the room so you two can be alone."

Rankin gave him a look of incredulity, but Cooper held his ground. And, in fact, he had meant every word of it. If Garcia wanted to throttle the life out of little Maizie Prichard, he would not only allow it, he would actually facilitate the execution. But Cooper knew the kind of man Sonny Garcia was, and when the deputy hesitated, looking from one anxious face in the crowd to another, he knew it was over. Garcia managed to take one more half-step closer, then his eyes fell squarely on Maizie and he deflated like a balloon.

Just then, a gale of laughter from outside drew every eye to the corner window. Beyond the glass, a group of girls came dancing gaily into view down the middle of State Street. Tracy Coggins. The Denton girl. The Chadwick sisters. Amber Gleason. A couple of others Cooper knew only by sight. The girls chased each other around and around until a *whoop!* from one of the others galloping through the darkness drew them away, and then they were gone. But not before everyone in the Sheriff's Station had the chance to see what they were carrying. Just like the kids outside the Elk's Hall, every last one of them was armed. Some had knives. One had a crowbar. Another had a screwdriver. Two others had tire irons. Little Amber Gleason, the darling of Jesper Street, was brandishing a machete.

Through the chorus of horrified gasps, Cooper announced, "Okay, then. There's no more room for doubt. All that *other* crazy shit has turned into *this* crazy shit."

"I saw some stuff on TV," Mindy-Lou offered, meekly. "I think it was Russia. They were shooting at kids. China, too, I think."

"Stinkin' commies..." Rankin growled, but Emma quickly set him straight.

"They're on the other side of the world," she told him, grimly. "Maybe they're just farther into it than we are."

"Yeah? Well, maybe it's time we did some catching up, huh?" Garcia harumphed.

To this, Grace responded as only Grace could. She looked the man warmly in the eyes, even offered him a glimmer of a smile, and saying nothing, she brought up a hand and cuffed him sharply on the side of the head.

"Okay," Cooper started over. "Short of murdering every child in Keeter's Bluff..."

"Not just Keeter's Bluff," Emma reminded him.

"Alright, then," he snarled. "Short of murdering every child on the entire *planet*, does anyone have any actual suggestions?"

"Stun guns?" Grace suggested.

"Not nearly enough. Next?"

"The Staties have those riot guns that fire beans bags,"

Rankin suggested.

"Bean bags?" Emma scoffed. "On *children?* You might as well just put a bullet in their heads."

"Again, sounds like a plan," Jermaine chimed in, eliciting a gentle scowl from her man.

"It's a moot point anyway, seeing as we have no way to contact anyone outside the 'Bluff," Grace grumbled. "Besides, I'm sure the Staties have problems enough of their own."

"Okay, what else?" Cooper pointed to each of them in turn. "Austin?"

"Uhh... tranquilizer darts?"

"Do you have those?"

"Yup! Sure do! Uhh... in the truck."

"Next. Jermaine?"

"How about a restraining pole? You know, the pole Austin and I would never use for even the angriest of dogs? The thing with a loop of rope at the end? A restraining pole probably wouldn't be lethal to a kid. *Probably.*"

"And you have one of those?" Cooper asked.

"Sure do!" she replied, then she, Cooper and Austin all finished the statement as one.

"...In the truck."

"We'd need hundreds of them anyway," Cooper huffed. "Alright then. Miss Wong, your turn."

Instead of answering Cooper directly, Emma Wong dropped back to her knee and laid a gentle hand atop Maizie's, still duct taped securely to the chair.

"Maizie, can I ask you something? Do you love your mom and dad?"

The girl said nothing. She simply beamed the same happy smile.

"How do you feel right now, Maizie? Are you happy? Sad? Angry?"

Nothing came back. Just the smile.

"Are you hungry, Maizie? Thirsty? Can I get you a glass of water, or a Coke or something? How about a hamburger, a side of fries, and a chocolate milkshake? Would you like that, Maizie?"

Again, nothing. But then came the million-dollar question.

"Maizie, what if I were to let you go right now?"

The girl jumped up and down as much as the restraints allowed and squealed an excited, "You're going to play with me? Yay! It's such a *fun* game!"

Emma patted the girl's hand and looked back to Cooper.

"All she knows is the game," she told him, plainly. "She wasn't afraid when I instructed your deputy to throttle the life out of her, and she hasn't complained once about being abducted, bound, and taped to a horribly uncomfortable chair. She doesn't know thirst, she doesn't know hunger, and she has no idea that she's done anything wrong. I seriously doubt that she understands a single iota of what's going on any more than we do. All she knows is that she wants to play. She wants to play the game."

"You mean she wants to kill," Cooper corrected her. Wrongly, as it turned out.

"No. She just wants to play the game."

"Sounds like *we're* the game," Garcia snorted.

"Be that as it may, all this little girl knows is that she wants to play. And if it's true for her, it's probably true for all of them. They aren't killing, at least not from their perspective. They're just playing a game."

"Miss Wong," Deputy Rankin stepped in, "When we

catch one of the yokels driving home drunk, all he's doin' is goin' home. If we pull him over, he gets a DUI. If he runs a stop sign, maybe he gets a ticket *and* a DUI. But if he runs a stop sign and takes out a school bus, he goes to jail. No ifs, no butts, no coconuts. Same offence, very different penalties. And why? Because that dumb bastard heading home with a snootful just caused a loss of life, and every life is precious, Miss Wong."

Her point made for her, Emma simply looked from one deputy to the other and said, "Yes. Yes, it is."

Cooper accepted the stalemate with a sigh.

"Alright then, what do you suggest, Miss Wong?"

"Oh, I don't have a clue!" she admitted freely. "But I do know that this won't be stopped with tranquilizer darts or lassos or bean bags. This isn't just about Keeter's Bluff, Sheriff. This is the world. This is *Gaia*."

Grace looked to the heavens. "Oh, not this shit again."

"Wait, what?" Jermaine suddenly perked up. "*What* shit? Gaia? What's a Gaia?"

Cooper explained it to her and to everyone else in his own way.

"Miss Wong has a theory..." he began, but when Emma raised a hand in protest, he corrected himself. "Beg pardon. *Actual* scientists have a theory, to which Miss Wong may or may not adhere. The theory goes that the planet Earth is a living organism, and we humans are akin to a virus. As long as we lie dormant, Gaia abides us. But if we cause so much as a sneeze, Gaia shrugs."

"Well, there's a *little* more to it than that," Emma harumphed.

"New age, hippie-dippy bullshit," Grace grumbled aloud.

"Oh, I don't know," Mindy-Lou piped up. "It makes a certain kind of sense, doesn't it?"

"A living Earth?" Garcia scoffed. "So, what, the old gal woke up on the wrong side of the cosmos this morning and decided on a whim to turn every child into a psychotic killer?"

"No, no, you're looking at it the wrong way," Granger piped up. "I've heard the theory too, and it doesn't suggest that the Earth is a living, conscious entity, just that it is a highly complex ecological system of checks and balances. The system has maintained itself for billions of years, through ice ages, global warming, asteroid strikes, solar radiation... There was even a time referred to as 'Snowball Earth', when the entire planet was covered in ice. And yet, life flourished."

"Then, along came man," Emma chimed in, grimly. "At first, we were just another animal eking out our place in the world, but the time eventually came when we began to *change* the world. We planted crops. We dug metal from the ground. We cut down forests and filled the air with smoke. We helped ourselves to Gaia's bounty without a thought for any one of those checks and balances. And still, for thousands upon thousands of years, Gaia abided."

"We all knew it was a matter of time." This, from Granger again. "I mean, we had to, right? In a single century, we've sucked all the oil from the ground, used every bit of it to pollute the air, and went from inventing plastics to dumping enough of it in our oceans to kill off entire ecosystems. And in all that time, all anyone has ever done is wring their hands and say that something ought to be done."

"We used to be a part of this world," Emma summed it up for all of them. "Now, we're an infection. It took seven billion of us to do it, but we finally did what no other animal could ever have done. We gave the Earth a fever."

Cooper listened to it all without a word, but now he simply had to ask, "And you believe this nonsense too, Austin?"

"Checks and balances, Coop. That's what nature is. Every bit of nature is all about checks and balances."

"When I was a kid in Sunday School, the idea of being wiped out by forty days and forty nights of rain scared the hell out of me. Now, I believe I'd take that in a heartbeat."

"Careful what you wish for, Coop. Who says that's not coming next?" Granger replied, ominously.

"First, she sent the wild animals of the Earth," Emma said to no one in particular. "Bees. Rats. Snagglepuss..."

Cooper spared a thought to old Jedediah Smithers and tacked on a silent, *Bears.....*

"...but it backfired. There were just too many of us, and we are just too damn good at killing. So, she upped the ante. She turned our own four-legged friends against us. Dogs. Cats. Horses. And when *that* didn't work, she upped the ante again. She sent in troops we wouldn't be able to gun down quite so efficiently. This time, she sent the children."

In a world turned upside down, even the insane could be considered reasonable, but Cooper knew that something in what she'd said was wrong. Rankin knew it too, and so did Garcia. He could see it in their faces. No doubt Emma would have figured it out too, given a little more time.

In fact, that was exactly the sticking point. Time.

"Jake the snake Peluso was killed last night," he said, plainly. "And not by bees or dogs or rats."

"Meaning?" This, from Mindy-Lou Rankin.

"Meaning," Grace *goddam* Tolliver spoke up for the sheriff,

"If this Gaia bullshit is true, she didn't just up the ante. If this new age hippie-dippy bullshit is actually real, then that heartless, nasty-ass bitch was all in from the deal."

CHAPTER

XXXVII

A sudden explosion shook the building down to its foundations as a fireball lit up State Street. Everyone ran to the windows to see Deputy Greenleaf's cruiser burning brightly atop the median, half a block away. In the flickering light, Cooper could make out no fewer than a dozen children dancing and cavorting nearby, cheering on the flames as a column of black, acrid smoke reached for the sky.

"Shit. They've discovered fire," someone said, but it was worse than that. Cooper saw one of the dancing children point past the blaze to the Sheriff's Station, and a gunshot rang out as a hole erupted in the window, mere inches from his head.

Everyone dropped to the floor, but then Cooper dared to climb back to his knees and sneak a careful peek through the corner of the window.

"That was a 9 mil."

"Henry's holster was empty," Garcia told him. Needlessly, as it turned out.

"I know. But even if it's his, that one Glock would be a proverbial drop in the bucket. How many other guns are there in town, you think? Hundreds?"

"At least. Maybe thousands."

"Fucking bumpkins," Emma huffed aloud from under Grace's desk.

"Guns don't kill people, Miss Wong," Garcia reminded her in a growl.

"No," she answered back. "Apparently *children* kill people. And thank God you bumpkins were around to teach them all about guns."

"No, Miss Wong, Hollywood did that. All anyone here ever did was try to teach their children how to handle those guns responsibly."

"B'sides," Rankin called up from the floor. "It ain't exactly rocket science. You just point and shoot!"

"The problem is, all of those responsible gun owners will have seen the news all day, just like Dean Pritchard," Cooper grumbled to no one and to everyone. "Now, all of those guns that normally spend their lives locked safely away are out, fully loaded, and within easy reach. Hell, everyone's so keyed up, I'd be surprised if even one of those weapons still had the safety on."

"So where does it end?" This, from Grace, currently sharing the sanctuary under her desk with Emma.

Austin Granger took the floor, albeit just enough of it to let him keep huddling face down in the corner.

"The infrastructure's already breaking down. With no adults to run the show, the rest will follow. It's just a matter of time. "

Time. Just a matter of time...

The first faint glimmer of an idea skittered through Cooper's mind, but before he could even begin to consider it, another gunshot pierced the air, and he dropped back down to his belly. But this time, no window shattered. Then another shot rang out, and another, but there was still no damage. No new holes in the windows or the walls, or more importantly, *them*.

Cooper climbed cautiously back to his knees and peeked through the corner of the window, followed immediately by Garcia and Rankin, spread out along the front.

"It's not the kids shooting," Garcia said.

"No, it ain't," Rankin agreed.

They were right. It wasn't the kids doing the shooting. With the fire finally grown hot enough to cook off the rounds in Henry Greenleaf's mag pouch, the gunshots were coming from *inside* the burning cruiser. But even as that remarkable man made his last stand from the far side of forever, the children dancing around the car only whooped and hollered more. Then, at last, the fire reached the shotgun in the trunk, and a series of almighty booms crescendoed with one last thunderous *bawumph!* as the gas tank erupted.

The back end of the cruiser leapt into the air and came crashing back down in a ball of flames. Three of the children were thrown through the air by the shock wave, and several more suffered burns and lacerations, yet they all carried on in their wild revelry. They picked themselves up, they ignored all of the cuts and singed hair and bleeding eardrums, and they whooped, they hollered, they laughed, and they danced as if this was the most exciting show in the world. He could even hear little Maizie Pritchard back in his office, bouncing up and down in his back-breaking relic of a chair, laughing to beat the band.

When the last of the fuel was spent, the fire began to die down and darkness swallowed the children back up again, one by one by one. The boy with the pistol was the last to vanish. The last Cooper saw of him, he had stopped all play and was standing stock-still at the very edge of the waning circle of light, looking straight across at the man he couldn't possibly have seen behind the glass. He fired the pistol one last time, punching another ragged hole through the window, then the light was gone, and so was he.

But none of them went far. Or maybe they did, and others had come to take their place. There was just no way of knowing. All Cooper knew in the world was that death was waiting out there in the inky black. It came on a thousand tiny feet and in a thousand bright, shiny faces. It came quietly, and it came with giggles and hoots and the merriest of laughter. It came by knife, by gun, and by fire, and it came by whatever else the mind of a child might dream up in this world of nightmares. All Cooper knew was that when it came, it came as surely as it would have had there been an adult's hand wielding the weapon.

He thought back to the hospital, and to Harlan Abrams' tow truck sitting in the road, and to the too-quiet Elk's Hall, and with that first faint glimmer of an idea still bouncing around in his head, his agile mind began to connect the dots.

"Sonny," he said, one eye glued to the window and a hand on his pistol. "Break out the flashlights, and draw weapons for everybody."

He expected a round of protests, but there were none. Suddenly, it seemed, they were all on the same page. The same awful page of the same damnable book.

There were guns enough for all. Jermaine selected a

shotgun, and stuffed her pockets with shells. Austin Granger opted for a Glock and one of the spare duty belts. Cooper himself showed him how to adjust the fit, and made sure he had a few extra magazines tucked away. At first, Emma declined a firearm, saying that the stun gun was more than enough, thank you very much. She even added a rather empathic, "I forgo the use of a firearm, Sheriff," but Cooper wouldn't have it. He loaded a pistol, showed her how it worked, and held it out, butt-first.

"No!" she declared, holding up her hands, "It's forgone! I forwent it!"

He screwed up his face.

"Forwent? Look, just take the damn thing," he demanded. Then he quite literally shoved the pistol at her until she had no choice but to relent.

"I won't use it," she advised him, even as she stuck the thing away in her jacket, opposite the stun gun.

"I know. You forwent it. But better to have it and not use it than to need it and not have it."

Grace Tolliver shoulder-checked Garcia away from the gun locker and selected her own weapon. It was the station's one and only Colt AR-15. Lightweight. Magazine fed. Gas operated. It was the semi-automatic version of the US military's AR-16, strong enough to be run over by a truck and still be able to shoot through a brick wall.

"You sure, Grace?" Garcia cautioned her. "That's a whole lotta gun you got there. Wouldn't you rather have something a little easier to handle?"

"Fuckin' kids," the woman scoffed, snapping in a magazine and chambering a round like a pro. "You think this is my first rodeo, Sonny-Boy?"

"Reckon not," he replied with a grin, and let her be.

"So that's it?" Emma fixed Cooper with a glare. "We're back to blowing them all to Hell and letting God decide?"

"That's not my intention, but such things are not up to me," Cooper told her squarely, then he announced to the group as a whole, "According to United States law, any person may use deadly force if they reasonably believe that the subject poses a significant threat of serious bodily injury or death to themselves or others. That said, with the world apparently on its way to Hell in a handcart, the word *reasonably* is open to a massive amount of interpretation. I will not stand here and tell you what you can and cannot do. All I will say is that it is up to each and every one of you to act according to your own conscience."

The silence that followed may not have been stunned, but it was most certainly shaken. Emma broke it with a hand raised in the air.

"Umm... shouldn't those of us who haven't already been deputized... you know... *be?*"

"Sure," Cooper said, obligingly. "Consider yourself deputized."

"Cool! Do I get a badge?"

Cooper unpinned his own star and handed it to her.

"There you go. Congratulations, Sheriff Wong."

She wasted no time in pinning it to her jacket.

"Awesome! Does the job come with a good pension plan?"

"No, but there's a police discount at Jeeter's."

He turned to Austin and Jermaine with an apologetic," Sorry, I only have the one," but Austin waved it away as he stuffed one more loaded magazine in his hip pocket.

"Badges? We don't need no stinking badges."

Cooper nodded and pretended not to see Jermaine roll

her eyes.

"That look on your face tells me you have a plan, Sheriff," Grace said from behind her desk, the AR-15 laying atop the blotter with its business end pointed toward the door. "If so, I'd sure like to hear it."

In fact, it wasn't a plan at all. It was a collection of dots, nothing more. But still, he laid it out for them as best he could,

"Humans are social animals," he said, checking his own Glock and slipping a few extra mags into his pockets. "It's hard-wired into us, just like most other animals in the world. Safety in numbers, and all that. We like to think we're fine on our own, but when push comes to shove, we'll always look for company." He waved a hand around the room to take in every one of them. "Case in point. And no one is more social than a child. They want to be included. They want to be part of a group. Even now, with whatever they've been turned into, when Henry's car was burning, every kid in the area joined in on the fun." He hooked a thumb into his office, adding, "Even little Maizie there."

"Sure. Makes sense." This, from Austin Granger. "But I don't see how that helps unless you *want* to get a bunch of the little hellions together."

"That's *exactly* what I want," Cooper said, and then he told them the rest.

When he was done, silence descended again. And this time, it was most certainly stunned. Stunned, disbelieving, and fully prepared to call the men in the white coats to come and take Sheriff Tom Cooper away. But then a few of the others started tossing in the odd tweak or question or tarnished pearl of dubious wisdom, and the dots actually began to coalesce into something vaguely resembling an actual plan.

"It'd have to be big," Mindy-Lou offered. "Like, *seriously* big."

"I know just the place," Cooper assured her.

"Do we even know how much it would take?" Emma asked.

"We'd have to take the environment into consideration," Austin shrugged. "Wind, terrain, and whatnot."

"It's the whatnots that concern me," Emma admitted.

"We'll have no way to communicate," Garcia reminded Cooper. "Once we leave this building, it's every man for himself."

Four coughs made in unison had him quickly amending his statement.

"Beg pardon," he autocorrected. "It's every man and *woman* for himself. Uhh... and *her*self."

"Better," Jermaine said.

"Barely," Grace huffed.

"How long will it take?" This, from Mindy-Lou.

"No idea."

"How long will it last?" Rankin asked.

To that, Cooper only shrugged.

"You sure he's got it?" This, from Austin.

Cooper narrowed his eyes. "Define *sure*."

"Sure. Certain. As in, you have direct, first-hand knowledge that such is the case, or at least have reasonable grounds to believe it to be so."

Again, Cooper equivocated.

"Define *reasonable*."

Granger threw up his hands.

"Oh, we are *so* gonna die."

"Look. This is a shot in the dark, but I have nothing

else," Cooper admitted. "If anyone has any other ideas, *please* speak now. Anyone? Anything? Anything at all?"

This time, the silence wasn't just stunned, it lay across the room like a dead, rotting mackerel.

"Alright then," he concluded with a nod. "Let's give it a go."

The bright blue Ponies rode high on Emma's brow.

"Seriously? That's your rallying cry? 'Alright then, let's give it a go'?"

"You never coached football, did'ja Sheriff?" Garcia asked, deadpan.

"What about Maizie?" Mindy-Lou had to ask.

"She'll be safer in here than out there. If this works, we'll be back soon enough. If not, then Keeter's Bluff dies and none of it matters. Anything else?"

Austin Granger stuck up his hand.

"Uh, since the Honda appears to be down for the count, I was wondering..."

Cooper unhooked the keys to Kelly Andruchuk's Challenger from behind the counter and tossed them to him.

"Try to avoid parked buses."

Jermaine snatched the keys out of the air.

"I will."

With that, the whole group filed up to the front door and waited for the cue.

Cooper took one last peek through the window, then he said, "Alright people, let's rock 'n' roll."

As one, Emma and Deputy Garcia rolled their eyes.

"He really sucks at that, doesn't he?" Emma said as the door flew open.

Garcia threw her a wink.

"Good thing there's a new Sheriff in town."

CHAPTER

XXXVIII

T he first part of the plan was as simple as it was dangerous. Grace piled into her big old Buick, Sonny Garcia took to his cruiser, Carl and Mindy-Lou Rankin jumped into his, the Granger's made a mad dash for the Challenger, and Cooper and Emma ran back to the Sheriff's car. None of them needed a reminder to make sure that their windows were up and their doors locked.

"Shouldn't I be driving now?" Emma mused, fiddling with the shiny new star on her lapel. But just then, a trio of boys came tearing through the parking lot, banging on the car's windows, wrenching on the door handles and ultimately roaring off into the night, and she recanted with a shaky, "Umm... Never mind."

Cooper flicked on his headlights and led the parade out of the parking lot. Once on the street, each vehicle went its own way as per instructions, and Cooper and Emma were alone again.

"Sheriff, do you really think this has any chance of working?"

"Honestly?"

"Honestly."

"No, I don't."

A pair of boys tore across the road in front of them, but Cooper kept his foot off the brakes and held his breath. Emma gave a frightened squeal as the big car missed both of them by mere inches, and as the boys stopped dead in their tracks and turned to watch them go by, she took note of what they were carrying. One had a hammer. The other, a knife as long as his forearm.

Cooper watched the boys recede in his rearview mirror, the glow from his tail lights turning them both an eerie shade of red.

"Honesty is overrated," Emma managed through gritted teeth. "From now on, feel free to lie your face off."

A larger group of kids appeared in the headlights up ahead, so Cooper took the next right to avoid the inevitable.

"Look, this isn't a fix," he said, inching the cruiser past a Black Top taxicab left abandoned in the middle of the road. The driver's door was open. A dark shape was slumped across a front seat awash with blood. "Even if it works, it will only buy us time. All we can do then is hope."

"Hope for what?"

"That you're right," he harumphed, "Or that you're wrong. That whatever's going on has its limits. That I'm actually asleep and this is all some botulism-fueled nightmare brought on by Jeeter's questionable meatloaf."

"Or that it really is a twenty-four-hour flu bug from Hell?"

"Pretty much."

"So, a miracle then."

"Honestly?" he asked, pointedly.

She didn't bother responding.

As they drove north on Burbank, a tiny shape appeared in the roadway at the farthest limit of the headlights. As they drew close enough for Cooper to make out Amber Gleason's tight blonde curls, he had to fight to keep his foot from jumping from the gas pedal to the brake. Instead, he aimed the car directly at the girl and dropped his foot to the floor.

He almost closed his eyes. It would have been such an easy thing to do, to close his eyes, to feel the slightest bump as the tiny girl's body was turned into pulp, and be done with it. One less killer child to worry about, and not a moment lost. But he couldn't. He was the sheriff, after all. And more than that, he was a man. If he was truly going to run this little girl down and leave her shattered corpse lying in the roadway, he'd damn well be man enough to pay witness to her end. He would watch that tiny body come apart on his bumper, and he would carry that horrible image with him for the rest of his life. However short it might be.

At fifty feet away, Emma grabbed the dashboard and dropped her eyes to the floor. At thirty, Cooper etched an image of that adorable, smiling face in his mind, and braced for impact. But at twenty, the face changed. The smile vanished, the eyes grew big, and the darling of Jesper Street hurled herself to the side at the last minute, letting the cruiser thunder past with barely an inch to spare.

When no impact came, Emma chanced a nervous peek out of the tops of her eyes and asked, reluctantly, "Is she...?" She swung around to see what manner of carnage lay in their wake. "Did you...?"

"No," Cooper told her. "She jumped out of the way."

"But you were going to," Emma said. It wasn't a question, and it wasn't a statement. It was an accusation. If her tone hadn't told him as much, the hardness of her glare would have.

"Yes," he admitted, and said nothing more.

What else could he say? She was already scared enough. Did she need to know how devious the children were getting? Would it help if she knew that they were trying to get him to stop the car? Would she be better off knowing that if he had stopped the car to keep from running Amber Gleason down, a dozen other kids with hammers and knives and guns would have come pouring out of the darkness to finish them off? Would it truly have made her day the least bit brighter to know that he had just saved their lives by almost killing a child?

They drove on in silence.

Eight minutes later, they were there. Abrams Auto, the sign read. Behind it squatted an ugly, windowless building. Worn clapboard siding. Sloped roof, sagging at the corners. Old junkers lining the side of the place, and more behind. Some almost intact. Others cannibalized down to the chassis.

He pulled the cruiser as close to the bay doors as he could get, and they both piled out.

One good kick got the office door open. He stabbed a flashlight into the darkness, swept it from one side of the room to the other, and stepped in, waving Emma in behind him.

"The shop's back here," he hushed, leading the way to a grungy door behind an even grungier counter.

And there they were, right where he'd had no reason to believe they'd be. Eight big, beautiful steel cylinders, ten inches in diameter and nearly as tall as a man. Nitrous Oxide, the labels read. Then the warning stickers below. Contents under pressure. Do not expose, blah, blah, blah.

It was one of Harlon Abrams' sidelines. Every kid in the 'Bluff wanted to be a badass, and Harlon Abrams was only to happy to oblige. For a hefty fee, of course. In every car, the amount of power the engine can produce relates directly to how big of an explosion the spark plug can create in the cylinders to drive the pistons. The force of the explosion relates directly to how rapidly the fuel burns, and the rate of burn relates directly to the amount of oxygen present in the system. Normally, this is a constant. But for the wanna-be badass yearning for more power, one could either cool the air being drawn in to make it denser, or better, add a supercharger or turbo to compress the incoming air.

Or one could go old school, just like Cooper had done with his old Chevy Nova way back when. Harlon wasn't around then, but his old man was, and for two hundred bucks, he'd fitted that old Nova with a NOX system that'd had Cooper owning the streets all through senior year.

"Let's load up and get out of here," Emma hushed. "This place gives me the creeps."

Cooper couldn't agree more. With Emma at one end and he at the other, they wordlessly set about manhandling those eight cylinders onto a nearby cart, but no sooner was the transfer complete than Emma put a finger to her lips and a hand on Cooper's arm.

He could see it in her eyes. Fear, as plain as day. But not just fear. Something else was in there, too.

Certainty. That's what it was. Certainty. This wasn't the willies creeping up on her. This was a real and absolute thing. Somehow, Emma Wong was sensing something beyond what they could see in their flashlight beams. Cooper turned an ear to the stillness, and now he could hear it himself. A soft, subtle scraping sound, coming from somewhere in the darkness.

Something was there with them, inside those very walls. He was sure of it. He knew it as well as he knew his own name. Something was there in the darkness that filled this ugly, squat little building that smelled of oil and gasoline and a thousand other corruptions. It was following them. Shadowing them. Stalking them.

He shone his light in every direction, but he could see nothing. Everything in the whole grubby place was either shadows or echoes of shadows. But wait. Back there against the far wall. Was that a person? No. Just a shadow in vaguely human form. Nothing more.

Or was it?

He grabbed hold of the cart and waved Emma cautiously onward to the bay doors.

Wait! There it was again. A soft, scraping sound, like shoes scuffing on cement. Or, more to the point, shoes trying *not* to scuff on cement. He aimed his flashlight to the corner of the shop where he thought the sound must be coming from, but he could still see nothing.

He unsnapped his holster, hardened his heart, and pushed the cart the rest of the way to the bay doors.

With no power to raise the door, Cooper would have to again go old school. A looped chain ran down one side of the door from ceiling to floor. It was dirty and oily and beginning to rust in places, but it looked like it would still do the job.

"This is going to be noisy as hell," he hushed to Emma. "Once I start hoisting, the clock starts ticking. So stay sharp, Miss Wong. We'll have to move fast."

She nodded and grabbed hold of the cart, but just as Cooper reached for the chain, she gave a tight little gasp and spun around, shining her light to the farthest corner of the shop. Cooper quickly joined her light with his, and they both stood absolutely still and silent as they struggled to make out what it was they were seeing.

An old El Camino sat over a grease pit in the last stall, obscuring much of what lay beyond. Cooper could make out a pair of oil drums tucked into the corner beside a metal tool cabinet, but the rest of it lay in shadows. He took a cautious step closer to get a better angle, but Emma grabbed him by the sleeve to stop him. She held up a finger, then she slowly and silently lowered herself to her knees. Once down, she bowed forward to get her eyes as close to the floor as she could, and shone her light directly underneath the El Camino.

A second gasp revealed the culprit.

Flushed out from his hiding spot, a young boy suddenly jumped up and waved into the light with an all too cheery, "Hi, Sheriff! I'm playing a game! Wanna play with me?"

Cooper recognized the kid. It was fat Conor Brady's boy.

"Not particularly, Daniel," he replied. "How about you come out here with your hands in the air. No sudden moves, now. Just come out nice and slow."

Emma snorted and climbed back to her feet with a scowl aimed directly Cooper's way.

"Seriously?" she scoffed, then she called out to the boy in her gentlest tone, "Hi Daniel. My name's Emma, and I would *love* to play a game with you!"

"Really?" the boy bubbled over with joy. "Oh, it's such a fun game!"

"I'll bet it is!" Emma bubbled right back at him. "I just

love games. Why don't you come over here and show me how to play it?"

The boy rounded the back of the El Camino with one hand tucked behind his back. Cooper kept him fixed in the light and moved a hand closer to his holster.

"What do you have behind your..." he started to say, but Emma waved him off.

"Oh, that's just part of the game, isn't it Daniel?" She waggled her fingers at the boy and took a single step forward. "Come on, Daniel. Come and show me how to play the game."

He took a few more tentative steps around the back of the El Camino, and Cooper's hand clutched his pistol grips.

Emma might not have seen it, but he had. It was a glance. Just one single glance into the shadows as the boy rounded the back end of the car. Then the boy's smile grew even brighter, and he took one more step closer.

"Daniel," Cooper called out, his eyes darting left and right and everywhere at once, "Where's your sister?"

An eruption from behind had him spinning around just in time to see Colleen Brady come tearing out of the darkness with a blood-slickened butcher knife in her hand. She launched herself at him, blade-first, and it was all he could do to backpedal away and try to keep his distance. But the girl kept coming, slashing the air back and forth, back and forth, at times coming close enough that he could feel the tip of the blade tugging at his shirt front. Then Emma uttered a stifled little squeal, and he knew that she was in a fight for her life too.

Cooper batted the girl's hand away again and again, then one lucky strike to her wrist knocked the knife loose and it clattered to the floor. But it wasn't over yet. The girl bent down to retrieve the weapon, and Cooper acted on impulse. He raised a boot and connected a furious kick to her backside, sending her somersaulting end over end across the room.

Colleen Brady's tiny round head made a sound not unlike a coconut striking rock as it bounced off the concrete, but Cooper paid her no mind. He kicked the knife to the deepest, darkest corner of the place and ran for Emma, currently in a wrestling match with an octopus.

Daniel Brady might have weighed all of sixty pounds soaking wet, but he was his father's son. He was all arms and legs, and when he fought, he fought for real. Emma had a good lock on one of his wrists and looked to be holding her own for now, but she was having a devil of a time just blocking the chisel in the boy's free hand as he punched it towards her belly time and time again.

But there were levels to this young woman Cooper was still discovering. Even as he rushed to her aid, he could see that she wasn't just fending off his attacks, she was using them. Every time the boy lunged, she crept the hand holding his wrist just a little higher up his arm, and every time she increased her leverage, she reeled the boy in just that much closer. Then, with one last almighty lunge, it was over. She grabbed the boy by the collar and spun him around, and before he even knew what hit him, she had the stun gun out of her pocket and pressed to the back of his neck.

It was like hitting an off switch. One second, the boy was an octopus, all arms and legs and deadly intent. The next, he was a crumpled pile at Emma's feet. She squatted down and felt for a pulse, then she relieved the unconscious boy of his chisel and sent it sailing as far as she could into the darkness.

"Emma Wong, one. Baby rhino, zero," she said, stepping

over the crumpled boy and stopping to quickly check the sprawling girl's pulse before returning to the job at hand.

Cooper grabbed the chain and began hauling. And as he'd warned, the process was far from silent. Every hand-over-hand pull of the chain raised the door another inch or two, but they were costly inches. Each pull came with enough clanking and rattling to wake the dead, and he knew that every kid within earshot would be stampeding toward the sound. But the trade-off was acceptable. As long as the kids were coming after him and Emma, they wouldn't be going after anyone else, so even if none of this craziness actually worked, he might still have managed to save a life or two. He could think of worse ways to go, but right now, he had no intention of going at all.

The door crept up the rails with a deafening and agonizing slowness. When it was at her knees, Emma dropped low and watched the gap, but Cooper doubted that even she knew what she would do if five or twenty or a hundred children suddenly came bursting through. The stun gun could only be in so many places at once, and a Sheriff's badge protected nothing. She had a gun in her pocket, but that Glock she'd forwent would never make an appearance. He was sure of it. Emma Wong would die with that thing right where it was.

And what about the erstwhile Sheriff Thomas H. Cooper? What would he do? When push came to shove and all that other shit, what would this sworn public protector do if and when the rush came? Would he let those little hellions tear Emma apart, or would he swap a few of their lives for hers. And when they came at him, would he let them come and leave Emma alone and at their mercy, or would he defend them both to his utmost ability.

The questions were unanswerable. All he could say for certain was that he would know what to do when the time came. And to keep that time from ever coming, they had to be rid of this place fast.

He redoubled his efforts, and the gap widened another inch. Then another, and another. At last, it was high enough to let the cart through, so he looped off the chain and pushed the cart out to the waiting cruiser even as a chorus of hoots and giggles and excited laughter closed in around them. They hand-bombed the cylinders from the cart into the back seat of the cruiser, then they jumped in and swung the doors closed, stopping to catch their breath only when Cooper hit the master switch to lock all the doors.

And just in time. No sooner had the locks clunked before the first bunch of kids came tearing around the phalanx of junkers lining Abrams Auto. They came at the cruiser in a wave, trying the door handles, pounding on the glass, and grinning in at the wide-eyed occupants. Then a few of the more intrepid boys climbed bodily onto the hood and the trunk and up onto the roof, and the outside world nearly disappeared completely.

Cooper keyed the car to life, shifted casually into drive, and showed his passenger which two buttons to push. She hit the first, and the light bar on the roof turned that ugly little corner of Keeter's Bluff into an instant rave. Red and blue lights flashed off of a dozen fresh, young faces, and those faces all turned upward to meet it. They laughed, they hooted and they cheered, and for a few seconds, every last one of them forgot all about the two grown-ups behind the glass. Then Emma hit the second button, and the rave got its music.

In the starkness of the night, the blare of the siren had

clearly caught Emma by surprise. Cooper had seen it a thousand times before. Everyone thought they knew what a police siren sounded like, but most people only ever heard one as a lonesome wail in the night, or as a cop car tore past on the freeway. Up close and personal, that hundred and twenty decibels was just shy of the human pain threshold. It always caught people short. Even raw recruits. Most jumped in their seats. The good ones managed not to cover their ears. Emma Wong didn't do either. Her eyes widened by the narrowest of degrees for the briefest of moments, then she merely watched the children scramble back down the windshield to the hood and bound to the ground. When the last of them was off, she tossed her chin toward the windshield and Cooper shot the car through the narrowest gap between a throng of tiny bodies.

He watched the children in the rearview mirror, but they didn't recede. They came after the cruiser in a wild rush of hoots and howls and laughter, and as the rave swung past the junkers and hit the main road, every one of those happy, smiling children chased right along behind.

Just like Cooper had hoped.

CHAPTER

XXXIX

I t was the Pied Piper as even the people of Hamelin could never have imagined. With the cruiser's lights flashing and siren wailing, every child within earshot was drawn in. And Cooper let them come. He kept the cruiser at a crawl, and he let every single one of them come. When they came from the front, he steered straight at them, veering away only at the last second. When too many started to fall behind, he took his foot off the gas and let the cruiser coast for a while so the main body could catch up. And when they came close enough to make a grab for the door handles or swing something heavy at one of the windows, he goosed the throttle just enough to keep them in his dust.

And all the while, he kept them moving. He kept them moving precisely where he wanted them to go.

Emma was more than a passenger now. With Cooper focused on the road ahead, she was his eyes and ears for everything else around them. When one or more kids came streaming down from yards and houses and alleyways to join in on the slow-motion chase, she alerted him. When she thought they were getting too close, she told Cooper to hit the accelerator. And when one or another child appeared out of the gloom to aim a gun their way, it was all she could do to not reach her own foot across and slam the pedal to the floor. In this way, with Emma calling the shots and Cooper leading the pack, they made their way in fits and starts to where they could only hope the others were waiting.

When they reached Laurel Drive, Cooper made one last turn, put his foot to floor just enough to leave the pack in his wake, and pulled the cruiser halfway up the hill, just past the old McIffrin place.

Grace Tolliver was already there, leaning across the roof of her Buick with her AR-15 cocked and ready. She didn't say a word as Cooper angled the car across the road and he and Emma piled out. She simply checked the watch pinned to her blouse and tapped it with her finger.

Cooper checked his own wristwatch and cursed inside his head. It had been thirty minutes already. That bullshit at Abrams Auto should have made them the last of the pipers to arrive, but they were the first. What that meant for the others was anyone's guess, but it couldn't be good. Garcia and Rankin were brave men, but brave men could die just as easily as cowards.

But then, Cooper got his first miracle. Grace growled, "Finally!" as Sonny Garcia's cruiser crept slowly around the corner from the east, mere yards ahead of a hundred or more children racing along behind. At a mile's distance, he hit the gas to leave them all behind, then he roared in behind Cooper's car and jumped out with his shotgun at the ready.

Cooper clapped his deputy on the shoulder, nodded

once, and said nothing. Moments later, he got his second miracle when another car came into view. It was Carl Rankin's cruiser, leading another pack as large as that already there. The cruiser wheeled onto Laurel, laid down a strip of rubber to shake off its tail, and screeched to a stop nose-to-nose with Cooper's car.

Grace checked her watch.

"If my calculations are right, we have exactly two minutes."

Cooper took her at her word.

"Two minutes!" he called out, as several weapons came up and sighting down at the crowd tearing up the hill.

There were hundreds. Literally, hundreds. But even as they came charging up the hill toward Keeter's Bluff's last few defenders, their numbers continued to swell. Then a sound like rolling thunder echoed through the night, and Cooper's third miracle arrived in the form of a souped-up Challenger roaring around the corner to the north, mere feet ahead of a pack that might easily have doubled the crowd. And just that quickly, this lonely street in a backwater little corner of the 'Bluff became the deadliest piece of real estate on the planet.

"One minute!" Grace called out.

Garcia leaned across the roof of his cruiser with his shotgun, snarling, "They'll be on us in half that."

The Challenger screeched to a stop behind Grace's Buick even as Cooper worked through the calculations in his own head. Garcia was right. There were too many. They were too close. There wasn't enough time. But since this insanity had approximately one chance in a million of working anyway, it made little difference. He flung open the rear door of the cruiser, took a deep breath, and began opening the valves on every one of those eight big metal cylinders currently laid across the back seat.

It started with a hiss. Just a gentle hiss, like air escaping from a tire. Then the hiss grew into a breeze, and by the time the last valve was opened, the breeze had become a full-blown gale. And every molecule of that gas that had once fueled an old Chevy Nova to the status of legend flowed downhill into the parcel of land that had subsided a good thirty feet below the surrounding area, way back when.

This was the Dip. No wind blew through the dip. The air was heavy. Unmoving. Cloying, even. And for this ludicrous plan to have any chance at all of working, that was exactly what they needed.

Cooper ran awkwardly back to the others, releasing his breath in a gush.

"We have to slow them down! We have to keep them in the Dip!"

On cue, Garcia let loose a volley from his twelve-gauge shotgun, but when all eyes turned to him in horror, they found him holding the barrel of his weapon high in the air. Again and again he fired, sending four rounds of double-ought buckshot into the sky, but the thunderous blasts did nothing to slow the advance. In fact, it only spurred them on. Now, instead of a thousand or more armed children dancing steadily up the hill, those in front broke into a run and came charging at them, laughing and whooping and brandishing every manner of weapon imaginable.

It didn't take long. The nitrous oxide that had turned his old Nova into a rocket with the flick of a switch all those years ago had another, more beneficial use. Now, with a gale of hospital grade anesthetic rolling downhill in a torrent, the rush slowed back down to a walk, and then to a slog, then the first boy dropped to the ground and curled into a ball, shaking Emma Wong to the core.

"Are you sure he's just asleep?" She grabbed Cooper desperately by the sleeve. "I mean, you can't control the concentration, right? How do you know it's not too much? How do you know he's not dead? How do you know this isn't going to kill every last *one* of them?"

Cooper regarded her through dark, narrow eyes.

"Honestly?" he asked.

"Yes," she said adamantly, releasing his sleeve and preparing herself for the worst. "Honestly."

He shrugged, and told her the God's honest truth.

"I don't."

Another boy dropped to the ground, and others quickly followed. Two. Five. Ten. More, and then more still. Like a toppling row of dominoes, children began dropping like stones in a downhill wave toward the lowest point in the Dip. Many times that number managed to stay on their feet, but they were all clearly showing signs of exposure. Some began wandering about in aimless circles. Others became suddenly confused, and either went running off, chasing after ghosts, or simply planted themselves where they were and stared blankly up at the night sky. And of course there were many others who demonstrated with crystal clarity how nitrous oxide had come by its nickname. For some, it seemed, this so-called 'laughing gas' made the whole situation the funniest damn thing they had ever seen.

The horde's advance had been slowed, but even in a place where no wind blew and stale air hung like a miasmic pall, it wouldn't be enough. The nitrous was cleaving a wide enough path down the middle of the pack, and those well inside the Dip had nowhere to go, but there wasn't enough gas to fill the Dip completely, and dozens upon dozens of children were high enough up the hill to be above the level of the settling gas. Even now, they came rushing the last few yards armed with knives and stabbing tools and chunks of rock and brick, and there was nothing anyone could do to stop them.

This wasn't how it was supposed to go. Even with a game plan that was more of a hunch sketched out on a soiled napkin, Cooper had hoped for better. Three quarters of the plan had come together seamlessly. The gas. The Dip. The roundup. But like a three-legged chair perched at the edge of a cliff, it was only a matter of time before the damn thing toppled over. Now, with this giggling, murderous, ravenous horde descending on eight defenders with hearts simply too big to ever wage war on children, Cooper looked to his comrades and wondered if any of those incredible people would live to see another day dawn in Keeter's Bluff.

Since none of them were going to lose the fight by winning it, the smartest thing they could have done was run, and it would have been an easy enough to do. The whole lot of them could have piled back into their cars and fled, but then all of this would have been for nothing. He had known most of these people for a lifetime, and though he had only met Emma Wong a few hours ago, he thought he knew her well enough too. They would never go. None of them. Even if he ordered them back to their cars and backed up his resolve at the point of a gun, he knew they wouldn't go. They were needed here. Though it was surely going to cost them their lives, each and every one of them would stay precisely here and try to keep the horde from running off in a hundred different directions. It was the only way the crazy plan had any chance of working, so here they would all stay, no matter what.

He looked to Emma, and to Garcia, and to Carl and sweet little Mindy-Lou, and to Jermaine and Austin, and his eyes finally settled on Grace *goddam* Tolliver, just as she checked her watch and announced, "Any second now!"

Another shotgun blast boomed, catching Cooper by surprise. But this wasn't Sonny Garcia with his barrel held high. This was Jermaine Granger, doing the unthinkable. She was firing directly into a group of twenty or more boys streaming in from the left flank. But no. Thank Christ, she wasn't firing directly into the crowd. Her aim was low, almost at ground level. As the gun boomed again and a boy tumbled to the ground, clutching his leg, he breathed a mitigated sigh of relief when he realized what she was up to. With twenty or more adrenalin-fueled murderbots mere yards away, she was taking careful aim slightly to one side or the other of those in the lead and knocking their legs out from under them with precisely targeted shots. So good was her aim that only one of the nine pellets of lead in any round found its mark. Painful, undoubtedly, but far better than either alternative.

Grace Tolliver quickly followed suit. Then Sonny. Then Austin. Then Carl Rankin, with Mindy-Lou tucked safely into his back. But even with five guns blasting away at a flurry of tiny legs, it wasn't enough.

The first wave reached the line of cars seconds later. They swept over and around the vehicle with their knives and their screwdrivers and their hammers and their chunks of rock and brick, and they came straight at those eight poor souls who had been foolish enough to think that they had ever stood a chance. But even with death staring them in the face, those eight fools stayed true to themselves. They fought, they wrestled, they hit and they punched, but not one of those eight brave fools crossed that most invisible of lines.

But that was bound to change. The next wave would be on them in seconds, and from then on, it would be every man, woman, and child for themselves.

Cooper tore the machete from Amber Gleason's hand and threw it and her in opposite directions. As she crumpled to the ground unconscious, he caught the Denton boy in midair as he came flying over the hood of the Sheriff's cruiser and tore the knife from his hand. Emma delivered the coup de grâce in the form of a million-volt zap to the back of the struggling, giggling boy's neck, and managed a reasonably glib, "Nighty night, Damien," just as the next wave crested the hill.

But then, Cooper got his final miracle. A loud *whump!* shuddered through the air, and a tiny dancing light appeared in one of the age-rippled windows of the old McIffrin place.

Grace Tolliver clunked the Chadwick sisters' heads together, and as they fell away to either side, she checked her watch and shrugged, "Sorry, Sheriff. Guess I was a little off."

It started at the back, where Grace had been instructed to pour the gasoline and leave a cigarette burning, standing on its filtered end. Once that Lucky Strike burned down to the nub, the rest was inevitable. The flame took to the old Mciffrin place like a drunkard to a wine cellar, and within seconds, the whole place was ablaze.

A sea of rats came pouring out of the flames, and Cooper let them come. But contrary to his fears, not one spider emerged, and for that, he gave a nod of thanks to whichever god it was that watched over idiots and arachnophobes. As the fire spread across the main floor and began licking at the old paint of the upper floors, he gave a silent cheer as every child in a group that still numbered in the hundreds forgot all about the sights and sounds that had brought them there, and became enraptured by the fireworks of the old McIffrin place going up in flames.

The last of the nitrous bottles hissed itself dry, and now it was up to the laws of physics to dictate the rest.

This was the Dip. No wind blew through the Dip. The gas from eight big bottles had settled to the ground, and with the old McIffrin place going up in flames, every child too far up the hill to be affected by the gas began to run back down to where the fun was, whooping and howling as they went.

Emma Wong came up beside Cooper as she tucked away her stun gun.

"Nitrous is extremely flammable," she said. "How did you know there would be enough to knock out the Children of the Corn without blowing them all to kingdom come?"

"Honestly?" Cooper asked through the corner of his mouth.

Emma said nothing.

The old Mciffrin place burned, hundreds of children whooped and hollered and danced around it, but the inevitable was well underway. They were all gathered at the lowest point in the Dip, and they were dropping by the dozens. By the time the old McIffrin place collapsed in on itself in one last triumphant eruption of smoke and embers, most were either unconscious or too befuddled to know where they were or why they were there.

But not all.

With the blazing spectacle turning quickly to ash, those few children who had stayed far enough up the hill to be spared from the gas turned their attentions back to the last of the grown-ups. Little Frankie Sumner led the charge, and the rest followed. The Slattery boys. Wanda Gamble. Tommy Wilkins. Kaylie Beaudrell. Mae Chappelle. Tommy Doogan. Tracy Coggins. And there, two others that Cooper knew all too well. Daryl and Maggie Brannigan, still in their Sunday best, and still brandishing a bloodied steak knife in each hand.

Sonny Garcia took careful aim and sent a few rounds over their heads, but the children kept coming. Carl Rankin sent enough nine-millimeter rounds downrange to kick up a cloud of dust at each of their feet, but it proved just as useless. Spurred on by the game, the children broke into a run and came charging at them with wild abandon.

Frankie Sumner had a hammer in one hand and his father's Colt pistol in the other. He fired off a couple of rounds that pinged off of the Sheriff's cruiser, then he stopped in his tracks, raised his father's pistol again, and took careful aim at the precise center of Cooper's chest.

After all that had happened, after all of the terror and all of the blood and all of the near misses, Cooper knew that this was it. His time was up. The plan worked, the children had been virtually tied to their collective beds, and now it was time for the piper to pay. He was completely exposed. He had no time to move, and nowhere to hide. In less time than it would take to draw his next breath, he'd be dead, and there wasn't one damn thing he could do about it. All he could was die.

But there was room for one more miracle, and this last one came courtesy of Grace Tolliver. She didn't flinch, she didn't hesitate, and she didn't pause for even the briefest of seconds. With one of her boys facing imminent death, Grace *goddam* Tolliver simply did what none of the others could ever have done. She sighted down the barrel of the AR-15 to a spot in the exact center of Frankie Sumner's skull, and let the bullet fly.

The boy collapsed in a heap, and with the rest of the children overpowered readily enough, Emma Wong gave them each a million volt jolt so they could join the others in slumberland.

But not so, Frankie Sumner. Austin Granger did his due diligence by checking for vital signs, but there was no point. The major part of the boy's cranium was gone. Whatever Frankie Sumner had been, and whatever he might have one day become, every last bit of that lost young life poured itself out onto that dark little patch of ground in a backwater street in a little nowhere town.

With the crisis over, Grace Tolliver threw her AR-15 to the ground, then that infuriating, insufferable, incredible woman dropped her face into her hands and burst into tears.

There were no words. She had just saved his life, but Cooper had no words. He simply wrapped his arms around the woman and let her bury her face in his chest, and the others all gathered around to share in her grief.

"So, what now?" Mindy-Lou asked no one in particular.

"Now we get all of the injured children to the hospital," Granger told her.

"What about the rest?" Jermaine asked.

"I have a trunk full of zip ties," Garcia hitched a thumb over his shoulder. "While you guys ferry the worst of them to KBG, Carl and I'll disarm the rest of them and string 'em together like paper dolls."

"And then?"

"Then we hope," Emma jumped in. "We hope that I'm wrong. Or that I'm right. Or that this is all a nightmare brought on by bad meatloaf."

Rankin uttered a confused, "Huh?"

Cooper set the record straight.

"We hope that there's been enough death this day to satisfy Gaia's bloodlust. Or maybe that enough people did the right thing to make her show a little mercy."

"And if not?" Jermaine asked, pointedly.

"Then none of this matters," he told her, just as pointedly.

But even as he surveyed the destruction, he knew those words weren't true. No matter the outcome, what he and those few brave souls had done this day mattered. Even if it only postponed the inevitable, it mattered. They had done their moral duty. They had saved lives. While the rest of the world was busy tearing itself apart, the brave men and women of this forgotten little town in the middle of nowhere had put their own lives on the line and done the right thing. If Gaia was keeping score, maybe it would tip the balance. If not, then so be it. Whatever that heartless, nasty-ass bitch threw at them next, she would never be able to take that from them. What they had done this night mattered.

As for what came next, he could only fall back on the wise words spoken by the only woman he had ever loved.

They would deal with tomorrow, tomorrow.

CHAPTER

XL

"Hiya, Sheriff!"

Cooper waved to beautiful, gap-toothed Janice Redman from his cruiser, and continued reluctantly on.

As it happened, when the sun came up on that distant tomorrow, it brought with it an end to the bloodshed. And as the world held its collective breath, another tomorrow came and went, and another, and another, and things slowly began to go back to some semblance of normal.

Two months after the day the world almost ended, much had changed in Keeter's Bluff, but much was still the same. Life went on as it had before, but perhaps now with a new unspoken bond that drew the entire community even closer together. What had happened had been horrendous, but it didn't take more than a glimpse at the nightly news to see how lucky this backwater little town had been.

Worldwide, the death toll was massive. Hundreds of

millions dead in twenty four hours of madness. Once it all shook out and a real tally could be had, that number was expected to double.

In Keeter's Bluff, the final tally was three hundred and fourteen dead, times two injured. It was tragic, to be sure, but there was much to make the people of the 'Bluff feel like celebrating rather than mourning.

The morning after the day the world almost ended, the children of Keeter's Bluff awoke. Some awoke with a headache, some with nausea, some with severe injuries and some caked in their own vomit, but aside from Frankie Sumner, they all awoke. They awoke as if from a dream, and however nightmarish that dream had been, they all awoke as their old selves with no memory at all of those horrible events. And for that, the town celebrated more.

No cause for the madness was ever discovered. Some maintained that it had been a terrorist attack. Others swore up and down that it had been a communist plot. Every pundit and blogger and columnist had their own pet theories. Aliens. Chem Trails. The Illuminati. Any and all alphabet agencies of a hundred different countries. Cooper even heard the word 'Gaia' mentioned once or twice in those first few days, but that particular branch of new age hippie-dippy speculation was quickly pruned. A few even argued that a killer gene was in the children all along, and that it had just been waiting for the right conditions to manifest, but they were easily outshouted. Then a new war erupted in the Middle East, and the day the world almost ended was all but forgotten.

But it wasn't forgotten in Keeter's Bluff.

Despite the fact that most of the townsfolk had saved themselves by trussing their own children up like Christmas geese and barricading themselves in their homes, and despite the fact that hundreds of other heroes had emerged during those awful hours, including the spectacularly heroic staff at KB General, the Town Council declared Sheriff Tom Cooper as the 'Bluff's savior. They even planned a gala event to celebrate their hero and hand him the key to the town, but when it came time to attend the ceremony, Cooper was home, hovering over a boiling pot of spaghetti and another pot of what he hoped wouldn't be too garlicky a sauce for the delicate palate of one Kira Melanson.

"I'm not sure, Doc," he said, staring gloomily into the pot.

Kira snuck in between him and the stove, and kissed him warmly on the lips.

"I am," she cooed, and the deal was sealed. From that moment on, whatever happened, for better or for worse, they both knew that they would go through every bit of it together.

A wedding was hastily planned, and having escaped the carnage at the Elk's Hall by the skin of his teeth, it fell upon the town's leading citizen to do the nondenominational deed. So it was that on a bright, sunny day, late that August, Judge Horace Whittaker scowled up at Cooper and asked the words, "Do you take..." But that was as far as he got.

"I do!" Cooper blurted out, raising a chorus of laughter from the thousands of townsfolk gathered in the square.

"Me too," Kira said, reeling Cooper in for a kiss so passionate that it sent every one of those thousands into an absolute uproar.

And in that crowd of thousands, no one cheered louder than Emma Wong. She was sitting front and center beside Bethany Lagrange, the two of them holding hands as if they had been together for years. On either side were the others. Carl and Mindy-Lou. Sonny Garcia. Austin and Jermaine. Even Grace *goddam* Tolliver was in attendance, alternately dabbing at her eyes with a balled-up Kleenex and cheering on her eldest idiot son who had finally made good.

"Then I guess that's it," the Judge concluded with a huff. "I pronounce you man and wife. All that's left is to cut the cake. Fancy?"

On cue, Fancy Whittacker appeared, juggling an ornate silver platter as she bulldozed her way through the crowd.

"I hope you're lactose intolerant, asshole," she said, handing Cooper the platter and beating a retreat that could never have been hasty enough.

Cooper took one look at the half-melted ice cream log pooling on the tray, and burst into laughter.

He bent down to the pretty little girl at Kira's side in her bright pink dress, holding her basket of rose petals, and he showed her the prize.

"I hope you like your ice cream mushy, kiddo."

"Yum!" Maizie Pritchard squealed, beaming a smile as bright as all outdoors.

Despite the warmth of the day, Cooper felt a cold wave ripple through his bones.

It was such a fleeting thing. So fleeting that Cooper himself couldn't be sure. It might have been his imagination, but for one second, just one single, solitary second on this happiest of days in that idyllic place under a clear, cloudless sky, he could almost swear that he'd caught sight of something dark pass behind the girl's big, blue eyes.

KEN STARK was born in Saskatchewan, but has called Vancouver home for most of his life. He was raised on a steady diet of science fiction and disaster movies, so it seems right that his first published book series be about the zombie apocalypse. In his spare time, Ken tries to paint like Bob Ross and play poker like Doyle Brunson, but results suggest that he might have got it all backwards.

Tweet Ken @PennilessScribe

Website: www.kenstark.ca